THE WORLD GAME

by

Allen Charles

The World Game
by
Allen Charles
Copyright © 2011 Allen H. Charles
All rights reserved.

Allen Charles may be contacted at
allen.h.charles@gmail.com

Earth image in cover art courtesy of NASA.
Cover Art By AUSome Llc. graphic by design gifted to
Allen Charles

Published by Ausome Llc.
6606 Park Heights Ave, Suite 3A
Baltimore MD, 21215 U.S.A.
info@ausomegraphics.com
Available on Amazon.com Kindle Books.

ISBN 978-0-9850518-0-8

Ed: 12-03-12

THE WORLD GAME

CHAPTER 1

5785 Years ago - somewhere on Planet Earth

The tall, thin figure materialized in the shadow of a fig tree, blending in with the dark and light dappling. It did not move and was invisible to the slender woman who was totally absorbed in touching and examining the fragrant fruit of another tree, scant feet away from the apparition.

The woman had glinting tresses of golden hair and was perfectly formed, as perfect as if she was the only woman in existence. Which on this particular planet, she was.

She suddenly balked and tensed, sensing the presence of something unknown. Feeling eyes upon her. She looked about without fear, just curiosity, scanning past the being and instantly swinging back, the gaze of her brilliant blue eyes fixed upon it.

"Who are you?" Her voice was pleasant and lilting, her smile innocent and enchanting. Her intuition told her that this thing did not belong. "You are not part of this place. Where did you come from?"

The apparition cocked its narrow, scaly head to the side and stared at her silently through tiny, round black eyes that were ringed by vivid yellow circles.

She walked towards it, without hesitation, to examine this new living thing that had presented itself.

It spoke.

"I am Snake." it whispered, its sibilant tones bringing a shadow of something cold into the air, new in the world and not pleasant. "This place is wonderful," it hissed, "to whom does all this belong?"

The woman raised her hands and looked about, shaking her head in wonderment. "It must belong to the Creator of all things. I have no knowledge other than this place and of my other who is like me, my man."

"Who is this Creator?" it asked her.

"Creator made all this and put us here to enjoy all of His work. There is no other reason for us to be here."

Snake moved his head to the opposite angle. "So you will wander about this garden for eternity, thinking about the Creator, with nothing else to achieve in your existence?"

She shook her head, a little puzzled. "What is better than such an idyll? You too are part of this creation." It tucked its head under a stubby arm trying to stifle a snigger of disdain. A thought flushed through its mind, "That's what you think, human!"

It looked up at her, now composed, and asked, "Wouldn't you like something more in your life? Something to challenge you and give you goals and ultimate satisfaction of success."

"What do you mean? My man and I have one challenge that our Creator gave us. A simple rule that if followed, allows us satisfaction in all else. We are grateful to our Creator for giving us this existence."

"And what is this rule?" it sneered at her.

Having never encountered aggression, she was somewhat taken aback, replying "We are instructed not to eat the fruit of one particular tree. In fact not even to touch the tree." she added, even though the latter comment was her own invention to insulate the real rule from the apparently belligerent Snake.

Snake knew she referred to the Source Tree. His instructions were clear: get one of the humans to violate the Rule. "This is just too easy." it chuckled to itself. "Lady, why do you think the Creator made this rule?" He paused a moment for effect. "It is because if you absorb the essence of this tree by eating its fruit you will become the equal of the Creator. You will no longer be a prisoner in this garden."

Snake walked out in the open. "Look here," and approached the Source Tree. The woman moved closer to see what it was talking about. It moved fast and bumped her while she was off guard and fell towards the tree, grasping the trunk to steady herself.

"See you are touching the tree and nothing has happened to

you. Now look closely at the tree and see the small things that are unlike any other tree. These are the things that make the Creator all powerful over this garden - and you! Take the fruit and hold it!"

She hesitantly reach out to a fruit and touched it, then held it. She saw small round, shiny spots in the tree bark, and tiny, sharp silvery wires, where twigs should have been.

"Go on, take the fruit and taste it. You will see what the Creator sees." hissed Snake.

CHAPTER 2

In a galaxy far away.

A thought flashed inside an instant galactic neural entertainment network. "Hey! Who put that snake into the scene? No direct interference allowed. Rule breaker!"

A reply bounced back, "I did. I had a wild card I won from the last World Game edition. So there!"

"The Rules say you can't use a wild card without first announcing. I say you forfeit the wild card and there is a set back to the performers by mind wipe and get rid of the snake."

"Don't be a black hole!" the disdainful thought came back. "The wild card rule is that it can be played without warning provided it was won during a Universe's Got Talent program sector and there is a public posting of use notification within 72 hours after the play."

"That means you can cheat on the betting, you overblown interstellar gas bag?"

"No need to get antsy with me you comet fart! The wild card player is not allowed to bet until after the 72 hours, just like anybrain else. Anyway, what are you watching? Any tips for a good bet right now?"

There was a sudden influx of attention in the network as audience consciousness throughout the universe strained to eavesdrop on the answer.

"Cain and Abel are looking good for a blow up."

* * *

1000 years after Game Start.

"Hey! Worm Hole!"

"Watcha want Boiled Brains?"

"Wanna bet on that Og giant hanging onto the back of Noah's Ark? 5 to 1 he falls off and drowns!"

"You're on!"

* * *

Around 2000 years after Game Start.

"Are you awake Globular Cluster?"

"You leave my cluster out of this. Go play with your Celestial Pole!"

"Ha ha! Haven't had one of those for over six Game Editions."

"So what cooking good-looking?"

"I'm watching a little altercation between some King Nimrod who's trying to cook some guy Abraham in a furnace."

"Any odds on it?

"Well... I'm a bit wary on this one. You took me to the cleaners on the Og thing last time and this guy should have been toast by now. Something strange going on and I don't have any more wild cards in play."

"So ya wanna bet or not?"

"Aw, OK, but evens! I'll take that he walks out of the furnace alive."

"Done!"

* * *

Around 3500 years after Game Start.

"Hey, Quasar Fluctuation?"

"Who you calling a Fluctuator, you Ecliptic Brain?"

"OK! Let's be nice. I was watching this bunch of descendants of that Abraham fellow we bet on."

"Oh! I've been watching a group called the Chinese and that general area. Have they EVER developed some amazing ways of killing each other. Whatcha got in mind?"

"D'ya think this World will go anywhere the same as the last six World Game Editions?

"Depends on the Talent segment at the end. Who are the Judges for this one?"

"Don't know yet. Too early to guess."

"Well I want some excitement; a really good bet. Haven't had anything since our Abraham wager."

"Anything happening with the Chinese?"

"Nah. Just the usual slaughter when they're not farming for survival. How about your lot?"

"Now that you ask..."

"If you had any hands you'd be rubbing them together and grinning with the face you don't have either. Right?"

"Maybe..."

"So the odds on this one had better be really stacked my way or no bet."

"Don't wet your brain pan. How's 5 to 1 sound?"

"It sounds like 10 to 1 to me."

"OK. But I am taking the Abraham descendants. You get the Egyptians."

"Agreed!"

* * *

Around 4000 years after Game Start.

"Are we betting on this one?"

"Naw! We know how many people a hungry lion can eat. This lot has been overfed."

"Oh brain! I thought the Chinese had it down for killing people. These Romans take the prize."

"Quick, tune in to the main arena in Rome. Something is happening there. Bets! Now! Quick! What's the Emperor going to do. he's run out of prisoners and gladiators and there's nothing to feed the lions! The crowd is getting restless."

"Ten thousand credits he throws the first rows of citizens into the arena!"

"Are you nuts? His own people?"

"20 to 1 odds!"

"That's 200,000 credits if you lose. Have you got that much?"

"Course I have. Been betting against you for how many Games now?"

"Middle finger if I had one! Deal!"

* * *

Around 5000 years after Game Start.

"Hey Naked Singularity!"

"Watcha want ya Maclaurin Spheroid?"

"I wanna win back the ten thousand credits."

"Keep dreaming you Main Sequence Turn Off."

"Good thing you're just a brain or I'd show you Turn Off!"

"So hit me with your latest losing bet!"

"I'm watching the Crusaders fighting the Saracens for Jerusalem. The last few Games the crusaders won. I'm betting on the Saracens for this time. Interested?"

"Let me have a quick look at the performance. Wait a mo!"

* * *

5794 after Game Start. Year 2034 by Earth count.

"Network announcement! Attention all subscribers!"

The neural network went from a busy rumble to an eerie silence as everybrainy turned attention to the broadcast.

"General Edition World Game access in now suspended and Universe's Got Talent Seventh Edition has commenced. Our judges will be announced momentarily..."

The network broke out into a palpable, excited hum.

CHAPTER 3

Korean Hegemony, Pyonyang - 24th June, 2034

Lun Jong Il was seated at a large conference table. An image floating before him changed as he pointed and made a flicking motion with his finger. The positions around the table were occupied by his cookie cutter, expressionless, subservient government ministers.

His voice was intense and shrill, fitting with his moon face and clownish hairstyle, as he ranted about the threat of the Iranian Islamic Empire. "They have more nuclear capability than we do. We cannot tolerate the threat of nuclear destruction that hangs over us. What is even worse," he stood up going red in the face, in almost apoplectic rage, and screamed "THEY ARE USING THE TECHNOLOGY WE SOLD TO THEM TO THREATEN US!"

Jong Il collapsed back into his seat with an exhalation and sudden evaporation of his anger. He continued calmly, with just a little screaming, "We have Japan, China and Western powers paying us not to use our nuclear capability. Paying us tribute! They are SCARED OF US! Now these Iranian upstarts come along and tell us to move out, THEY ARE MOVING IN!"

He placed his small hands on the table and slowly scanned the faces of his ministers. "This means war my friends. Something we have been able to avoid all these years by making the rest of the world think that I and my father and grandfather were all maniacs cut from the same cloth. We have done well until now, but these Iranians really are insane. We did it for the money. They are doing it in the name of religion. There will be no stopping this madness." He was silent for a moment and his hard expression turned to one of forlorn, abject sadness. A real tear, the first of a lifetime, trickled down his cheek, evoked by the thought of the loss of all that easy wealth. "Prepare the army and the population. Arm all our satellites and missiles. There will be no winners in this war."

In a far corner of the conference room, a patch of paint on the wall imperceptibly changed color and fluidly altered shape.

Jong Il raised his head. "Does anyone not concur with my

assessment?"

Half way down the table Jun Park, a cousin and close adviser of Jong Il stood. His tone was aggressive. "How can we be so sure that the Iranians will strike first, or even strike at all? We risk everything just on your word? Where is the intelligence information that leads to this conclusion?"

Park stopped and stood, leaning on his hands on the table, staring at Jong Il, waiting for an answer. Jong Il whipped his hand up and a flash of red light slashed across the room, inches above heads and across the neck of Jun Park. With a brief spray of blood Park's head tumbled off his standing body and clunked onto the table, rolling erratically down the middle, the neck almost cauterized by the searing heat of the light blade. The body collapsed back onto the chair and then slid out of sight under the table, just the fingertips peeking up from the arms wedged into place.

Mouths and eyes were wide open in shock all around. Park's dead eyes stared at them all as the head finally came to rest, teetered on the table edge and thudded to the floor. There was a collective sigh of released breathing as the ministers turned as one to see the fingertips dip out of sight.

"Does anyone else have something to say?" Jong Il peered around, the white faces swinging back to him, as he waved circles in the air with the deadly light blade finger. His voice was icy. "There is no room for the faint hearted or the doubter at this table. We cannot afford to be wrong. We MUST first strike!"

The patch on the wall moved again, contracting into a perfect disc shape.

CHAPTER 4

Greenbelt, Maryland- 24th June 2034

Announcement:

NASA's Goddard Space Flight Center and Skyhook Terminus is home to the nation's largest organization of combined scientists, engineers and technologists who build spacecraft, instruments and new technology to study the Earth, the sun, our solar system, and the universe. Goddard is the Earth based control center for the International Space City and the Skyhook Transport System, a direct evolution of the early International Space station, which is an unprecedented achievement in global human endeavors to conceive, plan, build, operate, and utilize a permanent, self sustaining habitat, in space. With the assembly of the space city at its completion and the support of a permanent population of one hundred and sixty, a new era of utilization for human expansion is beginning. During the space city assembly phase, the potential benefits of a closed cycle space-based habitat were demonstrated; including the advancement of scientific knowledge based on experiments conducted in space, development and testing of new technologies, and derivation of Earth applications from new understanding. The Skyhook System has reduced the need for costly orbital launches, conserving resources and making near space available to all. (See net.skyhook.vid for more information.)

The newly developed Dinkshif FRF Ion Drive will be transported to the ISC for proving under real space conditions. The brainchild of Euro-Russian scientist, Nylast Dinkshif, the ion drive is capable of accelerating a large mass (small asteroid size, 20 to thirty yards across.) up to and beyond light speed using Frame of Reference Focus theory. Dinkshif claims to have conceived of this radical mathematical anomaly while swimming laps and staring at the black line on the bottom of the Goddard pool. Micro model testing of the FRF Ion Drive has so far verified the validity of Dinkshif's discovery. We are on the threshhold of interstellar and possibly interglactic travel.

On a different note – 20 award winning students from around the country have joined us today at the Goddard Space Flight Center to prepare for a ride of a lifetime on the ISC Shuttle, to visit the ISC for two weeks.

Hosted by the Goddard Education office, NASA scientists, engineers, educators and astronauts will engage these top students in areas of science, technology, engineering, and mathematics (FRF Theory). Students will have the opportunity to experience Earth science, planetary exploration, astrophysics, heliophysics and more through Skyhook travel and two weeks of hands-on activities in the Space City.

Media interested in attending can contact Elliott Worthington, Goddard Public Affairs Officer. Goddard Release No. 34-112

CHAPTER 5

Goddard Space Center - Skyhook Base. 24th June.

20 teenagers sat in the two front rows of the new Goddard auditorium quietly chatting and getting to know each other. This was the first time they had all come together since individually winning places in the Space City Experience competition. Evenly balanced between boys and girls, all the candidates were dressed casually, the regimentation of schools and uniforms left behind. The ethnic mix was comprehensive and demonstrated the intergration of diverse racial origins that has built the USA into a great, free and cohesive nation.

Suddenly the buzz stopped as all attention was drawn to a tall man who had appeared at the podium. He smiled warmly, revealing perfect white teeth. His eyes sparkled with intelligence and were edged with lines of natural humor, further accentuated by strong features and a perfectly groomed head of silver hair. His voice was rich and warm.

"Ladies and gentlemen. Welcome to Goddard Space Centre. My name is Lt. Col. John Fuller and I will be your liaison officer and instructor throughout your stay here at Goddard and Space City.

Firstly let me congratulate every one of you on winning your placement. There are no short cuts to achieving this goal and your diligence and hard work has been noted and recognized. Your reward is being here today, about to enter the adventure of a lifetime." He paused and surveyed the eager faces before him. "Before we proceed with orientation and Space Boot Camp, do any of you have any general questions?"

There was silence before a hand went up. An Asian girl.

"Yes? Please stand and state your name, then your question."

"Amy Young, Sir. As can be clearly seen, we are from many different places, backgrounds, religions and ways of life. We are all high school graduates and young adults and I for one would hope to make friends and develop relationships within our group. Will there be any restrictions upon our private relationships here or on Space City?"

Fuller's mouth twitched as he suppressed a grin. He had anticipated this type of question further down the track, just not right on the chin at first contact. He put his hand up to stifle a staged cough and then looked up with a straight face.

"There are rules in living together in close quarters. These rules apply to all personnel on Space City and generally follow the normal routines of daily life. Married couples live together, with their children. Single people have individual living quarters and date and interact within the bounds of the rules. Space City is not the place to develop a private relationship and the Council will enforce the rules." He put his arms out and shrugged and allowed a little smile to show, "So no nooky-nooky on the City. OK?"

The group burst out in laughter and Amy made a wry face and swung her arm in an exaggerated shucks. She sat down.

Fuller signed for quiet and continued. "You will all receive a coms file of the rules for Space City. You will need to read them, know and understand them before we ascend. You will be tested on these rules. The only acceptable result is one hundred percent. Any more questions?"

There were none. Fuller moved from the podium. "If you will all follow me, we will pick up youniforms and equipment and I will show you to your rooms here at Goddard. For the next two weeks you are in Space City Boot Camp. Your attention to detail is crucial. It will save your life in space." He stopped walking after three paces and turned back to face the crowd of students. "From now on we get serious about this people." He turned and led them out of the auditorium.

They came to a large, long room with lockers down one wall. Each locker had a candidate name on an electronic security touch panel on the locker door. At the base of each locker, below the main door, there was a small hatch.

"Find your locker and stand along side it to the left. As of this moment we are under strict military discipline." Fuller marched along the row of standing cadets and assumed a harsh, instructive tone.

"You obey all instructions immediately and without question.

There will be no please, or thank you from myself or other staff. You will be addressed as "cadet" and by your last name, which must be visible on your uniform at all times. You will acknowledge instructions with "yes sir" or "no sir" as the case may be."

Fuller paused, looking along the line of dumbfounded faces. "Anyone who does not wish to comply with these instructions should depart now." The silence was tangible. A few cadets looked at each other in horror, wondering what they had got themselves into. But no one spoke, or left.

"Right, let's get on with it then. Open your lockers, read the instructions on the door, and become familiar with your youniforms and equipment. You will note the small hatch at the bottom of your locker. That is where your personal buddy parks itself when not active. You will get to meet your buddy shortly. For now, touch the green "screen" button, follow the directions and change into your youniforms."

As each cadet pressed the button a green fabric modesty screen ejected from the locker door frame and curled around and back, enclosing just enough space to change clothing.

"Cadets." called out Fuller, everything off down to the skin. That means plasdaids, feminine hygiene, 1-eye-v lenses. Anything. Your youniform will take care of all those matters as soon as you put it on. Your youniform is the ONLY piece of clothing you will wear 24/7. Together with your buddy, it cleans you and itself, and will take care of you if you take care of it. Hurry now. Another thirty seconds and the screens go back ready or not."

There were some noises of panic from a couple of the screens and one screen bounced as the occupant tripped over his own gear. thirty seconds later the screens retracted leaving most of the cadets standing straight by their lockers, looking smart in their deep blue youniforms. One of the boys was in a complete mess with his youniform on backwards. Fuller sauntered over to the backward youniform cadet and looked him up and down.

"Well, what are you going to do about this cadet?"

"Umm, yes sir. Ermm, no sir, I don't know sir."

"Do you know where your butt is cadet?"

"Yes sir."

"So why isn't your butt in the butt end of the youniform cadet?"

"It was sir, when I put it on. It keeps turning around on its own sir."

"How did you put it on cadet?"

"I pulled it over my head and slid my legs in sir."

"Did you read the instructions on how to put on the youniform cadet?"

"Sort of sir."

"You did not see them or you ignored them cadet?"

"I couldn't read them clearly without my contact lenses sir, so I guess I ignored them sir."

"That could cost you your life cadet. NEVER ignore instructions. Follow them to the letter. The youniform is made of DNA keyed allo-iso-skin. The youniform is YOU cadet. Read the instructions now." There was a short pause as the cadet squinted at the few lines. "The instructions state clearly, what, cadet?"

"Sir they say, put your fingertips of your right hand on the corresponding fingertips of the youniform and press the yellow Form-on button. The youniform will flow onto your body automatically and seal itself into place. To remove youniform put your right hand onto the youniform holder and press the red Form-off button."

"Well cadet?"

The cadet looked at the red button, then back at Fuller, his face a mask of horrified realization. "But sir..."

"DO IT!" There was muffled laughter coming from the others as the cadet hesitantly put his fingers onto the holder and pressed the red button. The youniform immediately began to flow back off his body into the storage unit as he turned around so only his bare butt would be totally and embarrassingly exposed. The muffled explosions of mirth from the cadets were met by an icy look from Fuller as the last vestiges of the boy's modesty were dragged back into the cabinet. This was one cadet who always read instructions from now on.

Suddenly the girl standing next to the hapless cadet pirouetted on her toes and slammed her hand onto the green screen button of his cabinet. With a grateful look the cadet pulled the screen around until he could reacquire his youniform correctly. Moments later the screen retracted and a fully clad cadet stood there with a straight face and at attention.

Fuller almost let his stern expression slip into the smile of amusement that was trying to surface. He looked at the girl cadet. "You, cadet," he beckoned with a thrust of the chin, "step forward."

The girl confidently took a step forward, a look of defiance on her face.

"What is your name cadet?"

"Felicity Hannaford, sir!"

"Cadet Hannaford, who gave you instructions to interfere with the cadet's situation?"

"No one sir."

"You will report to my office after we dismiss, cadet."

She took in a deep breath. "Yes sir!"

Fuller walked the length of the locker room, inspecting each cadet and allowing time for the tension to dissipate.

"I now draw your attention to your buddies. Does anyone know what a buddy is?" He stopped pacing and looked up and down the ranks. He was surprised when the cadet of backwards uniform fame stepped forward. He walked up to the cadet and got right into his face, nose to nose. "Your name cadet?"

"Gerald Shaw, sir."

"Cadet Shaw, for all present to hear, explain what a buddy is."

Shaw looked straight ahead and spoke up. "Sir, a buddy in any context is a personal, close friend, someone you can rely upon under any circumstances. The NASA personal buddy is a biobot derivation of semi-organic hybrid protoplasm that has been enhanced with human stem cells for intelligence, earthworm DNA for structure and organic armor growth from deep water sulphur based life forms found around volcanic activity in the Mariana Trench and the Red Sea. The organic strains have been refined and defined to be self-replicating and repairing. A buddy can pair with one human being by thought induction over a cerebral cortex link. The buddy is essentially impervious to heat, cold, vacuum, corrosive substances, radiation, biological hazards, projectiles and virtually anything outside of an immediate nuclear blast."

Fuller pursed his lips and shook his head. "Impressive cadet Shaw. Very impressive." Fuller looked up and down the line. "Can anyone add to cadet Shaw's description. Someone tell us how the buddy actually functions and interfaces?"

Felicity Hannaford stepped forward. No one else moved a muscle.

"Hmm," Fuller mused. "we seem to have a vaudeville duo with these two. OK cadet Hannaford, let's hear what you have to add."

"Sir. The buddy coexists with its host as a beneficial symbiont. It takes intellectual nourishment from the host thought processes and grows with and into the host. The buddy physically attaches itself to the host forming a helmet like covering over the whole head, but able to leave facial areas clear. The rest of the buddy forms a molecular mono layer over the whole host, creating total coverage and integrating with the youniform.

The buddy is able to anticipate the needs of the host by knowing the thoughts and emotions of the host through the cerebral cortex induction link. The buddy will form a total cover of the host, including face, eyes, ears and nose, and will provide oxygen, water and nourishment to the host as long as raw materials are available to the buddy on the outer surface. The buddy will work with the youniform and create clear panes for sight, with polarization to control light intensity.

The buddy will empathize with other buddies, providing instant communications for the host, and finally, the buddy will neutralize and recycle all host waste materials, including exhalation in a closed situation. The buddy takes waste that the youniform creates and shreds that waste back to molecular size. It then reassembles the molecules into whatever can logically be made and is needed by the host or for its own survival."

Felicity stopped. There was silence. Fuller looked the cadets up and down once more. "It is time to meet your buddies. Facing your lockers, press the blue button on the top right edge of your shelf and then look straight down. It is imperative that you look down and make eye contact with your buddy the instant it emerges. This is the critical bonding stage. Anyone who fails this stage will leave the program. Understood?"

"Yes sir!" came back in unison.

"Cadets, about face and do it!"

CHAPTER 6
The White House - Situation Room. 24th June.

"Mr. President, Madam Secretary, please watch this recording of the Korean Hegemony cabinet meeting some two hours ago. I must warn you that there are extremely violent and distressing events recorded." The director of the Asia - Iran Intelligence Group pressed a button and a fully three dimensional image of the Korean conference room materialized. The President and Secretary of State watched from a viewpoint above the conference table, and heard everything that had taken place in Korea two hours earlier.

At the execution of Jun Park the Secretary of State collapsed back retching in horror, barely keeping her lunch down. The Director paused the recording until she recovered. She apologized for her reaction and bade him to proceed. to the conclusion of the meeting. From the recording angle, Jun Park's dead eyes stared up at the camera from the floor the whole time.

Shaking her head and fanning herself with a sheaf of top severet documents, she asked, "Director Hanes, is it out of line for me to ask how you obtained this recording?"

"Madam Secretary, our technology has allowed us to see into all our allies and enemies alike for quite some time. I would not have breached security today had this matter not been of the gravest concern. The only location we do not have a permanent facility in place is the central government of the Iranian Islamic Empire. Since they went to extreme fundamentalism and reverted to tent life, we could not place a long term facility in a non permanent structure, their council tent. Due to the nature of the technology, we have to rely on secondary intelligence from the fixed structure homes of high officials."

The President tapped his pen on the desk blotter absentmindedly. "Do we have confirming intelligence that Jong Il is right about Iran? Are they ready to strike? A whole nation of suicide bombers. It is beyond belief. Has God abandoned us completely?"

"Mr. President, we have sufficient intel from Iranian officials speaking out of place, casually, in their homes for our analysts to say that there is an eighty percent certainty that Jong Il is right. Korean Hegemony must have a mole planted high in the Iranian Empire to be so sure of himself. Recall that it was the former North Korea that supplied the materials and advisors for the Iranian nuclear establishment. He would certainly have embedded sleeper spies during that time. The sad matter is that our President back in 2010 had the opportunity to strike and demolish Iran's fledgling nuclear capability and he didn't. Today we are about to reap the poisonous fruits of that failure."

"Director, is there any indication when there would be a first strike from Iran?"

"Mr. President, we are watching the mobilisation of the Iranian Empire armed forces and the placement of their nuclear missiles. Our assessment is that a strike will occur within the next 72 hours."

The President shifted to the edge of his seat, his knuckles white as he gripped the armrests, listening intently, jaw clenched.

The Secretary of State picked up the thread, "So we have to assume that Korea will strike immediately if their threat analysis is the same. Mr. President, Director, I need to leave now and call a meeting of the Joint Chiefs. We should raise the Homeland Security alert to Red. Mr. President, do you have any other instructions for me?"

"Other than get the Joint Chiefs in here fast, no."

The Secretary of State left, racing out the door.

"Chuck, what are our options here. Before the brass turns up. I don't want this to become a war of words and I can't chop off heads like that psychopath in Pyonyang. Do we need to do a double header and take out Pyonyang and Teheran right now? Do we have satellite capability to knock down any missiles they fire? Straight Chuck. We have been friends for a long time. No bullshit."

With just the two of them in the room, formality went out the door.

"OK Tom. We have some defensive satellite capability. We can take out a small number of missiles during flight, but to attempt to cover the whole shooting match between these two, well, quite a few are going to get through.

We do have test ready one of our new AMD devices we could use as a last resort. An Anti-Matter Device would take out all the missiles and everything else in the air. It would destroy the ozone layer in its effective destructive region and maybe send us the way of the dinosaurs. Its untested, we just don't know what it will do."

The President shook his head and threw up his hands. "Damned if we do and damned if we don't. Chuck, we are talking about Armageddon here. The possible end of the world. Because of two lunatics. Sheesh. We can't even throw some blame at Israel for it this time."

The President looked up at his friend suddenly, squinted in thought and grabbed the telephone off his desk. "Get me Rafi Ben-Gurion right now," he ordered the operator, then replaced the phone. Thirty seconds later it trilled and the President snatched up the handset. A deep voice came through, "Ben-Gurion here Tom, what can I do for you today?" asked the President of Israel.

CHAPTER 7

Goddard Space Center - Skyhook Base. 24th June.

"Stand at ease cadet Hannaford." Fuller walked around her, hands clasped behind his back. "Cadet Hannaford, by what authority did you interfere in my direct order to another cadet in a matter that was no business of yours?"

"It was my business sir."

Fuller raised an eyebrow. "Oh! How do you see that cadet?"

"Sir," she took a deep breath, "it is clearly obvious that we must look out for each other at all times. At what point does this obligation to look out for the other start? I believe at every point sir. Even the most insignificant point... Sir." Felicity paused to gather her thoughts.

"If we are there for our partners in a physically dangerous situation then we should be there to help against anything that may be detrimental. I saw that Cadet Shaw was being shamed enough by his own negligence without having to undergo the embarrassment of standing naked in front of the whole group, sir. I made the decision to protect cadet Shaw by the only means at hand. Sir."

Fuller rounded his desk and sat down. He cocked his head to one side. "Cadet, now that you know that such impulsive behavior will result in disciplinary action, how will you act in future similar situations?"

"My action was not impulsive sir. It was calculated to cause the least possible immediate and long term harm to our group. I would do exactly the same thing again, sir."

Fuller allowed a tiny smile to turn up his mouth. He reached out to a drawer in his desk and took out a small box. "Step forward cadet Hannaford." He paused as she took a step forward. "Let's make that Second Lieutenant Hannaford for the moment." He held out the box with the rank insignia. Her eyebrows raised in surprise, just a slightly. Regaining full composure she accepted the box and stepped back.

"Thank you for your confidence sir."

"You are the squad commander of your group as of now Hannaford. Your rank is only good within your group. Not in general personnel. I will call upon your recommendations for promotion of other members in conjunction with my own observations. We will structure into five squads of four cadets per squad. This will be completed by 0600 tomorrow. Promotions will follow in due course. I will announce your position at dinner in one hour. Do you understand cadet?"

"Yes sir!"

"You may return to your quarters."

CHAPTER 8

CIA - AIIG Division 24th June, late afternoon.

"Director Hanes, Madam Secretary." The senior operative acknowledged their presence as they waited for the Joint Chiefs of Staff to assemble. The Secretary of State looked ruffled after her rushed task to call the Joint Chiefs. She had out a small mirror and a lipstick as she watched the operative.

He launched into his analysis conjuring up images of buildings that floated before him with transparent walls showing room interiors down the most minute detail. Looking closely, human figures could be discerned moving about.

"We are looking into the governmental palace of Jong Il in Pyonyang in real time, currently early morning of June 25 in Korea. It is our understanding that Jong Il will instigate a nuclear attack within hours, just as fast as he can arm his missiles, so we are following him 24/7.

He will push the button himself. Our Psych profile on him makes it clear that he could not allow anyone else to do this. He has admitted on more than one occasion that his apparent belligerence and madness is feigned, as was that of his father and grandfather. It was all showmanship and brinkmanship contrived to destabilise the region and milk surrounding nations and of course us, for all the money they could collect. That run has now ended because the real lunatics, the Iranians, have achieved nuclear capacity and they will first use it on their old ally and supplier. Iran perceives the Korean Hegemony as the only threat to their plans for Islamic world domination. Our threat assessment has increased to 98% certainty that Iran will press the button. That is what Jong Il has concluded and he really does know his old playmates well."

The operative stopped for a breath and the Secretary of State asked, "How can we be so sure that Jong Il really knows for certain? Where are we getting these live feeds from? I had no idea of our capability until I saw the recordings a few minutes ago!"

The operative looked to Director Hanes for a cue. Hanes nodded for him to answer.

"Madam Secretary, Jong Il has had deep cover operatives embedded in the Iranian nuclear project for over a decade. These operatives are Iranians who believe they are working for the West. Some think it is Great Britain, some think for the United States. Jong Il was very clever about that as he anticipated that any Asian operatives in the project would be purged, which in fact happened about a year ago. His operatives have given him intelligence from the innermost circle of Iran's nuclear development group." The operative gave the Secretary a moment, but she sat silent and indicated he should continue.

"Our methods for intelligence collection are highly classified. So much so that outside of these walls, only the President and three of the Joint Chiefs know about it, and only on a "need to know" basis. You are the fifth person outside of this directorate to see this in action. Director Hanes, I ask you now to state the level to which I should disclose our surveillance technology to the Madam Secretary."

The Secretary huffed with anger at this "in your face" bypass of her authority. The Director waved his fingers to calm her down and said, "Agent Gordon is following strict procedure Madam Secretary. He could not do otherwise and would be criminally negligent had he gone further without my authority. You have my authorisation for full disclosure Agent." Hanes pulled a communicator from his pocket and spoke a few words in a low tone. A similar device now in the Agent's hand gave one beep. The Agent looked at the authorisation code record and acknowledged the Director.

"My apologies Madam Secretary."

"Accepted and not required. Please continue."

"Madam Secretary, over the past two decades the USA has developed the concept of molecular sized robots far beyond what is known publicly. We have all heard of nanobots and the good they can do medically and in a host of other applications. We decided to try to create spybots and succeeded far beyond the original concept.

Our solution is a nanobot based wall paint. On the premise that every building has some paint in it, even the most dank and basic prison cell in Pyonyang, once we infiltrate the paint based spybots into our target they remain virtually invisible and undetectable.

The present generation of spybots are based upon those used by NASA for their Astronaut Buddy systems. These are, and I quote the NASA handbook, biobot derivation of semi-organic hybrid protoplasm enhanced with human stem cells for intelligence, earthworm DNA for structure and organic armor growth from deep sea sulphur based life forms.

We took these biobots and made them self sustaining scavengers that could be controlled by signals from satellites. To ensure an ongoing replenishment of the biobot spybots we made their base sustenance paint. They eat paint. And of course in doing so create a need for repainting.

We are able to control the spybots to form lenses and audio amplifiers and they transmit on a nanofrequency radio range that is undetectable by any present technology outside our own."

"Excuse me Agent," The Secretary interrupted, "How can you be so sure about that?" The Agent gave a little smile.

"Madam Secretary, if they knew about the transmissions or the spybots, we would have been the first to hear about their discovery as we watch them 24/7. They know nothing. The can of paint looks, smells and acts exactly like a can of paint. The air drying activates the spybots and they have an effective life of six months. We move them around so the same patch is not being painted over time and again. They are quite mobile and almost invisible. They change color with their background just like a chameleon lizard.

This view is being rendered through a new method recently perfected. The spybots have distributed themselves as a lagrange mono layer throughout the whole building complex. Each molecular biobot is equidistant from its six neighbors effectively covering over a million times the area that the same patch of paint would cover. The downside is that the biobots will fail within 48 hours rather than six months. They cannot find nourishment on their own."

"At the risk of sounding ignorant, how can we take such a risk, of losing our long term coverage?"

"Madam Secretary, the threat level is so high and the use of nuclear weapons so certain, there is no point in not taking this action. However we have one more trick up our sleeve Madam Secretary."

Gordon looked to Hanes once again and the same short ceremony went down with a beep to Gordon's communicator.

"We have kept aside several strategic, concentrated patches of spybot paint in key locations of the presidential palace. Jong Il has the nuclear activation keys close at hand and amazingly enough, his nuclear activation fail-safe system does rely on antiquated metal keys that need to go into keyholes. These key locks are behind an hermetically sealed safe door that we have not yet been able to crack with the spybots. We are waiting for Jong Il to open this door and give us the chance to flow a spybot patch into the locks, where they will self destruct and fuse the locks closed. He will not be able to launch his attack."

"Phew!" The Secretary made a most unladylike noise. "So the fate of the world hangs in the balance on whether Jong Il will turn the keys immediately or give you time to run your plan."

"Not entirely Madam Secretary." Gordon did not lose his composure or miss a beat. "I did say we had several patches of spybots in place. We may not have been able to get into the safe, but we did get to the keys themselves. Both keys have a coating of spybots. We change these coatings every four to six weeks to make sure they will always be active. They were changed one week ago. Jong Il has handled the keys with the spybots and suspects nothing. We have three options with the spybots on the keys. We could build the spybots up in the keyway channel and prevent the key entry. This could be overcome by a strong push into the keyway.

We could build up the spybots and change the key profile, so preventing the key turning while the ally spybots flow in. Or we could self destruct on the keys making them turn red hot for a moment, burning his fingers and delaying him enough for the flow in."

"So Agent Gordon, before I say that I am still not convinced, do you have any more magical tricks that you have not told me about? I do recall that you could not penetrate the Iranian high command tents."

"Well Ma'am," he grinned "we could theoretically kill Jong Il any time we want to with the spybots, but our assessment is that the destabilization would set off the nuclear exchange even faster. Jong Il is a ruthless bastard as we have seen, but he really does have some very scary people around him. As to Iran, we are working on infiltrating tent pole paint but we have run out of time."

The Secretary looked at Hanes for clarification. "Charles, where does it go from here?"

"June, it goes nowhere but back to Iran. We may be able to stop Jong Il, but we also need to stop the Ayatollahs. That's not so easy. We don't have too many paint patches in that neck of the woods and as stated, it is extremely hard to paint the inside of a tent."

"Tom was talking to Rafi Ben-Gurion earlier. We should go and find out what he has in mind."

CHAPTER 9

Teheran. Presidential bunker. 24th June, late night.

President Arjmand sat scowling at the end of the conference table. His thinning hair was slicked back with craggy eyebrows accentuating a straight, pointy nose. His eyes were black and smoldering with anger.

"Who did this? Again! Our systems were supposed to be completely isolated and foolproof! The Israelis got us once with a computer virus back in 2010. Didn't we learn anything from that? It set us back years, and now it has happened again?" He stood up, glaring at his security council. The ayatollahs who sat there did not flinch under his angry gaze, but the military staff were all gut churning and trying to look away. Only one man stared Arjmand back, eye to eye.

Arash Zardooz was the head of nuclear development, known as Iranatom. On the surface, developing nuclear energy resources for domestic use. In fact, as the whole world knew, developing weapons of mass destruction, and some of not so mass destruction. Zardooz was a scientist with an unusual secondary function. He was also a Colonel in the state secret police. The fact that security had failed did not seem to bother him even though it was apparent that his own neck was on the line.

Arjmand walked around the table and got into the face of Zardooz. He spat out one word.

"Explain!"

A cold smile crept across the face of Zardooz and he snorted a laugh.

"Potemkin!" He calmly uttered this one word. Potemkin Village. A legendary place that looked prosperous but was an empty shell.

Arjmand froze. His eyes widened and his head slowly tilted.

"Yes?"

Zardooz shook his head slightly, indicating "not here."

Arjmand nodded agreement and pushed back from Zardooz. He looked up and surveyed the council members, noting expressions and reactions.

Wondering if one was a traitor.

He looked back to Zardooz and indicated his private office with a slight move of his head.

"No one is to leave this room. There will be no calls made. Just sit and wait. Do not talk." Arjmand led Zardooz into the small office and shut the door. The facility was swept for listening devices daily. It was as secure as possible. They leaned towards each other over the deep walnut finish of the freshly varnished desk and Zardooz began explaining.

"After the Israeli virus attack on our installations in 2010 we realized that nothing was safe. We needed the internet, and our computer systems are Western technology. There is always room for an enemy to insert a passive "back door" access that is undetectable, so my deceased predecessor devised a plan that has worked. There are only ten people today, now with you, eleven, who know of this plan.

From 2021 onwards I took my most trusted technicians and scientists and created an inner circle and a second, secret production stream. This team meticulously copied every step of the "real" production but manually, using over ordering and insisting on warranty parts with the main equipment orders. There was no internet connection, ever. We reasoned that even if there was a back door built into the secret production facility computers, it would not matter. You need a path outside the door to go somewhere. There was nowhere to go. We have a secret facility, one tenth the capacity of the compromised facilities, but we built a stock of fissionable material, currently enough for around thirty war heads, and *our* computers are uncompromised."

Zardooz leaned back in his chair, a smile across his face, as he watched Arjmand contemplate this news. After a few moments Arjmand looked up at him.

"So we sacrificed the Potemkin many for the sake of the few. As Allah wills it. An expensive decoy. We have strike capacity. Limited but sufficient to knock out the Korean threat. With such a small number of warheads we must strike first and hard. We will have no room for error and no defence if we fail." Arjmand paused and squinted at Zardooz.

"So how did this new virus attack get in? Do you know?"

Zardooz shrugged.

"No idea. But that is why we set up the secret facility."

Arjmand rubbed his hand over an edge of the desk, polishing a spot on the varnish.

"Keep looking. There is a traitor here somewhere!" The varnish shined and appeared to ripple in the reflected light from above. "OK let's go back in. We say nothing."

A patch of the varnish raced down the inside of the desk leg and onto Arjmand's highly polished black shoe.

Zardooz rose and touched the desk top. "Nice job."

They went back to the conference room, Arjmand hard pressed not to show his elation at Zardooz's revelation.

He would launch against the Korean Hegemony immediately. Council and traitor be damned.

The varnish remaining on the recently vacated desk coalesced into a distinctly dish shaped disc. A micro burst nanowave communication flashed through concrete, rock and soil towards a satellite far overhead.

CHAPTER 10

Goddard, 25th June, 6 am

" All cadets present, Sir." Felicity Hannaford announced in her new role as squad leader.

"Cadets." Fuller surveyed the squad, all in a perfect line and all dress in order. "We are going to do a dry run of our Space City launch today. We will be boarding a Skyhook transport shuttle emulating exactly the same ground stages and preparation as the actual launch day. Except that today we will not be going anywhere.

Today you need to look and listen so you understand all launch safety protocols and evacuation procedures. After that we will learn the procedures for emergency post launch atmospheric and vacuum survival.

Cadets, I stress to you that at all times, you remember that your buddy will take care of you and your youniform will protect you. Never panic. In the unlikely event that an emergency situation should arise, you will be able to follow the steps you learn in the coming days. Cadets! Learn and live! Live and learn. Any questions?"

Fuller waited a few seconds. No one stepped forward. "Cadets, follow squad leader Hannaford and board the shuttle.

At that point the semblance of military discipline evaporated and the group moved off towards the shuttle launch bay as if to a picnic, Felicity Hannaford leading. Fuller called out to the group, stopping it in its tracks.

"Cadets, your performance today will determine promotions within your group. I will be watching you closely. Carry on." The group immediately smartened up.

They reached the Skyhook transport bay where a sleek, round nosed tube awaited, straddling the horizontal approach rail of the sky tram. Fuller always stopped for a moment whenever he saw this. He likened it to a giant toothpaste tube. But what the heck, it got the job done.

Unlike the earlier generation of Space Shuttles that had flown their last mission way back in 2011, this new mode of orbital entry did not use huge reaction mass rockets and boosters. It was simply a tram-car into space, and used the Skyhook project as it's final launch platform, incorporating small, but effective, reaction mass engines, for free space flight.

The 27,000 mile long, or high as you look at it, Skyhook is a mono layer, mono filament, constant diameter carbon fiber tube extended from the Goddard Space Center to a gravity neutral point 27,000 miles in orbit, a geo-stationary point where major gravitational influences of sun, moon and planets cancel each other out, leaving only the gravitational pull of Earth itself to overcome. A counter mass, actually a tourist space restaurant, attached to the space end of the Skyhook keeps the tube taut and extended, just like a child whirling a weighted string around its head. Thrusters on the counterweight make constant minor adjustments allowing for spurious gravitational effects on the imperfect physicality of the structure. The forces involved in this edifice were so great that the added stresses of a space transport propelling itself up the apparently solid tube made little difference to the structural integrity of the Skyhook. Take away the counter weight and the structure would collapse like a nylon stocking without a leg in it. Once deployed and firmly extended, induction magnet cabling was attached to the inside of the tube without compromising the mono layer. A monatomic bond glue was used for this purpose, with constant vigilance and maintenance the order of the day. A controlled magnetic induction sequence would then propel the permanent rare earth transport magnets to the 27,000 mile destination in around one and a quarter hours of one gee acceleration/deceleration. The return simply used earth gravity and regenerative induction braking, returning some of the energy back to the system.

The public restaurant was serviced by slower, more luxuriously appointed internal tram cars that ran up and down the inside of the great tube. Paying passengers would lie back in their seats and enjoy the 4 hour ride each way at 0.1 g. Unlike the space force transport, the public tram turned about 180 degrees at the half way point. The carbon fibre mono layer was totally transparent and as clear as diamond, affording the clientele a perfect view of the Earth receding or approaching, and the panorama of space all around with little distortion. The tram windows were anti glare and the tube material itself protection from cosmic rays and solar radiation. Opaque blinds were available for sufferers of vertigo or other phobias and cocktails in squeeze bottles were served in first class.

Fuller herded his cadets across the walkway and into the transport at an entrance just behind the control cabin. He looked to see who was driving and was pleased to see the blond curls of Janine Carver spilling out under her commander's cap as she concentrated on pre launch checks, even though there was no trip scheduled. The old days of bulky flight suits and pressurization were long gone since the advent of youniforms and buddies.

A few years younger than Fuller, Janine was a career astronaut and transport pilot with the experience of dozens of trips behind her. She was also stunningly attractive, lively and available. He smiled to himself, looking forward to a great day and maybe an interesting evening.

"Cadets, find a seat, strap in and listen." The group sat themselves in the center seating area and buckled the safety webbing, as if the transport was really going to move off. Tendrils from each buddy extruded and penetrated small punctures in the webbing, drawing water and nourishment from capillaries integrated in the weave. At the same time, each youniform, sensing the environmental change and the new location, grew a protective helmet, including a faceplate and anti glare shield. Unlike the luxurious internal trams, the transport was spartan and functional, designed as a workhorse and temporary survival platform for space city staff.

The final jump to space city, a mere 500 miles from the Skyhook terminus, was by reaction mass thrusters as the transport left the tube rails behind. That last 500 miles was Janine's real task.

Fuller surveyed his charges carefully, ensuring that no safety detail was overlooked while Janine checked the passenger fault display panel.

"We are not going anywhere today." he announced. "This is purely an orientation session. Look around you and touch nothing. In the event of any emergency your familiarity with equipment, emergency escape exits and first aid equipment could save a life. Even your own. Look towards the..." Fuller's lecture was interrupted by a heavy bump to the transport accompanied by a loud thump as something heavy made contact. Fuller looked to Janine who signalled secure Buddy communication.

"That was the next supply upload being secured in the cargo bay at back." She thought to Fuller buddypathically. "The next run takes general supplies and four of the new Dinkshif drives up to the City. As soon as you guys have finished here I'm scheduled to deliver this lot. Wanna come for a ride?" Out of sight of the cadets, Janine winked at Fuller. He controlled a smile and turned back to his charges.

"Cadets, Commander Carver informs me that the noises we just heard are from loading the supplies for space city. In this payload are four Dinkshif drives that will be used on the new deep space explorer being built on a captured asteroid at Space City. Now back to basics. Please activate the safety view-card on the seat back in front of you and we will review evacuation procedures.

CHAPTER 11

Somewhere in Iran - Secret Nuclear Facility. 25th June

After a four hour flight, Zardooz and Arjmand stood small as ants next to a huge missile. This was something far larger than any intercontinental ballistic missile in the secret arsenal. The rest were less than one quarter the size of this monster.

"This my President, is the Jack Hammer missile. Something that not even you knew existed. This is the missile that will destroy the Great Satan, America."

"What is it? How?" Arjmand had his head back, slack jawed at the sight, peering into the gloom of the silo to see the top of the missile.

"Let's go back to my office and I will explain." Zardooz turned about and led the way up the mesh walkway through steel blast doors, to the office complex. It was a fair distance away as all the infrastructure around the missile would be vaporized at launch.

"Please take a seat President. I will call for coffee."

While Zardooz went out, Arjmand looked around the large office. The walls were covered with schematics of missiles, with one standing out, labelled clearly "Jack Hammer". On another wall were full projections of maps of the world and a single, detailed map of North America. There was a yellow dot on the map right on Yellowstone National Park, with Global Positioning coordinates written on the dot. Arjmand returned his attention at Zardooz came back in.

"We are going to destroy the Great Satan by blowing up some bears in a national park Zardooz?"

Zardooz smiled and laughed. "Something like that Mr. President. Let's start with that map then.

Zardooz went over to the map and lifted it, revealing a geological cutaway schematic. "This is a diagram of one of the world's largest magma plumes, Mr. President. It lies beneath Yellowstone National Park. If this plume were to erupt to the surface it would cause the largest volcanic explosion in recorded history. It would be so big that it would blanket North America in ash and make it uninhabitable for years to come. It would destroy the Great Satan and much of the rest of the world." Zardooz paused and flipped back to the world map. He walked over to the Jack Hammer schematic and continued.

"We are not capable of taking out the Great Satan without help. We need leverage. Certainly we can take care of North Korea, but once we launch against the Hegemony, the US will come down on us with everything she has and we will be obliterated. If we strike the US first, at the exact same time as North Korea, we will stop the retaliation. In any case the US will not react immediately as the Korean Hegemony is not their ally. They will react against a threat that may turn on them and only slowly at that. It is their way to absorb the first blows and then hit back. Our strategy depends upon this weakness of their leadership.

By the time the US reacts we will have nothing left of our thirty missiles, so Jack Hammer has to launch against the US at the same time as the Korean strike and blow out Yellowstone."

"Surely the US will destroy our missile in flight?" Arjmand asked.

"It is possible Mr. President, however we have devised a strategy that should fool the US defense systems and delay their presidential decision long enough for Jack Hammer to do its job. Look at this diagram."

The pored over the schematic that Zardooz had rolled flat and Zardooz continued his explanation.

"Jack Hammer is not a sub orbital ballistic missile. It is an orbit capable launch vehicle and will put our payload into an apparently benign low earth orbit. The US would be aggressors to shoot it down. They cannot afford that tag. So they will wait for absolute certainty.

The first section of the payload is a replica of a Space City supply transport. We have obtained genuine transponder codes from a NASA employed American Iranian whose parents are in our tender care, and to all intents, this will appear to be a Space Transport in distress. The rest of the payload are ten, fifty megaton nuclear devices each mounted on its own missile."

Arjmand was entranced by what he was seeing, coffee by his hand untouched.

"We launch the Jack Hammer 90 minutes before the attack on the Korean Hegemony. This puts Jack Hammer into a computed orbit over Yellowstone at the exact moment of the launch against the Korean Hegemony. Jack Hammer releases the Transport replica which is sending out emergency signals and may-days. The US focusses all its attention on this situation as the transport appears to be crashing into Yellowstone National Park, directly over the magma plume. As soon as the transport drops to atmospheric level and begins to heat up, it will appear that a tragedy is unfolding as pieces break away. The nuclear tipped missiles will then be launched straight down the throat of the magma plume at fifteen second intervals. The missiles themselves are hardened against the blast of the previous warheads and each one is programmed to penetrate deeper into the earth's mantle. By the eighth blast there should be a volcanic release as never before, with one or two more missiles left to make sure the egg is well and truly cracked. This emergency will overwhelm the Great Satan."

Zardooz stopped and looked at Arjmand expectantly. The questions came.

"How sure are you that this will work Zardooz? We are risking everything on this."

"What does it matter Mr. President? Until a few minutes ago you were going to launch twenty conventional missiles at the Korean Hegemony and hope that there would be no world power retaliation. If this plan works our great nation has a chance of surviving. It is the will of Allah."

Arjmand stared hard at Zardooz and then slowly nodded his head. "You are right my friend. You are right. Maybe those 72 virgins will have to wait a little longer for me. I am here to make this happen. Show me the launch sequence. It is time."

CHAPTER 12

The Situation Room, the White House 25th June, 8 am

"Mr. President, it is Rafi Ben-Gurion for you. He says it is urgent, life and death."

The President snatched up the phone, "Rafi, it is Tom. What is the problem?"

"We have lost track of Arjmand and Zardooz. We suspected and have confirmed a secret facility that we were unable to penetrate. Our analysis suggests they have around 20 secret nukes and they are about to launch against the Korean Hegemony. We stopped the 200 known missiles. The two of them just vanished off the map about half an hour ago. We are sending you their last known coordinates."

"What can the US do Rafi? What evidence do we have that they will launch?"

"Watch this recording Tom. You will have no doubts after that. I see you disabled the Korean missile launch Tom. Nice paint job. Our desk varnish is on Arjmand's shoe but unable to penetrate the rock overhead. They are deep. Very deep."

The President watched the meeting between Zardooz and Arjmand recorded by the Israeli desk varnish nanobots a few hours earlier. He needed no further convincing.

"Immediate meeting, all Chiefs of Staff still present. Situation room. Ten minutes." he rattled off to his secret service liaison. He picked up his communicator and pressed for the Secretary of State and Chuck Hanes to join him immediately.

A siren screamed, scaring an adrenaline jolt and making the President's heart race. Without ceremony the secret service grabbed the President and began rushing him out to the lawn where Marine One was just landing. Trained to obey without question, the President moved with his protectors, all the while frantically plugging at his communicator to find out what the threat was. The director of the NSA came on line.

"Mr. President, we have detected a missile launch from Iran."

"How many missiles?"

"Just the one at this time sir. It is not following a logical missile trajectory sir and appears to be an orbital launch of a multi stage vehicle."

"Is it a definite threat to us"

"It is too early to say sir. We must get you airborne in Airforce One now sir as we will not have time to respond if indeed this is a threat."

"OK NSA. This is POTUS transferring to Airforce One. I want SecState and Director Hanes on board with me."

"We will do our best to comply sir."

The helicopter had landed and the President was rushed forward by the guard detail. Strapped in tight, Marine One took off with two identical ships nearby and headed for Andrews Air Force Base where Airforce One and Two were ready to go.

With padded earphones stopping the engine noise, the President regained communications with his chiefs of staff who now awaited him in the situation room.

"I will not be joining you gentlemen but we will proceed as if I was present." He heard some responsive grumbles of acknowledgement and then went on. "In the past few minutes I received a warning call from the President of Israel, Rafi Ben-Gurion, that a secret Iranian nuclear facility and launch base has been identified. Arjmand and Zardooz both went deep underground and off the map suddenly. I have incontrovertible evidence that Iran is about to launch against the Korean Hegemony. We have physically disabled Korean missile capability and they are unable to initiate, nor retaliate to, an attack. Israel disabled the primary Iranian missile arsenal but was completely unaware of the secret Iranian base until a couple of hours ago.

The launch we have just witnessed from Iran appears to be an orbital vehicle. We have no evidence that this is a weapon platform. The recorded conversation of the Arjmand and Zardooz makes it abundantly clear that this must be taken as a weapon. We have the launch location and assume that the remaining estimated 20 missiles are in close proximity. Gentlemen, as commander in chief I must be the one to authorize hostilities against Iran that may plunge our planet into a world war from which no one will emerge. Advise me wisely. Advise me now. You have ten minutes."

The helicopter had closed on Andrews and Airforce One and Two, Boeing 888 flying wing space planes, which could be seen like two tiny corporal chevrons on a field of gray concrete, growing larger and larger. Their immense size now became apparent as human figures awaited the President's arrival by a portable escalator.

CHAPTER 13

Iran - Secret Launch Facility Bunker. June 25, afternoon

"You see Mr. President! I told you they would be paralyzed. The Great Satan has not reacted and soon it will be too late regardless."

"Zardooz - I never doubted you." Arjmand clapped Zardooz on the shoulder as they stood together alone in the launch control room. The countdown sequence on the twenty conventional nuclear missiles was ticking down the ninety minutes Jack Hammer needed to achieve orbit and position.

"Now Mr. President, allow me to show you the safest place on Allah's Earth while all this is happening. Deep below us is the command bunker capsule, a fully self contained survival shelter that can sustain a small group almost indefinitely."

A small section of the varnish patch on Arjmand's Gucci shoes had flowed off and up to the desk corner. There was not a lot of varnish and the weak signal this small patch could put out was not getting through to the satellite. As the two men left, the patch autonomously spread itself to achieve a longer wavelength of signal that would penetrate the rock. It was at capacity for such a small patch, but the satellite came on line with a weak signal and it sent the recorded session via micro burst. The men were gone now. No motion or body heat detected. Shut down.

Zardooz led Arjmand to a narrow elevator door, just wide enough for one person at a time to enter and room for maybe four adults in the car. Zardooz pressed the lower button. There were only two buttons.

"We are going down just one level?" Arjmand asked in an unbelieving tone.

Once again, Zardooz laughed. "Yes my friend, but what a level. One thousand feet down to the first and only floor."

After a ride of perhaps 45 seconds, the car decelerated and stopped. The door slid open to reveal a brightly lit white corridor that disappeared into a perspective dot far away. Zardooz pulled up a roller cover to reveal an electric 4 man cart. He turned a switch and a green active light came on. Maneuvering the cart into the walkway, he beckoned Arjmand to get on.

"It is a long way to the capsule. One mile with seven blast doors in between the elevator and the capsule, just in case someone decides to drop a nuke on us."

"Won't we be buried down here forever if that happens?"

"Mr. President, we have tried to cover every contingency. Even if we are buried, we have a rock borer in our inventory and unlimited nuclear power. We can survive here for years."

Arjmand shrugged his shoulders. "And what of the 72 virgins. How many of those are there down here?"

Zardooz smiled coldly once again. "Mr. President. Every contingency. Every."

CHAPTER 14

Goddard Skyhook Space Transport. 25th June, 8.15 am

Janine whipped around in her seat, a look of alarm on her face. "John! John! DefCon 1 There is some emergency. I have instructions for immediate launch. No delays. Make sure your babies are strapped in good because we are going right now."

Fuller, also in the DefCon loop, reacted immediately, eyeballing every seat belt and making sure nothing loose was going to become a missile during the run. He strapped himself into the nearest seat and gave Janine the OK to launch.

"Cadets, what is about to happen is not a drill. I repeat that this is NOT a drill. There has been a security alarm that requires this transport to launch immediately. There is no time to off load us so we are going for a ride to Space City. I will advise you what the emergency is as more information comes to hand. Over to Commander Carver."

"Thank you Col. Fuller. In the last few moments I was advised that the USA has entered the highest Defence Condition due to an Iranian Missile launch. The President is aboard Airforce One. Our standing orders are to get off planet as quickly as possible. We launch in 20 seconds."

CHAPTER 15
Korean Hegemony, Pyongyang, 25th June, 9.15 pm

Lun Jong Ill was enraged. Unable to turn the keys for the missile launch sequence, he had called for maintenance to bring a diamond bit drill and drill out the locks, not realizing that it wouldn't help. Two headless bodies lay on the floor nearby with the head of the facility commander staring sightlessly at the heels of his own shoes as it lay under the desk. The other body that of a guard who had stepped in to help his beleaguered commander, and paid the ultimate penalty.

Jong Ill was prancing around bashing consoles and screaming his head off. Blood from the corpses was splattered everywhere as he slapped his shoes into the pooling gore. Other staff in the area cringed and shrank down in chairs trying to disappear under desks or slinking behind file cabinets.

A terrified maintenance worker came into the launch console room and after one look vomited up his last meal. Jong Ill thought better of adding the poor man to the corpse count as he needed him to work the drill. He grabbed the hapless worker by the collar and dragged him through the blood and vomit to the launch console. The stench was overwhelming and the worker shaking in terror, unable to hold the drill steady as he cried and whimpered.

Jong Ill took the man's head by grabbing his ears and stared him in the face.

"If you do not drill these locks exactly as I tell you we will all be dead in minutes. Iran has launched nuclear missiles at us. These locks are blocking our defense! DO YOU UNDERSTAND?"

The worker calmed a little and nodded yes. Jong Ill released him and pointed at the console. The worker took a deep breath of the fouled air and positioned the bit right on the barrel groove in line with the tumblers and started drilling.

Senses stunned by the intense whine of the drill an officer came running into the room, not seeing the mess on the floor and slipping into a flying back flop on the floor with an audible crack of bones breaking, coming to a sliding rest under the console. He groaned and shook his head to clear some of the pain, gasping to deliver his message. Jong Ill tapped the drill operator and signalled him to cut the power.

"Supreme Leader," the officer grimaced with the effort, "We have confirmation of an Iranian orbital launch of one rocket only. It is not targeted on us." He gave a look of relief at Jong Ill and collapsed back, unconscious.

Jong Ill pursed his lips and looked thoughtful for a moment. He gestured to the worker, "Keep drilling! Fast as you can!" There was no doubt in his mind that this was part of an Iranian scenario to take out the Hegemony. He would try to first strike, but he wondered what else was going to fail to operate.

"Hurry! Hurry!" The poor worker looked at Jong Ill, cowering like a beaten puppy. Chasings of hardened alloy steel powder flew from the drill bit and acrid smoke permeated the air with the smell of burned metal. The penetration of the bit was just so slow that it appeared not to be moving at all. Jong Ill's impatience was getting the better of him and he began to lose control, flicking his laser sword on and slicing pieces off the nearest office chair. The drill operator, already in a bad way, was now shaking in uncontrolled fear causing the drill bit to chatter wildly.

"Watch what you are doing!" shrilled Jong Ill, beating the hapless worker with the rolled up coding papers. The man cracked, released the drill and fell to the floor, curled in a fetal position as the drill went silent. Jong Ill lost it completely and started slicing the worker into pieces with the laser sword, the screams of agony and terror dying into a gurgle as guts spilled across the older gore and another head rolled away. Behind Jong Ill, a desk worker had hefted a solid paper weight and crept up on him as he panted and looked down at the butchery he has just done. The man slammed Jong Ill in the back of the head, crushing in his skull like a raw egg and the body just dropped like a rock, without a sound. There was an audible sigh of relief from everyone in the room. Everyone looked about when the realization of what had just occurred hit home. So used to being followers, there was no one who could take charge. No one to stop the madness. No one to call out to the world for help.

One by one, and then as a group, they fled the room and the complex. The message spread. Jong Ill is dead. The Iranian nuclear missiles are coming. Run for your lives!

CHAPTER 16

Aboard Airforce One. 25th June, 8.15 am

The President, Director Chuck Hanes and Secretary of State June Beauvais watched the live nanobot paint feed from the Korean center. June retched at the gory slaughter, but this time was able to control herself.

"With Jong Ill out of the way and no succession we may be able to turn Korea around." the President suggested as he watched the staff fleeing the control center. "Provided of course that there is still a Korea left to turn. What do you think people?"

"Mr. President," replied Chuck, "Korea is not our biggest problem right now. Our own safety and whatever Iran is up to are the immediate concern. Our analysts have projected the orbit of the Iranian vehicle for the next 24 hours. In around thirty minutes it will be over the center of the United States. We need to take it out now." Chuck was intense, the stress levels showing.

June concurred. "I agree Mr. President. We cannot risk waiting to find out what they are up to. I would wager that they are banking on our policy of delaying overtly aggressive moves as we have always done in the past."

"What are our options Chuck?" the President was unruffled and holding himself together, calming Hanes.

"We really have only one sure fire option that will leave no doubt. An AMD. It is drastic and dangerous, but not as much as underestimating the Iranians. We can target and launch on your command Mr. President."

"June?" the President queried.

"I agree Mr. President. We have to be 100% sure of a knockdown."

"So be it. I order you Mr. Director, to initiate the destruction of the Iranian orbital vehicle using an Anti-matter Device without further delay." The President signalled the "football" carrier to approach and unlocked the briefcase containing the launch codes. June, as the next most senior official present had verification codes. The appropriate numbers were punched in to the traditional suitcase computer which transmitted to a satellite and bounced

---

to the Virginia launch center. Within two minutes a missile silo in the fields of Wyoming slid open and the missile was ready to fly.

The launch sequence counted down, 10, 9, 8, 7... suddenly klaxon alarms screamed for an abort, officers ran to preset positions screaming out "Abort! Shut down! Abort! Abort"

Aboard Airforce One the abort was noted and a reason demanded by the President.

The Chief of the Air Force appeared on a wall screen facing the President and his assistants.

"Report General!" the President demanded.

"Mr. President, we have detected a may-day signal coming from the same orbital region as the Iranian vehicle. It is not precisely the same position, but very close, say within 200 yards. The transponder identification indicates that this is one of our Space City transports in trouble." The president was about to interject with a question when the General cut him off and continued.

"Please wait Mr. President. The only Nasa Transport in transit at this time left the Goddard Skyhook launch terminus when the DefCon was raised. As per protocol under DefCon 1, the Transport launched immediately and should be climbing the Skyhook - it should not and could not be where this signal is originating. The situation is that the 20 high school guests at Goddard were aboard for orientation with their instructor, Lt Col John Fuller and pilot Commander Janine Carver. We are not sure about anything from the may-day origin vehicle, except that the transponder codes are genuine. We are trying to contact both Carver's transport and the one issuing the may-day to sort this out."

"Stand by General." The President turned to Hanes and Beauvais. "Sacrifice the few for the good of the many?"

Hanes and Beauvais looked at each other and then back at the President, neither wanting to be the one to condemn innocent children, even for the sake of the many. The President's shoulders sagged as he weighed and made his decision.

"General," the General nodded, "Take out the Iranian vehicle."

"Yes Mr. Pres... wait...ohh..." there was a pause for a few seconds as the General listened intently to his ear bud. He looked up.

"Critical developments, Mr. President. We have identified activity in the launch origin area of the first vehicle. We believe up to 20 concealed silos are being prepared for launch. Joint Chiefs suggest we target the ready AMD on Iran and launch immediately Mr. President. It appears that the first launch is in fact a decoy."

June and Chuck both released pent up breath in relief and waved accent to proceed with the General's suggestion.

"You have my authority to divert the AMD to the new coordinates, but prepare another missile for the orbital vehicle and take it out as soon as you confirm the May Day as a hoax decoy. Please try to double confirm by locating our transport, but that is NOT a priority. I will send new release codes momentarily. Thank you General."

The President keyed a new sequence into the briefcase computer and sat back. He looked at Hanes and Beauvais and said "Now what?"

CHAPTER 17

Missile Control, Denver. 25th June, 7.25 am central.

The AMD missile lifted on a billowing pillow of roiling cotton white clouds and blinding exhaust gases, tracing a chef perfect, creamy piped vapor pillar into the cloudless blue sky over the lazy wheat fields of Wyoming.

"This is NSA, Denver Colorado, Mr. President."

"Yes Denver. This is the President, Secretary of State Beauvais and Director Hanes. What do you have for us?"

"Mr. President, we have been unable to confirm the identity of the may-day source which leads us to believe it is totally a decoy. At the same time we have contact from Commander Carver that the Space City Transport is on the Skyhook at maximum acceleration and more than half way to the terminus. The recommendation is to eliminate the Iranian vehicle without further delay."

"Thank you NSA Colorado. Air Chief of Staff will be advised momentarily to initiate launch."

The president swung back to the wall screen where the General now stepped back into the picture. "General, are we ready to take out the Iranian vehicle?"

"Mr. President, the missile is in the last few minutes of programming for launch. As we are not using an AMD our targeting must be precise. We are about three minutes away from launch."

"Thank you General, authorization codes are …. now what?" Once again there were screaming sirens and flashing lights, with people racing all over the place behind the General. He listened again and then looked up, concern written over his face.

"We have multiple launches from the Iranian vehicle Mr. President. They are on short trajectory non orbital paths accelerating straight downwards as orbital mechanics allow. Target projection is Yellowstone National Park. There are ten incoming bogies in a stream with computed 15 second impact intervals. First impact in ten minutes."

"Can we take them out General?"

"We may be able to stop the last few, but our launched defenses will not bear on target in time to prevent initial impact Sir."

"Why Yellowstone? Yogi Bear can't hurt Iran." The President shook his head with an expression of disbelief. "This makes no sense at all."

"Unfortunately, yes it does Mr. President." Chuck had been Google searching his tablet computer and pressed a "RUN" button. A voice and hologram appeared over the screen.

"Yellowstone National Park is the epicenter of the earth's next super volcano, the same as the one that may have wiped out life on earth 160 million years ago. Under Yellowstone lies a great magma plume that penetrates the earth's mantle and closes with the surface, showing itself as hot mud geysers, earthquakes and limited eruptions. It is the "Big One" waiting to happen. Nature will sooner or later touch it off, or maybe man will do it sooner. However it happens, life on earth will change if not vanish entirely."

"That's the Iranian target Mr. President. The magma plume. They want to set off a super volcano and bury us."

"Every fighter plane, every missile, anything flying in range... get it into the area. Stop these things. General are you moving on this?"

"Yes Sir. Everything close has been scrambled. Civilian aircraft have been redirected by ground control into the area without being informed why. We have to choke the air space and we may stop some of these. Our nuclear guys are estimating 40 to 60 megaton warheads on each device based on penetration required and interval. If we can stop at least three of them we have a slim chance."

"Will the warheads detonate if they are intercepted General?"

"Our best guess under the circumstances is that they will burn up and cause some fallout, but they will be programmed for timed detonation or their sequence would not work. The warheads must be made safe until detonation."

"Proceed General and may God help us all."

The AMD was hypersonic, eating the distance to the target area at fifteen times the speed of sound. It would travel for around half an hour before it turned its trajectory downwards to commence a stealth approach to the Iranian border towards its target and detonation.

CHAPTER 18

Over Yellowstone Park. 25th June, 7.34 am central

The string of nuclear tipped missiles marched down through the atmosphere, nose cones glowing with the friction heat of re-entry, the first warhead thirty seconds from impact.

"This is VacAir Flight 67 out of Baltimore en route to Casper Natrona International Airport. Do you read me Casper Natrona flight control?"

"VacAir 67, this is Air National Guard. There is an emergency situation. You are required to hold your position until advised. Please circle at your current altitude. What is your fuel situation Flight 67? Over."

"Air National Guard, we have fuel for 20 minutes holding. We are at the end of our flight from Baltimore. Over"

"Flight 67, we anticipate a hold of not more than 5 minutes. Over"

"Thank you National Guard. What is the nature of the emergency? Over"

Before the National Guard could reply, the aircraft shuddered and the pressure dropped. Oxygen masks fell from the ceiling and loose papers whirled away towards the back. There was a rending and screeching of tearing metal interspersed with the muted cries of frightened passengers.

The pilots fought for control of the airplane, but the Iranian missile, the first in the stick coming down, had sheared off the tail plane and the whole rear end of the craft. It plunged to its doom with no survivors.

The missile was entangled in aircraft debris, undamaged externally, but no longer aerodynamic. It began to tumble out of control and did not burn up, but it did hit the ground off target and sideways, making a kinetic energy crater thirty feet deep, cracking its casing that was designed for nose impact and coming to rest, leaking radiation and fuel, in its crater.

Fifteen seconds later the second missile impacted 1000 feet away, drilled down its 400 programmed feet and exploded. The surface effect of the nuclear blast was muted by the depth, but the bubble formed by vaporization of rock, mud and water was instantly blasted full of magma from a side plume unknown to the Iranians. A huge, hot magma swimming pool awaited further warheads with the pressure buildup below pumping the super volcano far more than ever anticipated. This was a disaster of unimaginable proportion, and end of life on earth, but that life just didn't know it yet.

Approaching the secret launch site in Iran, the AMD missile was seconds from detonation, the first time an Anti-matter Device had been used, let alone used in anger. There was no warning. The missile was under the radar and moving too fast.

The Iranian silos were poised to spew out their messengers of death, with the lox vapor roiling out of the openings. The roar of multiple launches and plumes of billowing white exhaust gases were overwhelming, making the arrival of the AMD insignificant.

The AMD detonated.

There was no overpowering blast, no blinding flash, no mushroom cloud. Just a "pop" that no one was around to hear.

A silvery ripple, like a mercury spill, but without a source of liquid metal, started as a spherical shape at the detonation center and rapidly expanded outwards into an all consuming pancake at around 500 miles an hour.

Every thing beneath the consuming edge turned into a smooth and reflective silver surface, flat, featureless and formless. Matter, the missile silos, the missiles and the people inside met anti-matter and became pure energy that was sucked into the earth surface, uniformly raising the potential in the region by millions of volts. A lightning show began with small discharges flashing evenly spaced throughout the expanding region. The rapidly increasing lightning strikes were running out of cloud cover to balance potential and the growing earth charge had to seek other means to distribute itself. The recently uniform potential had nowhere to go but outwards as it repelled itself from the center of the glassy plain. The edges of the ripple now glowed with the building energy of millions of volts. Long, continuos tendrils of electric arcs probed ahead of the wave looking for a resting place. The silver front had become an anti-matter energy tsunami devouring everything in its path. Nothing slowed it down.

In Wyoming two of the first three warheads had penetrated the makeshift air shield and detonated, all seven remaining having been taken out by military aircraft missiles. But just the one warhead had really been enough to tip the instability of the magma plume.

The initial nuclear rock-vapor bubble was now filled like a ripe pimple on the earth's face, one touch and it would spurt out the pus of magma to relieve the pressure. But this was no acne pimple volcanic release. The magma from far below, with the pressure of the whole planet forcing it out, was gradually rising up its main pipe and forcing more molten rock through smaller secondary arteries. The two extra warheads that did get through simply accelerated the process a little, widening the open wound to allow the earth's heartbeat to pump out the red hot, bloody magma that should have been deep down inside the planet.

The shock wave of the nuclear detonations and the upsurge of magma had set of another reaction that no one had ever anticipated. There was enough of a jolt to the North American tectonic plate to set off a domino effect against the Pacific plate subduction. As the North American plate slid beneath the Pacific plate, the formerly balanced forces were now in turmoil, like flicking one end of a large rug and smashing up into the Pacific plate edge. Earthquakes unknown in magnitude were firing off around the Pacific Rim of Fire and immense tsunamis were racing towards the shores of every continent. Islands vanished with cities and populations, in a blink. They just were not there any more. The Yellowstone eruption was like a growing, suppurating, flesh eating bacterial infection on the Earth's face.

The anti-matter front was expanding outwards at the speed of a jet liner, to devour Russia, Europe and Africa while the super volcano and its earthquake support cast demolished the Americas and the Eastern Pacific. Two cataclysmic forces, each in itself capable of total planetary destruction, inexorably racing towards each other. Mutually assured destruction.

CHAPTER 19

Aboard Carver's Transport. 25th June, 8.55 am

Janine Carver had cut the news feed from earth, or whatever remained of it among the static screens and whistling speakers, as stations shut down, or were simply abandoned in the haste of flight from danger.

The cadets were strapped in and with no windows in the transport hull, unable to see the fireworks on the surface that were clearly visible. The cadets were totally stunned by the limited information they had been exposed to, sombre and silent. Fuller was observing them constantly on the cabin camera to make sure no one freaked out and headed for an air lock. He periodically took a look at earth at a sharp angle behind the ship from the co-pilot position. Janine had been pushing the ship to its speed limits on the magnetic rail. It was capable of double the regular acceleration, but she had to consider the novice passengers. At one and a half G's, they were well into the deceleration phase and the transport was two thirds the way up the Skyhook, about eighteen thousand miles from earth, their acceleration couches turned about to keep them sitting comfortably. They were well into zero gravity space.

"What happens if this anti-matter stuff hits the Skyhook?" he asked Janine.

"We become a real space ship. No drama in that because we can release at any time. The question is, where do we go? Back down to earth or head for Space City?"

"I think we need to wait and see what is really going on. We need information and options if we are going to survive. This is so far beyond war as we understand it. No one really knows what an Anti Matter Device event will cause." Janine stopped for a moment as she adjusted a communication channel, then continued, "It was postulated that an AMD event would initiate a self sustaining energy wave that would destroy everything on the surface of the earth. Our guys put their money on energy dissipation and damping by large bodies of water and atmosphere, so they went for it. I guess we are going to find out if we move off to Space City."

"Sounds to me like you've answered your own question. We go on. That is in our emergency protocol directive anyway. Complete the mission." Fuller scratched his head. "Although protocol be damned. We save our skins first."

He looked out at earth again and shook his head in despair. "What have we done to ourselves? Is this the end of humanity? Look at our home. By God, look there... New Zealand is half gone. How can it be possible? The tsunami's can't possibly have reached there yet. Oh! Look! Hawaii has vanished. Oh Lord! Millions of people, just gone. Look at California. The West coast is missing. This can't be. Look, Alaska is drowning in front of our eyes. Oh God! What have we done?"

"John?" Janine looked at him, tears in her eyes, "we have to carry on. Think about it. We may have the most precious cargo of any ship in the history of humanity. We have the survivors and the means to survive - for a while anyway."

He shook his head in despair. "We can't help them down there, that's for sure." He looked up at Janine. "I need to go and talk to the cadets. My gut tells me we should disengage from the Skyhook sooner than later. We have enough reaction mass to get to Space City. If a shock-wave hits the Skyhook it could flick us off like a swatter whacking a fly. I'll leave the final decision to you."

"OK go talk to them. I'm watching the comms from earth base. The moment I see anything change I will release. The longer we can hold on to the hook the more margin for error later."

Fuller looked thoughtful for a moment. "I have an idea."

"OK, what?"

"Stop the deceleration and reverse it. We are not in a standard situation so our detachment vector and release can be brought forward."

"You're right John! I'll do the calculations now. An early hook detatchment at higher velocity uses Skyhook magnetic energy and reduces reaction mass use which is one of our biggest concerns under the circumstances. I'm on it!" Janine's eyes sparkled with intelligence and excitement.

Fuller paused and looked back at the cadets. They were all preoccupied with their own thoughts. None looked his way. He leaned over and planted his lips on Janine's. She responded with warmth. And then got down to the math.

CHAPTER 20

Aboard Air Force One. 25th June, 9.00 am

"Mr. President." Chuck Hanes touched the slumbering President's arm to gently rouse him. He gave him a short moment to shake away the cobwebs of much needed sleep and handed him a steaming mug of coffee. The President rubbed his eyes with his free hand while he took a sip of the reviving brew.

"What have you got for me Chuck?" he yawned, the last tendrils of sleep dissolving away into heightened alertness. "You're not looking happy!"

"We may have a problem Mr. President."

"Oh, cut the Mr. President crap again. Tom. Here I am Tom, OK?"

"Aw. OK. Tom." He stopped to gather his breath and thoughts. "We have a potential problem about to arise that has never been seen on this planet and you are going to have to deal with it."

"What could be worse than what has happened so far Chuck?" Tom looked Chuck in the eyes.

"How about the end of the world? That is the problem."

Tom raised an eyebrow. "End of the world huh? I make the right decision, whatever it is, and the world goes on. I make the wrong one and no one knows about it anyway. So hit me with it."

"Our science advisory board at NASA has been monitoring the progress of the anti-matter wave front. It is not dissipating at all and it appears that it will totally engulf the globe. That's the good news."

"What! That's good news. I don't want to hear..."

"So while we have been watching the wave front from satellite live cameras the analysts noticed that whenever the wave front reached areas of caverns or active volcanic fissures it actually penetrated into the earth's crust and created voids that could not hold the energy charge. They witnessed huge explosions, greater than any seismic activity ever recorded and then the wave front kept penetrating into the newly exposed regions. Where this activity is most advanced the mantle of the earth is being undermined and detached. The wave eats away underneath but does not move back up. We are getting country sized segments crashing in on the voids and feeding the trapped wave. They don't know when, or even if, this process will stop."

"So what can we do about it? I don't see any decision here."

"That is not all." Hanes looked grim. "The scientists are trying to predict what will happen when the wave hits the Yellowstone magma plume discontinuity. It is so deep and wide now that they fear the wave will penetrate to the core of the planet."

"Now you are going to tell me the planet will explode?"

"Something like that Tom."

"So what can I do? What can anyone do?"

"You have one decision to make Tom. Go down with the planet or save yourself while you can."

Tom gave Chuck a wry look. "It was my decision to set off the AMD in the first place so I am responsible for this whole mess. A bit heavy to have the fate of humanity and the world on your shoulders. Sounds a bit melodramatic but dammit! I do have that responsibility. Do I run or do I die with my decision and our home?"

"Tom, it is a no brainer. We have to save as much as we can, survive as long as possible. That is our charter. That's the duty of the President of the United States. Survive and rebuild."

"Eight billion people wiped out Chuck. How do I live with that. The President of the United States, the greatest mass murderer in history." He shook his head and tears ran down his cheeks.

"Tom, we may not survive this at all. You have to try."

The President shrugged and sighed. "How do we survive Chuck? What magic have we got?"

"We have a Skyhook Transport in emergency transit to Space City. We divert it and rendezvous in low earth orbit. Air Force One can't make it to deep space on its own."

"What happens to Air Force One?"

"Autopilot to attempt to land back at Andrews. If there is an Andrews."

The President gave a defeated shrug of his shoulders, the weight of the world visibly pressing him down. "OK Chuck. We survive. Do it."

Hanes rose to organize the directives to the Transport. Air Force One was already on its way to low earth orbit and rendezvous with a Space City shuttle. He glanced out of a window at the visible rim of earth and stopped suddenly in his tracks, sucking in a breath of shock. "Tom, look. Look out the window!"

The President lifted himself on one elbow to get a view through the nearest port. "Good Lord! What is that?" A silver grey rim covered the edge of the horizon. Featureless and visibly rolling over the earth's surface, leaving a blank, gray face in its wake. On closer examination flashes of sheet lightning and tendrils of high voltage plasma could be seen, even against the direct sunlight.

"That is the anti-matter wave front Tom. That is the end of our planet as we know it."

"What have I done?" The President was crying, tears streaming, as he clenched the arm rests. "What have I done? What have I done." He repeated over and over, his voice diminishing to a whimper as he buried his head in his arms.

"Tom?"

The President looked up at Hanes, eyes red and face wet with tears. His expression morphed into the hard, decisive visage Hanes was used to seeing. He sighed a gasp of relief. The President was back. "I'm good now Chuck. I'm good. I will handle this... Like a President."

CHAPTER 21
Iranian Presidential Survival Bunker

"Zardooz, you have outdone yourself!" Arjmand lay on a reclining couch in his underwear, his clothing scattered around on the floor. Two young women knelt beside him offering plates of sweet grapes and exotic fruits. Trained from childhood to accept any abuse from men, neither of them flinched as Arjmand groped and fondled them without shame, his erection straining his shorts and his breathing fast coming rapid and shallow. He started moaning and pulled the nearest girl's hand to his member, pushing down his shorts with the other hand. In seconds he was flopping about like a landed fish as the girl's touch brought him to a messy, climactic spatter. The atmosphere was rank with his odor as Zardooz watched on with a smirk of condescending amusement. He thought to himself that the few so called virgins he had installed were going to remain virgins with Arjmand around.

Zardooz beckoned to one of the girls who came over to him. He quietly told her to clean Arjmand up and get him dressed. Arjmand had a broadcast to make to the world.

Arjmand sat in front of a sophisticated video camera array that transmitted in 3-D. His hair had been slicked back and he now wore a traditional djabella and keffiyeh.

"On 3, 2, 1..." one of the young women, acting as producer, pointed at Arjmand signalling he was transmitting.

"I am addressing the world, in particular the United States and its lackey Israel. The great Iranian Empire has destroyed the aggressor North Korean Hegemony and our doomsday bomb has collapsed the very landmass of the United States.

These same United States started this aggression by attacking the Empire of Iran with a weapon of mass destruction, an anti-matter device. The leadership of the United States should be tried and condemned as they did to our valiant neighbor Saddam Hussein all those years ago!

They called our brother Osama Bin Laden a terrorist for fighting a limited war, and then they killed him. No longer will the Iranian

Empire be subservient to any other nation.

We have retaliated to the use of the AMD with our doomsday bomb that is destroying continental USA even as I speak." Arjmand paused, red in the face with excitement and emotion.

"Whoever is hearing and seeing this broadcast, take up your weapons, seek out the enemies around you and destroy them in the name of Allah!"

CHAPTER 22

Goddard Space Center - Skyhook control.

"Understood Mr. President. I will repeat your instructions. Load all available Skyhook transports within the hour with whatever supplies are available. Board all Goddard personnel and whoever else is on site and wishes to make a one way trip to Space City. Launch all transports within 90 minutes and instruct transport pilots to disengage from the Skyhook thirty minutes after launch." The General's voice was steady as he controlled his emotions. He knew exactly what was coming. "Mr. president?" He allowed his humanity to slip past the steely military armor.

"Yes General?"

"About our families? Our wives and kids?"

"General, I can't tell you how to handle things down there. That is your job alone. However if you can get your families into the transports within the time limits then do so. There is no shortage of passenger capacity and Space City has plenty of room. The only risk is that there are no survival suits for all the passengers and only the vehicle integrity will protect them. I guess that is better than staying behind. General, go do what you have to without delay."

The General's shoulders moved maybe a quarter inch in relief as he acknowledged. "Thank you Mr. President. See you aboard Space City Sir."

The General issued the orders, with carefully worded instruction regarding families to be brought into the facility. He warned the Goddard security team leaders, those that he could trust, that there may be violent reaction to his orders. Within moments of issuing the orders there was screaming and crying reported from several areas of the complex as some staff members who commuted hours each day saw their loved ones were doomed. The security details had to restrain three women and one man, all who had broken down emotionally, the man becoming violent when approached. Sedated, the four were taken aboard the first available transport. Freedom of the individual was no longer an option.

Three transports were being frantically loaded. There was no time for safety checking or the niceties of inventory control. Crates were strapped down wherever they would fit. Pallets of food and assorted essentials were slipped randomly into pallet bays while bales of soft goods were piled into every available gap and held in place with duct tape. Mechanics hauled hoses to reaction mass tanks and started the filling process while the three designated pilot commanders watched for obvious disaster in the making dangers that had to be corrected.

Within minutes the first staff members without incoming family attachments started to file into the passenger loading area and flight crew hurried them on board and strapped each one in. There was little talk between the passengers who did not have space suit protection or any experience of space flight and the inherent dangers. But better a reasonable chance of survival than none at all.

The first three transports were loaded and locked down ready for launch. There was no delay or traditional countdown from Goddard Launch Control. The transports simply left one after the other and three more railed in to take their place and loads.

The activity was becoming frantic with less than 45 minutes until the shock wave was due to hit Goddard and the Skyhook. The semblance of discipline and order was beginning to break down, with military and staff realizing that this was the last chance to escape certain death. People started pushing and shoving to get aboard the transports, the wailing of injured punctuated by the shouted orders of the few military controllers still trying to maintain order.

The bales and supplies were being thrown in now with no attempt to secure them or balance the loading. The three pilots huddled together in conference, looking at timepieces and comparing with the wall screen data on the shock wave approach. They came to a decision and broke away to their respective transports, each now with sidearm in hand and plain sight. They knew that there was only 8 minutes left until they had to leave to achieve the minimum thirty minutes until separation from the Skyhook.

Just meeting those constraints was no guarantee of safety or survival. No one knew how the Skyhook would react when the shock wave hit the base of the twenty seven thousand mile long tube. Such a catastrophe had never been anticipated and never tested in theory. They were soon to find out.

At thirty seconds before lift off, the three pilots activated emergency alarm sirens in their transports, loudly wailing klaxon warnings. Enough to make everyone freeze in their tracks and look for the source of the danger. In that instant the pilots closed the doors automatically, over-riding the safety switching that prevented bodies, limbs or objects from being crushed or severed in the doorway. Screams came from two of the transports as people struggling to get in were caught in the doorways. Arms and torsos were severed and dropped inside the air lock as the former arm owners writhed in agony and bled out on the gangway rolling in the bloody pools of guts and legs of those maybe more fortunate to have been killed outright. The crowd withdrew in horror at the shock of the violence and the abrupt end of life before their eyes.

After a few seconds of silence within the strident alarms, the collective anger of the mob grew, suppressing their individual will to survive, and as one they fell on the outer hull of the transport, hitting it with bare fists or anything at hand. The bloody smears and impacts did nothing to a metal skin designed to withstand meteorite impact.

The pilots saw that there was no way to push back the angry mob, so they engaged drive and started launch with seconds to spare. The grasping hands slid away as those closest to the first transport were dragged by friction against the gangway safety fence, then the transports were free and the crowds fell forward off the gangways onto the rails. Those fallen on the rails at the first and second gangways were crushed by the second and third transport as they passed. Blood flowed like water between the rails as the remaining people looked on in horror as the red streaked transports, with their only hope of survival, drew away and vanished up the Skyhook.

An engineer in the crowd, his face contorted in raw, animal

anger, screamed out "Why should they get away? Look what they did! They need to pay! They need to come back and get us all or they should die!" The crowd turned to him. A single voice called out "Come back or die! Come back or die!" The engineer screamed "Follow me! I can turn off the power to the Skyhook. We can make them come back!"

The crowd parted allowing the engineer to lead the way and then surged after him, oblivious to the fact that their existence was limited to the minutes until the shock wave struck. They started chanting "Come back or die!" as they ran behind the engineer who was heading for the master control room.

The pilots of the first three transports that had left had no idea of what had occurred. They had reached the minimum separation point and from then on every second on the Skyhook was a bonus. They were monitoring the approach of the shock wave and decided that five more minutes was as much as they could consider. They had calculated to be at least ten thousand miles from the Skyhook when the shock wave would hit.

The pilots of the second group did not have that luxury of decision. They were working on separation seconds before the shock wave hit, at the very minimum thirty minute separation point.

The pilot of the second transport in this group was reporting an air lock error due to an object jammed in the doorway. He decided to put the transport on auto pilot and to go and clear the blockage. He was not looking forward to what he was likely going to find, but he activated his youniform and buddy for vacuum activity and left the flight deck. As he passed through the passenger cabin he saw the expressionless, stunned look on every face. There was no talk.

He cycled the inner lock only to find that it was deactivated due to vacuum in the air lock. The outer door was not sealed at all. The only way he could fix the problem was to open the inner lock manually and allow the cabin pressure to drop as the air was sucked out in the time it took for him to move into the air lock and close the inner door again. He clicked on his internal intercom mike and spoke to his charges. "Ladies and gentlemen, we have an emergency. We will be experiencing a drop in cabin pressure momentarily. To ensure the fastest recovery to normal pressure, please look around you and secure any loose objects of paper that may be drawn into the vacuum and prevent door closure. Do this now. RIGHT NOW!" he screamed the last to shock the passengers into action. When was satisfied that loose items and debris were secured, he turned to the inner door manual opening sequence. Peering through the small view port he could just see a lighter slit where the outer door should have been closed. The slit was interrupted towards the lower half by an object blocking the light. He hated to think what that object might be. In any case his view was obscured by the fine mist of gore that had deposited all over the air lock.

The problem he faced was simple. Either he could clear the blockage and close the outer door, taking the risk that the mechanism was damaged and all the atmosphere in the craft would vent, or leave it alone and take the chance that the inner door would hold. The inner door was not designed to withstand the forces that the outer door would routinely encounter. It was simply an emergency second defense and air lock mechanism rated for six hours of continuous vacuum. Space City was more than six hours away. Much more.

CHAPTER 23

Skyhook Control, Goddard.

The engineer had reached the control center at Goddard and along with three others who had come forward professing knowledge of the power system, were looking at the grid schematics presented in 3-D before them. The engineer had found the VR gloves that made the virtual reality concrete. He had them on and was working through the grid turning off every switch he could find. Gradually the green conduit lines represented were all turning red, until finally he narrowed down the Skyhook feed to three possibilities. Without any hesitation he shut down all three – and the lights went out. There was screaming and howls of fear from the blinded mob, the darkness total and almost tangible. Then even the sounds of terror were smothered by an increasing rushing sound, like a train coming out of a subway, hundreds of trains. The shock wave had arrived!

CHAPTER 24

Aboard Carver's Space Transport.

Fuller and Carver were glued to the comms screen. They were aware of the six transports following them up the Skyhook, but they were watching the shock wave approach Goddard and the Skyhook base.

"Time to release!" Carver stated decisively. "We need to be far enough away from the Skyhook to avoid whiplash effect, regardless if it is just energy wave transmission or a complete severance of the Skyhook from its ground anchors."

"What are the likely outcomes?" Fuller asked.

"There are two principal disaster scenarios presented in flight study. What we are facing is orders of magnitude greater than anything ever anticipated." Carver flicked a switch and spoke an override code into her youniform microphone. A noticeable force of acceleration pressed the cadets back into their seats as the reaction mass engines kicked in. The transport was now a free flight space craft. Watching out the window, Fuller saw the apple sized earth swinging away under the belly of the craft, the blue of the oceans and the dappled colors of continents now mostly a uniform silver, interrupted only by cloud banks.

A further turn of a few degrees revealed the Skyhook behind them, dwindling away to an invisible point on the surface, attached to a small wedge of surface that was visibly being consumed by the silver cloud as it rolled forward. There were clearly only minutes to go before the shock wave met Skyhook.

Fuller, still mesmerized by what he was seeing, whispered "What were the two outcomes?"

Janine glanced at him, never having seen him so close to losing it. "Are you OK?"

"Yes, I'm fine. Shocked, but fine. Please tell me."

"OK. Scenario one. Closest to an energy transfer. A transport or a meteor strikes the Skyhook. We only need to consider the low altitude strike now. The carbon mono filament shell will hold integrity up to an atomic explosion, but the energy transmission

---

will cause a ripple to run along the Skyhook in both directions. The ground anchors will dissipate the downward force. The upward ripple will behave like the ripple of a skipping rope. If both ends are held firmly the ripple will be absorbed by the holding points and transmitted to an energy sink. It goes away. Our problem is that we do not have a fixed energy sink at the top of Skyhook. It is held in place by some clever Lagrange mathematics. When the ripple hits the top, it is going to flick like a bull whip tip. And toss off anything on the Hook as the ripple travels. That is the good news John."

He rolled his eyes. "Give it to me. The bad news."

"Scenario two. The Skyhook is severed at some point. In this case at the base. What happens when you have a bucket of water on the end of a rope being swung around horizontal to the ground, which negates gravity for our intent?" Janine paused, seeing that Fuller knew exactly what she was getting at. "The rope stays taut and the water remains in the bucket under centripetal forces just as long as the velocity of the swing is maintained at a certain minimum. You can swing faster and the tension on the rope becomes greater. Then you let the rope go. The bucket goes flying off and becomes subject to other forces that were negligible compared with the centripetal force. It takes off and the rope follows it, bucking and twisting as it is affected by localized forces around it.

The Skyhook is a huge bucket on a string, with the bucket in vacuum and the string end in atmosphere. If it gets sliced it is going to take off at some extreme velocity with its directional vectors dictated by the tail. Kinda like the tail wagging the dog." Fuller gave her a half hearted grin. "So it takes off? What's the danger?"

"The theoretical directional uncertainty from the Skyhook vertical position is a planar arc of around thirty degrees. Like a narrow fan. Space City is the bulls eye of the target. We have to hope that the tail wags the dog enough to miss Space city."

He looked at her. "We have nowhere to run. We can't risk Space City until this is over." He put his head in his hands. "Oh, God help us!" he murmured.

CHAPTER 25

Yellowstone National Park.

The super volcano was belching magma and ash into the atmosphere in never before seen volumes while molten rock spewed into pyroclastic rivers that carved new pathways through what had once been lush nature reserves, now scorched landscapes with barely a tree stump smoldering. There was no living thing within a hundred miles of this boiling landscape. Multiple craters pocked the area as magma surfaced through cracks and melted new vents. The earth mantle was like a giant sponge oozing out liquid, but without the resilience of a sponge. As the magma pipes grew wider and more numerous, the infrastructure of the crust was being compromised to the point of total collapse into a super crater. Rivers which drained into the region boiled and vaporized their total flow, adding superheated steam to the miasma and forming mud-rain as it liquefied in the atmosphere.

There was no one to see it, not even from space due to the ash cloud, as the center of the cataclysm simply sank into the surface. The dimple grew as the edges followed into the boiling lake of lava that was exposed. In the centre of the molten lake a new phenomenon appeared as the liquid lava drained downwards into the earth. A whirlpool appeared, only explained by the enormous number of vents that had allowed the internal magma pressure to drop to the point that reverse flow was possible. Unheard of in geological theory, but there it was. The earth was suffering a wound like a flesh eating bacteria on a body.

The collapse raced outwards at the edges at sixty miles an hour and not appearing to be letting up and passed out from under the ash cloud, finally visible to those in space.

Aboard Air Force One, now in low earth orbit, the President and anyone who could be spared from immediate duty were glued to the windows, watching events unfold beneath them as their orbit took them over the volcanic region. Far over the horizon to the east they could not see the silver wave front as it approached Goddard and the Skyhook. The shock wave would reach Yellowstone in about 25 minutes when their orbital position would be down on the horizon to the west. The other side of the wave would soon be racing past them in the opposite direction as it totally engulfed the surface.

"What is happening down there Chuck?" The President asked Hanes. "Have we got anyone on board who can explain this?"

"We are in contact with Space City. There are geologists up there but they are not in viewing range now. We sent up the imagery and we are waiting for interpretation."

The President sighed and went back to looking out the window.

A flight officer tapped on the cabin door and entered, handing a note to Hanes, who scanned it and sucked in his breath.

"Tell me Chuck."

"Oh man, Tom. This is not good." He looked up with a wry grimace, realizing the silliness of the comment. "The geologists are saying that the super volcanic region is collapsing in on itself. Because they cannot see the epicenter due to the ash cloud, they are theorizing that a lava lake is forming. One of them is of the opinion that crust collapse is imminent and the lava lake will implode and be sucked back into the earth. The other two discount this as a remote possibility. They all agree that the lava lake will expand until cooler geologic formations are encountered that will stop the melt."

"Do they say where it will go from there? What about the shock wave when it hits?"

"None of them have any certainty of what happens next. The one who suggested the implosion does say that the shock wave could travel down into mantle and cause massive fragmentation as the energy of the wave is bottled up and concentrated. He says the earth itself could shatter."

The two looked at each other, the flight officer still standing by listening in shock. Chuck turned to the officer. "Not a word. There is nothing anyone can do. There is no point in starting a panic. Report back to your station."

"Yes Sir!" The officer turned smartly, composure regained, and left.

Hanes looked at his watch. "Twenty minutes and we find out who was right." They went back to staring out of the window.

CHAPTER 26

Aboard the Space Transports

The strident scream of sirens punctuated by the shouted orders over the PA system "Strap in! Strap in or find a hand hold! Skyhook release is immediate. Power failure emergency!" The steady acceleration that had held everything in place had ceased and loose items floated about in the weightless environment. Bits of paper fluttered in the ventilator breeze while potato crisps ballooned into an out of control cloud. Bodies floated, arms and legs flailing for control. Without weightless training there was only panic.

All six transports had separated successfully. Aboard the fifth transport with the jammed air lock, X5, the co pilot had handled the separation while the pilot had grabbed onto the air lock handle as the artificial gravity disappeared. His intention was to examine the air lock jam and then decide on a plan to fix it or leave it alone and rely on the inner door. That option was not to be. As he grabbed the handle the residual momentum of his body twist took the handle around or suffer a broken wrist.

An ominous hissing sound started as the lock released and only the internal cabin pressure held the door closed. There should not have been any leakage.

The pilot's mind went into trained auto drive mode, analyzing the problem and deciding that some debris must also be trapped in the inner lock seal. The extra pressure of the lock itself had controlled the leakage until a moment ago. Now the craft was tumbling in free space out of control with the limited air slowly leaking out. His body was now flattened against the door pod due to the acceleration of the transport. He couldn't open the door to clear the blockage because the outer door was unsealed. He doubted if he could open it against the cabin pressure on his own any way. His own youniform and buddy would keep him alive even if the atmosphere ran out completely, but his passengers were good as dead if he could not do something very quickly to stop the leakage.

Could he turn the lock handle back and slow the leak or stop it? Without some purchase to push against he was helpless.

He scrabbled his feet about, feeling for a projection or anything he could push against. His toes found a protrusion and he jammed his foot hard against it, hoping it was not just some weak, plastic molding. He applied pressure gradually between the lock handle and his foot. Fortunately the direction to close the lock was away from his body, so he was pushing the handle. The projection at his foot held so he applied more pressure to the handle.

Suddenly the hissing increased as the lock dogs failed to engage their holes in the frame and pushed the door gap wider. The air was now rushing out disastrously.

CHAPTER 27

Aboard the remaining five transports.

Aboard the other five transports things were going smoothly. The first three were thousands of miles higher than the second and closer to their objective, space city. The last three were at a point that significant reaction mass would be needed to escape earth's gravity well and reach the City.

Air Force One was at low earth orbit waiting for a pick up shuttle from Space City.

"Attention all stations! Attention all stations! This is Commander Janine Carver on Skyhook Transport Designated X7. Warning! Warning! Our calculations show that if the Skyhook is severed at the base by the anti-matter shock wave, the probability of the Skyhook terminus mass sling shooting into Space City with some level of significant impact, is in the range of 25% to 35% probability. Failing higher authority or executive direction, it is my recommendation that Space city be immediately evacuated until the danger has passed and that all Skyhook transports stand off out of range of whiplash effect of the Skyhook and do not approach Space City until danger is cleared. This message is now on automated loop repeat on guard channel."

Janine put the comms back to local. "What do we do now?"

"I was thinking about that while you were transmitting. What's our reaction mass state?"

Janine brought up the display which showed 99% full tanks. "We are full. Just a little used for the separation. What do you have in mind John?"

"Space City needs to evacuate and take as much survival material as it can ship. They need the shuttle that is picking up the President. We have to wait about for the hit or miss and we have reaction mass, so we could go get the President and release the shuttle for evacuation. We can recharge reaction mass from Air Force One if you don't mind loading volatile fuel instead of water. The reaction mass thrusters do not have any ignition system so the mix should be safe, just a little less effective in thrust due to the lower density of the fuel. Is that feasible?"

"It has never been done before to my knowledge John, but it makes sense. Shall we go meet the Pres?" Janine said with a cheeky grin.

"Let's talk to them!" he replied.

Janine flicked the comms to Air Force One and the Space City Shuttle in a three way link. "Air Force One and Shuttle C2 acknowledge link." She paused waiting for responses.

"This is Air Force One X7 acknowledged."

"Shuttle C2 acknowledged"

"Commander Janine Carver here Air Force One and Shuttle C2. Here is what we have in mind..."

CHAPTER 28
Goddard Space Center Skyhook base

The silver cloud of the anti-matter shock wave steam rolled in at five hundred miles an hour towards the Skyhook base. In an instant the base was obliterated and the Skyhook sheared off clean, leaving nothing behind except the silver surface. The tail of the mono filament tube flashed away into the sky, its end being devoured by the silvery anti-matter that slowly increased into an anti-matter doughnut rolling up the tube.

It was if Goddard never existed. The people never existed.

The Skyhook tube flew off into space, dragged by the counter mass of the terminus twenty seven thousand miles away. The impact of the shock wave had send a directional energy wave up the filament, causing a wave amplitude to travel up the tube. The bump of the wave was small at first as the cut end of the filament offered no resistance to the energy, but as the anti-matter torus grew in size and mass, the filament began to taughten again and the travelling wave amplitude grew in proportion as the end stopped flailing. It was already a mile above the filament axis. The three lower space transports were just moving away from the unpowered hook when the anti-matter struck the base. They were just miles from the Hook with the wave heading towards them at over one thousand miles an hour, the amplitude growing and doubling every two minutes.

Transport X3 was in trouble losing atmosphere. The co pilot had called for help from the near by X2 and X1 Transports to close and mate locks to allow clearing without air loss, but that would require a rendezvous and cessation of travel away from the Hook. They would be in range of the wave as it travelled up the Hook. They would be smashed like bugs on a windscreen. Or X3 would lose its air and all aboard would die.

The race was on.

CHAPTER 29
Deep beneath Yellowstone National Park

The anti-matter wave front dove down into the fractured earth, devouring magma and rock like a superfast gangrene infection. It worked its way into every crack and pipe, eating and widening, fracturing further and isolating micro particles to island size chunks of the mantle that tumbled about like silver nuggets in a sack. If they ever found virgin rock the anti-matter coating transferred itself and started a voracious new path of destruction. Like a giant mosaic in three dimensions the earth was crumbling into tiles of anti-matter coated rock. The silver plague reached the molten core and started to spread over the liquid interface, starting the creation of a single silver ball being orbited by the scattered pieces of the mantle.

Each rock fragment, no matter the size, remained stable once it was completely coated by the silver anti-matter screen. The silver surface shimmered and rippled as pieces came together, but were repelled before collision. Battleship sized juggernauts drifting into each other that should have smashed themselves with violent momentum never touched. They slowed down and then steadily accelerated apart a two like poles of magnets repel.

The few who were watching from space saw a surreal vision of the shell of a silver ornamental ball gradually shattering and the myriads of pieces expanding outwards, leaving a smaller, perfectly spherical silver core at the centre. The planet earth was gone. In its place floated an alien construct. The few left in space were the sole remnants of the human species. A species without a home.

Somewhere floating in this expanding shell of debris was a modest chunk of earth that used to be part of Iran. Inside that morsel was the survival chamber where Arjmand and Zardooz waited out the expected retaliatory strikes after the broadcast some hours earlier.

The pair sat looking for communications which had ceased completely. They had no outside contact. Arjmand grabbed the arm rests of his chair and started pulling down on them. He looked uncomfortable, almost panicked. "What's happening Zardooz? I am feeling light headed. I feel light all over?"

Zardooz was being more focussed. "We are getting lighter. I also feel it. There is only one explanation that makes any sense. Gravity is reducing. We are in some form of free fall like astronauts in space."

"How could that be? We are hundreds of metres below the surface."

Zardooz was silent as he scratched his chin in deep thought. "The last thing we saw on the outside video," he began slowly, "was a silvery cloud rolling towards us from the epicenter of the AMD the Americans dropped on Teheran. I am not really sure what this cloud was, but if it was an anti-matter front then it would explain what is happening now." He looked Arjmand square in the eye in a detached way. "Conclusion!"

"Yes? What?" Arjmand was half out of his seat burning for the answer.

"The earth is disintegrating. Blowing up. Coming apart."

"No! I don't believe you! That couldn't happen. Not from one bomb."

Arjmand smiled revealing browned teeth and a wide gap between the front pair. "Oh, you're just trying to scare me. You're joking." He flapped his hand in negation and sat back grinning and shaking his head.

"No I'm not joking with you. This is real. We may be the only survivors left from our planet."

CHAPTER 30

Near Earth Orbit.

Far above, from several vantage points in orbit, survivors of the human species peered down at the spectacle of their unrecognizable home world. A world that a few hours ago had been blue with oceans, green with forests, white with ice caps, brown with deserts and all interspersed with grey and white clouds.

All they could see now was a silver ball covered with cracks and fracture lines that multiplied in real time, with segments moving away from each other and gaps visibly increasing. There were frequent flashes of electrical discharge between the gaps and whatever lay beneath them. There were no cities. No ruins. No radio or TV signals.

Just an alien world.

Over a period of hours it became apparent that the shattered surface segments were moving away and outwards, some heading directly for the last human outposts. Nothing would be spared from the destruction of collision and absorption of the anti-matter shells. The movement was relatively slow at this time, powered by the repulsion force of the anti-matter upon itself, but countered by the gravity of the remaining earth core. There was time to formulate a survival plan.

Aboard Air Force One the crew watched as Janine Carver's transport nudged in to dock. The locks mated with a slight clunk and showed all green to open between the craft.

Crew and staff from Air Force One had assembled all possible useful materiel near the lock. Only those items that could fit through or be broken down to fit. In the world of technology a hand to hand chain passed the items through to the cadets on the transport. While this was going on, Fuller, with an auxiliary oxygen bottle clipped to his belt and a jet-pack on his back, was space walking on the airfoil of Air Force One with a reaction mass transfer hose which he plugged into the under wing valve. The other end was already attached to the Transport fuelling system and simply unwound to accommodate the reaction mass supply

---

tank. The transports suffered no performance disadvantage in carrying apparently superfluous equipment as they had relied primarily on the Skyhook propulsion system. That luxury was now a life saving feature for a large part of the human species.

When Fuller saw that the reaction mass tanks were topped up and the auxiliary tanks filled, he headed back inside the transport via the front air lock and called Carver to save time.

"Commander Carver, do we have any other containers available for reaction mass storage on board the transport?" He was on open channel so was being formal.

"Wait Col. Fuller. I will ask the cadets to look and check if Air Force One has anything we can use. How much mass is left in the tanks?"

"The pilot tells me that they are still half full of jet fuel. I am reluctant to take this inboard due to the volatility, but the benefits far outweigh the risks." Carver stopped as a voice interrupted in the background. "Col. Fuller, Cadet Hannaford would like a word with you."

"Go ahead Lt. Hannaford." Felicity couldn't stifle her grin of pleasure at Fuller's use of her rank, even under the gravity of the circumstances.

"Sir, I have been discussing the issue of the reaction mass with Cadet Shaw and how we could preserve it. Cadet Shaw had a great interest in Air Force One, both the current craft and its predecessors and if extremely familiar with the engineering and structure of this craft."

"I am listening Lt Hannaford. This is a timely intervention on your part. I was just discussing bringing as much reaction mass as we could store, on board."

"Sir, Cadet Shaw believes we could save all the remaining reaction mass. May I get him to explain his plan directly?"

"Absolutely. Let's move. The anti-matter clock is ticking."

"Shaw here Sir. I am working from memory of the schematics of Air Force One. The reaction tanks were placed and designed for fast removal and replacement in case of emergency. Each tank has an internal rigid bladder that can be collapsed when empty but retains a firm shape when extended and even partially filled. We could lift the bladders out and tow them behind us sir. This may give us time to move out of the path of the anti-matter fragmentation. We can consolidate the reaction mass when we are out of danger."

"Do you know how to remove the bladders Shaw?"

"I studied Air Force One in depth sir. In theory I know. In practice…?"

"Take Hannaford and any others you may need to the rear air lock. I will meet you there in one minute. Make sure you have any tools or equipment you may need." Fuller turned his attention to Carver. "Janine, what have we got for a tether for the reaction mass bladders?"

She looked thoughtful for a moment. "There is a coupling on the hull just behind the rear air lock you will be using. Our refueling hoses are the only things long enough to do the job, but if we damage them all the reaction mass in the universe is no use to us."

"All I want to do is impart sufficient momentum to the bladders to get them moving in the right direction away from the anti-matter storm. We can pick them up later and tow them on a short leash. The plan is to attach the hoses and pull the bladders out of their housings. We move away from the anti-matter and Space City and impart enough velocity to the bladders to outrun the anti-matter, then we untether and put the pedal to the metal as my old Dad used to say."

"Risky, but I guess we don't have any option. Can your cadets handle free space with no training?"

"That's not a question I am even thinking about. There is no option. The Air Force One guys don't have youniforms or buddies. They hadn't planned on a space visit. These kids are good. They will do fine."

Fuller kissed Janine and backed out of the flight deck. He saw the human chain still taking goods aboard from the doomed Air Force One while far down the end of the cabin he could see Hannaford and Shaw waiting for him. As he passed the first lock one of the chain members fumbled a large package that floated away from him. Fuller reacted and seized the slow moving missile, stopping its progress by planting his feet on the cabin roof. He handed the package back to the crewman with the comment "You have to be careful mister, we don't get two tries at this."

The crewman accepted the package, and Fuller saw the President's face peeking around it grinning. "Yes sir! Won't happen again!"

"Mr President!" Fuller was speechless.

"Carry on Col. Fuller. You are in charge here, not me."

Fuller threw a salute and kept on towards the waiting cadets.

Shaw and Hannaford were accompanied by Amy Young, the three cadets unencumbered by any equipment other than a universal multi tool carried by Shaw.

"Is that all you will need Shaw?" queried Fuller.

"Yes sir. According to the Manual there is only one type of fastener in use and this will handle it. I am more concerned about the anti-matter sir."

Fuller looked sharply at Shaw. "What is the issue Shaw?"

"I crunched the numbers on the fragment velocities with Felicity sir. They are very approximate, but there is a distinct acceleration due to internal repelling forces between the segments and the core. As much anti gravity as it is anti-matter sir. What this means is that we do not have as much time as we thought sir."

"How much time do we have?

"In reality sir, none. No matter what we do, some anti-matter is going to overtake us based on a delay to recover the reaction mass and our maximum acceleration away from the danger. If we do not pick up the reaction mass we will run out and will not escape the anti-matter. If we do pick it up we cannot outrun it. We are done both ways."

Fuller looked thoughtful. "Did you get a scan of what anti-matter is heading directly our way?"

"Yes sir." Hannaford replied. "There are two large fragments that have a high probability of impact with us. Fortunately there do not appear to be dust particles of anti-matter. They annihilated themselves in the atmosphere and were a major contributor to the electric discharge we saw. Other fragments are on close trajectories but will clear us by sufficient distance. These pieces are masking whatever may be behind them."

"If we could deflect the two segments, we could still take an escape trajectory so that other faster segments will fly right past us. We may then be able to outrun anything coming up behind. Question is, how do we deflect these things?"

There was silence for a moment then Shaw nodded his head and drew shapes with a finger in the air. He squinted one eye deep in thought. Just as he was about to speak, Felicity held up her hand and looked him in the eye. "That will work."

Fuller frowned. "He didn't say anything."

"He doesn't need to. I know what he is thinking." Hannaford turned to Fuller. "Really sir, I know what he is thinking. He knows what I am thinking. It must be our buddies."

"OK we will look into that later. Right now, someone tell me."

Hannaford gestured to Shaw to explain. "Sir, we have the reaction mass of jet fuel on Air Force One and reaction mass of water on this transport. The fuel will not ignite without oxygen and as reaction mass it will only give up its kinetic energy potential. As jet fuel it will give up its chemical energy potential, hundreds of times more bang. On earth, an air-fuel device turns fuel into an aerosol mist and disperses it into an optimum volume of air to provide oxygen. Once ignited the explosion is devastating.

We have the oxygen we need in the water on board, but we need to break it down to hydrogen and oxygen. I believe that if a layer of water is propelled towards the anti-matter fragments immediately followed by a dispersed layer of fuel, the anti-matter surface will dissociate the layer of water into oxygen and hydrogen, maybe their anti-matter equivalents, as a vapor layer ahead of the fragments. The fuel will hit this vapor layer and form a fuel air effect. We just need to ignite it if it does not ignite itself. The resulting reaction will either deflect the fragments, slow them down or even shatter them. Depending on the outcome, we may have to dodge particles, but they will be regular matter."

"We have some RPG's on board from Air Force One. A rocket

propelled grenade should ignite the mix." Fuller beckoned an Air Force One crewman over and instructed him to locate and bring the RPG and launcher. "We need a method to shoot the water and fuel at the fragments. The travel time of the water and fuel is critical. We can use the refueling pumps and spray it out of the hoses at high pressure. We have to make sure our aim is right.

How much can we use without leaving ourselves short?"

"If this works sir, it really doesn't matter. Where are we going to go?" Hannaford asked.

"Sir, the energy release will be significant. I think we should risk half our mass. After all, we lose completely if we fail."

"You are quite right Shaw, so here is how we will do it…"

CHAPTER 31

Carver's Transport, Space Walking.

The four figures floated near the hull of the transport, the only indication that they were not in atmosphere were the darkened faceplates extruded by the youniforms. They each had a small oxygen replenishment pack on their utility belts.

Young and Hannaford were hauling at a long fueling hose that was coiled into the hull. Their task was to fix the hose outlet at the center of gravity of the transport facing directly into the oncoming fragments. Any deviation from this fix point would cause the jet effect of the high pressure water to impart a spin on the transport. Instead, this rocket effect would add to the velocity away from the fragments. On Air Force One which was still coupled to the transport, Fuller and Shaw were doing the same thing with the jet fuel, however their nozzle was an improvised spray head.

"Are you ready Hannaford?"

"Yes sir. We have secured the hose to a docking pylon that is close to the centre of mass point. Ready to open the valve on your command."

"Shaw, you have the calculations. You give the order."

"Sir." There was a moment of silence. "On my count release on three Felicity. You will shut off at my call and I will release the jet fuel exactly fifteen seconds later. Starting count. One, two, THREE."

Felicity pushed the manual valve lever and a solid jet of water shot straight out into the void. A fine mist of particles dispersed around the edges of the nozzle and gradually formed a slow moving cloud that shrouded the glistening shaft of water which became a fine line in the distance and then vanished from view.

The fifteen seconds flashed by and Felicity pulled back the lever on hearing "CLOSE NOW!" from Shaw. Instantly a new stream appeared, not as a solid pillar of liquid but as tendrils of noodles and buckshot, all gradually spreading out as they charged towards the oncoming anti-matter coated fragments that used to be earth.

The World Game by Allen Charles   Page 92

CHAPTER 32

Inside the Iranian Bunker fragment.

"Zardooz, tell me what is going on. What can we do?" Arjmand was hyperventilating upon the realization that Zardooz was in no way joking with him. The reality and finality of the destruction of the earth was too much for anyone, and certainly so for the unstable Arjmand.

Zardooz was holding himself into a chair, knees jammed under a computer console, doing nothing. Just staring at the snowing screen. Thinking.

A pen slowly drifted past his hand. He poked it with a finger and it started to spin away. His analysis of their situation led him to believe that at least two of the corridor blast doors had maintained their integrity as he could see their green safe indicators on the panel. It could be that others had held but the electronics were damaged.

He grabbed the errant pen from the air and pulled a note pad from a drawer, sending a shower of paper clips into orbit. He started scribbling figures and calculations and drew a diagram of what he believed the fragment would look like. As he had designed the bunker, he had a good handle on the geology of the area. He had put the bunker into the core of the hardest single mass of granite he could locate.

The blast doors were one hundred and fifty meters apart, so he had at least three hundred of meters of rock in that direction. Assuming some symmetry to the fracture and integrity of the granite node, Iran now consisted of an orb about six hundred meters in diameter. The problem he faced now was how to get some eyes working on the outside to see where the fragment was located and where it was heading.

"Arjmand!"

"Huh? Yes. What?"

"I need you to do something so we can see what is going on outside."

"But I don't have any training in this. What can I do?" Arjmand was visibly shaking with fear.

"You just have to go down the corridor and look through the view port at each blast door. You will see a green light at each door indicating that the next section is intact. When you reach a door that has a red light or none at all, you need to look very carefully through the panel and report back to me what you see. Here, take this flashlight with you. You may have to shine it through the port if the segment power is out."

"Why don't you go!" Arjmand demanded.

"I have to stay here and monitor the corridor segments. I can warn you if there is any danger ahead. Like you said, you have no training in this. I helped to design it all."

"Send one of the girls." Arjmand was trying to assert himself while his knees knocked together.

"No, I need you to do this. You may have to follow some precise instructions when you reach the dead section. What you do could mean life or death. Do you really want to give this over to one of the girls?"

Arjmand's eyes were swivelling from side to side in panic, like a trapped animal. His breath came in short sharp gasps. "I.. I... I'll g... g... go." he at last stammered." He took a deep breath and calmed down. There was still a vestige of presidential strength of character deep within him, probably the last particle he possessed, but he dredged deep, getting up from his chair gingerly and grabbing available protrusions as hand holds.

"You will have to angle off the walls using any joins to move yourself forward. Be careful not to go too fast." Arjmand just nodded and pushed off in the direction of the door. He had slipped the flash light inside his shirt to free his hands, the robes he wore drifting and billowing out around him.

His first flight left him holding on to the top of the door frame as momentum swung his body through the opening. Strung out facing the wrong way and holding on tight, he squirmed his body around and calculated his next jump, a long one down the first corridor segment. There were few hand holds in sight, and none he could grip to get a push off.

Zardooz watched on the security camera as Arjmand worked into a squatting position and placed his feet on the wall next to the doorway, ready to push off. "Not too hard now." Zardooz murmured to himself.

Arjmand grimaced and then pushed off, much too hard for his first attempt. The angle of thrust was all wrong and he bounced and caromed like a billiard ball, the knuckles his hands over his head for protection getting skinned and leaving bloody streaks on the walls.

He finally came to rest floating near the first lock, curled into a ball, shaking and whimpering. Over the speaker system Zardooz coaxed him.

"Come on now Arjmand, you need to get hold of yourself and do the job. There is no danger to you if you think about the next step. Come on now." The unusually gentle goading by Zardooz began to have an effect. Arjmand stopped his whimpering and peeked out from his protective arms, like a kitten from under its paws. He saw he was stationary and where he was supposed to be, perking up immediately and unfolding from his protective ball. "Go look through the window and tell me what you see." continued Zardooz. "You are looking for lights on in a normal corridor and green indicator lamps on the air lock console."

Arjmand puffed out his chest and worked his way to the view port. Everything looked normal, so he signaled to Zardooz with a thumbs up.

"OK Arjmand. You need to open the air lock and move into the next section. Do exactly as I tell you."

Once again Arjmand gave the thumbs up, not realizing he could use the intercom system by the lock."

Thousands of miles away Fuller and his team of cadets prepared to launch a water fuel bomb towards the approaching earth fragments. Contrary to all the laws of probability, the Iran fragment was the leader of the fragment pack heading directly at Fuller's transport, with the US President on board.

In another quadrant of space, the whiplash of the severed Skyhook was flailing its way like a trapped snake as it trailed the

Terminus which was now a tangential missile heading towards Space City, its trajectory being controlled at whim by the Skyhook tail that itself was being consumed by the anti-matter like a stocking being rolled up a leg.

On Space City the people were visibly frenetic, but disciplined as they rushed to load and board the transports. There was enough room for everyone, but time was the issue, not space. They knew that the Skyhook Terminus was hurdling in their general direction with a follow up of anti-matter coated fragments.

Altogether, not a fantastic moment for the remnants of humanity.

CHAPTER 33

Aboard the X3 Transport.

The air rushed out of the lock dragging at the pilot's body as he clung on to his precarious hold. With a loud crash the escaping atmosphere stilled as the object blocking the outer lock was sucked out into space and the lock slammed shut, the dogs fully engaging.

The pilot released his death hold with a gasp of relief, unable to move or react for a few moments. He recovered enough to cling to the view ports and peer through to the outer port as the black of space was replaced by a gray, uniform glow. With a shout of alarm he realized what he was looking at.

He keyed his communicator to the co-pilot, "Go! Go! Blast everything we've got. The Hook is coming. MOVE!" He was screaming now as he watched the pulsating gray bear down. The sudden acceleration of the transport pulled him away from the port and he scrabbled about to regain a hold and a view of the oncoming menace.

The other transports had fled minutes earlier and were out of immediate danger. Just X3 was left in the Skyhook kill zone.

The pilot peered over the edge of the view port as he dragged himself up against the thrust. He could make details on the Skyhook surface as the carbon filament Tsunami rolled inexorably towards X3 despite the gallant attempt to outrun it.

"Oh God!" He gasped as he saw the end seconds away. "Oh God save us!"

"Hah! Thirteen thousand credits to my account you meteoric turd!"

"OK, you win you black hole." came back a grudging reply. "I never expected he would invoke the Deity Clause. Where did he get placed?"

He and the rest on that ship were saved to a category three stasis. There was some wreckage left to keep things going. These ones take the first thirty positions of Saved for Game Eight."

"Can you believe it. Game Edition Seven. This was one of our longest running Games. Five thousand eight hundred of their Earth years. That's gotta be a record."

"Wanna bet on that?"

"Oh go vaporize yourself. You're addicted to this betting." There was a pause in the thought stream. "What odds?" There was a babble of thought noise in the network as bets were placed across the galaxies. "Quiet down you lot! I haven't finished here yet! What are the rules now? Its been so long since the last destruction that I forgot what the play is."

"By gosh, you have the intellect of moon dust. Post destruction rules are that all survivors are classified as conditional winners. We don't interfere until they are about to die and then we save them to stasis and rank their position according to the time frame of being saved. If any two are saved at the same instant we flip for the ranking. Last two standing are the Grand Winners. Got it?" "Yeah, got it. Wanna put something down on the Iranian fragment against the US Transport? I'll give you five to one that the Iranians win this one."

"They're your credits sun zit! I'll take it and your bet on the time record."

The galactic channels buzzed once again with wager and counter wager.

CHAPTER 34

Aboard Carver's Transport.

Fuller and his small team made their way back into the Transport and strapped in. Carver checked all security and systems then announced, "Everyone brace for maximum acceleration. We're getting out of here!"

The immediate thrust pressed everyone back into their seats at three time Earth normal gravity. Faces distorted as cheeks tried to flow back in faces. Breathing became difficult with the pressure and eyeballs felt like they were being squeezed out of their sockets. Raising an arm took major effort and standing was impossible. Fuller's normally 200 pound frame now weighed the equivalent of six hundred pounds.

The youniforms and buddies could partially compensate for the extreme artificial gravity by adjusting pressures across the body and assisting breathing, but there were now passengers aboard, including the President, who did not have the added protection.

Fuller was watching the President closely. He could see the physical distress and was keeping Carver informed.

"John there is nothing I can do about this. If the fuel bomb doesn't work and we don't outrun the anti-matter we are all dead."

"I hear you. How long until the bomb hits the fragments?"

"Approximately three minutes. Is the President good for that?"

"I don't know. He doesn't look too good right now, but none of us do. Wait a second!" He peered around the edge of the seat back in front of him, as far as he could move. There was movement in the aisle.

"Janine, Hannaford has somehow got herself roped up to a wall brace and has managed to lower herself and an emergency aid kit down to the President. She is giving him oxygen. She must be weighing in at four or five hundred pounds. Amazing kid. I can see the President is responding. He is signing her to help others if she can."

"Great John. Two and a half minutes to impact."

The one hundred and fifty seconds ground by so slowly.

"Fuel bomb impact in ten seconds. Nine... eight... brace! Brace! four... three... two... one... IMPACT!"

The cloud of water spray engulfed the surface of the fragments coming directly at the Transport. There were some visible sparkles and a grey fog of dissociated hydrogen and oxygen molecules formed a mini atmosphere. Nothing more happened.

"What's happening Janine?" John gasped out.

"Nothing yet. Wait. Wait! The fuel has just hit. I can see flashes. Ouch that was blinding, even with the youniform. The whole surface has ignited. My doppler radar tells me the fragment has slowed a little relative to the former velocity vector. The explosion must have been quite a kick."

"Has it affected the anti-matter?

"I can't see yet. Everything has gone dark." Carver checked herself. "Hang on. If it is dark and I can't see the silver of the anti-matter then maybe we just killed it? My radar tells me the fragment is still there, although the profile has changed. Actually it is constantly changing. I think we not only slowed it down but we also put a spin on it."

"How is the relative velocity? Is is still gaining on us?"

"Yes it is gaining, but at about a third of the previous rate. I can take our thrust down to one G to maintain our escape and keep it at a distance. We can't veer from this course because of the other fragments."

As the heavy acceleration throttled back to one G and Earth normal gravitational effect, people started moving, rolling over and groaning with pain from bruised and cramped limbs. Carver issued instructions for everyone not providing aid to others to stay strapped in.

Fuller clambered across and up the seat backs to check on the President. Hannaford had settled in against the seat frame and was quietly checking the President's vitals with a BioMeter. She smiled at the President, "All looks good sir. You just need to rest now." She looked over to Hayes. "May I check your vitals Mr Hayes?"

He looked at her gratefully and held his arm out across the President's lap. The President turned his head slightly. "Aw Chuck.

Didn't know you cared!" The three of them started laughing until Hannaford looked up and saw Fuller.

"All in order Colonel. Mr Hayes is looking good." She took the BioMeter and packed it away. The President nodded at Fuller. "You have quite a team of young lions here Colonel Fuller. I understand that they are our best High School graduates with no formal space training and yet here they are taking over our survival. The young man behind us with his fuel bomb and reaction mass conservation, and Miss Hannaford here keeping us out of trouble a few minutes ago. Congratulations Colonel. An outstanding effort."

"Thank you Mr President. We all have to look out for each other now. You and your staff were at quite a disadvantage without youniforms and buddies. We will have to rectify that as soon as we can. Please try and rest now while I go and check on the rest of our passengers."

The President and Hayes, both recovered from the ordeal, were quietly talking. Shaw, sitting directly behind, could not help overhearing their discussion about the failure of the Anti-matter device. Neither the President nor Hayes had the scientific background to accurately analyze the catastrophic outcome and determine a reason for the calamity. Shaw reached over the seat back and touched Hayes on the shoulder.

"Excuse me sir. I don't mean to be eavesdropping, but I couldn't help overhearing. I have a theory as to why the AMD caused the effect, not that it really matters now. May I explain?"

Both men half turned to see Shaw. "Go ahead cadet... Aren't you the young man who devised the fuel bomb?"

"Yes sir."

"OK. Let's hear your ideas please."

"Mr President, Mr Hayes, can you think back to the days of terrorist threats of dirty nuclear bombs? This is before my time of course, but I have read about the concept. It is not a nuclear explosion in a real sense, but a conventional explosive used to scatter deadly radioactive material over a wide area, causing slow radiation sickness and devastating the population and land.

Now to the AMD. The Laws of Conservation state that the energy produced when matter annihilates anti-matter is defined by the Einsteinian equation of "Energy is equal to the mass times the square of the speed of light." In theory the amount of energy release is huge and absolute with no radioactive fallout, but it is finite. The explosion should happen and finish.

In this case, the first time an AMD has been tested and unfortunately in real use, we have had a design flaw and ended up with the equivalent of an AMD dirty bomb.

I believe that the reaction between the matter-anti-matter masses was too slow and that equal particles of both matter types were dispersed into the atmosphere. The matter was inconsequential however the interspersed anti-matter particle cloud was the danger.

Anti-matter exists is our universe in infinitesimal amounts, but clearly enough for our scientists to have gathered mass for the AMD. There is a theory, which now seems to have been substantiated in the worst possible way, that anti-matter is created and constant in the universe. Every time one particle is destroyed, a new particle "appears". The physics behind this theory is challenging and I could not begin to explain it here, but it supports the concept of "creation from nothing." Sounds like magic but it is real. Any questions so far?"

"Please go on Mr Shaw." The President said.

"The constant creation theory could not be tested at this time as we still have no idea where the replacement anti-matter will appear in the universe. Furthermore, conservation of energy dictates that the replacement anti-matter must maintain the energy balance and take in energy equivalent to half that released at the point of annihilation.

Sirs, I believe that the silver cloud we see is the creation interface of anti-matter replicating and absorbing energy from the surroundings, thus the lightning flashes. The anti-matter interface should be at extremely low temperature, possible close to absolute zero, as the energy is converted back into anti-matter.

What puzzled me the most is why the creation front kept growing. Why didn't it stop? It appears that the anti-matter is increasing and not staying constant. I have a theory about that based on statistical particle physics. There appears to be a sympathetic reaction between subatomic particles that defies our conventional idea of space time relationship. Experimenters over 20 years ago were able to strike a particle with a gamma particle and the particle pair in a remote location would emit a photon at exactly the same instant as the photon emission from the target particle.

Based upon these real observations, I am postulating that the concentration of the AMD explosion has caused a nexus in our universe that attracts the sympathetic reaction of remote anti-matter destruction throughout the universe. We have attracted all the anti-matter in creation like a magnet attracts iron filings. Past this point there is no projection as to where things will go. That's it Mr President."

The President took in a breath and looked at Shaw in astonishment. "Pardon me for asking, and I do not doubt you Mr Shaw, but how old are you?"

"Eighteen sir."

"And how did you reach this level of knowledge and capability that people twice your age do not achieve?"

"Sir, only because you ask, my assessed IQ is 195. The tests did not cater for my level of IQ and eidetic memory. I have a God given gift and I intend to use it. My associate Felicity Hannaford is not far behind me sir, and the rest of the cadets are all the top of their schools. We have no shortage of intelligence, just a lack of experience."

"Well Mr Shaw, I guess we are all in the same boat as to experience right now. I am grateful that we have you and your group as survivors. Maybe we have a chance."

"Thank you sir."

The President scratched his nose in thought for a moment. "Mr Shaw, I didn't miss your comment of "thank God". Did God do this to us?"

"Mr President, we had a society based upon belief in God that had its roots stretching back thousands of years. We believed in the Bible and the stories of the Flood, the Exodus and all the miracles that accompanied this theology. Why should we stop believing now? This is as valid in human existence as were the Ten Plagues in Egypt or the splitting of the Red Sea.

There are no half measures. One either believes or does not. I choose to believe that our situation is God's will."

"All the population of Earth destroyed? God's will?"

"Sir, He made us, He can do as He wants with us. It remains to be seen if the population was destroyed or sent to a better place. Your questions reveal self doubt and internalization of this catastrophe. See I used a negative word, catastrophe. It is one from our perspective, but we are like fish in a goldfish bowl. We can't even imagine what is outside the bowl. A net comes in and scoops up some fish. The others run away and wonder if those lost are cat food. In fact they are in a much larger tank with great freedom. Who knows? So I choose to follow the belief in God that is supported by a philosophy of non-interference unless absolutely necessary."

"And you don't see this as necessary?"

"I am not God Mr President. Neither are you sir."

"The President looked back at Shaw with a smile."I hope I never have to run against you for President Mr Shaw. I wouldn't stand a chance."

Shaw grinned and then turned suddenly at a cry of distress from behind. It was Amy Young who had been going around checking the presidential staff. She was clinging to the aisle seat frame next to the Secretary of State. "I need emergency care here. Oxygen and defibrillator. I do not have a pulse and my BioMeter is telling me thirty seconds to brain death."

"Amy!" Shaw cried out, "Do exactly as I tell you! Put your fingers in her mouth and pull her jaw open!"

Amy clambered over the arm rests and secured herself precariously, taking precious seconds. "OK I've done that." She called out.

"Put your mouth over her mouth and pinch her nostrils closed, then blow into her mouth to inflate her lungs. Let the air come out naturally. Do this three times quickly."

Amy frantically applied the breath transfer while trying to fight the acceleration drag. "Done!"

"Pull your youniform hood over her head and apply the breathing again. Felicity is heading your way with a HeartStart. What is the BioMeter saying now?"

"We gained another thirty seconds. Wait. The youniform seems to be flowing over her and my buddy is working on her too. The BioMeter is saying there is blood flow and pulse but no heartbeat. The time to brain death has gone and she is showing as critical stable. Here's Felicity."

Felicity crawled over the adjoining seat back and slipped the HeartStart cable under Beauvais's clothing, allowing it to attach just below the sternum. It released chemicals into her blood stream and wire tendrils penetrated into her heart muscle. There was a beep noise and a spoken warning, "Stand Clear. Electric Shock."

Felicity cleared but Amy was still attached by the youniform and the buddy. She calmly said "Go ahead Felicity. Activate it manually. The youniform will protect me." Then in a whisper "I hope..."

There was no more time to lose. Felicity pressed the green button on the HeartStart and Beauvais's body convulsed with the shock. Amy was driven clear of her hold on the seat and attached to Beauvais by the youniform, face to face like lovers kissing. Amy's body came down hard across the seat back in front as acceleration took over and she blew out a gasp into Beauvais's face as if punched hard in the stomach, which in fact was the case. The youniform had reacted to the impact and frozen to prevent major damage, but not before the intrusion of the seat back had doubled her over and cracked a couple of ribs.

"Aaahhg!" Amy moaned, before the buddy could kick in and suppress the pain of the bruising cracked ribs.

"Aahhg yourself." came a whispered reply from Beauvais.

"Oh thank God you are OK!" Gasped Amy with a grin, even around her now decreasing pain.

Felicity moved herself into a position to support Amy and lower her into the now vacated seat in front of Beauvais. I need to get the BioMeter onto you now Amy. The HeartStart is taking care of Secretary Beauvais.

Felicity put the BioMeter onto Amy's arm and after a few seconds read the diagnostic screen. Two cracked ribs and bruising trauma to the diaphragm. No action to be taken other than rest and analgesics. The buddy was already taking care of that part of the pain management.

Fuller had reached the group and in all only sixty seconds had passed since the first alarm.

"Madam Secretary how are you doing?" He asked.

"Colonel Fuller," she answered in a small voice, "you're cadets are quite amazing. I feel weak but fine now. I blacked out and then the next thing I remember is being attached face to face with this young lady who seems to be in some distress herself."

"Amy will be fine Madam Secretary. Her equipment protected her from major injury and she was able to save you under Shaw's instructions. These are exceptional young people and are here because of their abilities. I think you should rest now and let the HeartStart do its job."

Beauvais looked up at Fuller gratefully and relaxed. Her eyelids dropped and she fell into a deep, curative sleep aided by the HeartStart.

Fuller looked at the bio-stats on the HeartStart screen. Beauvais had been clinically dead for at least five full minutes prior to intervention. The warning to brain death should not have happened. Technically, the HeartStart should not have worked. Beauvais should be dead.

He carefully looked around. Felicity was busy with Amy. He reached out and cancelled the read-out.

Beauvais had an empty seat next to her, so he summoned another cadet to make her way over and instructed her to watch Beauvais. She would be relieved in four hours. Fuller headed back to the flight deck, walking up chair frames like a ladder. He poked his head into the cabin, "Room for one more Commander?"

Janine looked back over her shoulder, "Take a seat Colonel Fuller." He could see the weariness in her eyes and the stress in her gaunt features. "We seem to be reaching an equilibrium velocity to outrun the fragments. How far ahead of the pack do you think we should position ourselves until we can calculate for evasion if it is possible? I could throttle back the acceleration and give some relief to the passengers, as well as save reaction mass."

"What does the math look like for the direct fragments?"

"Since you guys blew away the main ones heading for us and slowed them down, there is a dimple in the expanding ball of fragments with the unaffected pieces moving faster than the dimple. That will put us into a one ended cone of fragments for some time. The problem is that we don't know if there is an end to the fragment stream, although common sense says there must be. We are trapped inside this tunnel effect until the expansion of the fragment ball is sufficient for us to be able to navigate between the pieces safely and maybe get behind it. Because there are probably specks and dust size particles out there, we take a risk moving off this vector at any time. Your young genius Shaw may be able to shed some light on all this."

Fuller just sat silent for a moment, decompressing. "I wonder what happened to the other transports and the Space City shuttles?" he murmured.

CHAPTER 35

In the Iranian Fragment just before the fuel bomb impact.

Arjmand had reached the final active lock, the third one, so there were two segments of safe corridor before the vacuum of space broached the bunker safety. He was full of self confidence now and acting without detailed instruction from Zardooz. He pulled out his small flashlight and muted the corridor illumination to see beyond the air lock window. It was black. Just black. He pressed the flashlight against the viewport and turned it on. At first he could not make out what he was looking at. Was it inches from the glass or feet away? The glow of the flashlight was completely refracted and diffused as it tried to penetrate the darkness.

"What do you see?" came Zardooz across the intercom.

"I - I'm not sure. It looks silvery and fluid but I can't tell if it is on the other side of the glass or far away. It seems to suck up light and is the same in all directions. There is nothing to give it perspective. What is it Zardooz?"

"The Great Satan used an Anti-Matter Device on our glorious Empire. We are seeing anti-matter as close as we ever want to see it I believe. There is nothing more for you to do there, start heading back."

Arjmand turned up the lights again and prepared to kick off back down the corridor. It was this braced position that saved him from injury and probable death as the fuel bomb water vapor precursor struck the fragment. Part of the vaporization reaction caused a slight jolt to the constant velocity vector. Zardooz, although not knowing precisely what was about to hit, screamed across the intercom "Arjmand hold tight!"

There was no reply and fifteen seconds later the fuel hit and ignited, making the fragment stand still in the mass of fragments and blasting away the anti-matter coating around the fragment. The cloud of the blast coalesced as a trail behind the fragment, neutralizing the anti-matter coating of smaller pieces that slammed into the Iranian fragment like billiard balls. But the nett effect was that the main fragment had been slowed down relative to the remaining masses that formed the expanding shrapnel effect. Behind the main fragment front there was relative emptiness as the earth's crust had blasted away and left the core in place as a coolly glowing planetoid coated with anti-matter. There were scattered pebbles and particles following the main masses and then a clean vacuum.

In the corridor Arjmand was being flung about like a rag doll, his arm hooked under the grab bar by the air lock at Zardooz's warning. The pain was excruciating as his shoulder was dislocated in one direction and then popped back in by the follow up impacts. Blood flowed from his broken nose and one ankle was twisted at an unnatural angle. During the impacts the lighting had flickered and gone out, but it came back on again as the violence ceased. Arjmand was still conscious but in terrible agony.

"Arjmand?" came Zardooz. "Are you there? Are you all right?" Zardooz could feel a sensation of weight against his chair.

"Ooooohhh. I'm hurt so bad. Help me." he whimpered. "Please? I'm dying."

"Arjmand! Get hold of yourself. Where are you hurt?"

Arjmand groggily lifted his head and looked at his ankle. He screamed from the pain in his shoulder as he tried to take his arm from under the bar. He felt like he was pinned to the wall and was no longer in free fall. He panted for breath and gasped "I have a broken ankle and I think my shoulder too. My nose is broken and I'm bleeding everywhere. Please come get me."

"Can you see outside from where you are?"

"I can't move at all Zardooz. Come get me for the love of Allah!"

"Answer my question. Can you see outside? Then I will come get you."

Arjmand slowly twisted his head around. He was almost hard against the viewport and the bloody smear on the glass attested to where he had smashed his nose. He looked past the mess and blinked his eyes in disbelief. He looked again.

"Zardooz, are you there?"

"Yes, what do you see?"

"I can see stars, and the moon off to one side. All slowly moving.

Now please come get me."

"I'm coming." Zardooz grabbed a first aid kit and threw in a syringe and a couple of ampoules of morphine. He took one more look around the control center and then bounced out against the tiny gravitational force. In the outer room the bodies of the two female attendants had drifted and settled against the far wall, broken and bloody from the frightful impact injuries received. Zardooz shook his head. "Such a waste." he whispered. The safety harness in the control seat had engaged automatically at the first impact and saved him from any injury. "Just me and that swine Arjmand now."

CHAPTER 36

Aboard the Space City Shuttles and remaining Transports.

The pilots were frantically computing reaction mass data and relative velocities of ships, fragments and moon to try to outrun the fragment swarm and hide behind the moon. The Space City shuttles would have no problem making the distance, however the two remaining lower altitude transports did not stand a chance. The fragments would overtake them half way. There was just not enough reaction mass to complete the equation successfully.

The other three transports X1, X2 and X3, could not run to the moon, but would take their chances shielding behind the bulk of space city. They were gambling that the missile that Skyhook terminus had become would miss Space City and leave it as a shield of sorts.

"X6 come in, this is X4. Over" the pilots were reduced to simple radio communications ship to ship, now that all infrastructure was dust.

"X6 here. What do you have in mind Corcoran? Over"

"If we do nothing we have no chance at all. I was thinking about what Carver did, picking up the Air Force One reaction mass. I think we should rendezvous and take on all your passengers and transfer your reaction mass to this transport. That would give us a fighting chance to either get behind Space City or run for the moon. If any of the other transports have reaction mass to spare they could leave it at pre arranged coordinates for us. We have to make contact with them and tell them what we are doing. Two of them could do the same and definitely have excess reaction mass. We lose the resources of a ship but what's that compared to immediate lives saved? Over"

"I agree Corcoran. We maintain this escape vector to keep running ahead of the fragments and we rendezvous in ... say thirty minutes. We will be ready to transfer to you lock to lock. None of my passengers have youniforms or buddies and I have a full house here, so it is going to get a bit cramped. Over"

"What's your reaction mass status Martin? Over"

"Fifty-five percent. Can you take that on board Corcoran? Over."

"We run parallel until we are both under fifty percent then transfer. We cannot waste a drop. Over."

"We need to crunch the numbers to see if we can run for the moon with the extra passenger mass aboard and then let the other transports know how much reaction mass we will need to finish the run. Corcoran, do you know the location of reaction mass depots on the moon for an unguided landing? Have to be on the dark side and we would need to move fast if the anti-matter spreads on the moon like it did on earth. We could fuel up and haul off a load of reaction mass so we don't get stranded. We can pick up six times the mass we could haul off earth. Might get all the transports out of trouble later. Over."

"Nice idea Martin. We need to tell the others to do that as soon as they reach their way points behind the moon. Do we have a depot chart on the on board system? Over."

"I do not believe so Corcoran. That is the problem. We need to contact the Space City shuttles and see if any of their people know the location by dead reckoning coordinates. Over."

"How do we contact anyone with these dinky little radios? We need to get past the Skyhook tube between them and us and Solar interference. Over."

"Corcoran, do you have any laser equipment aboard? Over."

"It was quite a mess throwing everything in sight aboard when we left so I'm not sure. I think I saw a corporate logo for Lasmine equipment on a couple of the boxes. What do you have in mind? Over."

"We do not have direct line of sight with any other craft that we know of. If you look back what do you see? Over."

"I see a terrifying sight of silver coated missiles heading for me. Over."

"You got it Corcoran. We have mirrors coming at us, and mirrors reflect, so we can get past the obstacle of the Skyhook. We just have to hope that someone is watching at the other end. Over"

"How do we turn mining lasers into communication lasers?

Over."

"It's a good thing I'm a History major. Back in the beginning of radio communications and line of sight light communications there were simple codes used. One of these was called Morse Code and became the default standard. My historical re-enactment group learned Morse code, so I can flash a coded laser message and reflect it off the anti-matter in the general direction of our other transports. Over."

"And then what? Over."

"Then we pray to God that someone sees our message and figures out it is Morse Code. Over."

"It's a long shot Martin, but I'll find that equipment. Over."

The two transports continued on parallel courses for a further twenty minutes until reaction mass on both was less than fifty percent. They had still not accelerated sufficiently to outrun the fragment swarm which was gradually drawing closer. They had less than one hour to complete the personnel and reaction mass transfer.

The two pilots skillfully mated the transports lock to lock and opened the hatches.

The passengers on X4, Martin's craft, were to move over to X6. They began to drift over and congregate near the air lock and the first person began to climb through - to be met at the other side by a bear of a man wielding a piece of metal tubing as a club.

"Get back where you came from or I'll smash your skull in!" he growled in a voice that matched his coarse appearance. His face was red and unshaven and his arms bulged with muscle under the tattoos that he wore like skin tight sleeves. "And tell ya friends to stay right there. There ain't enough room on this here ship to begin with. We don't need you lot as well."

"What's going on here?" Corcoran the pilot had come down to supervise the transfer before space walking with Martin to move the reaction mass. "Stand aside and allow them to come in!"

"Not bloody likely. Who are you anyway you pussy uniformed prick?"

Corcoran paused and looked around assessing the mood of the

other passengers. He decided this was a stand alone troublemaker that had to be dealt with. "I am the Commander of this transport and what I say goes, without question. Now put down the bar and stand aside."

"Or what you big pussy. Wotcha gonna do to me if I don't? Huh?" The brute lifted his face in a sneer and menacingly tapped the bar in his palm. The other passengers edged back as best they could in weightless conditions.

"Unfortunately for you we are under full martial law and I will kill you without hesitation. Now stand aside or suffer the consequences."

"Come and get me mister pussy soldier."

"I don't need to." Corcoran raised his arm, hand clenched into a fist and turned down. Suddenly his youniform emitted two fine streaking missiles that took the troublemaker in the throat. Corcoran backed off a lethal solution at the last moment and had his buddy simply paralyze the target, whose eyes bulged as he gasped for breath. He released the bar which drifted away and his legs untangled from the wall harness. His already red face was now crimson as he choked for breath.

"I can let you die right now or you can behave yourself. There are not enough of us left to waste the life of even a fool like you. Your choice, live or die."

The terrified man was gagging, holding on to consciousness and signalling he would give in. Corcoran not entirely convinced on the sincerity of the capitulation under duress, reeled back the buddy and watched as the offender slowly recovered.

"Get that transfer happening now. We have no time to lose."

CHAPTER 37

Far away in another galaxy.

An expletive soiled the thought waves. "Putrid offspring of excreta! Damn and a supernova up your etherial arse! I could have sworn that he would kill him. I just lost a heap on that bet."

"You cheated again didn't you!"

"Rubbish. How can you accuse me of cheating? I lost the bet."

"Yes you lost, but you stimulated the brute to mutiny. Everyone else was cooperating so the probability of a single mutineer is so slight as to be zero. You did something, I just haven't figured out what yet. When I do figure it out I am going to call for a penalty payment as well as the bet amount. You really suck with this cheating. First the snake, now this. Twice in one game."

"But I'm down over seventy thousand credits on this game. If I lose any more I won't be able to pay my subscription for the next series. I'll go nuts with nothing to do during penalty wait out. It happened to me once before and it ain't no fun."

"Which series did it happen?"

"I think it was Game Series Four. I always bet on the good guys, they all seem to be called the Allies in most series, winning the main war of the series. Problem was in Game Four...."

"Yeah I know. The Fartzi Party won that one and them blew up the world almost straight away testing their nuclear bombs. Short Game that one."

"How'd you do on that?"

"Oh, I watched where you were putting your credits and bet the other way..."

"Why you..."

"Language old son! Language!"

Across the universe the network hummed with bet and counter bet.

"Aw give me a break will ya? Have you got a form guide handy?"

"You haven't had hands for at least twenty five thousand years blob brain. Handy my hippo campus! Anyway, what do you expect to find in the form guide. It is updated every hour and is obsolete the

---

moment it is published to the network."

"Just wanna know if that Carver Fuller team is a stayer or if they fade on the home straight."

"Don't need the form guide for that. Carver fulla Fuller is a stayer. Hah! I'm just sooo funny I crack myself up! Yeah, those two are good for a win. Put something down on Shaw Hannaford. I'm hedging between those pairs for the winners. Gosh, Carver almost makes me wish I had a body again. She's hot!"

The network almost glowed with the overload of bets being made.

"Talk to you later man! Having a brain massage in ten. Gotta go."

CHAPTER 38

Aboard Carver's Transport.

"Look at that will you!" Fuller was looking at the rear view 3D platform where a now blackened and scorched earth fragment appeared to be falling towards them. He could see the visual aspect of the rock changing as it rotated about an axis perpendicular to the fuel bomb explosive force. The bomb had not hit evenly and the unbalanced explosive force had imparted a spin to the micro-planet of Iran.

"Janine, is there any way we can check the vector of that big rock from before and after the blast?"

"I was tracking it with doppler radar so we have its earlier path. Because of the spin on it the reading will not be as accurate now, but yes, I can run a new track."

"Please do it now." Fuller was staring at the rock with intense concentration, as if he were looking right into it with X-ray vision.

Janine ran the tracking and a 3D vector diagram hovered in front of her. "I made the older track red and the new track green. There's not a lot of the new track yet, but I can see that the path has a divergence since the explosion."

"Can we do a multiple scan of all surrounding fragments to see if there will be a collision between this rock and other anti-matter coated pieces?"

"That's a hard one for our little on board nanobrain. I'll give it a try but we are pushing the limits."

Fuller said nothing and just nodded, still furiously thinking and calculating. Shaw may have the IQ but Fuller had the experience. Janine had instructed the nanobrain and the display was showing a tiny 3D rendition of the Solar System as a please wait clock. Seconds went by. Then a minute. Another thirty seconds.

"It's not happening John."

"Give it some more time."

There was a sweet little tink noise and the solution began to appear as a 3D wire image. Once the image was complete the solid objects were colored in, brown for the rock and silver for the fragments. Red dots represented detectable micro particles of anti-matter that were as dangerous as any large mass, given time. The transport itself was represented in miniature. Once the scene had finished rendering, it moved into relative motion showing the objects relative to the transport, projected forward in accelerated time. Carver and Fuller watched the majestic lumbering of the infected earth fragments as they expanded ever outwards. Only the brown rock, slowed down and being overtaken by the surrounding fragments, did not follow the parallel path. Even as it was being left behind, its skewed trajectory looked like it would take it into collision with other fragments.

They continued to watch this space ballet, tension heightening as the rock was fully passed by the rest of the fragment cloud - and missed collision. They both had been holding their breath and let out a whoosh of relief as even the micro particles flowed by.

"You know what this means Janine?"

"We can get behind the fragment cloud and use the rock as a shield if any particles are straying towards us."

"More than that. The rock is reaction mass. It was a chunk of Earth. It may contain elements, minerals and trapped gasses essential for our long term survival." Fuller stopped to think again, tapping his finger and spacing out. "I wonder?" he said to no one in particular.

"What?"

"Huh?" Shaken out of his deep thought he said, "I think we could do something with this rock. What's its mass? Can we calculate that?"

"Approximately. We don't know the overall density or composition so it will be a high end estimation."

"That's fine. Anything less than our initial estimate is to our advantage. We are moving mass so the less we have to move the easier it is."

"Moving mass?" Janine looked at him expectantly.

"Maybe. If my idea works and the equipment works."

Janine's face lit up as the light bulbs in her brain turned on. "Hey Mr Fuller. Not a bad idea at all. I'll call up the specs for the

Dinkshif drives and get the mass estimator working."

"I'm going to bring Shaw and Hannaford in on this. I will need some competent help to pull it off."

"How about the President? Are you going to fill him in?"

"I was thinking about that. Honestly, what is he the President of any more? He's just another survivor without any skills to add to our survival chances. I respect the fact that he was the most powerful man in the world until a few hours ago, but now it is you and me. We command absolute authority on this vessel. I think we need to proceed and advise him of what we are doing, but not ask any permission to proceed."

Janine screwed up her face and squinted at Fuller. "Wow. I never considered it in that way. When you live your life accepting the power and prestige of the office of President you don't consider that it may become a position of nothing overnight. I guess the issue is that this craft is still US property and subject to the authority of the Commander in Chief of the US Armed Forces, and that is the President. But protocol and Marine Law is that the Captain of the vessel under way wields supreme power at all times." She stopped to think for a moment and came to a decision. "You are right you know, but break it to him gently Captain Bligh."

Fuller grinned at her, took her chin gently and planted a kiss on her lips.

"Hmm..." came a happy response. "You fink Mr Fuller," came muffled by the kiss, "that there's a two hour motel on dat dere rock?" as she pulled away and looked in his eyes.

"Bloody well hope so!" His long departed Australian dad's expletives bouncing into his mind for no apparent reason.

They held on for another long twenty seconds and then reluctantly separated.

"I'm going to have a chat with Shaw and Hannaford about the idea. Isn't it crazy that these children are our greatest experts? Scary." He made his way out of the cabin, only having to work against one G of acceleration.

CHAPTER 39

On the X6 Transport.

"Everyone is on board now Corcoran. We do the reaction mass transfer now."

"We both have to go EVA for that Martin. That leaves no one in authority on board and I'm worried about that clown you had to zap."

"If we don't move smartly we won't be worrying about anything if the fragments hit us. Read them all the Riot Act Corcoran and let's get moving."

"Better to say nothing. Maybe the idiots on board will not notice we are missing. After all, without us they are all dead."

"OK, let's go. Checklist the tools. We only get one chance now."

"Auxiliary oxygen canisters, you and me. Welding and cutting laser, wrenches, de-icing spray."

"Check." Martin opened the inner lock and they both moved in with their equipment. The buddies went into EVA mode and the youniforms transformed into vacuum suits. He hit the remote dock separation switch and they saw X4 gradually drift away from X6 through the view port. "Ready for EVA Corcoran?"

"Go."

Martin opened the outer air lock and they could see X4 now about ten feet away, the separation drift slowed by automatic compensation jets. The two pushed off into space and headed for the reaction mass holding tank cover. Martin released and slid back the cover over a keypad and keyed in the unlock code. The cover popped up along one edge and then swung back and out, lying flush with the surface, revealing a brown, translucent bladder.

"Looks like my grand-dad's old water bed guts from the 1980s." laughed Corcoran. "Hope it doesn't puncture as easily." He poked at it with a finger and it rippled away from the indent. "I'll get the handles on this end."

They each took one end of the huge bladder and began gently lifting while keeping tension across it, simply by anchoring their feet under the locked down hatch cover. The half full bladder began to drift up at the two ends ever so slowly, the center gradually following.

"Funny thing happened to my grand-dad once. I was just a little kid sleeping over with the grands. All of a sudden I hear this running and screaming in the night and its gramps racing around yelling that he is dying, he's been stabbed and he's bleeding to death. Scared the crapola out of me being a kid. Never forget that."

"So what happened?" Martin asked.

"Oh, we got gramps calmed down, sat him down in a chair in his very wet, brand new red pajamas and looked for the stab wounds. There weren't any. There was nothing. The water bed had sprung a leak and the dye in his new jammies had run everywhere and looked like blood. He hadn't washed them before wearing as you had to do in those days."

Martin cracked up laughing, almost sending his end of the bladder off into space and grabbed hold again just in time. "OK. OK." he said still giggling at the image conjured up, "No more comic relief like that until this is done."

"Wasn't so funny at the time. He thought grams had stabbed him and she wasn't too pleased about that. They got over it but things were a bit strained from then on until the day gramps passed on."

"Aw, that's a shame. Why did it go that way?"

"Gramps was a bit of a wild boy and like to chase the ladies. Guess he had a guilty conscience and thought grams had found out about one of his conquests."

"Did he really do that?"

"Naw. I reckon it was wishful thinking. He was eighty-six when the red pajamas happened. Blimey. If I can still get it up at eighty-six I reckon my wife would tell me to go for it just so I would leave her alone!"

Martin cracked up with laughter again but held the bladder tightly. The tension of the past hours was lightened and the two of them carefully drifted the bladder clear of the hull. Corcoran jetted to the umbilical feed hose and wound off the connector above the automatic safety valve.

"Should I shut the hatch?" he asked Martin.

"It's not as if we're coming back to the transport. Don't waste time we do not have."

They imparted a velocity to the bladder to take it to the X6 reaction mass hatch and with Martin herding, Corcoran jetted off to open the hatch.

There was no provision to have both bladders connected so all they would do at this point is store the X4 bladder in the space available. Another EVA would be needed to move the feed line from the empty bladder to this one when the time came.

"We have to move Corcoran!" Martin warned, "The nearest fragments are only twenty minutes away."

"OK. We're done here. Didn't need any of the tools. That's a thought!"

"What?"

"Have we got stuff on board we could jettison in the path of the fragments? It will reduce our reaction mass consumption and maybe slow down the fragments a bit."

"Once we get under way we can physically check inventory. It won't be as effective as throwing it back now, but we can't wait. Good idea though."

The pair made their way to the entry port.

"Damn! Will you look at that!" Corcoran exclaimed.

The window of the port was filled by the ugly, red face of the big troublemaker. He held up a handwritten sign which said "f--- off and die pigs!"

"What are we going to do about this Martin? We only have about eighteen minutes left. This idiot is going to kill us all."

"We have only one choice that may give everyone a slim chance. It depends on how many are with this fool and how fast we can gain entry."

"I see what you are thinking," said Corcoran calmly as he watched Martin turn on the welder-cutter and head for the entry lock. Even with the inner lock open, if the atmosphere in the lock evacuated the inner lock would automatically slam shut. Martin was counting on only the bad guys being in the lock or in the way of the inner door. It was going to be very messy.

He applied the cutting arc to the glass port as red face inside screamed in berserk rage and beat on it with bare fists.

CHAPTER 40

Inside the Iranian fragment.

Zardooz had sedated and dragged Arjmand back to the living quarters where he strapped him into a bunk. While Arjmand was out cold he took the broken ankle and savagely jerked it straight to set it. An inflatable splint did the rest. There was a huge cache of medical supplies aboard so he set up a morphine drip into Arjmand's arm. When he came out of the sedation he was going to need it.

Zardooz went out to the control room where he had left the corpses of the dead girls, one settled under the desk and the other draped over a command chair. He stood still holding the door frame to counter the coriolis force that pushed him sideways, as he considered what to do with the bodies.

"Bodies!" he muttered to himself. "Where are the bodies. There was no sign of them. Not a bloody mark or scraping of skin. They were gone. "Just gone...? Just... gone?" he kept repeating to himself.

He worked his way around the room looking for some explanation and then went through to the communications center next door, shaking his head and muttering to himself, "Must have made a mistake. Have to be in here. Could swear they were back in the control room.

He couldn't see them anywhere. He even looked inside the unused staff lockers. Nothing.

Suddenly he brightened up. "Of course!" he vocalized, "They were not dead at all, just unconscious. They have come to and gone to clean up in their quarters. That must be what happened. Thank Allah they are all right!"

Zardooz returned to the living quarters and headed for the women's section He called out their names in hope of hearing something, but the silence chilled him. He looked into every room, pristine and untouched, until finally he was back where he had started, shaking his head in disbelief. He slumped down onto a bunk in defeat. "By the beard of the prophet, where could they have gone? I am a scientist. People do not vanish into thin air!"

Usually not one to lose his cool, there was no one to see him as he beat the bunk and tore up the coverings, screaming and thrashing, crying with spittle flying everywhere. There was no one to hear him. As precipitously as he had started his tantrum, he suddenly stopped and a huge grin took over his features, more a grimace than a grin.

"I am a rational man and a scientist. There has to be some logical explanation to this. I will follow scientific method and put this anomaly aside until the situation reveals the answer. Yes, I have lost things before and then found them some significant time later. I can do this. I refuse to believe in the irrational. I am not mad."

"Hey how many contestants are left poofteroid?"

"Who's calling me a poofteroid jerkaroid?"

"So how many?"

"We're down to one ninety-nine since we lifted the two girls."

"Right! That means we can go to the final Game Segment, Universe's Got Talent. This is the part I like best because we get to interfere with the contestants."

"Hang about! You've been interfering since the game started. You did the snake thing and set the poor blighters on the way to this mess."

"Quit ya whinging!. You made good money on that penalty payment I had to fork out."

"Come on you gas giant, get on with it. Who are the judges for this section?"

"We've got three. There's Peepers from Morgana Galaxy, Charonelle from Osburn Galaxy and Howley from the Mandelbrot quadrant."

"How does the game go now?"

"The judges decide who gets taken out and put in stasis until there are only ten or less remaining. That is when it goes to the viewers to vote and decide who wins."

"I reckon Carver and Fuller."

"I think Shaw and Hannaford, but I'll take your money anyway."

CHAPTER 41

Aboard Carver's transport.

"We have four Dinkshif drives on board that were going to be used in the first stage experiments of approaching light speed. The goal was to capture a reasonably symmetrical asteroid in a particular mass range, attach the drives on the perimeter around the center of mass and then accelerate in a straight line from that point."

Fuller drifted in front of the small group and pointed at his makeshift white board. Carver, the President and all the cadets were seated buckled in around him. He pointed at the diagram drawn on the bulkhead, depicting relative positions of their own transport, the shattered Earth and the pursuing fragment, the moon, the Skyhook with its attached terminus, Space City, and a guess at the positions of the remaining transports and shuttles.

"This diagram represents what I believe to be the whole remains of the human species. Not a lot. We are out of immediate danger right now and we have the time to consolidate ourselves and work on long term survival. Our resources are finite so we must try to capture anything that comes our way. The only thing coming our way at this time is the earth fragment with which we have matched velocity. We have the opportunity to close with this fragment and dock with it. We will then attach the Dinkshif drives at precalculated locations, stabilize the rotation and the fragment becomes our new home and space travel vehicle. With the Dinkshif drives engaged we have the capability to exceed the speed of light many times over, contrary to Eiensteinian physics. Yes Shaw?"

"Sir, the Dinkshif theory has never been tested and flies in the face of all accepted theory and observation. What happens if we expend all these irreplaceable resources and the drives do not work?"

"Commander Carver and I have examined all the parameters of this course of action, including the scenario of total failure. We believe that the risks involved are far outweighed by the possibility

---

of finding another home planet. NASA would not have funded the Dinkshif project unless there was a high probability of success. We need to have some confidence in that. On the flip side, if it is a failure, we still have sufficient reaction mass to make a run for the moon and meet up with other survivors. That scenario does not have a great ending because of limited resources. Sooner or later we all die and humanity becomes extinct." Fuller paused and saw that the President has a question.

"Mr President?"

"Colonel Fuller, what is the time frame to reach another planetary system if Dinkshif works? And just by the way, I signed the order to implement the Dinkshif Drive project. Nylast Dinkshif was clear and convincing in his presentation and mathematics. I do have some understanding of the theory."

"On an approximate time scale we have calculated around fifteen hundred days to reach Alpha Centauri which is four light years from us. We will exceed the speed of light by a factor of two during our acceleration deceleration stages. If we simply passed by Alpha Centauri we would achieve that in around four hundred and fifty days' but we would be travelling at four times the speed of light and would not be able to stop or even observe that system."

Fuller looked for more questions. There were none so he continued. "Dinkshif theory does not ignore relativistic effects. There will be time dilation involved. He predicted that the time dilation would be logarithmic just like the Richter scale was for earthquakes. Each factor of light speed would cause a many hundred fold increase in the time dilation calculation. Our roughly four year journey will take us four years, but some thirty thousand years will pass in the regular universe." There was a gasp of dismay from one of the cadets as she covered her mouth and tears filled her eyes. The others looked stunned."

"Wake up people. You will not see any difference between now and thirty thousand years once we are four light years from this location. We are giving up the remote possibility of meeting up with the other survivors and maybe lasting a few years. We have the best chance of long term survival and continuing our species.

You are the ones to renew our race."

The President signaled Fuller that he wished to speak. He half turned in his seat to face the cadets. He gave them a warm smile to put them at ease and began speaking. "I owe everyone an apology. I owe humanity an apology. I made a decision to try to protect our way of life from a dangerous terrorist regime which was taking humanity down the road to war and possible extinction. I decided that we had to try to knock out this threat at the source. The only resource I had at hand was an untried weapon using anti-matter. We chose this path to prevent radioactive fallout and to cut off the threat with overwhelming force.

I based my decision on past experience of our country in dealing with irrational, Islamic terrorist regimes. They negotiate from the front and stab you from the back at the same time. It is the irrational minority that rise to the surface and take over these nations. Not just Islamics. Nazi Germany, Stalinist Russia, Red China are all examples of regimes that have abused human rights and murdered millions.

The threat assessment on the Iranian Islamic Empire was so extreme that it was a case of "them or us". I had to protect us. Unfortunately the scaling back of our military resources by past Presidents reduced our options to only one. I had to use the AMD which was an initiative of my terms in office, a fast fix to patch the huge gap in our defences while we rebuilt the military as it should be, as distasteful as that sounds.

Had we the time we needed for testing and refinement, our AMD would have become the deterrent as designed and kept the madmen in check. We were not given that time and here is the catastrophic result. There is no point in blaming others, but if we should survive and rebuild ourselves, I would like to ensure that even the President cannot reduce our ability for self defence. The rot started in 2008 with the election of a President with doubtful roots, no matter what the denials. There was appeasement and accommodation of radical Islam with a corresponding wind down of our military resources. Britain's Chamberlain did this with Hitler in 1938 and plunged the world into war with a maniac in power in Nazi Germany.

Our President in 2008 started the same process with the Islamics, deliberately or other wise we will never know. I was elected to reverse the damage, but it was too little, too late.

My friends, I hope God is with us and we all survive to rebuild humanity. Please learn this lesson and build in rules in the new society to keep us free and morally decent.

I apologize to every one of you and to all our lost souls for my action. I now resign my Presidency and become one of us. There is no more Mr President, just Tom. Our leaders are Commander Carver and Colonel Fuller, who have brought us thus far.

Thank you."

Tom sat down and strapped in. The group just stared at him, stunned. Fuller acknowledged him and began clapping his hands. Everyone followed and the reaction became a standing ovation. After a minute or so, Fuller nodded to Felicity. She worked her way forward and held position before the group.

"Mr President, I could not call you Tom sir, we have discussed this possibility among ourselves and with our commanders. We came to a consensus that no one could have done a different or better job of handling the Iranian threat than you did. We are collectively not experienced enough to form governance for our small group and we request that you join with our commanders Carver and Fuller as a leader of our community. We hope you will lead, teach and nurture us so that we can become leaders of the future. We would like to continue to address you as Mr President."

Felicity went back to her seat and all eyes turned to the President. He looked to Fuller and Carver who nodded assent to Hannaford's proposal. The President gave a cheezy grin and shrugged his shoulders.

"OK I guess." He looked around at the smiling young faces. "Wish all my elections were that easy to win!"

The group laughed until Fuller signalled for silence.

"Delighted to have you on the team Mr President. Let's get back to the matter at hand. Dinkshif Drives, survival and thirty thousand years. You all have the outline of the plan so now I am opening the meeting to questions and comments. Please raise your hand and I will call each person in order. State your first name so we all get to know each other."

Fuller pointed at a cadet. "Yes?"

"David sir. Let's say all this works and we get to Alpha Centauri and there is nothing there for us. What is the contingency plan? When will we run out of resources that if we did not go, might allow us to survive here much longer and look for a survival path right here, in our own solar system?"

"Commander Carver and I considered that scenario and examined every aspect we could think of. Each time we thought we had a viable plan the issue of the anti-matter fragments in our vicinity posed an unknown risk. We have an artificially created concentration of this stuff in our neighborhood. We don't know how it will replicate but we do know it did not self destruct with an equal quantity of matter. We also know that the mass of anti-matter is steadily increasing as it draws like particles, I guess the term should be teleports, particles from all over the universe. We believe that our solar system is too hot with anti-matter for us to risk our best chance of survival. Given time it is probable that the whole system will revert to anti-matter.

Alpha Centauri is our closest galactic neighbor. If we fail to find a new home, there are other more distant star systems we will be able to reach in our lifetimes. We will keep searching. As to resources, just as we are going to pick up this "disinfected" earth fragment, we will certainly find more raw materials on our journey."

Fuller was silent and waited for David. "Thank you sir. I believe I understand." He settled back in his seat.

"Yes." Fuller pointed to Amy Young.

"Sir, you will recall the question I asked that long four days ago when I still had a family..." she broke down into tears for a moment and then visibly fought off the gnawing emotion. "... and a home and a planet. Sir, we are all that is left of humanity, along with a few other ships which we don't even know if they made it. Sir, I don't want to die without having experienced love and sex and having babies like God designed me to do. I know there needs to be rules, so I am saying we should come up with these rules now, that will allow us to live together and to satisfy our physical and emotional needs, right from the beginning."

"Amy, all of you, and I include myself, Commander Carver, Mr President and his associates. The most important matter at hand is to latch onto the fragment and get away from here as fast as we can. I can't say there are not risks involved, but with diligence and hard work we can be on our way and we will have around four years of space travel in which to define a workable social system. I have no doubt that love and sex will play a major role in that time. Please, each and every one of you maintain self control as you may never have done before. We cannot afford discord in our small space and you are all the most precious individuals in existence. For certain we will want to make babies and diversify our gene pool. You are the parents of a new humanity. We are Adam and Eve again. Come and help me people. We have a Garden of Eden to find."

The meeting broke up into designated teams and the two commanders went to each team, handing out concise instructions that were recorded by the buddies. Each group had a prioritized task, but the whole plan was accessible to every cadet.

Fuller approached the President. "Mr President..." the President cut him off mid-sentence with a slash of his hand.

"In private I am Tom, this is Chuck and June. OK? No argument."

"Soooo..." Fuller stretched out the word. "Tom, Chuck, June. We need to find youniforms for you and see how we can get three more buddies while the cadets are locating the equipment. We need to do this before the docking attempt to ensure your safety."

"Look" said Tom, "if there are no suits or buddies we will sit and take our chances. We've had our lives. You make sure these kids make it."

Fuller pulled a half smile. "I believe you don't understand my motive Tom. Your genes are as important to our diversity and long term survival of humanity as any of the cadets."

"Sorry to disappoint you John. I had a vasectomy nine years

ago. Shooting blanks now."

"We'll find a way to reverse it. You're getting suited up. That Mr President Tom, is an order." Fuller beckoned to two cadets who had been detailed for this job. They were clumsy in the weightless conditions, but were slowly getting the hang of free fall movement.

Because the transport had undergone orderly loading before the crisis, every item was documented and locatable. Fuller's buddy transmitted the information to the two cadets and they drifted off to find the uniforms and buddies, spares designated for the ill fated Space City.

"Please wait here for the cadets. I have to get back to Janine to work the approach."

CHAPTER 42

Aboard Carver's Transport.

Fuller and Carver had their heads together as they pored over the surface scan of the fragment. "Looks fairly uniform," Janine observed. "Shouldn't make much difference where we set down."

They continued to look for another minute when John pointed at the image and said, "What's that?"

They both craned forward, looking intently at a tiny black spot on the surface. Janine reached out and expanded the picture with a reverse pinching motion, a carry over from the ancient touch screen days. The black spot grew and began to resolve with edge detail around a deep black centre. Janine pulled a virtual ruler from the tool bar and aligned cursors on each side of the spot. "About three meters across. What do you think it is?"

"If was a cave or part of a cave complex I would expect to see more holes and craters. If it was part of a city or structure same thing. This appears to be isolated. It could be a volcanic tube or a missile silo. Even an isolated mine shaft." They stared at the spot for a few more moments. "As that is the only thing we have found on the surface, I vote that we land next to the anomaly for further investigation. Come to think of it, is there any way we can work out the mass of the fragment? Can we see if there are cavities in it?"

"First thought is that we can't do that. We don't have the computing power or ground penetration radar equipment to work an average density calculation. We will be able to explore this hole. Land first then we can decide."

Fuller leaned back and stretched with a yawn. "I think we should both get some sleep before we try the landing. I'll put Hannaford and Shaw on watch. He checked his communications and was pleased to see that the President and his friends had found youniforms and buddies and were wearing them. He put in orders to Hannaford and received acknowledgement. "G'd night Janine." She has already leaned her seat back and drawn the eyeshades in her youniform.

"Mmm John." came the quietly murmured reply.

The persistent buzzing of an alarm awoke the pair some hours later. John yawned and stretched again. "Coffee?"

"Absolutely! You expect a girl to land a space transport on a tiny speck of rock without first having her morning coffee?"

"That's one thing they could never get to work with these youniforms. They do everything else for us but they can't make a good cup of coffee. Back in a moment."

She flashed a smile at him and turned back to examine the console. The fragment almost filled the view port as they had drawn towards it during the hours of sleep and she could see detail of the surface as it slowly tumbled in a multi axis rotation, a wobbly, three dimensional movement that was clearly going to be difficult to stabilize. The force of the explosion had applied unevenly across the face of the fragment above the axis of rotation. Random explosive forces had imparted multiple secondary spins in different axes and the fragment was tumbling like an out of control beach ball, but here there was no friction to slow it down.

Janine was good, one of the best pilots around, but she could see that without a supercomputer she was not going to solve this docking equation, and right now she just did not have one handy. She was startled out of deep contemplation of the problem by John returning with an insulated bulb of fresh coffee.

"Thank you." She took a careful sip of the aromatic Columbian roast and then lifted it. "The things we take for granted that are going to be used up and disappear forever. I wonder what the last cup of coffee in the universe will taste like? Who will drink it?"

John shrugged. "Use it while we have it. Enjoy. It will be something to tell your kids about and a legend to your grand kids." He took a pull at his own brew and gestured towards the fragment landing equations that were sliding up the viewer at an unreadable rate. "We're not going to get there that way Janine."

"No we are not, unless a miracle happens and the fragment motion stabilizes."

"So what would your great great grand pappy have done in these circumstances?"

Janine gaped at Fuller in disbelief. "You're not suggesting we just do it by the seat of our pants? My great great grandpa flew Tiger Moths in the Great War of 1914. He made up his own rules for landing on the fly. My great gramps flew Marine Corps off flattops in the next war. He told me when I was a little girl that he landed comms blind on more than one occasion and lived to talk about it. I guess he was my inspiration to become an astronaut."

Fuller pointed at the calculations again, and then at the view port. "Were your grandpa's better pilots than you? Was your Dad a pilot too?"

Janine smirked, "You want to hope that the ability can skip two generations. He and gramps were dentists and Dad got airsick on a second floor balcony." She stared out at the fragment again. "Yeah! That's just a piece of dirt moving in a straight line. Its not an aircraft carrier in rough seas in the black dead of night, and this baby isn't a Tiger Moth biplane." She turned to Fuller, her face intense and eyes burning with excitement.

"John, I can do this. I can!"

CHAPTER 43

On the World Game Network.

The whole World Game network was quiet as the three judges introduced the first two quarter final acts. Peepers from Morgana repeated the rules for the galactic immortal audience.

"My dear amorphously blobbish friends, some of you are winners from the earlier editions of the World Game and you have a true and real appreciation of the emotions in play during your performance. These are the essence of what we are able to take from each game and these intense feelings sustain us and are our reason for existing."

"Parasites!" came an unidentified transmission from a back galaxy. There was a network uproar as the dissenter was shouted down.

"Quiet please! Let me do my job..." The noise gradually abated. "We have two magnificent acts running simultaneously and as much as they both deserve to get through, only one group will survive and one group will go into stasis as it dies."

"Our first act is led by Martin and Corcoran. They are presently locked out of their space transport by a madman inside and they have less than eighteen minutes until an anti-matter fragment strikes them."

"The second act is the stage for Carver and Fuller who are about to attempt a hands on landing on what could only be called a bucking bronco of a fragment. On top of that, the Fuller team is unaware of the presence of the Iranians inside the fragment and of course the reverse is true. My fellow judges and I wish you great betting success and trust you will get the kick you need from the performers' terror and emotion as they face a certain and possibly horribly messy death. Enjoy! Let's begin!"

CHAPTER 44

Aboard Transport X6

The glass of the view port glowed cherry red and began to swell out into a bowl shaped bubble. Martin played the cutter around the neck of the super tough flask. The maniac inside had backed away from the intense heat and he and his three ringleaders were the only ones in the air lock, but the inner door was open.

Martin backed off with the cutter as the fused quartz rapidly cooled. The mutineers moved in closer and pointed at Martin, slapping their thighs and laughing. Suddenly their mirth turned to outrage and terror as Corcoran approached with a huge wrench from the heretofore unneeded toolkit. He could see them screaming and mouthing "NO!" as he brought the wrench down hard on the weakened flask neck.

The internal pressure exploded the quartz into razor sharp missiles that went hurtling off into space to become cometary bodies in their own right. Hard on their heels came the still screaming mutineer leader who was silently shredded as he was sucked through the shattered quartz edges. Globules of blood and shreds of flesh expanded outwards to join the glass cometary objects. The body shot off into the distance until it dwindled to a speck and then vanished as if it had never existed.

The inner door had slammed shut as designed with the remaining mutineers trapped in the vacuum mouthing like fish and rapidly turning red and then almost black in the face as their oxygen starved bodies shut down.

Corcoran and Martin waited a few more moments until the bodies had stopped thrashing and quickly opened the lock. They dragged the corpses out and gave them a good shove in the direction of the oncoming fragments.

"Waste not want not!" said Martin as he cracked open the emergency repair box attached to the air lock wall. There was always the possibility of a meteorite strike on the quartz view panel that could cause any degree of damage. He rolled out a flat nano panel of clear gel and flattened it over the hole and fractured edges. The nano particles went to work as designed, to fuse with the quartz and create a perfect seal. The panel hardened instantly that the seal was formed and provided a slightly distorted view of the segments fast bearing down on them. Martin paused for a moment expecting to see a flash as the bodies of the mutineers impacted with the fragments, but nothing occurred. He was just a little puzzled and put that snippet of information to the back of his mind. The two pilots hurried, gliding as fast as they could through the internal lock and headed for the control cabin. The passengers shrank back from them as they passed, having seen how the pair had dealt with the mutineers. No one wanted a piece of that action.

"Sit down and strap in NOW!" screamed Martin as he went by. "If you want to live just DO IT!"

While the people struggled to get back into their seats and harnesses Corcoran and Martin prepped the transport for emergency takeoff. The fragments were almost upon them and they had to orient the ship away from the threat and blast at full acceleration to have any chance of outrunning the danger.

"We have about one minute until impact." Corcoran said coolly. "Engines ready."

"Hit it!" Martin pushed the ignition button and held the accelerator over-ride down to the last stop. They were thrust back in their seats by the huge force of the engines. There was nothing else to do except pray which Martin muttered to himself as he watched the aft view monitor. The closest fragment already filled the screen and the smooth, silver anti-matter surface became clearer and more detailed as it closed in on them. The acceleration was not enough. The closure rate was lessening, but there was not going to be an umpires decision on this race. There was going to be life or death.

BZZZZTT!!!

The disapproval buzzer sounded from one of the judges. It was Charonelle from the Osburne Galaxy.

"Why did you buzz them?" asked Peepers.

"Yeah! Why?" echoed Howley.

"Boring!" replied Charonelle. We saw the other group outrun fragments and beat them. There's nothing original here. I think they should be eliminated and put in stasis immediately. They were good at the beginning when the mutineer got sucked out and the others asphyxiated. That was exciting and somewhat original, but they've lost it now."

"I disagree." said Peepers. "I personally find this present knife edge counterpoint to be invigorating and exciting. It is physics and a moment of truth as to which way it will go. What do you say Howley?"

"I'm with you this time Peepers. You see, if they survive this event, then we all get a warm and fuzzy emotional tingle which we haven't had for some time in any of the acts. If they get taken by the anti-matter and they all die in some horrible way, we get to absorb the emotion of terror and hopelessness. We need that aspect of these acts to appreciate the whole gamut of emotional nourishment and entertainment we will gain from this series. I think we should put it to the viewers to vote on this one. Do we have time?"

Peepers consulted his assistant. "Yes plenty of time for a vote. At least ten seconds. All right viewers, to vote to allow the Corcoran and Martin team to perform to completion vote one and to take them straight to stasis vote two. You have four seconds to get your vote in from NOW!"

With the thought processes of the intergalactics working at instantaneous speeds, the four seconds of relative time were like hours for the judges. The votes poured in on the network, limited to one per viewer. The instant reflexive counter was ticking over in a blur faster than even a neural connection could discern the outcome. It was going to go to the cut-off time limit. Some voters were waiting until the last moment, watching the scene of the fragments approaching the craft and trying to calculate a win or lose for Corcoran and Martin. With less than two hundredths of a second to go a last surge of votes came in and then the counters stopped. There was an eerie network silence.

"Well?" came a comment. "Who won?"

"Split decision!" announced Peepers. "Judges have the deciding vote. Charonelle started this with a vote against. I am still for allowing them to finish. Howley?"

"I don't know now. I was thinking for earlier, but I don't really enjoy messy deaths and gore. On the other hand..."

"Howley! Vote now!" Shrilled Charonelle. "There's no time for your ramblings or washing your conscience. Get on with it!"

"I - I'm going to go with my first intuition. I vote for!"

A huge uproar invaded the network and Peepers tried to settle all the viewers down. "We have our decision. Let's watch the show and see what happens. These boys are really finalist material and deserve to finish their act. Here we go!"

CHAPTER 45

Aboard X6 Transport.

Martin had the manual override clamped down in a death hold. His knuckles were white with the strain of defying the enormous thrust of the engines. Every body on board was flattened back into the seat and every little imperfection in clothing or seat fabric became a stabbing pain. All faces pulled back in a rictus showing bared teeth and bowels and bladders voided, fouling the cabin. A few passengers with physically weak hearts or brain aneurisms just died without anyone noticing. Each person was too absorbed in countering the terrible force that made breathing almost impossible and sight completely unfocused. No one noticed the bodies vanish as life left them.

Martin exuded terror of the condemned as his youniform partially defeated the overwhelming forces. He could still see the fragment approaching and the landing proximity reading was now registering the distance and relative velocity.

"Corcoran," he struggled to say, "we're not gonna make it. By about half a second. Only chance is to do a forced jettison of some mass."

"Do it! Do it!"

Martin hit the emergency reaction mass dump and saw a stream of fluid globules stretch behind like a comet tail. They impacted the fragment surface with a fireworks display. But more importantly, the proximity counter was now winding the other way. They were leaving the fragment behind.

"How much mass did we dump? asked Corcoran.

Martin waved a finger and the reaction mass reading came up. "Ninety percent gone. We have enough to run at this rate for another four minutes then we are stranded."

"We're already outrunning the fragments. Cut the acceleration now. We're safe for the moment."

Martin cut the engines and the crushing force suddenly ceased. The moaning and cries from the cabin were pitiful. The two pilots looked back and saw the shambles and mess. The people looked like they had all been in a street brawl, with bloodied noses and burst eardrums. The stench was unbelievable as the gore and waste pooled at the end of cabin.

"I think I better say something to them," said Corcoran.

"Ladies and gents, you have all been through a terrible ordeal and we need to clean up the ship. We are safe now and running ahead of the fragments. We have a plan but we need you to get things shipshape on your own. Tend to the injured as best you can." Corcoran paused and looked hard into the cabin. He muted his communicator and said to Martin, "I'm sure there were no empty seats when we left. We lost the four trouble makers, but I count at least ten vacancies. Where are the people?" The two looked at each other and then at the pool of gore and feces at the end of the cabin.

"No way!" shuddered Corcoran. "We would see bones if they had been liquefied. There's something weird going on here. Come to think of it, I didn't see the impact of the bodies on the fragment earlier and put that down to that I just missed it. Nah! Something is going on here. Don't ask me what. God only knows."

"So what is this plan we have that I know nothing about?" Martin asked.

"Oh? That. I just said it to shut them up. Without that reaction mass we can't do much of anything. The little we have left won't let us get behind the moon but we may just squeak it in for Space City. It will be a very close call again. As long as we maintain our present escape vector we can add angled thrust to put us crossing behind the city just ahead of the fragment strike. The other transports were headed there when all this started because they didn't have enough reaction mass to get to the moon, same as us. Maybe if we can get there and ride out the fragment storm we could hook up with one of them and try for the moon at a slower rate."

"What about the laser Morse Code idea. We could still do that. Try and let the others know that we will be flashing past like a jack rabbit and hope they can snare us."

"You should do that anyway Martin, and hope, because once we burn for the Space City attempt we have nothing left. We can't even slow down. I have to work these vectors and thrust so that the fragment swarm passes us by while we are crossing behind Space City. We come out the other side unless someone gets the message and they have some way of plucking us out of trajectory."

"Regardless, we need to jettison every non-essential item on board to increase the effectiveness of our reaction mass. Hmm?"

"What Corcoran?"

"All that vile bilge down there could be reaction mass. It is ninety five percent water. We can't afford to waste anything now. What else is there that we can use Martin?"

"Technically? Anything liquid or gel. If this doesn't work we're all dead anyway and won't need it, so we may as well take the advantage. But it's gonna be fun getting this mob to go along with the idea. They are not going to get it that there is no choice. I think we will have to bang some more heads together unfortunately."

Corcoran shook his head. "This is like the Israelites coming out of Egypt all over again. Army to the back, sea to the front and nowhere to run. God we could do with a miracle right now!"

The Galactic network screamed and clamored. "Deity Clause! Deity Clause! They get a pass! Free pass and automatic to the semi finals!" The hubbub was almost unintelligible as the viewers all hit their comment button. Peepers was signalling down the Game Compere, Nickle Gannon, to restore order. Gannon hit the mute control and blocked all the comments. The silence on the network was absolute. This had never happened before.

"Thank you Nickle." Peepers responded and then consulted with Charonelle and Howley until the muted uproar had subsided. "Viewers, it is clear to me that this act has captured your imaginations and your very existence. There IS a Deity Clause rule in the World Game, but it generally only applies until the finals commence and we are well into the finals at this time.

However. There is always room for flexibility. I have had a fast meeting with the other judges and we have unanimously agreed that these two, Corcoran and Martin, deserve the Deity Clause and yes, they will be automatically brought in to the semi finals. Provided they survive of course."

There was a more controlled cheering from the network that Peepers was able to stop. "Let me finish please. Let me do my job. The issue remains, that Martin and Corcoran do not need the others on board and they certainly do not deserve to go on to the semi finals, so we have decided to lift them out into stasis, but there will be NO mind wipe of Corcoran or Martin. They invoked the Deity Clause so we will allow them to think along those lines. We believe that you, the viewers, will gain much more from these two acting alone, and with the Deity Clause in play, you will all be able to absorb and enjoy some very new and original emotions and faith emanations from these two, the like of which has not been seen since the incident mentioned by Martin, about the Israelites. Be truly entertained by this act as it goes forward. We will now go back to the Fuller and Carver troupe."

The applause down the network was wild, a galactic ovation for a wonderful decision by the judges. Aboard the X6 Alex Corcoran and Jeff Martin were moving into the now passenger devoid cabin area to start gathering jettison items. Every single passenger had vanished.

CHAPTER 46

Aboard Carver's Transport.

"Are you ready John?"

"As I'll ever be. Let's do it!"

They had spent several hours plotting the exact motion of the fragment and detected a repetitive pattern running on a three hundred and five second frequency. By plotting the spatial position of the tunnel mouth, they now had a real time wire model of the relative motion of their landing zone. It was not the best position on the fragment, but because it was the only easily visible reference point and Janine was flying by the seat of her pants, it was the best compromise.

Their plan was two fold. The major axis of spin was in the same plane as the forward motion of the fragment, as expected from the frontal explosion. The Transport was not designed for hard planetary surface landings, but it did have the rail undercarriage which was like a series of claws that gripped the Skyhook rail. Janine was hoping to plant these claws into the fragment surface to act as a braking anchor while she applied "upward" thrust to drive the claws into the rock face. This would result in an effect like an ancient ground car skidding on an icy road out of control until the snow chains took bite. Except here the forces were a mite larger.

They would follow the rotation of the fragment by going in to a tight, fragment synchronous orbit in the same main rotational plane. Once they held that orbit, which would really be chewing up reaction mass at a gluttonous rate, they would see the tunnel mouth oscillating from side to side below them with the same period but varying amplitude of oscillation and drawing a flower petal shaped path.

They knew the exact count and pattern of the movement and would attempt the docking at the smallest oscillation, when the motion vector was comprised of north west components, rather than the one huge west directed wobble. Conservation of energy and good old Pythagorus to the rescue.

Janine sat tight with concentration and tension as she manipulated the thrusters to rotate the craft. The fragment was now "above" the transport so that the centripetal forces of the orbit would keep the "down" vector as pressure into the seat. The inner ear was going to play a big part along with the seat of the pants. Keeping it "normal" would enhance Janine's judgement calls.

She activated the main reaction mass engines at five percent thrust and used the docking jets to apply constant orbital acceleration. Even though the relative speed over the fragment surface was matched, the circular orbit required a polar acceleration thrust.

"Got it!" she muttered to herself. "No, just a little more torque. Not going to drift away. Ummm. On target."

Fuller sat silent, ready to do whatever Janine asked of him but not breaking her concentration.

She had her couch tilted back as far as it would go and was looking "up" at the fragment surface. Her head moved from side to side in time with the motion of the tunnel entrance dot that waltzed across the view port. Her next maneuver was the easy part, bringing the transport down to just above the surface in a region that did not have undulations greater than around one meter in height. This landing was going to be like skiing over moguls sideways with a blindfold on.

As the surface came closer and the angle of view lessened, the black gaping maw of the tunnel raced in and out of the view port, sometimes from side to side and often diagonally. Janine thought back to her experience as child, swinging in an old car tire tied to a tree branch, spinning and swinging at the same time while she reached out and tried to grab the candy from gramps hand as he stood teasing her.

This wasn't so hard. The tunnel mouth was the candy. She just had to grab it. That was the easy part. Before she could grab it she had to flip the transport over one eighty degrees so it could land claws down.

She had to perform this trick in a matter of five seconds, starting the turn before the edge of the level area located below the ship

---

and completing the controlled crash landing before the heavily roughened region encroached. There was no going around again. No second chance.

The finale to the performance was to apply sufficient thrust upwards to pin the transport in place until it could be physically fixed to and adopt the fragment's sickening motion. It was going to be a time of motion sickness like never before until they stabilized the fragment's spin to one plane.

Like an Olympic ski jumper at the edge of the ramp, Janine synchronized her breathing and her body motion with the movement of the tunnel as it swung in and out of view. She counted down to the sequence that was do or die.

"Three.... Two.... One..... NOW!" She shouted and worked the controls with an uncanny precision that could only be described as a symphony in frenzy.

The transport lurched into an accelerated ninety degree axial spin and just as rapidly decelerated. That was Janine's left hand control. Her right hand lowered the transport to a meter and a half above the surface and rotated it "upside down" so that centripetal forces would be like artificial gravity inside the ship. She was counting the seconds.

"Three... Four... NOW!" She slammed the transport straight down into the fragment and held the thruster jets on full blast while the sound of grinding rock and screeching of metal on metal vibrated and shook the transport until her teeth felt like they were falling out.

"You did it Janine! You did it!" John moved fast. "Hold it now while we get this thing tethered."

He drifted to the air lock where Shaw, Hannaford and the President waited, all carrying coils of nanocarbon rope, the same stuff as the Skyhook, along with titanium shell repair staples that had been destined for Space City, and mallets.

The first task was to tack the transport down, even temporarily, to conserve reaction mass. The idea was a simple tether at each end, anchored in the bed rock by the staples and slung over the top of the transport. The four exited the air lock and split into two teams.

They had to use belt thrusters to stay in place until they could get at least one staple down and secure. Holding the staple while their legs swam around in crazy patterns, they secured a rope end with several staples. The rope looked insubstantial and flimsy, but it was the anchoring that was the weakest point.

With one end of the rope secure, Fuller and Shaw propelled themselves to the opposite side of the transport, each pounding in a staple as a hand hold, and signalled Hannaford and the President that they were ready. Metal nuts had been attached to the other end of the rope to give it momentum. Now the pitching team of the President and Felicity stepped up to the plate in no gravity looking for a perfect tangential pitch over the transport. The pitch had to have just enough angle to it that when the nut extended the rope to its full length, it would begin to wrap around the transport and swing down towards Fuller or Shaw before the rebound brought the nut crashing back towards its point of origin. A delicate pitch indeed.

"OK Felicity," came Fuller's voice across the buddy empathic system, "you go first. Tell me when you release and not to hard a throw."

"I have my feet locked under a staple and I am sitting down, holding with my left. Ready to throw on three count. One... Two... Three.... uhhh!" She sat back watching the rope slither away as it followed the metal nut into space. "Hitting end.... NOW!"

The rope went taut for a split second and then slackened as the nut rebounded, but the small vector added by the encounter at the top belly of the transport was swinging the nut and the rope downwards as if there was slight gravity. Fuller could see the rope snaking around but couldn't locate the flying nut.

THWACK!!! It hit him in the head a glancing blow that tumbled him over and fortunately tangled around his outflung arm. He drifted, stunned, into the side of the transport.

Shaw was the only witness to John's distress. "John? Col. Fuller? Are you injured?"

John was for the moment, spread eagled against the side of the transport by coriolis forces. He gingerly touched his head where the nut had impacted. "Phew," they all heard, "bruised but not broken. Youniform does it again."

The buddy was already at work repairing the bruised area on John's cranium. He recovered his equilibrium and quickly reoriented himself to the task of tieing down the transport. "Shaw, Tom, go ahead and do your end and don't make my mistake."

He went to the staple he had set and slid the rope under it and looped it around the staple twice more. Shaw had captured his rope without mishap and followed suit.

"Janine, you copy?"

"Loud and clear John."

"OK give it a blast!"

Janine upped the thrusters to max for a moment, driving the transport down hard on its upper fuselage and allowing the ropes to slip through the staples as Fuller and shaw took up the slack. By now Felicity and the President had joined them and were pounding in more staples to lock the ropes in place. John twanged the iron hard rope and called Janine. "Cut the thrust now!"

"Roger."

The transport seemed to start getting up like a huge whale growing legs, as the former undercarriage claws reversed themselves and pressed down on the fragment surface. Then all movement stopped as the furniture cord thin ropes took up the strain. They were locked and down.

Four hours later the transport was securely tethered, looking like Gulliver tied down by the Lilliputians with gossamer strings. Many of the cadets had succumbed to motion sickness that even the buddies could not counter. It was imperative that the fragmentary motion be stabilized, or at least limited to two dimensional rotation.

A six person council of Fuller, Carver, Shaw, Hannaford, the President and Hayes sat harnessed in the first two rows of passenger seats, the front seats turned around and a tray table extended as a work desk.

Janine started. "I am calling this meeting as the Commander of this vessel under Clause 95a of the Articles of War of the United States of America. The proceedings of this meeting will be recorded for the sake of future generations and for continuity in the present circumstances if any one or number of us should become incapacitated or deceased. These ongoing records and instructions will enable our successors to take up the task of survival with full knowledge of prior acts. I link this first record of actions to the remaining knowledge base of human history and its contained philosophies, technologies and arts as a foundation for future generations. Our meeting today is as momentous, if not more so, than the creation of the Constitution of the United States of America by our founding fathers. We are more than the United States. We are the People of Planet Earth. This fragment is our Earth." She paused for a breath and to gather her thoughts. The others remained silent.

"Our first task, as mundane as it may seem and as complicated as it appears in the undertaking, is to stabilize the motion of Fragment Earth and place the Dinkshif engines. These engines are our hope for survival of our species somewhere else in this galaxy or maybe in another. It will be our imperative task to guard and maintain these engines for all time until a destination and new home for humanity can be found. Under the Articles of War previously stated, it is my sole duty to ensure the preservation of this vessel and the safety of all aboard her, to take the conflict to the enemy and to defend our territory at all cost. The plan I have outlined is an amalgamation of the salient points I have collected from discussion with you my fellow councillors and with the young people on board.

I further place on this record that my directives are not absolute and are subject to amendment my a majority vote of this council. I further propose that when Ms Beauvais is well and able, she join this council of seven to ensure a decisive vote at all times. As Commander, I will always cast the deciding vote in a hung decision. The meeting is now open to discussion which should be primarily directed at the question of motion stabilization.

Yes Mr Shaw."

"Commander, councillors," the concept of calling each other councillors took root then and there and stuck, "I have been studying the path and movement cycle of this fragment and with our extensive topographical mapping we now have a volume measure. While we were outside tethering I collected several samples of the rock that forms this fragment. From the average density of these samples I was able to extrapolate the expected mass of the fragment. I then took an estimate of the explosive energy of our fuel bomb based on the calorific output of the thermal reaction. This very rough calculation gave me an estimate of how much the fragment should have slowed down relative to our velocity.

If I may present an analogous example to explain where I am heading with this. Imagine you have two glass spheres identical in all external physical aspects, and you have two powerful, identical water pistols. The two spheres are rolled towards you and it is your job to slow or stop them by squirting water against them. You squirt equally at both spheres. One just keeps rolling and barely slows, the other slows down perceptibly at each water impact. What does that tell us about the spheres?" He didn't wait for an answer. There was no grandstanding here.

"It tells us that one sphere is probably solid glass and has great momentum, and the other that slows down, is probably hollow inside." This time he stopped to make sure everyone understood where he was leading.

"Councillors, by my even most inaccurate calculations, we should not be sitting here right now talking. We should have been molecules of anti-matter or vapor drifting in space. Our little bomb should have had little or no effect on this fragment. So that tells me that this fragment has much less mass that a solid of its shape should rightly have. This fragment is very hollow, and whatever process made it hollow, well, that is what saved us."

"Thank you for you insight Mr Shaw. That is a brilliant piece of detective work. Discussion please?" Janine opened the meeting to show of hand comment, signalling Fuller to continue.

"Mr Shaw, does this mean intuitively that the less mass we have to deal with the easier the stabilization will be?"

"I am not expert in these things sir. I just did the math, but logic says it will take much less energy to counter the unwanted spin. The downside is that there is a lot less reaction mass than we counted on for the run to Alpha Centauri. We may need to consider capturing more material from a safe source before we make the attempt."

Janine gestured to the President. "Councillors, I am humbled in your presence. I would have lost the Presidential race to any one of you." Said with a grin, the others laughed, the light hearted moment bringing a touch of relief to the constant stress they were all under. "I do have a question that we need to answer. If Mr Shaw is correct and we have an apparently man made tunnel penetrating the fragment, then it is probable that this is a man made cavity or tunnel system. So who made it? Is it ours or a foreign power? And a much bigger issue, is there anyone still alive in there?"

"Mr President," Janine hung onto her words for a moment. "Better yet, Councillor Tom. Yes, Councillor Tom. You have raised a very important question that with some time and hopefully a lot of good data, we will be able to calculate where the fragment originated by back tracking the recorded trajectories to the known celestial positions of all the planets of the solar system. We know where on Earth everything was at the point of disintegration. We should be able to do it."

Tom added "I think this needs to be a priority. We need to know if we are sitting on a friend or an enemy."

"I will take care of that immediately after this meeting Councillor Tom." replied Janine. "Time to figure out how we are going to stop this tumbling first."

Fuller signalled that he wanted to speak. "Yes Col. Fuller." Janine waved him on.

"I had a look at our cargo manifest and we appear to be most fortunate in the supplies that were brought aboard for the Dinkshif engine trials. We are carrying a quantity of demolition charges for deep space use as there was intention to attach the drives to an asteroid and run them up to maximum thrust. The charges were meant for leveling the asteroid on a balanced explosive force basis. I believe we could use these charges for stabilizing the fragment. We know the kinetic energy of each charge and now that Councillor Shaw," he paused and smiled at Shaw. who grinned right back, "... has worked out the mass of the fragment, we can isolate principal spin vectors of the fragment and nullify them with controlled counter blasts."

"Felicity?" Janine pointed.

"Councillor Fuller, how many of these charges do we have? We are looking at a very large mass of rock, even if it is partially hollow. It seems to me that the charges would be futile against this monster."

"Technically you are correct Councillor Hannaford, however we intend to calculate the exact force required to nullify at least two of the tumbling effect vectors. This will leave us with a major spin around one axis with probably some wobble left, but not enough to matter and something we can deal with in the long term.

The two major explosions will be augmented by placing reaction mass in the plane of the explosion. This mass will be rock debris that we will mine from the fragment in a place that is most beneficial towards our stabilizing efforts. We will collect this mass in cargo nets and place it over the charges. The effect will be like the difference between shooting an ancient projectile weapon with a bullet or with a blank cartridge. Our recoil is the force we are looking for to push back the spin. Councillor Shaw will do the calculations and Councillor Carver will verify them before we proceed." Fuller stopped talking and looked expectantly at the faces around him. "Any more questions? None? Let's get to it."

CHAPTER 47

Inside the fragment.

Zardooz awoke strapped into a control room chair. He felt stiff and disoriented by the erratic movement of the fragment. His balance was completely thrown and he felt as if he were drunk, a feeling that he knew well from the numerous times he had defied the prophet Mohammed's teachings. He slowly extracted himself from the webbing and worked his way over to the tiny galley area that serviced control room personnel. He pulled open the mini fridge and found a Turkish coffee self heat cup. Thirty seconds later he was inhaling the delicious aroma of the coffee and allowing the thick, sweet brew to spread its warmth through his whole body. The caffeine hit was rapid and began to counter the constant dizziness from the tumble dryer effect of the motion.

His head clearing, he started to think how he was going to get a view outside to see where he was and how much of Iran had come with him. His secondary issue was to stop the sickening motion somehow. He could not last long under such conditions. At the back of his mind was the violent action that had started the tumble and injured Arjmand. What had caused it?

He slowly savored the coffee and looked around the control room. His mind empty by choice, he looked for inspiration in the dials, screens and devices. Nothing struck him as exceptional or possibly harboring some obscure duality of use. He looked again and then a third time. Nothing.

Rolling up to a computer console, he commanded the computer to open an inventory list.

"Supply room log." he said.

A list appeared in front of him, text description and a small dimage next to the list. He scanned the column quickly, paying more attention to the dimages than the words. A dimage of a crate gained his attention and he rotated the dimage to see all four sides, then flipped it to reveal any hidden markings on the base. There were just three letters in English script stencilled on one side. He activated a check box next to the dimage.

"Show location." he commanded the computer. A grid appeared locating the object in three dimensions. The dimage showed ghost shapes of other containers indicating that this box was two rows in and three high in the storage. He wondered if the impact shock had moved the stacked supplies.

"Retrieve selected dimage object."

The computer confirmed its task. "Retrieving dimage object selected."

While the computer did its work, he looked through the list once again, occasionally flipping or rotating the 3D images that had become to be know as dimages when holographic displays became the norm. The most recent development in dimage technology was a shape matching electric charge projection that gave the hologram image an illusion of tactile solidity and allowed the rotation to work. Zardooz smiled to himself as he recalled the prank he had played on his lab assistant before fragmentation.

He had upped the charge voltage on their lab computer so that every time she manipulated a dimage her hair would spread out and stand on end while she received the tingle of an electric shock. Seeing her not withdrawing from the electric discharge and the silent scream on her face, he thought he had gone too far and did an emergency shut down of the system.

His assistant, and also his not infrequent sexual interlude, screamed at him to turn it back on. He had just shut down the best orgasm she had ever had without a man around.

Zardooz reminisced with regret that he would never get the opportunity to exploit this phenomenon. He had already planned the erotic dimages that would be sold along with the high voltage systems, with half the population of the world potential consumers and the other half gift purchasers for the first half. How sad.

He looked back at the computer. The retrieval was still in progress.

"Computer, show me surveillance schematic and live feeds."

A wire diagram came up showing the complex. There were the expected nodes showing for the inner section of the complex and the two active corridor segments. There was one odd node that appeared to be totally disconnected from the rest of the complex. It was blinking on and off, more off than on. This was very interesting. He touched the screen where the node was blinking and commanded the computer, "Isolate and expand."

The screen zoomed and filled with the blinking dot. "Details."

Two columns appeared, one with the node designation and position, the other showing technical details of the feed from that node. The designation was correct, but the position was a series of null dashes, because it depended upon non existent GPS satellites. This was an external node all right and the blinking was caused by ongoing attempts to locate the GPS signals.

Zardooz scrutinized the data before him. How could he circumvent the GPS feed? Was there some way of substituting? More importantly, could he make the node active and get a reading of the surface?

His thoughts were interrupted by the computer beeping that the retrieval was done. The box he wanted had been delivered to the receiving room which was two doors down the corridor. He slowly got out of his harness, refocused on the schematic. "Save page. Personal Zardooz."

Making his way to the receiving room with extreme care, he was confronted by a wooden case, about a meter long and half a meter on the sides. The stencil on the side that had been unclear on the dimage was fuel cell powered device warning. There was a lot of raw hydrogen compressed inside the package. He commenced unclamping the steel band lock ties until he could fold back the lid. Inside lay a gleaming, polished Robotic Automated Boring Instrument. Known as a RABI, all he had to do was activate the fuel cell and the device would become active and fully self operational, even from getting out of the box on its own. After that, it was commanded through the computer system.

Zardooz reached into the box and lifted back the activation switch cover. He keyed in his personal ID code on the pad and immediately the RABI came alive. It said, "System check." A few whistles and beeps sounded. "All systems working."

"Stand by for instructions RABI." Zardooz commanded the

Borer. He left it and headed back for the control room, already planning the first task for the RABI. The device had rudimentary facilities for performing low level repairs once it reached its target. He planned to send it to the operational surface node and attempt to disable the GPS search. Once disabled, the node would go into local mode and become operational within its immediate area. Whether this worked or not, he would have the RABI deposit a hand carried communicator on the surface with a direct line down the bore hole. Not perfect, but some type of solution with two, better than zero, possibilities of success.

Back in the control room Zardooz examined the schematic of the nodes imposed over the layout of the complex. He was looking for a point that the RABI could start its journey through the rock. He needed a place that could be sealed off to prevent atmospheric loss when the RABI penetrated into space. He wasn't overly concerned about proximity of the node to the starting point for the bore. The RABI had capacity for long distance tunneling which was not going to be tested.

He ran his finger over the schematic to focus on every detail, but after a few minutes he had exhausted all options and he sat back in his seat with a frown on his face. After a few more minutes of staring and thinking he began to nod and talk to himself. He tapped the screen on the access corridor where Arjmand had come to grief, the seed of a plan germinating in his mind. He had to try to jury rig some circuits in the dead part of the corridor for his plan to work, so he called up the electrical circuit schematics for that section.

A scream from the living quarters reminded him that Arjmand needed attention. He got up from the station and drifted in a wall bouncing path towards the cries of agony.

CHAPTER 48

Aboard Martin's X6 Transport.

"We can store all this stuff as reaction mass but we can't get it into the system without an EVA," said Corcoran, "and first we need to do the math to see if jettisoning it now will give us the edge with the remaining reaction mass. Every item we jettison will change our directional vector slightly. We have redundancy totalling about ten percent of the transport mass. That is a significant effect on our vector if we do it right."

"The transport has to be revolved so that the air lock is opposed to and in the same plane as Space City. For greatest benefit we have to push the stuff of at the center of mass and perpendicular to our present vector. If we miss the center of mass we will impart a spin to the transport and have to use reaction mass to correct, so we lose the benefit."

Martin brought up a calculation table and ordered a dimage of the transport showing center of gravity and the neutral points on the skin that would not cause rotation. The points formed a ring about two thirds of the way to the rear of the transport where the reaction mass and engines were located. "We have to take the stuff out of the air lock, down the side of the ship and pitch from that point on the ring." He pointed at a spot in line with the air lock. "We don't have to rotate for air lock alignment. We can trek at an angle to the pitchers mound."

Corcoran laughed at the thought. "It's going to be much easier if the lock is in line with less distance to drag everything. Don't forget that as we jettison stuff the center of mass position will change so the pitchers mound has to move. That's not a bad idea to set up something as a place holder."

"We will have to stuff the lock full to reduce the number of cycles. We will lose too much air other wise." said Martin.

"The air in the lock is conserved to ninety percent. We don't lose a lot each time and we don't really have an option. Let's do it."

The pair started by removing empty seats, which easily unclipped from their bases. They decided to discharge the gory

---

mess that was breaking into globules and floating about. The on board vacuum system took care of that, with the collection bag looking like a huge Scottish haggis by the time the job was done. Each load was tied into a bundle using fabric stripped from the jettison seats. They then started at one end of the transport and worked their way up checking the cartons and bales that had been haphazardly thrown aboard at the tumultuous take off. They separated out drinking water and food supplies, enough for about three days, which is what they had calculated as their maximum survival period, after which there was no point. A very fine balance indeed.

The pile of material was strewn down the aisle to the air lock. Martin entered the lock and Corcoran passed the first bundle in and closed the lock. He went to the control cabin and initiated the rotation of the ship to the optimum position, then headed back to the lock.

"You're good to go." Corcoran said to Martin over the lock intercom. He watched through the view port as Martin cycled the air out of the lock and opened the outer door. He struggled with the ungainly load which had snagged on the door sill and gave Corcoran a heart palpitation when the mass suddenly free and headed for the stars with Martin attached. He watched in helpless terror as he saw his friend being carried off, the primeval emotion drowning the cool logic and training of a professional astronaut.

Then he saw Martin's arm appear around the edge of the bundle and the rest of his body appeared as he swung himself around to the back of the pile of seats like a child on a monkey bar. Martin saw Corcoran and gave him a big grin and a quick thumbs up as he launched himself towards the air lock and grabbed the recessed handle. He had the bundle on a leash of seat fabric and waited until it had drifted to its full extent, then using the gradual extension of his arm and body, gently brought it to rest without shock. He then drew it back very slowly until he was able to grasp it and slow it down to a stop.

"OK!" He exclaimed. "Take two."

A relieved Corcoran peered through the port. "You scared the living crap out of me man! I thought I was going to have to go fishing for you!"

Martin turned his head and gave another cheezy grin that Corcoran could just discern behind the youniform visor. He turned back to the task at hand and gave the mass a small push in the correct direction, following it holding the tether with a little slack. There was no room for error now as there were no grab handles to prevent being dragged off into space. Only the engine nacelles remained between him and eternity.

The stately procession of junk on a leash leading the astronaut like a huge dog being taken for a walk made its way to the first "pitcher's mound" point. This was the tricky part, as Martin had no way of stopping the mass drift. He had rehearsed his moves in his mind over and over, but now it was do or die.

He released the leash and jetted himself around and in front of the oncoming bundle. He didn't have a bat and there were no balls or strikes coming up. He had to hit a home run every time. He had time to plant an adhesive base to the pitching point. The technology was ancient and had been called "Velcro" in its heyday. Every transport carried these patches to allow skin surface repair of the non-ferrous outer wall due to meteorite or other holing damage. Now the hook and loop material proved itself again.

Martin planted his feet to which he had attached the hook part of the system onto the loop base. He was secured to the ship sufficiently to be able to tilt himself about forty five degrees forward, as far as his human ankle joints would allow, ready to receive and bring the mass to a halt once again. In a way, his previous mishap has given him confidence as he now had a feel for the forces involved and the energy he needed to apply to stop the mass.

It came at him and he grasped available projections, using his legs and arms as shock absorbers through to the hook and loop anchor. He felt the immense strain on his legs and felt the ripping of some of the loops as the hooks were dragged free in a shearing action. His left foot was lifting and almost loose. He was in trouble!

The mass stopped in equilibrium and he heaved a sigh of relief as he carefully planted his left foot back on the loop base.

"Is everything OK?" Came a tentative inquiry from Corcoran.

"Just peachy old son. Just peachy. Watch for the pitch now."

Martin crouched down and tickled the mass overhead until he felt it was reasonably centered above him. He carefully placed his palms on solid points of the bundle and then pushed up with his whole body to impart a velocity to the mass perpendicular to the axis of the ship. It took off like a dog after a bone, the leash trailing out to the side in weightlessness. Martin also flew upwards, only arrested by the hook and loop tether looking like a dancer in an ecstatic fling. He followed the course of the mass, thinking of the dog and stick. Good thing there were no fire hydrants in space. He giggled to himself at the absurd thought.

He took a moment to rest, then squatted down. He had to do a back squat, one hand on the skin, while the other helped his leg pull away from the attachment. Once one leg was freed, he had to almost peel the other foot away to avoid bouncing away into space. He could use this pitcher's point five more times before he had to move it back towards the nacelles. The good part was that he would gradually have security points in case of further emergency. He called for timing from his buddy. Less than five minutes had elapsed since his near disaster. He probably had around fifteen loads to jettison. Fourteen more times doing this, he thought to himself.

"Eleven down, four to go Martin." Corcoran was elated as each cycle went without a hitch. He was monitoring the effect of the jettisoning on the relative velocity of the transport. The cumulative effect was now significant with a directional component towards space city. The final four loads would bring the shift to about half the required move. The final adjustment would have to be delivered by precious reaction mass thrust.

Martin had got each cycle down to around three minutes, gaining confidence and experience as he went along. As the pitcher's mound was moved farther back the extra time was offset by his ability to shove the masses at greater speeds as his confidence increased. Finally, a quarter hour later he cycled back into the lock for the last time.

As he came through the inner lock he imagined all the missing passengers clapping and cheering. "Not going there." he thought to himself. Corcoran grabbed his hand and actually gave him a hug, a very unprofessional and human showing of care. Martin just relaxed with a sigh in Corcoran's embrace and whispered, "Got to stop meeting like this man."

Corcoran pushed back and held Martin's shoulders at arms length. They both burst out laughing while the invisible crowd aboard escalated their silent cheering.

"Come on, its not over yet. We've gotta check the new vectors and plan the best burn. Then we can pray." said Martin as he disengaged and made his way forward. "That was five tons we just dumped."

"And all our passengers." added Corcoran.

CHAPTER 49

On the Fragment Surface.

"It's so difficult to stay in place on this thing!" exclaimed Felicity. "I used to do rock climbing, but this is extreme rock climbing, being flung off in any direction with an endless drop ahead. Creepy!"

"Just make sure you're double tethered Fel," came from Shaw.

She paused a moment and looked over her shoulder at him. "Fel?" she said with feigned astonishment. "Oh! OK... Ger!"

They both burst out laughing at this tiny interlude that had taken their relationship to a new level.

Fuller had placed twelve of the 24 explosive charges in a compact pattern about four hundred meters from the ship, at a point calculated by Shaw and confirmed by Carver as the optimum point to remove a major rotational vector that the fuel bomb had imparted.

Hand lines had been set up by Carver and Fuller who had some free-fall experience. It had taken several painstaking hours of virtual rock climbing across the tumbling surface to hammer in pitons and attach the ropes that had come with the explosive charge kits. Someone was looking favorably on this situation. A wrong move could mean being swatted off the surface like a blowfly on a hot day. There were no second chances here.

Once the lines were established, the charges had to be transported two at a time in a back pack to ensure a soft landing at the site, then Fuller had used a portable fuel cell multi tool to drill set holes and fixed the charges into place with self channelling rock spikes. These spikes allowed some directional adjustment so all the explosive force was focused to a narrow virtual cone that would be covered with slabs of fragment rock. The gap behind each charge base plate was reinforced with small pieces of rock that would be pulverized by the recoil, but it was the initial microseconds of intense force that would slow the tumbling vector.

Shaw and Hannaford were the second shift, mining slabs of

rock using a mining laser that had also fortuitously been loaded aboard for asteroid mining. They used a variation of an age old technique to shear out the blocks. Firstly they carved into the fragment surface in a two by eight grid of sixteen rectangles each a half meter by a quarter meter and to a depth of a quarter meter. These would be impossible for two people to move or lift under former Earth gravity, but here the blocks were weightless. The problem was their mass momentum and the tumbling forces. If a block got loose it would be a deadly, crushing missile, even at low speed the momentum would mash a human body into a bloody smear.

Ever the problem solver, Shaw had designed a rope rig that tethered each block by two holes lasered through opposing short edges. The holes were smooth and the angle through the edge acted as a braking force simply by tensioning the guide rope. It was going to be a long, slow process, but there was no immediate time shortage.

To shear each block, the guide rope was first threaded through and clamped to prevent the block escaping. The first block was the big test. Shaw and Fuller had made up sponge foam sealed packs that had a second ingredient of water. The edges of the packs were titanium alloy strips cannibalized from the seats and welded closed with the mining laser. Like the expanding wedges of freezing wet wood used by the Egyptian pyramid builders of four thousand years earlier, these packs would expand outwards as they froze. Jammed between the fragment itself and the cut out block, something had to give. Shaw and Hannaford hope it would not be the titanium rim.

"The pack has to go down to the bottom of the channel so we shear as close to the base as possible and we have about five seconds to place it from the insulated pack into the channel before it freezes. OK Fel?"

"Gotcha Ge...er!" Felicity exaggerated back.

"You two get serious!" came the chastising disembodied voice of Fuller over the buddy comms.

"OK Fel, on three exactly. We extract and place then pull back fast. Have you got your tether taut?"

"Tether is good. Start counting." Felicity had tucked one foot under the rope grid for purchase and watched Shaw intently waiting for the count and his motion cues. Her hand was in the insulated bag ready to yank out the pack.

"One.. Two.. Three!" They both sprang into action, ripping a pack out of its warm slot, swinging it over in slow motion and aiming at the crack in the rock like bread into a toaster. The slot was exactly two centimeters wide and their youniform protected fingers hit that measure at their bases. They pushed the packs in and jammed their fingers after to shove the packs down as far as they could reach.

"Out! Now!" Yelled Shaw urgently. "Back up!" They scrambled to push away from the block, the reaction of the forces involved now beyond theory.

Shaw turned back only to see Felicity still in place, her foot caught between a rock ridge and the rope grid. Her effort to push off had hopelessly caught and tangled her ankle.

"Get down! Get Down Fel!" screamed Shaw as a vibration shock of the block shearing rattled the fragment. The block bounced around against the rope restraint but held in place. It was a razor sharp shard chipped off by the shearing impact that did the damage. Even carbon mono filament nano technology has its limits. The keen edged mini missile of rock travelling at bullet speed sliced through Felicity's tensioned main tether sending her flying away from the surface in whiplash effect. The second tether was in place but that was not going to help her. She was about to be whipped around like a tennis ball on a string but she was not designed to bounce on impact. Even with the youniform and buddy, she would not survive.

"Gerald! Help me!" She drifted away, her arm outstretched towards Shaw who was frantically looking around him for anything that could be used to save her. He stopped for a second, clearing his thought and letting his incredible mathematical mind take over. He could see a solution that was a race he had to win at the risk of his own life

"What a great act!" Peepers commented. This is going to be a hard decision between the X6 act of Corcoran and Martin and these guys. If you are going to bet on this one you have the next three seconds to place your bets. Charonelle, over to you. What do think of these guys?"

Charonelle projected an image of delight, a disembodied pair of hands clapping. "Oh, Peepers, it is just too hard to call between X6 and this group. They are both fantastically entertaining and they both deserve to survive and become immortal, but I guess only one can win and the others have to die. But they don't really die now! They go into stasis and get another chance. Ooh! I just don't know... Hmmm... I would have to go with... Hmmm... FELICITY! Dear Felicity! What do you think Howley?"

"Okay! You know, Felicity is cute and Shaw is entertainingly different with his big brain, but their act is a little bland, flinging around on ropes and stuff, and calling each other "councillor". Seems a bit dull to me. Now Martin and Corcoran have got some pizazz! As a professional comedian I have to work hard to get all the bored morons out there laughing..." there was a huge uproar across the network. "... calm down everyone. Calm down. See I actually got some emotive thoughts moving in you lot. That's my job! That's all that ever moves in us disembodied brain pods!" The grumbling died down. "So! Y'know, these two, Martin and Corcoran, are the good guys too, but they are EXCITING! Look at the blood and gore spilled in the name of justice. Look at their ingenuity using makeshift stuff like chucking out five tons of junk. I have to say that these two will be the winners."

The network started buzzing again with bets and counter bets, odds and side wagers and the occasional psych brawl. The network police had to intervene in an unusual cerebral exposure perpetrated by an ancient who got too much ethanol stimulant when his automatic brain pod maintenance system went on the fritz. Turned out he had been a wild boy early in his bodied life during Game Series two. The police put him back in his brain pod and suspended the ethanol delivery until a certified repair coding was registered at *the police nexus.*

Nickle spoke up, "Get your bets in now friends. This is THE most exciting finish we have ever seen in all the World Game series. Who do YOU think is right? Charonelle or Howley?"

CHAPTER 50
Behind the Moon

The transports and shuttles from Space City were now milling around in the protective region that used to be the back of the moon, never seen from Earth. Reduced to line of sight ship to ship communications, it was taking time to determine who was senior and in command.

While they argued and sorted themselves out, the front of silvery fragments and particles moved inexorably towards the moon like a disciplined cavalry charge. No one had noticed the faint laser pulse flashes reflecting off the oncoming fragments that were oblique to the moon's umbra. The light was being scattered by the irregular fragment surfaces, but was reaching behind the moon. No one was looking for a signal like this.

Aboard a shuttle, Space City hydroponics engineer Jing Chu was sitting quietly looking out one of the few windows in the hull. She was watching the distant fragments that were just coming into sight at the edge of the moon's sharply curved horizon. Her head was lolling against the window in a half doze as she semiconsciously observed the unique display unfolding in front of her.

She suddenly felt dizzy and disoriented and her eyes opened wide, making the feeling worse. A feeling she had not experienced since she was a small child at a fair, when the flashing lights had set her off into an epileptic fit that turned into a grand-mal seizure. Medication had taken care of her childhood malaise and she had grown out of the condition by her early teens.

Now it was back and building in full force. She knew immediately what was happening to her and recalled her childhood control instructions. Shut your eyes and control your body. Force relaxation.

After a few minutes of controlled breathing the sensation dissipated. She peeked out of one eye into the cabin and felt no discomfort, so opened both eyes and looked around. No reaction. Jing now realized that something from outside had set her off. Regular flashing lights no longer had any effect on her, so whatever was coming in the window had to be unusual and very powerful to set her off again after all these years. She decided to experiment cautiously by covering one eye and taking a quick look out the window.

Nothing happened. She looked inside then swung back to the window a second time. Nothing. With trepidation, she prepared to uncover her eye and look out with both, intending to swing back immediately if she felt an onset in any way. She failed to consider that the fragments had moved closer in the last few minutes and the intensity of whatever had revived her long gone childhood epilepsy would be considerably stronger. In fact not in a one on one increase, but a squared value increase.

Jing looked out with both eyes open and immediately went into a grand-mal fit, thrashing in her seat restraints, eyes rolling back in their sockets and gasping for every breath.

"Medic! Medic!" came the scream of alarm from the passenger behind her. Her buddy was trying to counteract the fit but not succeeding, as one of the Space City medics drifted up to Jing's convulsing body. He immediately immobilized one arm slapped a BioMeter on it. The Meter flashed and made a pfft noise as it blasted a seizure calmative through Jing's skin and into her bloodstream. The medic watched as Jing gradually calmed and subsided into a fitful sleep, then he looked at the BioMeter and read off Jing's medical profile, noting that her epilepsy had been classed as full remission over twenty years earlier. He looked around and asked the nearby passengers what had happened.

The passenger who had called him spoke up. "I noticed she was looking out the window a couple of times. I guess I was a bit envious that she had the window which made me look at her. She was restless, looking out and back and she kind of shuddered once just before she looked the last time and went into the fit."

The medic queried Jing's buddy, rapidly putting the evidence together of an external stimulus that had set off the epileptic fit. He keyed in his privacy channel to the shuttle commander, Bob Evans. "Commander Evans, Medical Officer Hogan here sir with a report on Jing's condition and a strong recommendation."

"Yes MO Hogan?" replied Evans.

"Sir, Jing is now stable. She has suffered a grand-mal epileptic seizure that I believe was caused by external stimulus related to the approaching fragment swarm. Her buddy records indicate that it was purely a visual effect that resurrected her epilepsy that has been in remission for twenty years. based on this finding I recommend that all view ports on all ships be closed and secured while we investigate what the phenomenon is. It may be that even those with no previous history of epilepsy may be affected, including yourself and your copilots, sir."

"Thank you Hogan. Understood and being implemented immediately."

Evans went straight to the line of sight communications channel. "All ships! All ships! Cease all communications now and listen carefully. This is an emergency order." He continued to instruct the immediate closure of all view ports, including the pilot cabins, and then after a suitable pause for implementation, explained the reason why. "Has anyone else experienced passengers with any sort of fit in the last few minutes? Affirmative replies only please."

The speakers were silent. "Monitor and observe using electronic means only until further notice. I am taking command of this flotilla under Martial Law until further notice. Evans out."

"Sir!" the co-pilot signalled urgently, "One of the shuttles is on collision course with a transport and not responding to radio or guard frequency."

"Get the transport to move, emergency procedures. Keep trying to raise the shuttle." Evans activated the external cameras and gradually brought up the gain on the resulting dimage of the flotilla. There was a faint, pulsing interference of the dimage that he had never seen before, but that was not his concern right at the moment. He could see the errant shuttle heading towards the transport. Tiny puffs of jets from the transport set it moving off to the side, out of the path of the shuttle. It was going to be very close.

"Sir, I am getting something back from the shuttle comms channel. There seems to be screaming and incoherence... wait...

Yes shuttle, we hear you. What's going on there?"

The frantic voice was fading in and out, "Our pilot has collapsed for some reason and our co-pilot is having a fit of some sort. I had to subdue him to get to the comms. What shall I do? We are heading straight at another ship I can see ahead. Help us!"

Evans took the comms. "Stay calm. The other ship is taking evasive action so you do nothing. Now tell me your name and position."

"Yes. Yes. I am Sheila Johnson, Cook's Assistant on Space City. I don't know how to fly this shuttle."

"Sheila, this is Commander Bob Evans. I will help you through this. Firstly, make sure you do not look out the windows of your shuttle or you could end up like your flight officers. Something outside is causing the problem. I need you to shut all the view ports and then I want you to get the Captain and his co-pilot removed from the cabin."

"Y..yes sir." Sheila replied, voice trembling.

"Look on the console in front of the co-pilot WITHOUT looking out the front view port, and locate a symbol that looks like a pull down window blind."

"Found it sir."

"Press the button and hold it down. A selection of windows to close will come up as a dimage. The last one is "Close All". I want you to touch that."

Sheila followed the instructions and the window shields slid smoothly into place.

"Look at the diagram that should have appeared under the dimage. It shows the shuttle and all the window shields in place. They should all be green. Are they?"

"Yes sir." Her voice gained confidence.

"Get some help and remove the flight crew from the cabin. Get them medical care but YOU do not leave. Do you understand Sheila?"

"Yes sir."

"Move on it, fast."

Sheila peered out into the cabin area and beckoned four

passengers in the closest row to come to her. All had some space training for City living so they were able to move efficiently. They stopped just outside the cabin.

"You two take the captain and you take the co-pilot. Get BioMeters on both of them straight away."

"Yes SUH! And who put you in charge SUH!" The attitude coming off a large, square jawed man was almost tangible. "Who are you to order us around. What did you do to the captain?"

"Oh, for crying out loud!" Sheila used her old Australian namesake grandmother's favorite expletive. "There is no time for this bullshit. Just do what I tell you if you want to live!"

The macho man was a little confused, but still retained enough arrogance to be a problem, smirking and delaying the removal. "Want to live, huh? And what's an iddy biddy little girl like you wearing a cook's insignia going to do to save us, huh?" He stopped moving arms folded in defiance.

"Ooooh!" Sheila was getting angry. She suddenly launched herself at the man and flicked out her hand at his exposed neck. The look of surprise on his face was classic as his body became paralyzed by Sheila's application of Pirogi Cholent martial arts that was her leisure past time and exercise regimen.

"You!" she indicated, "Get over here now and help! Anyone else want to argue with me?"

The group moved with aclarity and the cabin was quickly cleared, The captain and co-pilot under medical care. Sheila resumed her seat at the console. "I'm back Commander Evans."

"Thank you Sheila. Is everyone OK?"

"Yes sir. One of the helpers slipped and fell sir, but he will be OK soon."

"Slipped and fell?"

"Don't ask, Commander."

"Oh. Oh well, let's get a move on now. Look at the console in front of you. To the right you will see a series of Flight related buttons. These will bring up a dimage of your shuttle and other vessels in proximity. Do you see the row of six buttons with shuttle shapes on them?"

"Yes sir."

"The top button has one shape that is your shuttle. Press it now."

A wire frame representation of the shuttle came up as a dimage in front of her.

"The next series of buttons represent other vessels in close proximity regions, like layers of an onion. We will stay with the default settings for proximity. Push the second button down now."

Sheila touched the second button and another dimage appeared next to the first. Following Evan's instruction, she traced a path from the single shuttle dimage to the red colored miniature on the second dimage. All the other shuttles and transports in the group were represented by blue wire frames, except for one which was pulsing between yellow and purple. It was also the closest and visibly getting closer. The path lit up and the words "confirmed I.D." flashed along the path. She told Evans who acknowledged.

"Sheila, this is where you become a pilot, OK?"

"Yes sir!" she replied, now full of confidence.

"I want you to place your pointing finger of your right hand on the red image of your shuttle in the second dimage, then trace a path in a downwards orientation, away from the moon, between the other vessels in your area, then stop the trace just outside the grouping. Do not remove your finger from the path end. Do it now."

She did as instructed, checking carefully that the path avoided all contact.

"Sheila, on the first dimage there should now be a response menu asking you to confirm the path. You have checked the path visually so please touch the confirmation menu with your left hand and wait for an activate menu message. Keep your finger on the path end through all this."

"Sir, the message is in front of me. It says "Path Confirmed. Action Move? Yes No"

"Shelia, touch the "Yes" menu entry, wait until the word "Yes" turns from yellow to green, then you may withdraw your right hand from the path and sit back for the ride. You should watch the dimage for your travel progress. If you see any danger approaching, you can use your pointing finger again and drag the path to change it. Only you can do so as the system has read your fingerprint for this move."

Sheila went ahead and activated the Shuttle manoeuvre. She felt the acceleration and direction changes as pressure on her back from the pilot's seat. The tiny shuttle in the dimage was on the move.

"Sir?"

"Yes Sheila?"

"Is the dimage supposed to be flickering or completely steady?"

Evans was cautious. "What are you seeing Sheila? Describe it to me exactly."

"The dimage is clear sir, but there is a flaring effect that flickers for about two minutes, then it stops for around fifteen seconds then starts again for two minutes. There appears to be a repetitive pattern within the flickering sir." She paused. "I am watching it now. I don't think it is random sir."

"What makes you say that Sheila?"

"I can see a rhythm to it sir. My Pirogi Cholent martial arts training emphasizes rhythm and flow, so I am very conscious of such phenomena in the world around me. I also hold a Ph.D in stochastic processes and I can interpret what I am seeing as definitely non-random."

"Ph.D huh?"

"Yes sir. That was my pre-requisite for being selected for the assistant cook's position sir."

"They couldn't make you the primary chef with a Ph.D in statistics?"

"No sir. The primary chef is a Gourmand Master Chef only. He didn't need a second discipline to get his job."

Evans rolled his eyes and chuckled to himself, only now realizing that his "pinch hit" pilot was possessed of an IQ that topped the charts. He felt a great deal more confident in the successful outcome of this evasive action. "Can you make anything of the pattern, Sheila?"

"I am watching it sir."

"Please call me Bob, Sheila. Forget the sirs for now."

"Yes siree Bob!" came back the laughed reply.

"OK. I am seeing something here. Crikey!" came out another of Granny's expletives. "It's code sir! Bob! Um."

"What code Sheila?"

"Stochastic processes are used for code breaking. My Doctoral thesis was an analysis of the development of code systems from ancient times to the present. I am seeing simple morse code from the early twentieth century here. Give me a moment to transcribe the sequence then I can translate it. It's a long time since I played with this stuff."

Evans, far away in his own shuttle, shook his head in amazement at how the right people surfaced just when they were needed. He told her to take her time while he monitored the path of her shuttle, now out of collision course with the transport, but on its way to infinite space. The one issue he had not checked was available reaction mass. Would he be able to bring the shuttle back to the group? Sheila was an invaluable asset, aside from the fact that there was a remnant of humanity at risk aboard the shuttle.

Four minutes later Sheila came back to him. "I have it Bob. The message reads "X6 transport near moon trajectory. Need capture. No reaction mass left. 2 aboard. No line of sight until..." the rest is time and I assume position at a certain time."

Evans took the data and plugged it into the onboard computer. The information was sufficient to project a dimage showing the X6 transport, currently eclipsed by the moon, and the trajectory and future positions and relative velocities of all concerned at the point of requested pick up. This was going to be a difficult catch, if it could be done at all.

"Sheila, this message is from Jeff Martin the commander of the X6 transport. He is in a trajectory that will swing him right past us behind the moon just as the fragment swarm reaches us here. His problem is that to get here he has used all his reaction mass so he can't slow down. He has only himself and Alex Corcoran aboard... Wonder what happened to the passengers."

"Bob, my shuttle is already heading outwards. Maybe I can

intercept them."

"Two problems Sheila. First is that the laser message they are using reflected off the anti-matter fragments is the cause of the epileptic seizures we have seen. The anti-matter is altering the radiation in some way. The second issue is that you do not have reaction mass to be able to catch them, let alone return here."

"It doesn't matter if we can't return immediately Bob, just as long as I rescue them. You will be able to take on more reaction mass once the fragment swarm has gone past and come get us. I think we can do it."

"You're pretty confident for a cook's assistant Sheila."

"It's me old Aussie Granny Bob. She always said you'll never know if you don't have a go. So how can we save them?"

Bob looked at his area dimage and gradually projected it forward in time. The reaction mass limitation and the relative velocity of X6 were being compensated so the extrapolation was reasonably accurate. The dimage showed X6 passing by Sheila's shuttle at around 200 kph relative speed, X6 passing under the shuttle at an angle of sixty degrees and distance four hundred meters. Both craft would be shielded from the passing fragment swarm, but after that they were headed for the infinity of deep space.

"Sheila, you must have some large mono filament cargo nets on board? Right?"

"Yes Bob. I saw them when I was coming on board."

"I have a glimmer of an idea. It is crazy but better than nothing. We're going fishing."

"But those nets couldn't possibly hold the X6 Transport. It is just too big."

"Not the transport, just Jeff Martin and Alex Corcoran. We only have a few minutes to work this out so hurry and do exactly as I tell you.

Deploy the cargo nets on long tethers, one for each corner, in the same direction as the travel of X6. The mono filament tether cables for ship docking are perfect for the job. Make sure the nets spread to maximum area. The mono filament cable must be at least three hundred meters long."

"The same direction as travel?"

"Yes. We are going to do some high risk bungee jumping, but I don't see any other way of rescuing the guys."

"OK Bob, I'm on it. I'll keep you informed through my youniform comms. My buddy needs a little space exercise. By the way, before I go EVA, could you kindly inform all aboard here over the public address system that you have appointed me as command. I don't want a mutiny on my hands from the ox I had to put out earlier."

"You what?"

"I had to subdue a passenger who objected to the cook's assistant being in command. He will be coming to about now and have a raging headache."

Evans smiled to himself again and shook his head in disbelief, thinking that he must meet this Sheila one on one. She was someone really special apparently. He keyed his comms. "Put me on the PA Shelia."

He heard the click as the comms switched. "Ladies and gents aboard the shuttle, this is Commander Bob Evans speaking. Enough of you will know me to understand that I am the senior officer in this region. We are under US martial law due to the nature of the incidents that have occurred. We are presently engaged in an attempt to rescue two transport pilots from X6 which has run out of reaction mass.

Effective as of this moment I am appointing Sheila Johnson, formerly cook's assistant and Doctorate is Stochastic Processes as commander of the shuttle. You are all to obey her instructions. Failure to do so or any insubordination will be dealt with under Martial Law. Time is of the essence in saving our pilots and a plan is under way. Do exactly as Commander Johnson tells you. Good Luck to all in this attempt. Commander Evans out." He waited until Sheila clicked back to the private comms channel.

"Thank you Bob, I think that will do it. I have the cable covers opened on the outside and three space trained passengers to assist me. We are gathering the cargo nets now.

What should we do about the laser transmission?"

"I have used the same technique as Martin and sent back a

message that we have received and understood, but on a different wavelength that should avoid the epileptic effect. That they should stop sending as it is causing epileptic fits, and be ready at line of sight to receive voice comms instructions for capture. They also know to get strap on jet packs ready. I will take a last confirming RODGER transmission as acknowledgement."

Evans told Sheila to stand by while he watched for the laser transmission to stop.

Suddenly the pattern changed and his translator showed the word "RODGER", then the transmission ceased entirely. "Sheila they have the message, go. Go!"

Sheila and her assistants deployed through the air lock each pushing a bundled cargo net. The three assistants attached their nets behind them for the moment and each deployed to a corner of Sheila's net. As there were only four tether cables available, they attached pre cut cable to the corners of the net and drew them back into a pyramid shape facing the shuttle. Sheila clamped the four ends together with the tether cable and added nano-glue to the junction for extra strength. The four of them each took a corner of the net and jetted outwards, making a huge square kite that they then drew away from the shuttle to the full five hundred meter length of the cable.

The cable had enough elasticity to catch a high velocity projectile and slow it down at a rate that a human body could just survive, even in a youniform.

The group repeated the task three more times and then they brought the kites together and formed one giant kite, joining and gluing at critical junctures.

Provided Corcoran and Martin could hit this forty meter square target, they had a chance.

"Target!" Shelia exclaimed as they jetted back to the shuttle. "We need to make the net highly visible. The guys will have seconds to correct any trajectory errors so they will not have time to search for the net if it is hard to see. Quickly into the lock. I need to refill my reaction mass and get back out there."

"What do you have in mind?" Came Bob across the youniform

---

comms.

"We have twenty four emergency visible light beacons on board and even more reflective safety patches for the City repair crews. We are going to attach these all over the nets."

"Great idea, but hurry. You have about twenty minutes before crunch time."

Sheila's group recharged reaction mass in their personal packs and went about gathering the beacons, patches and any other light emitting items. They EVA'd minutes later and each took an edge of the net, attaching six of the beacons to each side with nano glue. They worked their way in attaching reflective pieces which may or may not catch sufficient light to be useful, and then meeting in the middle, they clustered light emitting games, communicators and flashlights, all turned on to their brightest settings, to form a bulls eye for the target. It was crude but effective.

Evans came over "People, time to move out smartly now. You have four minutes until impact and three until they are in line of sight. Go back to the shuttle and wait inside the lock. Recharge your reaction mass in case you need to give assistance. Do not go out until the event is over, one way or the other."

"What are Martin and Corcoran supposed to do Commander Evans?" Sheila was formal now, with her team on the comms.

"Here's the theory. As the transport passes you at relative two hundred kph, they will orient so their air lock is facing back towards you. They will both be wearing emergency escape back pack reaction jets with extra reaction mass bottles for extended burn. I have calculated their best angle of egress to maximize the deceleration effect that the jets can impart, but also enough angle away from the X6 trajectory to bring them into your net at around one twenty kph. This should be very survivable for them provided they don't miss the net.

In the event of a miss, they will be able to slow down to relative eighty kph before their reaction mass runs out.

As soon as you see that X6 has passed by safely and the guys are flying and not going to hit any of you, take off in twos pulling a mono filament lifeline out towards any one who missed. You should be able to catch up fairly quickly and grab on. The mono filament will stop you in a second bungee jump attempt.

In theory!"

"Yah! In theory!" came back Sheila with grim humor. "Let's do it people!"

"It just goes from great to amazing! Now we have Martin and Corcoran in what could be their finale interacting with Sheila and Bob who have come out of nowhere and are really contenders along with the performers out there on the fragment!" Peepers was shedding endorphins of excitement that were churning through the network. *"Howley, who would you choose as the winner"*

"Peepers, I love all of them. They're fighters, they're funny, talented and they want to hold on to life like it was the most precious thing ever. You know, I wouldn't want to see any of these finalists get squished, blown up, vaporized or horribly asphyxiated, but keeping in mind that they do get a second chance in stasis, I'm still particular to Hannaford and Shaw.

I mean, this Sheila is great, coming out of left field like that, with her Pirogi Cholent martial arts taking down a guy twice her size in twenty seconds, but I just have a brain feeling that Felicity turns on my primeval engine."

"Thank you Howley. Charonelle, what do you think with this new development."

"Peepers," came across the warm sexy voice, *"Just when you think you've seen it all, well these groups pull out all the stops and raise the bar. It is too hard to call so I'm not going to try."*

"What she talkin' 'bout raisin' bars? She ain't got no legs for high jumpin' any mo! Fact is she just another blobby brain swimming in a glass bottle. Sheesh! It's me Nickle Gannon that's gotta keep a body going so's I can service all them brains and I ain't gonna jump no bars!"

"Settle down Nickle. You will get to join us as soon as this game is over and a new com-repair is trained and active."

"That's easy for you to say Peepers. You didn't have to hang around for five and a half thousand years with a sore back and a

---

blocked terlit!"

"Just think about all those emergencies you took care of over the time to save our people the discomfort of isolation. You can feel good about that."

Nickle gave a middle finger in Peeper's general galactic direction and went "Hmmmfff!"

CHAPTER 51

On the Iranian fragment.

Felicity was a comet swinging in a tethered arc towards the unforgiving rock ridges of the fragment surface. Shaw had seconds to attempt a rescue.

He quickly looked to his own second tether to make sure it was secure as everything he had calculated depended upon it holding.

"Felicity! I'm coming to get you!" He jetted forward at maximum thrust towards Felicity's tether which was now steel taut as it swung her around. He snagged the tether in the crook of his arm and then released, to slingshot him back the way he had come. Applying full acceleration to his jet packs again, his own tether was now dragging Felicity's down, shortening her arc of travel but also accelerating her velocity in compensation. Her splat on the surface would be even more severe if he has miscalculated.

"Felicity, you with me?"

"Yes!" came the panicked reply.

"Grab hold of my tether really tight and release yours!"

There was no time to talk about it. Felicity's gut took over as she ignored the fast approaching surface that would shred her to bloody ribbons. She hooked Shaw's sliding tether under one arm and used the other to flick the emergency release that had been redundant to this point. Releasing earlier would have shot her off into space with no hope of recovery.

Shaw saw the change over and immediately vectored for an upwards trajectory that started slowing Felicity's plummet to death.

"Use your jets now Felicity! Help me slow you!"

"Can't!" She moaned, her shoulder in agony from the twisting and pressure that the youniform tried to compensate.

She was already starting to swing into a parabolic dive, the question in Shaw's mind, was it too late to avoid impact?"

Seconds that felt like lifetimes had elapsed. Felicity saw the surface racing at her but now she was going to skim it at high velocity, hanging on to Shaw's tether like a knot in the middle of a skipping rope. Shaw was now travelling against her motion, slowing her horizontal velocity. She bunched up her legs anticipating impact. Her speed relative to the surface was now survivable if she could miss the worst rocky outcrops.

She hit, feet first that set her tumbling but ricochetted her off the surface and she lost her grip on the tether. She was now a space object, disoriented and flying away from the fragment at a much reduced speed. Shaw released his tethers, reversed his course and came jetting after her.

He caught up after a minute, still over the fragment but at some altitude. Felicity was spinning and tumbling, completely disoriented and barely conscious. He felt that if he grabbed her, his youniform would be able to compensate and stop the tumble effect she would impart to him, so he made a split second analysis and grabbed hold of her.

The stars and fragment started whirling around for him, but the youniform controlled the jet thrust to bring him under control.

He checked his remaining reaction mass. There was not much left so he would have to activate Felicity's thrusters to get them safely back to the transport. He held Felicity in a tight clutch and looked at her unconscious face through the youniform helmets.

Even under the dire circumstances, he felt the softness and femininity under his fingers and saw the simple beauty of her features in repose. A rush of warmth and care, sheer hungry desire, churned in him, his male human instincts unsupressable as his youniform stretched to accommodate an ill timed tumescence.

Felicity's eyes flickered as she regained consciousness and looked into Shaw's concerned face inches in front of her. She stretched her arms around his shoulders, adding to the pressure between their bodies as they drifted in space.

"Hmmm, Mr Shaw... Are you just pleased to see me?" She murmured, "Or is that a banana in your pocket?"

They both giggled at the reversed cliche and hugged together even tighter, sharing Shaw's erection through the thin youniform material.

Felicity wrapped her legs around Shaw and commanded her

buddy to meld the youniforms. The youniforms flowed into a cocoon around the pair, leaving them skin to skin as they kissed deeply with the passion that only sharing a near death experience could create.

And then and there,

In outer space,

Was again conceived,

The human Race.

"Shaw? Hannaford? Are you guys OK?" Fuller's concerned voice rattled in their ears. They looked at each other, nose to nose in the cocoon, relaxed after the rush of weightless, simultaneous orgasm.

"Yes Colonel, we are both fine, now." Felicity could not suppress another giggle. "We have merged youniforms to share reaction mass and will jet back at optimum velocity to regain the transport."

Fuller wasn't hearing someone who had just cheated death by a whisker. Something was going on here and he had a fair idea now of just what it was. "Don't do anything I wouldn't do." He hinted.

"We are fine sir." Replied Shaw who then whispered in Felicity's ear "And if we do I'm not naming it after him!"

Felicity broke out in a fit of laughter while Fuller's request for repeat, transmission unclear, rattled in their ears. They turned off the comms transmission and locked lips again as Shaw explored Felicity's warm, smooth body. They had at least ten minutes until they reached the transport. Felicity felt his erection harden again and looked at him with wide eyes. "Again?" She said with a cheeky grin.

"Forever..." Shaw answered breathlessly.

Far away across the World Game network Peepers could not get a word in as the voyeur audience roared with approval at Shaw and Felicity as they coupled in total abandon and bliss. If there was one emotion and sensation that could be vicariously shared with greater intensity than violent death, it was the peak of sexual climax and satisfaction. The immortal brains that made the World Game audience were all screaming in superlative ecstasy as they pseudo climaxed along with the human couple. The junction of vagina and penis ruled the universe as billions of immortals focused upon the intensity of sensation that controlled the two warm, copulating bodies. The pseudo orgasms were a mixed double for the audience, combining Felicity's rolling pleasure with Shaw's sharp and intense pulsations.

As the multiple climaxes faded and the two clutched together, slippery with hot sweat and body fluids, the hubbub of moaning and screaming across the network died down, giving Peepers a chance to regain control.

"Wow!" Peepers gasped. "Charonelle, Howley, are you ready to go on?" They too had all enjoyed the experience, but professionalism dictated they get back on the job. He received single word affirmative from his co-panelists but could hear them still gasping.

In the background Nickle was grumbling. As a full corporeal caretaker he was not hooked in to the network so he had missed the shared climax. He turned on his time out signal and ambled off to his private quarters to fix his problem.

"Well everyone! What do you think about that? That has to be one of the most spectacular events of audience participation for all times and editions. I mean, how could you beat that? Howley, what do you think?"

"Peepers, you know I don't like messy or dangerous things, but this time I felt that I wanted to be one of those little sperms swimming about weightless and being welcomed into Felicity's warm tunnel of love. I had an urge to seek out the core of her sex, her womb and to join with her half of the new life. I was wallowing in his semen and her lubricating fluids and actually enjoying it. Peepers, I have said it once and I'll say it again. These two are just so far ahead of the other acts, my money is on them. Phew! I'm still high from the endorphins."

"Charonelle, your comments."

"Oh Peepers. If I had a face I'd be blushing right now. I did something very naughty I think." There was a slight roar from the audience.

"Keep it down! Keep it down! Where in the galaxy is Nickle when we need him? Go on Charonelle, what did you do naughty?"

"I actually masked out Felicity's orgasm and just left Shaw's. I never, in all these millennia, experienced a male climax sensation before and I wanted to know what it was like, on its own, so the second time they coupled I did it. Wow, you guys get it short term but what intensity!"

"So Charonelle," asked Peepers, "would you want to come back as a male if you had the choice?"

"Oh no Peepers. I just wanted to feel the sensation. I wouldn't want to have to walk around with all that equipment hanging between my legs all the time. It has to get in the way, and in any case I still think that a female orgasm lasting much longer but at lower intensity if far more enjoyable than the quick flash bang of a male release."

"Interesting. Very interesting Charonelle. So your opinion at this time?"

"Oh, these two for sure! They've got it all going for them as an act with spontaneous action. They have cheated death several times now and unlike Martin and Corcoran, have given all of us something to enjoy besides terror and death!"

Nickle had come back by now, a beatific smile on his face. "Maybe not all of us. They is a few poofter-brains out there that would rather see Martin and Corcoran do something like this together!"

"Aw Nickle! That is just gross!" complained Howley.

"Ha ha!" Peepers laughed to defuse the moment. "Alright people, let's focus and get back to the Game." Peepers paused. "Where did you get off to when we needed you Nickle?" he asked on the private channel.

"Ah had to get off - as you say. I ain't no monk you know. Them two love birds was driving me crazy. OK?"

"Oh!"

CHAPTER 52

Inside the fragment.

Zardooz had sedated Arjmand and cleaned up his vomit mess. The tumbling sensation was wreaking havoc with Zardooz's gut and had made Arjmand completely sea sick in three dimensions. The nano-healing technology stolen from the former "West" was working as Arjmand's external injuries visibly cleared. The broken ankle was secure and appeared to be staying set, in spite of the shifting forces of the spin.

Zardooz made his way back to the control room. He was getting the hang of moving and knowing when he could safely move. There was a pattern to the tumbling that he was gradually recognizing and could adapt to.

He strapped in with the dimage before him. The RABI was ready to go. He traced some circuits that were shut down and sent a repair bot along the service conduit to reset the last outer door that had been damaged in the blast. He overrode the "no atmosphere" security warning and activated the dead section of the corridor, the lights and cameras all coming on. The corridor looked fine other than the atmospheric breach. The RABI would start from there.

He took the RABI dimage and placed it in the corridor in a position to allow the shortened journey to the surface node. The RABI could not repair the node cameras, but he would send a repair bot with a replacement module after the boring job.

The RABI moved in the dimage as it was transported to the closest point to the corridor. The security overrides would not allow it to bore from within the complex under any circumstances, but the corridor segments after the first two were exempted from this exclusion. The only issue was to prevent atmospheric loss as the RABI bored into the corridor section.

The RABI sent a signal that it was in position to bore to the corridor but could not proceed due to atmospheric breach. Zardooz set the emergency door locks on the room that the RABI waited in and isolated it. It was risky, but nothing ventured, nothing gained. Those locks had to hold. As a second thought, he activated the lock on the access corridor to the room as well. Then he overrode the RABI security. As the RABI was still in the complex no go region, he had to fool it into believing it was outside the area. There was only one way to do that and it was surely risky. He isolated all power circuits in the complex and left only the control room active. Arjmand would have to take his chances for the few minutes needed and was so pumped full of narcotics it didn't matter.

Zardooz flicked off all power except the control room and activated the RABI. The security warning was gone and only an atmospheric loss warning, the air in the room itself, showed and was easily cancelled. The RABI activated its boring head and went at the wall, chomping its way through the panelling until it hit the bed-rock. Then the real work began.

There was a small run of about twenty feet from the room to the corridor that would take ten minutes or so at two feet per minute. A cloud of powdered rock came blasting back into the room and swirled madly in the coriolis forces of the tumbling fragment. Ultimately the dust would cling to the walls as the flung layers built up and were held by static charge and a blast of fire retardant would set the deadly dust into a mud that could not foul the atmospheric scrubbers. Zardooz sat back and watched the RABI's path, ready to step in if the inertial guidance could not cope with the tumbling.

The RABI soon broke through to the corridor followed by a rush of mud and fire retardant blown out by the air pressure from the room. The once black RABI carapace was now dirty white with rock mud and Zardooz was able to watch it in real time as he guided it up the corridor to the starting point for the big bore to the surface node. He double checked the intended path and set the RABI on its way, once again rock dust spewing out behind into the corridor, soon obscuring vision and coating everything with dust. The dust was going to be one of his major problems.

While the RABI chewed and burrowed, Zardooz readied a repair bot with the new module for the surface node. He was going to lose some more atmosphere as he let the repair bot into the connecting corridor to the tunnel room, but only what was in the corridor itself. He could spare that.

He opened the tunnel room door and saw the residual mud and dust fly into the tunnel as the air whooshed out from the corridor to room to tunnel. At least the repair bot would have a fairly clean path ahead. The bot trundled into the room and Zardooz shut the door behind it. He did not replenish the air in the corridor as there was no need for it. He could see the dimage of the bot and guided it to the tunnel. Its rudimentary artificial intelligence told it there was a solid wall ahead so it came to a stop even though nothing barred its way. Unlike the RABI, this one was easier to fool as Zardooz took the structural plans and added a door and the tunnel and saved the changes. The computer system updated the plans throughout the complex and the bot took off into the tunnel without further ado.

Zardooz thought back to his decadent days as a student when western television still came to the internet, to the Road Runner Coyote cartoons where the Road Runner would paint a black tunnel entrance on a cliff face and run right through it, then the coyote would run at the same tunnel and bounce off. He was certain he had just done a Road Runner trick and snickered to himself at the idea.

The RABI was now some twenty feet into the fragment mass with around two hundred feet to go. About an hour and a half of boring. Zardooz decided to catch a nap and set perimeter alarms for the RABI and a wake up for himself. He had not heard a sound from Arjmand, so he laid back his chair, stretched out and instantly dozed off.

A violent jolt spoiled his peaceful nap which he saw had been for fifteen minutes. He looked at the heads up panel and saw no warnings. What in the blazes had bounced the fragment? Had it collided with another piece of Earth?

Something was very different however. What was it? Of course! He suddenly realized that he was not suffering vertigo and that down was almost down. There was still some slight tumble but the worst effect was gone.

Well, down was not really down. The wall was down. The floor was the wall, but who cared? He reasoned that another fragment must have clipped this one and stopped the tumbling. He looked at the RABI progress and saw a glitch in the path from when the jolt had occurred. It had taken a few seconds for the RABI to reprogram from its inertial guidance and it had gone into a loop of sorts for four feet then corrected.

Problem was that the RABI couldn't go around a corner in solid rock and that was just what it was trying to do. It did have limited reverse capability so Zardooz reset the program to back out. It slowly withdrew back into the tunnel and stopped, ready to line up again. Zardooz gave it a start command on the original track and off it went, leaving a large, side cavity along the tunnel where it had digressed from the set path.

He sat back once again, his mind churning over the possibilities that had caused the jolt, but relaxed in the return to normality, the nausea from the constant tumbling virtually gone. He was even more determined to get the node working to see what was going on out there.

The RABI bored on.

Back aboard the transport Felicity and Shaw had joined the council group to watch the charges being detonated. Fuller had decided that there was enough rock rubble mass in front of the charge for a definitive recoil effect. The blast was quite spectacular viewed through a remote camera as a silent, pyrotechnic display. The loose rock mass simply vanished in a cloud of dust that dispersed in the conical shape of the directed blast forces.

However the immediate, and welcome result was the change from tumbling to centripetal "gravity" in one direction. There was still some minute wobble to the rotation, but it was not significant, more like sitting in a rowing boat on a day of very slight swell, a pleasant almost rocking effect.

The group all looked up and around as the interminable vertigo and moving pressures on their body harness simply vanished.

Fuller cautiously unstrapped and stood up in the light, rotational gravity effect, and took some small steps. "Oh, this feels good to be walking normally again! Come on guys, get up and walk a bit."

They all unbuckled and stood. Felicity swayed a little unsteadily at first, still recovering from her ordeal at the end of the tether, and they milled around, smiling, hugging and remarking on how good it all felt. Shaw was next to Felicity like a magnet and held her when she swayed. She looked at him and gave the sweetest smile he had ever experienced. Forgetting the others about him, he whispered in her ear, "I love you!" She relaxed in his arms and just purred , "Mmmm."

"May I have the next dance?" Fuller again spoiled their reverie.

Shaw turned to look at Fuller with a huge face splitting grin he just could not suppress. "Get in line Buster!"

"Seriously, Gerald, Felicity. I think we need to have a quiet chat somewhere."

"I know what you are...." blustered Shaw.

"Not here Gerald." calmly interrupted Fuller. "Later, in the flight cabin. Just the three of us."

CHAPTER 53
Behind the Moon

"Here they come!" Screamed Sheila in tense excitement. The X6 was a rapidly growing point of light as it approached at two hundred kph relative velocity. Slow by space standards but fast enough to become a statistic if you happened to stand in front of it.

Shelia could make out detail now and saw that the entrance hatch was open. The orientation looked about right according to Bob Evans' instructions. She could just see the two men hanging in the doorway as the vessel rushed in.

It was exactly opposite her position now at the ejection point and she saw the pair launch themselves from the opening. They were travelling away from the ship but still away from Sheila's location, although at much reduced velocity. She watched in fascination as the slow motion drama played out. Her heart was in her mouth as Martin and Corcoran drifted away. Were they going to hit the target nets?

Her youniform alarm trilled and she launched off with the other three, all releasing mono filament tether lines. The danger of collision had passed and it was time to go catch their mates. As the four flew towards the nets, she saw one of the tiny figures tumble into the edge of the net and roll towards the center. The other missed entirely and flew on into space. She called "Contingency!" and drifted to her nearest companion. He released his reaction mass pack to her then braked his motion and started reeling himself back to the transport on the cable.

Sheila strapped the extra pack on her chest, oriented towards the dwindling speck and put the pedal to the metal. She concentrated on the speck of light that was her target and a warm, live human being in trouble. Gradually she drew up on the speck and could soon discern limbs and details.

With a shocking squawk her youniform alarm warned that the end of the mono filament was seconds away. In a snap decision she hit the release to the line and left the spool adrift with its small light beacon flashing. Relieved of even this slight resistance her acceleration picked up and she soon reached the inert figure.

"Hey there big boy! Who have I got here?" The short range youniform communication jolted the figure into action and it raised its head to reveal Martin's weary face. He cracked a smile for her and raised a hand in welcome. She drifted up to him and matched velocity, attaching her harness to him. She used her orientation jets to turn around so she faced back to the shuttle and re-activated her jets to decelerate them and start them back. But she hadn't been watching her reaction mass level and the youniform screamed another warning at her.

She checked all levels and computations for return to the shuttle. The extra reaction mass pack would just make it for one person, but not for the two of them. She would have to hope that her team would see her predicament and come out and meet her with another pack. She was out of youniform comms range to tell them.

Sheila released her expended pack and Martin's to reduce mass. There was nothing else expendable. She activated the jets to gain optimum effect. The deceleration phase would use around eighty percent of the mass, leaving only twenty percent to drive them back, but that was too slow to avoid Martin running out of recyclable air, even with his youniform working at full capacity. She would cross that bridge when she got to it.

They were going to drift for some hours based on the reaction mass calculations. Sheila brought up a schematic that showed she could reach the drifting tether line spool with a quarter of one percent mass left. "Hell, that's enough margin for error!" She thought to herself. Meanwhile she was cuddled up with Martin in the weightless version of the missionary position. This was getting interesting.

"Martin? Are you with me?"

"Y-yes." He replied weakly.

"Are you hurt?"

"No, not at all. Just exhausted. Haven't slept in like sixty hours. Can't stay awake, so tired."

"We have a few hours of travelling to do before we are back at the shuttle. Can you hang in there?"

"Don't know. My youniform says my air supply is reaching critical contamination. Think that's why I am so sleepy too... Hey, thanks for rescuing me. You're taking a big risk for a cook's assistant."

"How'd you know that?"

"Seen you on the City. Asked around."

"So how about cook's assistant Ph.D?"

"Yeah, that too. But you're much cuter as a cook's assistant. Not so scary."

Sheila laughed. "So what are we going to do to keep you breathing?"

"Well, whatever you think of, do it soon?"

"Yah. Here we go. Behave yourself!"

Sheila initiated a youniform suit meld to share her atmosphere with Martin. It would get them back to the shuttle with molecules to spare, but she was getting used to cutting it fine.

The suits reflowed around the pair, taking the thin barrier between their skins away and providing fully oxygenated air for Martin's oxygen starved body. He gradually became warmer and more coherent while Sheila enjoyed the feeling of his hairy chest stimulating her nipples of her neatly endowed breasts. She felt his hands slide down to her buttocks but didn't stop him, his unavoidable erection probing directly at her now stimulated vulva, wetly flowing with anticipatory juices.

Martin's eyes popped fully open and he tried to pull away from her, gasping, "I'm sorry! Can't help it! I.. I..."

"Martin, don't worry. I'm a big girl now. Let this happen. I want it. We have time."

Sheila felt him relax and then an urgent pressure as he slid inside her. They started gently pumping away together...

"Ahh!"

"Ooh!"

The screams meshed into a general uproar across the network as

---

the few remaining glands in the immortal brains reacted to Martin and Sheila's explosive orgasms, probably the most viewed and voyeured copulation in the history of the universe.

Hard on the heels of Felicity and Shaw's performance, this total release and abandon by Martin and Sheila, both so much more experienced than the raw, virgin pair, some of the brains that still had memory of corporeal bodies, genitalia and the associated sensations, couldn't take it any more. They went into sensory overload and Nickle's emergency board lit up amber spotted with a few red dots. The amber ones were viewers in severe distress requiring Nickle's intervention. The red ones, never before seen in six World Game series, were brains that had suffered aneurysm and were either dead or reduced to unintelligent mush. Not so immortal.

"Nickle! Nickle! Where are you?" Screamed out Howley losing his cool.

"Nickle? We need you!" Peepers monotone pretending calm did nothing either.

"NICKLE!!!" Shrieked Charonelle. "WHERE THE **** ARE YOU?"

"Oh look! I got blipped... NICKLE!!!"

Nickle was back in the rest room having released the vice that clamped his genitals in a state of extreme need. He muttered to himself, disgruntled at his lot and isolation. "Damned old fart brains, getting off on watching this shit. I gotta get back in the real life scene and find me a woman to do it with again. Screw being a brain or immortal. One good orgasm with your woman beats the crap out of this bullshit."

Nickle opened the control room door and was assaulted by the control board that for centuries had been pure green, and was now liberally scattered with amber and a few points of vivid red. "Crap!"

He rushed to the board not knowing where to begin, waving his arms about and repeating "Oh shit!" to himself, over and over. He looked up at the observation screen and saw that Sheila and Martin were now just resting, holding each other and dozing in post coital bliss. Looking back to the control board the amber lights gradually started reverting to green again, the metamorphosis accelerating at a rapid rate until there were a few manageable dots left and the red ones. "Hmm. Red ones." He said to himself holding his chin. He quickly selected the few remaining amber dots and ordered an infusion of adrenalin for all of them. They soon winked out to green.

"The red ones...shit!"

"Nickle?" It was Peepers on the private channel.

"Yah Peeps?"

"What's going on?"

"I got red ones Peeps. Never had red ones before. What can I do Peeps?" Nickle was almost crying in despair.

"Don't worry Nickle," assured Peepers, "They went out in ecstasy and exchanged immortality for sublime pleasure. The bottom line is Nickle, they are gone and there is nothing any brain can do for them. I suggest you send in the disposal unit and recycle the tissues."

"But them's is still living brains Peepers. Ah cain't trash them man!"

"Nickle, an egg is a living thing but you boil it and in your case, eat it. These brains that remain have the personality of an egg. The sentience is gone. I repeat, recycle them."

"Aw that's gross Peepers, calling them eggs."

"Nickle! Just do it!" Peepers switched the comms back to the network. "Well people! How about that! Two of our acts have turned in unparalleled copulatory performances, set the audience afire and yet even if the basics were the same their execution showed imagination and originality. I truly thought Shaw and Hannaford had this wrapped up, but it seems this newcomer, hee hee, get that... new comer... Sheila has come out of left field and put some heavy competition back in the game."

Charonelle interrupted, "Hold on there Peepers, you're being a bit chauvinistic isolating the woman here. Sheila certainly played her part and performed well - I know I got quite a thrill from her climax, but Martin had something to do with it all and we have to consider them as a team."

"True Charonelle, but I'm going by the results on Nickle's board and all the brain overloads occurred in male brains. I noticed one or two mild reactions in female brains that recovered very quickly."

"But.."

"Look Charonelle, that is not the point here! My job is to ensure the best possible entertainment for our audience and that is what this pair has provided. What I want to talk about is the fact that this happened twice in close succession and each time immediately following a near death experience for one or both of the performers. Howley, what do you see in this?"

"Huh? Huh? Wow! I'm still coming down from the high. Gads, if I still had a body I'd be taking Sheila home with me... OK, seriously? I think that the survival drive is so strong in this group and that they know there is nothing to go back to, well the relief of the spontaneous sex gives them the hope that their procreation will advance their group survival. Honestly, I do like humor in the acts, being a professional comedy-brain, but these guys have it all and I have no doubt we are going to enjoy many more hide the sausage acts before this game is over."

There was an immediate uproar on the net as Howley finished. Peepers was yelling at Howley that he couldn't say such rude things in public and Howley flashed back an image of eyes rolling up in distain. The roar settled into an intergalactic chant of "We want more! We want more!..."

"See!" was Howley's final word.

CHAPTER 54

The fragment swarm

Safe behind the moon, the anti-matter coated fragment shell that was once the crust of planet Earth, along with the flailing remains of the Skyhook, itself being consumed, the deadly materials flew on and dispersed as the ball expanded. The front still gathered more material as it encountered space garbage and then the asteroid belt. Much of the destructive material would vanish into the intergalactic regions to do no more harm. Some would encounter other planets of the Solar System and send them the same way as Earth. In a few decades, some would approach the mighty Sun.

The last sparks of Earthly life were on the fragment and behind the moon. The X6 transport had traversed the moon and run into the swarm. The empty ship was now a deflected anti-matter missile also heading for unknown reaches of space. There were now one hundred thirty five human beings left in the Universe, not counting Nickle, the World Game compere and guardian.

Behind the moon, Sheila had captured the tether reel with just a sniff of reaction mass remaining and had activated the haulback on the reel. She and Martin were getting an easy ride back to her shuttle. Now she had to get Evans to rescue the immobile shuttle that was still flying away from the group.

On the fragment, the team was placing the Dinkshif Drives on the ends of the axis of rotation of the fragment. The drives would counter-rotate to provide linear thrust, while the spin provided pseudo-gravity. Carver and Shaw had calculated a flight path that would take them through the fragment swarm front in the window created by the shield of the moon, a cone of ever expanding safety. The longer they waited, the larger the clear disc became.

However they would have to manoeuvre around the anti-matter coated moon and get behind it before they commenced their long journey to Alpha Centauri. They would achieve this by varying the thrust and orientation of the Dinkshif Drives in normal space drive mode. Aboard the transport, class was in session as they worked their way through the theory and technical side of the drives. Four prototypes that had never been tested upon which the fate of humanity was hanging. It was a tall order, but the team was not going to allow failure due to ignorance.

CHAPTER 55

Aboard Carver's Transport.

The front of the cabin was full. All the cadets and the President's party were seated, waiting for Fuller to begin. There were thirty five souls aboard.

"My friends," began Fuller, "I do not have to go over the situation we are in. As far as we can ascertain, there may be some other survivors behind the moon, but we won't know that for some time. We will proceed as if we are the sole survivors of our planet. Our goal is to do more than survive. It is to continue humanity and find another planet to restore our species.

There are two principal aspects to the success or failure of this goal.

The first is that these drives we are about to use are prototypes and have never been tested. Simply put, the theory is great, but the practicality may not work. We wait and see.

The second aspect is that for survival, we need the broadest genetic distribution. With so few of us, we will need to calculate and keep genetic records as we carry on normally and have children. We must breed and produce the next generation. And the next. We must minimise the risks of inbreeding for the sake of our future generations.

There will be no shortage of material resources for nurturing babies and growing children and our transit time to Alpha Centauri is quite short. Whether we find a habitable planet when we arrive is another matter entirely.

Our two jobs from now on are to learn about and maintain the Dinkshif Drives, and to find our first level mates and start producing babies. We have established a pairing register that must be maintained. There is one simple rule. You stay with your chosen mate until you have produced a child. You will then look at the register and choose another mate for the next child. The parentage of each child will be recorded to ensure maximum diversity when they mature and have children.

Friends, the old ways and institutions of Earth are gone. We have to survive. This does not mean we do away with love and loyalty to your partner. It simply means you will need to spread that love and be understanding to many partners over time, in order to suppress any jealousy that may arise. We will need to put aside our mores and concepts of modesty. We live in these cramped surrounds until we can make planet fall. Just as we eat together, sleep and every other activity that humans do, so we will learn to ignore a couple in intimacy or the nakedness of someone taking a physical shower to relax from the youniform pressures. Whatever develops from our small community will mold the society of the future. We learned the concept of "shame" according to the scriptures, from the Garden of Eden story. There is no more Garden. There is no more shame."

The group sat somewhat stunned. The content of Fuller's delivery had been carefully discussed and constructed by the council which included all the senior adults and Felicity and Shaw. That pair had attended Fuller's summons together, even though only Shaw had been requested, expecting to be reprimanded or worse for their extra vehicular activities. Instead, Fuller had talked the issue over and explained to them that their apparent breach of discipline was just jumping the gun on what was required.

Now Shaw and Felicity exchanged smiles as a buzz of subdued conversation came from the assembled student cadets and the President's secret service staff, who owed their lives to their job and dedication to the President. There was an even balance of men to women in the group, the president's detail always being half and half to take care of the First Lady and other female guests. Fuller had semi consciously marvelled at that fact, jesting in his mind that it was almost planned that way and not the chance of the draw.

"Ladies and gents!" Fuller called out, "Take your time, find the partner you can live and work with for the next year or so. Guys, find the partner you are prepared to take care of when she is carrying your child. Ladies, find the guy who is going to take care of you. But most of all, for all here, find the partner you can work with twenty four seven. It will not be easy."

There was a sudden turmoil from the back of the group as two of the girls bounced around in the low gravity effect and made like cats having a brawl on the backyard fence. They were kicking and clawing, shouting and screaming as they laid into each other. "he's mine!" Screeched one.

"I saw him first!" Yelled back the other as she pulled her opponent's hair. The object of their attention and conflict was one of the young secret service men who sat back and watched in amazement. The other cadets watched with amusement as did Carver and Fuller, who had to pull a straight face and break up the wrestling match.

"Girls!" He said in his best parade ground voice. "This will NOT do! We do not have the time to engage in petty rivalry. The pairing decision is not yours alone to make, so settle down." He had edged between them, and even then they tried to claw the other around him. He had no way of subduing or incarcerating them until they calmed down. The youniforms had prevented any physical injury to the pair and it was only their ego that was bruised. They eyed each other and sat down with the cabin between them. One looked at the other and hissed at her like a feral cat.

"Ladies and gents, let me have your attention." Fuller commanded the moment. "Anything like this happens again and all involved will be held to account. You will be locked up or disabled in some way if you disrupt life on this fragment." He looked at both girls in turn, a hard, penetrating stare that left them cowering. "DO YOU UNDERSTAND?" he roared.

Both girls curled up in their seats crying. They may have been the creme of intellectual youth to have won their berth on the transport, but they were still just children.

Fuller had turned attention to Dinkshif Drive theory and was explaining the principles of Faster Than Light travel based upon what was known as the Rampay Anomaly.

"You are all knowledgeable in contemporary physics or you would not be sitting here today, but for the sake of those who come from other walks of life, I am going to explain in simplistic terms and analogies so everyone starts on the same playing field.

Once there was a man named Newton who developed laws of motion, gravity and other physical constants that hold at relatively low speeds and theoretical non resistance. That works most of the time.

Then along came Albert Einstein who determined that nothing can go faster than the speed of light. That light speed was an absolute. He found that for conservation of mass and energy, energy is equal to mass times the square of the speed of light. The Theory of Relativity.

Then along came Neugee Rampay, an Indian Physics professor, who said that Einstein was only partially correct. He propounded that light is absolute in its relative universe. Take light out of this universe and all the Laws of Relativity fly out the door.

Neugee compared us to fish in a fishbowl. That glass is the boundary of the fishy universe and we are confined to the waters within the bowl. He therefore considered the means by which our fish could jump out of the bowl. Not just jump out, but also survive. We need to take our water with us on the jump. Where are our fish jumping to? That is the risk. We don't know what is outside the fish bowl, so we need a fail safe to be able to get back.

The speed of light is absolute only in this universe. This universe is our fish bowl, therefore it is reasonable to assume that there are other universes out there, other fishbowls, and maybe something else between them.

The Rampay anomaly states that if one sends a beam of light to say, Alpha Centauri, that beam is going to take about four years to reach its destination. Time dilation is not a consideration. However, if we are on a vessel travelling at light speed and we have significant mass, then time dilation aboard the vessel tells us that several thousand years have passed in the universe in the four years that the vessel took to reach Alpha Centauri. This theoretical paradox is the basis of the Dinkshif Drive. Frames of reference dictate the absoluteness of light speed. Dinkshif theorized that if the homogenous object of the light speed travel could be made subject to an alternate frame of reference, that is we jump out of our fishbowl, then we can travel at the light speed of that relativistic frame until we reach the limit. We then extend the same process to a third frame and so on. The inherent problem is in returning to our own, original universe at the end of the journey.

Dinkshif reasoned that just as he had to swim the length of the pool using individual strokes, small, incremental pulses, then so too should the reference frames be created, used and discarded incrementally, instead of using one full universe frame at a time.

The Dinkshif drive took this "fishbowl" idea to a new level. The nano-quantum technology looked to the micro level of particle physics and created "psuedo-universes" by looking into the micro universes from outside their fishbowls and altering the relativity of these flash universes. The resulting particle emanation from this relativistic dissociation was orders of magnitude faster than light speed in our universe, resulting in thrust faster than the speed of light.

Dinkshif then addressed the issue of mass becoming infinite as it approaches light speed by creating a charge field to contain the drive and its vessel, an egg shaped cocoon of captured "extra universal" particles that formed a shell, much like an electron shell on an atom, around the drive vessel. The only thing that could penetrate this shell were the particles themselves.

Inside the shell, other universe. Outside, this universe. A simple change of frames of reference.

The last effect of the Dinkshif drive was almost as astounding as the drive concept itself. The laws of relativity were never suspended or changed, at least not those of our universe, so the faster than light particles that left the shell as reaction mass had to suddenly conform to the laws of physics of this universe. As did too the very outer layer of the shell.

The infinitely small particles at many times the speed of light had to revert to infinitely massive particles limited to the speed of light. The outer shell and the reaction masses instantaneously transmuted into heavy metals and one heavy inert metal in particular. The Dinkshif drive left a trail of pure gold dust in its wake. The ancient alchemist dream come true.

Dinkshif had also taken a practical look at his creation. The Pseudo Universe drive was useless for close in manoeuvring, so he added auxiliary reaction mass thrusters that could be fuelled with any material that could be pulverized or liquefied. He realized that his drives would end up far away from home without a gas station is sight. Little did he ever imagine that not even home would be in sight, for eternity."

The network was shaken by an "X" buzz tone that was rarely heard. Peepers sent out an enquiry as to who had buzzed the girls' act. It was Charonelle. "Well! Go on Charonelle. Tell us why you buzzed that last act."

"Oh Peepers, I was of two brains about buzzing them. They are just so innocent and such yummy girls. Look at them! But on the other hand the whole act was too contrived. It lacked the professionalism that we expect by this stage of the game and I don't think they will go much further."

"You do recall we are not buzzing now, Charonelle?"

"Yes, but I just couldn't help myself. Some of these acts cannot possibly make it through. These two are wasting our time. I think they should be taken into stasis right now."

"If we do that the others will start questioning what is going on. Howley, what do you think?"

"I would like to give them one more chance. You have to consider that the previous two copulation performances have truly eclipsed all other acts before them, Now that Fuller has given the green light to unrestricted relationships, who knows what sensations these two might bring us. I am predicting a glut of sex acts coming up, so the best ones will have to truly be spectacular. You take these luscious little kittens out of the running and who knows what we will miss. I mean, look at the shlong..." There was another uproar on the net. "Come on! Excuse me! What am I supposed to call a reproductive organ of that size, people? Let me finish!... Look at the size of the shlong on that young man and think of the sensations he could provide with either of these two nubile, ripe, hot, oooohhhh... I've set myself off again just thinking about it. Hmmm? I guess that's all

I can do anyway..."

"Calm down Howley. Keep your dural membrane on! I tend to agree with Howley, Charonelle, so I am voting to keep them going a little longer."

CHAPTER 56

Inside the fragment.

Zardooz wakened from his half snooze with a shudder. Something was not right. He felt it in his gut, and he had trusted that feeling for all his life as he climbed the tenuous and sometimes deadly rungs of power of the Iranian Empire. He scanned the monitors and saw that the RABI was right on course. Nothing there. He got up and checked Arjmand who was now sleeping peacefully in the normal pseudo gravity. He returned to the control room and looked around carefully. Nothing.

The only place he had not looked was in the disabled outer corridor where he had turned out the lights once the RABI had started its boring job.

He flicked the lighting on and examined at the monitor that showed the corridor. He could see nothing out of order right to the blown out doorway open to space.

"Wait a second! What's that?" There was variation in light and shadow that simply could not be in the vacuum of space. It happened again.

Suddenly the image went black as what appeared to be a hand closed over the camera lens. He now heard the friction of scraping against the camera housing. Someone was in the corridor. But who?

In the corridor, the President, Fuller and Shaw were exploring the apparent cavern they had spotted before landing on the fragment. They saw it was man made immediately on entry and were working their way into the cavity when they hit the obstruction of the air lock just as Zardooz hit the lights. Being right under the camera they were not in view when the lights came on and gave them a fright. They reasoned that their motion had cause the activation, until Shaw spotted the camera and saw the red light on it.

"We're on show guys!" He said across his comms and pointed at the camera, at which the President instinctively reached up and covered the lens with his hand.

"We now they know we are here, if they didn't before..." said Fuller.

"Oops. What now?"

"I guess we tell them who we are, see it they identify and let us in." Replied Fuller. "Go ahead and talk to them. If they don't know who YOU are then they are aliens."

The President took his hand off the lens, stepped back and looked straight into it. There was no way to transmit sound in the vacuum, so after a few moments he stretched up and pushed his faceplate against the camera housing, assuming that there was an audio pickup hidden somewhere. "Hello in there! If you can hear me, please flick the lights off and on."

The lights went off, then on.

"Can we have a system that one flick means "yes" and two means "no"?"

One flick.

"Can you let us in?"

Two flicks.

"Is it a mechanical problem with the air lock?"

Two flicks.

The President paused to think for a moment. "Do you know who I am?"

One flick.

"Is there a political reason you will not admit us?"

One flick.

The President felt a tap on his shoulder and looked around, disengaging from the camera. Out of view of the lens, Fuller showed him a fire extinguisher tag written in Farsi. "Iran." Was his only word.

"Oh shit!" said the President. "This must be the secret base that Zardooz and Arjmand ran to. Of all placed for us to have to spend our lives, why this?" The President thought through his options and went back to the camera. It had to be Zardooz or Arjmand on the other end. Knowing Arjmand's profile, he worked the probability that it was Zardooz.

"Mr Zardooz." he said calmly, wondering if indeed it was Zardooz, what his shorts contained now. "The war is over. There is nothing left except a few survivors. Let the differences go. Allow us to enter and we will share with you for the good of all."

There was no reaction. The President knew he had it right. Arjmand would have done a light show.

"Mr Zardooz, we know it is you. we tracked you from the moment you left to launch the missiles. We tracked you to this location when it was Earth," the President bluffed, "and we tracked this fragment as originating from your secret bunker in Iran. It was our initiative that blasted away the anti-matter coating this fragment and the power of the United States that stopped the tumbling. We will enter the fragment. It can be as you friend or your enemy. One flick for friend, two for enemy, or nothing and we will take our chances. Be aware, Mr Zardooz, that this fragment is going to Alpha Centauri and there are no bus stops for you to get off on the way. Do we chase you like a rat, Mr Zardooz, or do you join us and live? Decide now."

Once again there was no reaction from the interior.

The group withdrew from the tunnel and returned to the transport. They called the council together to discuss this astounding new development. Of all people, of all nations, the very cause of the extinction of humanity was beneath their feet and the war was apparently alive and well.

The group sat around looking at each other with glum expressions. Janine broke the silence, "Isn't it just too much! We have the ultimate catastrophe in human history which a few of us survive and then it topped off with the survival of the very cause and we end up on top of them! Lord! What are the chances? Who wrote this script? I just don't believe this is random! Impossible!"

The President continued. "Yes, I guess when you put it all down in one place the probability of these events is a bit far fetched. I too agree that this is not random."

"So is it God doing it?" asked Felicity.

"That kinda sucks." answered Shaw. "What is His point in destroying everything and then putting us in this situation? Are we Noah's Ark all over again?"

"Naw." yawned Hanes. "No animals on board." This got the mood lighter with a laugh. "And Noah didn't have his worst enemy hidden away in the hold of the Ark."

"Beg to differ," interjected Shaw. "I read in comparative religion that the detailed interpretation of the Bible by the ancient Jewish sages says that a race of giants who lived very long lives numbering in the centuries, existed before the Flood. One of these giant called Og clung to the outside of the Ark and actually survived to the times of Moses, but became the enemy of the descendants of Noah, so Noah had one just like us."

"But we have no animals?"

"Au cointraire, again," Replied Shaw.

"Sheesh! Your French sucks Gerald!" scolded Felicity.

"So what? Show me France? Show me a Frenchman? Who will care? Anyway, about the animals, we already have hydroponic garden kits in the hold that were going to Space City and in the computer we have the genome mapping of virtually every living thing, male and female... and mushrooms which do have a third sex. Kinky huh?"

"So we really are Noah's Ark in a way. How do we deal with our giant pain in the ass?" queried the President.

Fuller raised his hand for silence. "We saw the reaction from presumably Zardooz. Of all the ruling elite of Iran, he was always the most inscrutable, the invisible man, but he wielded immense power through his secret police. When I came back on board I did some quick research on him, whatever our on board computers had in storage. There was not much, but the little I found lends credence to Tom's opinion that it is Zardooz we are dealing with and he is a pretend fundamentalist who was driven by money and the need to survive. The limited profile says that he is a moderate in Iranian terms and would be inclined to negotiate rather than confront if the risks do not justify the gains. It said that had he been born into any other society he would have been a nice guy.

My conclusion is that he has something up his sleeve and is therefore not negotiating. He has something to gain. Following

---

that line, whatever it is must have preceded our entry on the scene. We need to get our feet on the ground and look out. He is up to something."

Janine stood and activated a surface map of the fragment. "Now that we know where the fragment came from, while you boys were out playing I accessed the last planetary photography for that exact area and superimposed it over our fragment scan." She waved her hand through another control dimage and a photo dimage of the region ghosted on top of the harsh fragment representation. Another gesture zoomed in on the north east corner so they could see the fronds of the palm trees. "Eyes peeled everyone. This was supposed to be a totally deserted and untouched area. We are looking for any anomalies. Vents, unusual vegetation patterns, pathways, anything."

The image began a slow glide as at an altitude of about two hundred feet. No detail escaped scrutiny.

"Stop it there!" Demanded Felicity. Janine reacted and the image froze. Felicity went closer and peered at one palm tree. "Can you zoom on that tree?" she said, pointing to it.

Janine worked the dimage and the tree grew and moved off to the side a little. Janine edged the image across and they all began to see what sharp eyed Felicity had picked up. Unlike all the other trees, this one had a much greener central growth, the others all a dust yellow green specifically due to the dust. As the tree came into focus they could see that the core branches were artificial. In fact the whole tree was artificial. Now they could see the holes of the vents that the branches disguised from the ground, but not from close scrutiny above. The inrush of air kept the inner branches clear and had revealed the vent.

Janine marked the position with a red circle then turned off the photo overlay. The fragment surface was ordinary and homogenous with no special features, other than a small mound where the tree had stood. She zoomed in on the mound and they all looked carefully.

"There is a slight indent in the top, like a crater." Janine remarked.

"Think about it," added Fuller, "this was clearly a ventilation point. There did not appear to be any access points in the photo scan so I think we can safely assume that other than a hole down into the working, there is nothing here threatening to us. Good catch Felicity. Let's move on."

Janine activated the overlay and image travel again and they settled back. Nothing extraordinary revealed itself for long minutes.

"Bingo!" Shaw startled everyone. What had he seen that everyone else had missed?

"No you didn't miss anything guys. I just had an idea how to speed this up. Based on Felicity's find we need to zoom out and look for other palm tree vents using the color differential. If we find more, they will give us a rough topography of the underground installation and we can focus our search within and around the vented region."

Janine gave him a smile of approval and immediately implemented the move. The image pulled away like a ride in a hot air balloon. She stopped it abruptly when the pattern that Shaw had suggested became apparent. In the scatter of palm trees the artificial vents now stood out.

The President shook his head in despair. "How did our aerial analysts miss this. You guys saw it in seconds. This whole mess could have been stopped."

"No use crying over it now Tom. We had a specific, tiny area to examine. Your guys had millions of square miles. There's just no comparison. We were looking for the black jelly beans in the jar. They were looking for the needle in the haystack." Janine comforted him and patted his back.

"Yeah!" he sighed, "I guess you're right."

Janine went back to the map and played join the dots around the palm tree vents. The resultant area put the tunnel approximately in the middle with the whole region being heavily located to the north east quadrant of the fragment. Assuming that the venting addressed a radius around each vent and that the access tunnel provided a central vent, she drew slightly overlapping circles around all the trees with a larger one around the access tunnel until all the area was covered by the reach of a ventilator.

"This," she said indicating the total area, "is our search area."

Shaw moved forward and looked hard at the area, mouth screwed up in concentration and hand on chin. "I do believe," he said very slowly, "that we have a pattern defined by need here. If there are any observation points they need to be away from the fake trees so the trees can be under scrutiny." He traced the circles with a finger. "They would want minimum number of observation points for maximum coverage to avoid detection. Give me a minute." He sat down and closed his eyes in intense concentration as he worked complex geometry in his head as you or I would add two and two, and sometimes get four.

He stood abruptly, nearly forgetting himself in the miniscule gravity effect. "Here, here," he pointed and Janine added blue marks. "Here and one more here. OK, now let's zoom in around these areas."

Janine obliged and they all looked, the search now a bit of a competition. Again, Felicity's sharp vision pinned the tail on the donkey. "There!" She called out. The slight shadow was hard against the blue dot Janine had put down earlier. Janine pulled in on the shadow and moved the perspective. The irregular mound resolved into an artificial roof disguised as a sandy atoll with a three sixty degree all around overhang. From a little side movement the sharp shadow of a view port that had maybe a one inch exposure, stood out. Easily accommodating a rotating camera for constant surveillance.

"Look at the ground next to the camera port." Felicity pointed to a discolored patch of sand that now looked out of place and just a tad too regular in shape. There was nothing like it close by.

"Access door!" said Fuller, "Janine, show us what we have on the fragment for this one please."

The overlay faded again and the drab fragment surface materialized. There was an inverted bubble of lava like rock where the access door had been, but where the observation port had been was a deep shadow and a glint of metal. Close in the remains of a camera or support shaft could be seen.

"Here's my thinking," went Fuller. "You're an underground facility designed for nuclear fallout and direct blast. What do you need after the war is over?"

"A way to burrow back to surface and test it!" Shaw said excitedly. They have to have a rock borer down there or be trapped forever."

"And what is the first thing you would do if you were trapped inside a chunk of rock, weightless and therefore obviously flying through space, and probably blinded by external equipment being fried, boiled and blasted away?" asked Fuller.

"Try and find a way to see outside!" answered Felicity.

"So in all probability there is a borer working somewhere in the fragment right now!" added Shaw, "And I know exactly where it is!"

They all turned towards him astonished.

"When we were in the tunnel and working our way in by flashlight, I came across a hole in the wall that seemed to have no purpose. I put it down to an access panel that had blown away in the evacuation of atmosphere. When we came back into the transport just now, we all had to clean dust off our gear that we had picked up in the tunnel. I thought that was a result of our fuel bomb blast, but it's not. It came from the rock borer blow back from the cavity in the tunnel."

Fuller moved to the dimage schematic of the whole fragment and looked at the tunnel as they knew it and the surface plot of the vents and observation ports. They had found three observation points in total. Where would the borer head to be most effective? "We need to take a closer look at the three observation points. If I was controlling the borer I would head for the port that had the best chance of being reactivated or least damage to the control gear where a replacement camera could be mounted."

Fuller gave dimage control back to Janine who zoomed in on the next mound. The first was clearly destroyed. This next was quite different. The mound shape was obvious but there was no dimple in the top. It was a clean mushroom top but there was no observation slot around that appeared in the photo overlay. They would have to go out and investigate.

Fuller and Shaw had driven in pitons and were anchored next to the mound. They were tapping at the compacted sandy coating on the mound with particles and larger pieces being flung away by the spin. As the underlying structure was revealed it became apparent that the observation point was relatively intact and the camera view slot was soon clear. Squatting down, Fuller could see a red power light flickering in the dark interior. The camera appeared to be workable, although on closer scrutiny the lens and front end were crusted over with caked sand and the green active light was off. It was not active.

"This damage happened before the cataclysm." observed Fuller. "Look at the damage pattern. It doesn't go all the way back."

"Look under here, sir." Shaw pointed to a flap of metal that was angled in at forty five degrees. "I think this was a sandstorm guard that malfunctioned and left the workings exposed. It accounts for the damage pattern inside. Then the sand built up and clogged up the whole station so it was disabled and completely buried in the sand. When we were breaking away the sand cover I noticed that the compacted sand had something like spiderweb binding it. There shouldn't have been any sand here by now. It should have drifted away or been blasted off by our fuel bomb and I think that most of it was."

"So what is the binding stuff?" Fuller picked off a bit of the aggregated sand and peered closely at it. "Hmm. Maybe fire retardant foam. Has to be. When the camera went off line after the sand storm they tried to clear it by blasting fire retardant from inside the post. All it did was make a mush of the sand as it soaked outwards and glued it together. The sand shell coating is what saved the obs post from the anti-matter and gave it a sacrificial layer of protection from the fuel bomb."

Fuller stood up against the tether and Shaw followed. "This will be the place for the borer sir."

"No doubt. But if Zardooz is running the show then he will be anticipating us. That he did not reply to Tom is telling. He is going to fight because he thinks he has an advantage, but he will still be cautious as his machine emerges. He has to send a repair bot with a new camera so I think he will first send an anti-personnel device to make sure the area is clear."

"Why don't we just block the bore hole and stop the repair bot?"

Fuller looked at Shaw, "Because if he is half as cunning as I believe, he has already mined the tunnel with explosives to take us out if we venture back in. We need to take action here."

"He is sending a bot expecting to clear sand and fire retardant goo. We could put something much harder in his way, say a cargo crate over the obs post. The bot will have to be going very slow to hold itself down to the surface so it will not be carrying more than he expects it to need. Everything else will be reaction mass. We could capture the bot, sir."

"Sounds like a plan, Gerald."

They went back to the transport and hauled out a nano fibre cargo container after emptying the contents into other receptacles. Designed to withstand being hauled about in space and protect from cosmic rays and space debris strikes, the deceptively light folding container would not be breached by the repair bot in any great hurry. Not even a laser welder would make a fast dent in it.

Hauling the container over the mound, they tacked it down with the longest carbon fibre pitons they had been able to find, then retreated a distance away and set up an anchor station. They lay down flat to present the smallest possible target to any hostile emergence and waited. Tom and Felicity were to spell them in four hours if nothing happened. They were both armed with tether tendril guns that could be deployed on the hapless repair bot from a distance, shooting out sticky tendrils like the imaginary Spider Man comic of old, and binding the bot into a gooey cocoon. The tendrils had a curing time of around five seconds, enough to smother the bot and disable it before turning flexibly solid.

They waited.

CHAPTER 57
Behind the Moon

Sheila's small team hauled the cocooned pair back to the shuttle where Corcoran waited slumped into a seat, exhausted, but smiling to see his friend alive and well. Once in the air lock they had been able to revert to individual youniform configuration, but the intimacy lingered through memory and buddy interaction. Martin and Sheila were inseparably part of each other, beyond the brief, biological exchange of bodily fluids. The buddies merged elements of their psyches when they joined. Where love had meant a conscious decision to commit totally to a partner, love was now the absolute knowledge of a lovers intent.

There were now two empathically co-joined couples in the universe who understood what love really means.

Sheila left Martin to the team's care and headed for the cabin to advise Bob Evans and get a report on rescue for the shuttle which was fleeing away from the moon in the precise center of the safe, fragment free region, masked by the moon. Even as she contacted Evans, she could see the fragments sparkling like a diamond halo all around. The view of the deadly baubles from the now unshaded front window was breathtaking.

"Commander Evans, this is assistant cook Sheila Johnson reporting. Over."

She waited a moment but all she received was static.

"Commander Evans? Come in please?"

Nothing.

A mixed sense of panic and alarm sent a feeling of nausea through her body. She changed channels and tried again.

Nothing.

She stopped and took a deep breath to calm her racing heart, invoking the discipline of Pirogi Cholent martial arts that had brought her this far.

After a few minutes she opened her eyes, her body calmed and her mind focussed. She got out of the pilot's couch and drifted to the navigator's position where a simple slide cover revealed a roof dome for manual navigation by star sighting. Even under the circumstances, she reflected how nothing had really changed in thousands of years when technology was absent. At least the shuttle designers had the forethought to consider such an eventuality.

Looking back to the moon, the small region she could see due to the shuttle orientation, was enough to tell her what had happened. The moon itself was being devoured by the anti-matter as it coated the surface. It was already well around the rim of the dark side facing the shuttle, and was discernible against the black shadow due to reflection of ambient starlight. But tellingly, in the middle of the black iris, was a scatter of silvery specks that formed a faded pupil to the eye. The ships of the Space City evacuation and the transports that had joined them were turning into anti-matter. There had been a fatal miscalculation.

The gravity of the moon, mild as it was, had bent the path of fragment material in a sling shot effect. Gravity affected anti-matter in the opposite way of regular matter, but the anti-matter was a surface coating over regular matter which was present in far greater quantity. The larger masses flung around the slingshot and went off at various angles. It was the tiny, dust like particles that were bent into lunar orbit, and these had collided with the waiting fleet.

Only the Pirogi Cholent training kept Sheila from breaking down in despair. They were lost.

She looked out again and then it hit her. The shuttle had survived because it was running from the moon in the fragment free umbra. They were the sole survivors of the fleet, and they had to continue in the exact path they were following to avoid any particles that pursued them.

Sheila went back to the passenger cabin where Martin was now dozing and the rest of the passengers sat waiting and chatting to each other. She signalled for silence.

"I am afraid I have bad news." The faces before her were impassive. "The anti-matter fragments were slingshotted around the moon by gravity and some of them struck the fleet. They are all gone, turned into anti-matter and I don't know if anyone is alive inside the vessels. There was no answer to my call to commander Evans.

We must assume the worst and there will be no rescue for us. We are on our own and we must conserve every resource we have while we look for some way to survive. We are the last of humanity."

"That's bullshit!" The big troublemaker engineer stood up and pointed at Sheila. "We can't survive this. There's nowhere to go. I say that we are all gonna die right here, so let's PARTY!"

He pivoted around and grabbed the nearest female, clutching her and forcing a smothering kiss on her mouth, as she squirmed and struggled. His cronies saw the action and followed suit, some of the women willingly joining in, others struggling.

Sheila was aghast and called her team over. Two of them came, the other had joined the orgy. "We have to stop this. We can survive, but not like this."

"Tell us how." said one of her team.

"Tell us, we're with you." Corcoran and Martin had roused themselves and joined Sheila's group. They turned back to the passenger area where bodies floated in all directions, now mostly stripped out of youniforms and joined in animal hungry copulation where consensual, and screaming frenetic frenzy where rape was happening.

"Get the Bio-Meters, quick!" Sheila ordered.

They split up and sidled their way to the emergency first aid points. Each came back with a Bio-Meter in hand. "Set the Meter to manual and dial up anaesthesia." Sheila directed. "Choose the highest gas setting." They all complied. Sheila pushed back to the control console and set the atmospheric control to manual, then turned off the regenerative system and set circulation to maximum. "Set youniforms to space conditions."

The group of five suited figures moved around the melee of sweating, thrusting bodies and held the Bio-Meter nozzles towards the rabble.

"Go!" Shelia gave the command to release the anaesthetic gas into the mass of bodies. Guilty and innocent alike, they were all

---

going to sleep and would wake with enormous headaches in about an hour.

In rapid succession, the individuals succumbed to the gas and went limp, stuck in whatever position they had been in. The last to fall was the big engineer as he shook his unconscious rape victim, all the while himself weakening. Finally as the last vestiges of coherence left him, he looked around and saw Sheila and the Bio-Meter. He released his victim and flung himself towards Sheila, even as he fell fully unconscious, he drifted like a huge, pink walrus, arms outflung and his third standard deviation sized erection looking like a bulbous Americas Cup boat keel, but it too quickly went limp as the brain that controlled it switched of.

Shelia put out a hand to stop the brute from crashing into her or the wall, as much as he deserved to do so. "Truss this one up in a seat. Put an emergency diaper on him but no youniform. I will peel his buddy off right now."

The group started separating the entangled mass, making note on shoulder blades the status of rapists as opposed to consensual couples. Three more of the men were treated to diapers and buddy removal, as was one woman who was known to be homosexual and butch. The condition of the clawed off youniforms and the defensive marks on the attackers confirmed each status. The victims of the four male aggressors were moved to a separate area and made comfortable after being checked over with a Bio-Meter and post coital anti pregnancy protocols applied.

The victim of the lesbian was not in such bad shape and was also settled down in a seat.

The team had got all the passengers back to their seats and restrained them by one arm to the seat frame. They were going to stay in place when revived. The rapists were placed in the front row, restrained at arm and ankles, naked but for the diapers.

Shelia took one more look at her charges and then reactivated the atmospheric regeneration system. It soon cleared the gas and movement and moaning started to come from the passengers as they came up from the drug induced sleep. She checked the air monitor which had gone from red to green and told the team they could revert their youniforms to cabin status.

There were no weapons aboard the shuttle, so Sheila spread her team around the perimeter of the cabin, each with a Bio-Meter on manual and ready on subcutaneous anaesthesia. A quick press against the skin and lights out for that person.

Soon all the passengers were awake, but groggy from the after effects. The big engineer came to and started pulling at the restraints throwing his weight about and shaking his head in frustration. He swore and threatened Sheila, hatred burning from his eyes.

"That's enough from you!" Sheila exclaimed, and planted herself right in front of him, where he tried to head butt her. She grabbed his chin and kept his face just out of range and warned him, "I don't know who you are. I don't care right now. I was put in charge of this shuttle and I am going to do my duty for the good of all the passengers and to the best of my ability. And if that means putting a raping, foul mouthed bastard like you into space wearing just a baby's diaper, I will do it! Got me?" She stopped and stared him in the eyes. She felt his neck relax in defeat and he gave a single nod.

"Get me out of this diaper!" he whispered.

"I'll think about it." she replied. "You raped a woman. You have some justice to face."

Sheila got up and went to the front to talk to the passengers. "I'd like to start Ladies and Gentlemen, but there are few if any of those among you after what just happened." There was mixed reaction, some grins and some scowling. "I want to make something very clear. We are under Martial Law until further notice. I am in sole command of this shuttle by order of the fleet commander before the fleet was destroyed. this appointment still stands and I will not hesitate to exercise my authority for the good of all aboard. So I am starting with the ruling that any further instances of rape, attempted rape or assault of any kind, will be met by summary evacuation of the guilty party into space without a youniform. There are no more chances.

The second issue is that contrary to certain opinion," She looked pointedly at the hulking engineer, "this shuttle can be saved and can survive for an extended time. I will explain how we do this..."

"*Peepers! Now you buzzed this lot. You can't do that!*"

"*Howley, I can do anything I damned want to do!*"

"*Oooh! Peepers! You swore!*"

"*Since when did that stop you, Charonelle?*"

"*You're the one who said buzzing was a waste of time at this stage.*"

"*It was a lone stand of individual protest.*"

"*Against what?*"

"*Against boring, copycat performances that don't come close to the last two.*"

"*But Peepers, you've completely missed the beauty of this act. This was a group act that was driven by completely different emotion sets than the other two, which were purely motivated. This orgy had elements of violence, hate, lust... well just about everything you could name, except love.*"

"*Exactly, Charonelle, and in experiencing it I was not entertained in the common sense of the term. I felt like I was licking out the dregs from a filthy trash can, had I only a tongue. I can handle a good, messy death, or a predetermined rape and murder, but this was just not my cup of tea, so I buzzed it in protest.*"

"*Ohhh... Peepers, if you had a head I'd tell you to pull it in! Look at the warning board. All green and just normal chit chat on the network. You must be the only one who took offence at the orgy.*"

"*Charonelle! I was not offended, just disgusted and in fact the only high light of the whole rancid event was the way Sheila and her team put a stop to it, so their estimate has gone up even more in my eyes.*"

"*What eyes!*"

"*You know what I mean, you cow!*"

CHAPTER 58

On the fragment

"Look! There!" Shaw pointed to a tiny ripple in the aggregated sand, a small fountain erupting and curving away into space, even as he spoke.

"Zardooz is being very cautious as he breaks through the surface," Said Fuller. "I'll bet that he is crying inside about even this small disturbance that reveals his intentions."

The bore head of the RABI slowly revealed itself until the exit hole was about a foot in diameter. The plume of debris was a sure giveaway, but Zardooz had not anticipated that issue. All he could see was his schematic of the node area based upon the last known surface conditions and the sensory feedback from the RABI telling him that the foremost bore heads were clear of rock.

He withdrew the RABI back down the bore hole and hoped that the surfacing of the RABI had not been noticed by the Americans.

The repair bot was ready to go, but it had an extra little surprise as its first job. Zardooz had loaded a small anti personnel grenade in the bot's manipulator arm and positioned it ahead, arms up, so a flick of the bot's articulated joint would toss the grenade ahead, out of the hole. Just in case.

Fuller and Shaw had not been sitting by idle. Fuller was anticipating that Zardooz would do something violent to ensure the node area was clear. The hole was distant enough from the node that whatever Zardooz would come up with would not further damage the observation post. Fuller did not want to scare Zardooz back down the hole. He wanted the bot and the node replacement it carried.

The pair took the cover of the nano fiber case they had put over the obs post and wedged it down next to the new bore hole. Two cables were attached to the corners and now the pair moved well away from the hole and waited, ready to drag the cover over the hole to prevent the bot from escaping. They lay prone behind rocky outcrops as protection from whatever Zardooz may throw at them.

"Shaw, head down. He may do a recce first or just blast away blind. I'm betting a scope first, otherwise he might damage his obs post. Look for any tiny movement around the edge of the hole. If you see it, pull back into cover."

"He may see the cover on the obs post, sir. And possibly the trap over the hole, even though we put sand on it with static charge. The mono filament cables blend right in, but there are enough tell tales to warn him."

"Doesn't matter, we're committed and he has to make a move or remain blind... There! Head down!" Fuller commanded.

They both ducked behind their cover rocks as a tendril of fiber optic slid over the rim and peered around like a curious caterpillar. First it looked away from the obs post, then made its way around the rim of the hole. It actually slid over the disguised cover and Zardooz missed the textural change. He wasn't concentrating inches or feet in front. He was looking for the enemy. He ran the full circle and then the tendril stopped moving as he saw the cover over the obs post. They were there. Where? Where?

The tendril started around again more slowly. There! He saw scuff marks in the sand aggregate leading towards a large rock outcrop. "Got you!" he said to himself.

There was no gravity to return a lobbed grenade to the surface, so he had to calculate the detonation delay and angle of projection to take the grenade past and over the back of the rock before it showered its deadly shrapnel in all directions. The bot would make short work of the cover on the obs post, but now he thanked his enemies for protecting it from the shrapnel. The node was already damaged and it didn't matter if he damaged it further in ridding himself of some Americans. He prayed that the US President was behind the rock.

Calculations completed, he instructed the bot and trained the tendril on the outcrop. The bot flicked the grenade in precisely the correct direction. In slow motion the grenade travelled across the terrain until it exploded in a blinding, soundless flash beyond the outcrop, causing a huge dust cloud and ricocheting shrapnel to jettison off into space. He looked for evidence of shredded bodies but could discern nothing. He was committed now and started the bot out of the hole, activating two other cameras on its carapace as it emerged.

Behind two other outcrops perpendicular to the false trail Fuller had put down, the pair hauled on their cables and covered the hole. The bot appeared to swivel frantically, looking for the source of the threat, but not transmitting to Zardooz the reality of the entrapment.

It rolled about trying to get back to the hole which was now solidly blocked. Zardooz watched the three views, scanning between them. He saw the exposed cables that had flicked up dust trails and the two outcrops where Fuller and Shaw were concealed. He had no more weapons to deploy, just the bot's tool set, which could be used defensively at close range. He had to get the Americans close in. Then he would slice them with the welder.

While he kept his enemies occupied he would bring the RABI back up to cut through whatever covered the hole and then recover the bot as well. He commanded the bot to back up to the node and replace the camera as intended, all the while surveilling for any threat from the Americans.

The bot raised its cutting arm to slice away the container cover that Fuller and Shaw had dropped over the obs post. The carbon nano fibre was designed to resist the most extreme conditions imaginable. The Iranian regime had not seen anything like it and the little bot's cutting torch was no match for the impermeable covering. The patch heated white hot but retained its integrity. In fact the structure of the covered post was being damaged by the intense heat and Zardooz was losing his cool in frustration. Instead of stopping and backing off, he continued attempting to cut through and ignored the fuel warning for the repair bot's torch. Designed for small jobs, it flamed out and left the bot defenseless.

Fuller was hoping and watching for this. "Move now!" He yelled in his comms to Shaw. They jetted up and swept across to the bot, maintaining constant altitude despite the fragment's spin. They immobilized the bot with a cargo net Fuller had brought along for the purpose, all the while Zardooz trying to make the machine run away, an impossible task under zero gravity.

"Gotcha!" said Fuller. The pair put down anchor pitons and cables then turned off their suit thrusters. The bot was popping out all sorts of tools trying to cut free from the net. A few strands started to part as an exceptionally hard bladed cutter was deployed.

"Oh no you don't!" exclaimed Shaw as he whipped a piton weighted cable around in an arc to connect with the bot's articulated arm behind the net. Like wrestling a lion and avoiding the sharp cutting claw, Shaw held the netting to the arm as he wound the piton cable round and round. Now trapped by the net and the grounding cables, the bot was going nowhere and its cutting arm was trapped.

Fuller picked up the tendril camera and pressed it to his helmet for sound conduction.

"Zardooz! Give it up! We cannot be fighting any more. There is nothing left to fight over. There is no one left to fight! Join us and live!"

On the bot a small cover slid up revealing a view screen. Zardooz looked out at Fuller from the screen. Words started to appear. Zardooz typed, "I can hear you. You cannot hear me. You know I am here so there is no point in my hiding the fact. As far as I and all the people down here with me are concerned, the war will never be over, even if it is just one of us and one of you. The Great Satan will be destroyed and Allah will bring back all the faithful. Leave this place or I will destroy your vessel and you with it. I will detonate our last nuclear device and become a martyr for the sake of Allah. You have one hour to leave."

Fuller and Shaw looked at each other astonished. This fanatic was going to blow everyone to bits when there was nothing left? Fuller called up Zardooz's profile on his suit screen and quickly looked it over again. There was nothing that indicated suicidal tendencies and to the contrary, Zardooz exhibited an uncanny knack for staying alive in a dangerous environment and a tendency towards corruption and the gathering wealth and luxury. This was a bluff. It had to be. He was betting their lives on it.

CHAPTER 59

Aboard Sheila's shuttle.

Sheila concluded her explanation to the assembled passengers who were looking somewhat shamefaced in the main. "… and that will give us several months of survival time aboard this ship while we look for a more permanent solution. Questions?"

"You have made some huge assumptions in your plan. What if you are wrong?" A small woman from the Space City maintenance team asked.

"Then we are just as dead then as we would be by doing nothing now."

The woman screwed up her mouth and then admitted, "I guess you have a point there."

"Every one either strap in or take the position I assigned you. We get one shot at this."

Sheila buckled into the pilot's seat and looked over the controls. There was just a minute amount of reaction mass left in the main tank. Then there was a small auxiliary tank, like the last emergency gallon in an old internal combustion car, that had been overlooked because it had never been called upon in all the decades of space travel.

Fortunately the shuttle was facing the right direction for the attempt and there would be nothing wasted on thruster adjustment. She was going to move in close to the anti-matter coated fleet. All the particulate anti-matter had now been coalesced by the fleet or attracted by the gravity of the moon. The fragments were long gone past as had the flailing Skyhook remains, so they were safe as long as they kept some distance from the fleet.

She was going to take her time over the approach, using the little remaining in the main tank to decelerate relative to the fleet until it ran out. She had calculated that the auxiliary tank would be sufficient to complete the stop and the remainder would be used for a very slow approach back to the fleet, with enough mass left to stop them relative at about one kilometer distance.

This journey was going to take them some days, so during that time they were going to find a way to get past the anti-matter coating on the ships. With no comms from the fleet she had no idea if they were trapped inside alive or all dead.

Getting past the anti-matter. Now *THAT* was the rub!

It was four days into the plan. Sheila sat with a group of scientists and engineers as they analyzed the problem from the beginning and evaluated the properties of anti-matter. If one had to be stranded in space and facing such a problem, there was no better brains trust than these multi-discipline trained Space City scientists. They all had mundane daily tasks to perform on the city, like assistant cook, but they were all Doctorate level qualified professionals in at least one or more mathematical, science or engineering areas.

Even the big troublemaker had relented and apologized to Sheila. He was out of the diaper and back in youniform with his buddy and all his friends had followed suit. It was he who launched the conversation.

"I had some contact with the people who built the AMD. There was discussion about an instability in the matter-anti-matter self annihilation equations. They found a small factor that would not balance. The guys I was drinking with were worried about it and as I was cleared for Space City and we were looking at alternative power for the City using MAM as an energy source, they asked me to go over their calcs against our Space City math." He paused for a squirt of water. "Our process was fully internal and totally controlled, I guess you would compare it to a nuclear reactor of old times. We could theoretically control the process inside a magnetic bottle. Their idea for the AMD was simply crude. Throw anti-matter at matter and duck, so yes, there was an imbalance in their calculations. That error caused, for want of a better analogy, the equivalent of a nuclear meltdown that consumed everything in its path. That's where the analogy stops.

My recommendation to them was to stop and go back to square one." He shrugged his huge shoulders. "I guess they didn't take my advice."

"Thank you Graham," Sheila gave him a warm smile. "Is there any insight you have that could head us towards a solution?"

"People, I kinda let go when the shit hit the fan and for that I apologize. I guess I am carrying a load of guilt that I didn't stop them, but I never believed they would build an AMD let alone use it. I got sauced and lost it badly, so keep the booze away from me. That said, our research actually reached a practical test at particle level. We successfully collided one atom of positive matter gold with one of antimatter. The resultant energy release was contained in a powerful magnetic bottle effect using the almost absolute zero of space to cool the superconductor windings, also of pure gold, of the field generators. That collision delivered enough energy to power New York city for a week and then some.

What we did discover however, that may be useful here, is the behaviour of anti-matter when in contact with noble metals, such as gold, compared with its destructive effect on minerals and lower metals. The astonishing result of our experiment was that the collision did not destroy the two atoms. They reversed themselves and we still had two particles AND all that energy. The anti-matter became positive matter and vice-versa. We could not explain the phenomenon. When we introduced a pure gold surface to the inverted anti-matter atom it behaved like a ferrous magnet and was repelled away, even though one would think the opposites would attract."

Sheila was thinking intensely and blurted out, "But we could use that here." She tapped a stylus on her pad as she synthesized the boolean logic patterns that could tame the anti-matter. "If we can reproduce on a larger scale what Graham has described, then not only can we penetrate the anti-matter and survive, but we could power our systems for all eternity with the energy released."

"We need to understand what is happening first. This phenomenon is possibly the imbalance in the first set of equations. They never saw our results or had a practical test. We could make things worse."

"I think we have concluded that we couldn't be in a bigger mess in all creation." chided Sheila, "But we have a little time in hand.

Let's insert these variables and do the math again."

The group were heads down over a dimage of a cylindrical shape large enough to hold a second cylinder that itself could hold one man.

Once they had adjusted the equations by allowing an illegal mass retention factor that flew in the face of all known physics, the equations balanced. With working math loaded into the ship's small computer, Sheila had run a synthesis on one more important unknown that was critical to their success. The question was the interactive behaviour of the inverted anti-matter when placed in contact with first generation anti-matter. She ran the calculations three times, changing variables as they might change in reality. The invert anti-matter would interact with regular anti-matter like the real world of positive matter. It would be "normal" to its counterpart. The attempt could proceed.

First task was to make the two cylinders out of pure gold. Fortunately for Sheila and her group, gold foil was the main component of solar reflectors that gathered the light of the sun for energy. There was no shortage of these aboard and on the skin of the shuttle. Sheila went EVA with one of her team and stripped two of the panels from the outside of the ship. The panels were too large to fit through the air lock so she stripped out the gold foil and let the framework drift away with a gentle shove.

"Littering!" she laughed.

The engineers constructed the two cylinders out of the thin foil. They reinforced the flimsy shells by rolling excess foil into more substantial wire and fusing it solid with laser torches. They made the wire into circular hoops that fitted snugly into the outer cylinder to hold its shape. There was no question of welding it in as the foil was too thin to take the risk. Finally, they had two solid looking cylinders that would collapse at the slightest bump.

Sheila and the now very helpful Graham shifted the cylinders outside the shuttle and tethered the smaller one. The pair took the larger cylinder and jetted slowly toward the fleet, shiny with anti-matter coating one thousand meters away. They would launch the cylinder towards the nearest ship at very low relative velocity. Upon collision with the ship the gold cylinder should, in theory turn into anti-matter gold and stay attached to the ship. The anti-matter gold effect should be, in theory, a surface effect that would not enter the open end of the cylinder, contrary to the behaviour with mineral and base metal contact. In this respect the anti-matter behaved like a traditional electric charge when in contact with noble metals.

Once in place, Shelia was going to climb in to the smaller cylinder and be launched into the mouth of the larger cylinder. In theory, that's three "in theories", the regular gold cylinder should hold exactly in the center of the outer cylinder by the repulsion effect of the outer layer which was more like a non ferrous magnetic effect than an electric charge. The whole thing was full of contradictions but the equations worked. Once inside the larger cylinder, Sheila would be able to use a laser torch from a central point on the cylinder end and burn through into the air lock of the ship where they had placed the cylinders. She hoped not to kill anyone still alive on board.

In theory, the anti-matter should flow around the outside of the cylinders and the hole as the welder cut through. In theory the connecting hole should form an inner tube of regular gold, and outer tube of anti-matter gold repelling the inner tube and it should all penetrate the titanium skin of the vessel air lock which should (in theory of course) flow around the outer anti-matter gold as it flowed with the cut.

Sheila climbed into the cylinder carrying the cutting torch and other assorted tools that were anticipated to be useful. The cylinder hoops had loops and hooks formed on them to carry the gear and give Sheila hand holds. Behind her trailed an antenna wire for comms. Signals would not get out of the gold casing and certainly not out of the vessel if she was able to make entrance.

Graham and Martin were her support team and would be sliding the cylinder into the large one. The group had tried to get Sheila to step down and allow one of the other small women to make the attempt. They did not want to lose her leadership if things went wrong, but she was adamant that she would do this job. If things did go wrong, then they wouldn't need her anyway. They would need to pray.

The pair jetted out with Sheila in the cylinder towards the large cylinder which had just made contact. They saw a blue, electric haze engulf the outer cylinder as it touched the anti-matter. The light flared then died down, until only the faintest glow could be perceived against a shadowy, dark backdrop.

They stopped a few meters from the silver covered ship with its gold protrusion and waited a few minutes longer to see if the effects on the main cylinder would change, but everything remained static.

Sheila keyed her comms, "Let's do it!"

"Where did the energy burst go?" asked Martin.

"I think its still there." Replied Graham. "What we just saw I do believe is a reciprocating equilibrium between mass and energy. The contact and conversion released the initial burst which had nowhere to go. The energy level could not be sustained so it dropped back to mass which was our first anti-matter transformation. Some of the energy was released again and the process repeated itself. Now it appears to be in equilibrium and that explains what happened with the atomic level. It was just too small and fast for us to see what was happening."

"So is this good for us now?" asked Martin. "Is Sheila safe to proceed?"

"In theory, yes."

"Enough of this "in theory" bullshit." Get me moving before I change my mind." Sheila was up tight.

As Martin and Graham moved Sheila into position in front of the main cylinder, the electric charge expanded across the gap and engulfed the group without any apparent harm apart from tingling on the skin. The men gave Sheila's cylinder a careful shove and it slid straight into the main cylinder. Before it could rebound out, Sheila gave a slight burst of her thrusters and stopped it dead in position. She darkened her youniform face plate and readied the laser welder.

"Here goes nothing!" she called out.

She applied the laser focal tip to a mark on the cylinder drum head. It popped a hole immediately and the edges began to roll up and melt together. With the hole about one inch across she could see the outer cylinder held by repulsion just a quarter inch away. She slid a prepared tube of gold into the hole and with heart palpitating pushed it home against the foil of the outer cylinder which internally, was inactive.

In theory.

Nothing happened.

The tube sat jammed in against the repelling force, hard against the outer cylinder. Sheila carefully melted the protruding section of tube down to the inner cylinder face and allowed the molten gold to gently meld with the cylinder, forming a continuous pipe line to the outer surface. Then, holding her breath, she applied a very fine cutting focus to the center of the exposed circle. The molten gold of that surface should flow back to the titanium ship skin and form a seal against it with the reactive anti-matter only on the outside.

In theory.

The pinhole grew to the size of a dime and she could see the change in color of the metal beneath. Nothing nasty crawled into the hole and she breathed out in a sigh of relief.

"So far so good guys!" she reported back as she took a moment to steady herself and let the adrenalin rush wear away. She need a very steady hand for the next step. "All that cookie making as assistant chef has paid off. I just cut a perfect cookie!" she quipped.

"What flavor?" came back Martin.

"Anti-pasta! What else?"

She heard the groan at her pun. "I'm ready to install the evacuation hose."

Because they had no idea if the air lock was pressurized or not, Graham had designed a contingency device that would vent atmosphere past the cylinders without blasting them away from the skin of the ship. He had taken a good length of carbon mono filament tubing normally used for refuelling and cemented an attachment collar to the end of it. The collar had inactive, foaming nano-glue applied to the end of the rim, ready for Sheila to activate once it was inserted into the hole, against the titanium.

A hole in the collar accommodated another laser cutting head preset to variable depth for the titanium skin at the known cutting rate. All Sheila had to do was place the tube, activate the glue, reattach the laser to the new head and program it to start cutting when the glue had cured. She did not have to remain in the cylinder for this exercise.

That done, she called to be extracted. The men carefully dragged her back out, watching that nothing got snagged on the way. The trio moved away from the vessel and the exhaust tube which was likely to flail about if there was any air discharge.

There was a wait of about five minutes as the glue set, then they saw the laser glow from the carbon fiber join of the exhaust tube reflecting off the gold cylinder walls in an eerie light show. Graham was watching his counter for the breakthrough.

The cutting went on for a few minutes. No paper thin gold foil this time. This was Space Rated titanium alloy.

"It should be through by now." Graham said as they watched the end of the hose for evidence of air jetting out. The hose remained still and the light show winked out, setting the cylinders into deep, black shadow.

Martin moved in to the hose cautiously, expecting it to wake up and start flicking around like a demented cat's tail, but he reached it and it didn't move. He put a charge and leak probe near the tube without actually touching it. The small device, usually used for locating micro cracks in a ship's skin by detecting ionized particles, remained silent and green lit.

He put the probe away and took a coiled tendril camera from his pack. They had cannibalized it from the shuttle where it ran from the passenger section back to the control cabin and had opted to keep the fine metal coiled conduit around the mono filament optic fiber. That made it all the more bulky, but gave it the rigidity they required.

Martin started to slide the tendril down the exhaust tube. They were going to have a look inside the vessel they had penetrated.

The tendril camera went as far as Martin could push it. The trio floated heads together around the small view screen as the micro light in the camera head revealed a view of the inside of the air lock, that became clear as Martin drew the camera head away from the wall that had stopped it.

"There's the view port!" said Sheila excitedly. Look, there's light coming through!"

Martin manipulated the camera head so it curled towards the view port which was oriented to look straight down the axis of this ship. He pushed the tendril carefully forward as he adjusted direction, until the camera looked straight down the ship.

"Ooh!" gasped Shelia in dismay. "It's empty!"

"See! I told you not to pull the fleet people into stasis so quickly. Now the cat is really out of the bag, Peepers!"

"Look, Howley, I made a perfectly good and rational decision at the time. All the science pointed to the fleet being non-recoverable and essentially dead. The audience wouldn't stand for a hundred boring deaths by starvation, asphyxiation and natural causes. They had enough of acts like that for the past five thousand years..."

"The audience can't stand for anything, Peepers, they don't have any legs to stand on! Ha ha ha. Oh I'm so funny! No legs to stand on... Get it?"

"Howley, I would puke if I had the ability to do so. Your comedy is without humor. How did you ever make it as a comedi-brain?"

"No need to get personal, Charonelle!"

"She wasn't getting personal Howley. She was just being truthful! You suck as a comedi-brain. You are not funny!"

"Well, screw the two of you!"

Charonelle laughed, "Now THAT was funny!"

"Huh? What?" asked a confused Peepers.

"Imagine two brains screwing, Peepers! That's funny!"

"Yech! That is gross and slimy."

"Hmph! Wasn't supposed to be funny," Mumbled Howley. "But now that it is funny," his voice lit up, "can we get on with this act?"

"We are down to three acts left in the finals." Announced Peepers. "It looks like the Fuller Zardooz acts are going to either be vaporized by Zardooz with his supposed nuclear weapon, or they will get through somehow and meet up with Sheila's group.

As Sheila's act had interference from us by removing the fleet crews into stasis, I think it only fair that we balance the advantage by helping the other two acts in some way. What do you suggest, Charonelle?"

"Oh, Peepers! What can I say! There's only one thing that makes any sense..."

CHAPTER 60

On the fragment.

Fuller and Shaw hunkered down next to the little bot, watching the screen. Zardooz had taken a portable head wear camera and appeared to be transmitting everything he did. Right now he was standing in front of something that looked awfully nasty and was possibly a nuclear device. They saw a pair of hands open a compartment on the front of the device and key in a sequence of numbers. A timer started counting down from sixty. The sixty minutes Zardooz had given as his ultimatum. The image backed away from the device and they could see a work bench behind it. Fuller leaned forward and peered at the tiny screen. A smile creased his mouth.

Shaw was showing his uncertainty about the whole situation and asked,"How can you be so sure Zardooz is bluffing?"

Fuller looked up at Shaw and answered, "I'll explain after its all over."

"But..."

"If I'm wrong, it won't matter any way."

Shaw shook his head and resigned himself to faith in Fuller's assessment. They both went back to staring at the screen. The picture reverted back to Zardooz face on at his desk. "You are still there Americans? You are very foolish. You will be the cause of the destruction of all of us by your insistence on staying here. Be it on your heads. I will let you watch the count down, but you must direct the repair bot camera towards your ship. If I see it take off I will stop the detonation. Otherwise, enjoy your last minutes in this life."

"Shaw look at Zardooz's desk."

Before the image flicked over Shaw examined the screen closely, then it changed to the device with the work bench behind it.

"Now look carefully."

Shaw looked intensely at the screen with a frown behind his faceplate. Suddenly he let out "Oh shit! Now I see it!" With a huge grin replacing the frown. He looked up at Fuller who had a small smile curled on his lips. "Its a recording. A fake."

"Yes, and how do we know this?"

"The wrench sitting on the workbench at the back. It couldn't possibly sit there under these spin conditions, not unless Zardooz has glued it in place, and he wouldn't do that because he wants us to think it is real and leave. That's why his desk was empty. Nothing would stay put on it."

"Ergo..."

"He's bluffing! Phew, for a while there I thought you were gambling with our lives. You saw it straight away."

"Yes I did, but this does not mean that he does NOT have some sort of destructive device or self destruct system throughout the complex beneath us. But you know something..."

"What?"

"Two can play the same game. He want's to see our transport lift off, so let's give it to him."

"That means untethering and a lot of work. What's the point?"

"Has Zardooz seen our transport yet?"

"No."

"Then how will he know what he is looking at?"

"We have another transport available?"

"Sort of. We better get back to the ship and set it up. Leave the bot tied up here for now and slip a packing case cover over it. Keep Zardooz blind."

The pair jetted back to the transport, basically a small hop upwards and wait for the transport to rotate under them, then down again. Once inside, Fuller pulled up a full graphic of a transport. Not a wire frame, but a completely detailed representation that looked entirely real, except it was only twelve inches long. He then took the surface imagery and imposed the ship dimage onto it and ever so slightly in to the surface. Simulating the view that a tendril camera might capture, he launched the dimage ship which rapidly grew in size and appeared to fly overhead and then out of sight synthesized by the axial spin of the fragment.

Knowing that Zardooz would not take the launch at face value, Fuller continued the simulation for two more spins of the fragment until the dimage transport was lost in the blackness of space. He then had the computer add some particulate matter to the launch, creating a small dust storm that blasted out in all directions, clouded the view for the first critical moments and the dispersed into space like the spiral arm of a galaxy. The dimage movie then looped an empty fixed landscape with the stars rotating in time with the fragment. Exactly what Zardooz would expect to see.

The final touch was to add drifting tether ropes that had just been released. Fuller ran the complete clip, looking for any obvious errors. Finding none, he called the group together and ran if for them without explanation.

"Any errors?" he asked when the final loop cut in.

There was no comment from the group until Shaw asked, "How do we get that piped to Zardooz so he thinks it's real?"

"Oh, a little robot is going to help us." replied Fuller.

Fuller and Shaw were back with the repair bot. It didn't move and it appeared that Zardooz had given up on thrashing the tendril camera about under the cover. It was the only part of the robot that could still move, that had not been disabled by the pair earlier. Fuller pointed to one of the pitons that had been used to secure the cover over the robot.

Shaw knelt, secured by the tether ropes left earlier. He placed a pilot helmet in front of the piton with the heads up view screen facing the selected spot. He activated the image generator and had the starting loop running, with the transport sitting on the surface, apparently held in place by thruster control with discarded tether ropes drifting about, now only attached at one end. The scene was set for Zardooz.

Fuller took out a small, very sharp, pointed cutting tool and secured himself next to the selected piton. Just above the head of the piton, where it rubbed against the fabric of the cover, he worked the tip in between the weave of the carbon fibers, pushing them apart until a tiny hole appeared. He forced the lower fibers under the edge of the piton head, gave a quick upward shove on the opposing fibers and withdrew the blade. There was now a tiny hole that appeared to have been made by the rotational forces working the cover against the piton head. Too small for the tendril camera to get through, but large enough to get a view of the helmet scene. Except that to the camera the scene looked entirely real, if not somewhat distorted by the tiny hole it had to look through.

Fuller inserted a single thread of carbon fiber into the hole, as if the piton had managed to cut one, however unlikely that may be. This was the weakest part of the plan, but necessary to show when Zardooz found the hole. The thread would move and also occlude the view, forcing Zardooz to use the tendril head to hold the thread down, preventing him from extensive angling through the hole.

They settled back to wait again, certain that Zardooz would not blow himself to smithereens without one more attempt to see outside. They did not have a long wait.

Fuller was looking away at the real transport when Shaw tapped his shoulder, pointing to the thread which was jiggling madly. After a few gyrations and waves, the thread settled down to a slow movement as Zardooz tried to massage it out of the way. He used the tendril to roll the thread so that its natural curve tended down, out of the view, and then locked it into place with the camera head, exactly as Fuller had intended.

Shaw gave Fuller a look of admiration as Fuller said, "Give him another thirty seconds and then start the launch sequence." Fuller looked at his countdown timer. It was fifty minutes since Zardooz had given his ultimatum. Enough time elapsed for "launch preparation" and sufficient time left to show "fear" of the ultimatum.

Shaw waited the few seconds then keyed the remote control, setting the second seamless scene into motion. The image showed the retaining thrusters shut off and the lateral thrusters below activate, blowing away some debris. In a few seconds the transport appeared to fly towards the camera until it completely obscured all vision, then it abruptly vanished from view directly overhead.

They saw the thread move as Zardooz tried to watch the transport fly over. After a few twitches it settled back to the stable position as Zardooz waited for the next rotation. "Oh so predictable," thought Fuller.

The rotational sequence only took forty five seconds and went through five cycles, the transport image dwindling away each time until by the sixth time, the thread dropped as Zardooz turned off the tendril to conserve the bot's limited power.

"What now?" Shaw asked Fuller.

"My only concern is that he may use the bore hole to send another bot, if he has one, or possibly cut through in another location and all of that does not take away the possibility that he does have a self destructive device down there. We need to go on the offensive and neutralize him as quickly as possible, before we consider taking off for Alpha Centurai. Let's get back to the ship and see what we can do."

CHAPTER 61

In the transport.

In the cabin, Fuller and Carver pored over the cargo manifest looking for something that could be used as a weapon to stop Zardooz. "I would prefer to use non-lethal methods," remarked Fuller, "but if all we have is lethal, then so be it."

"Look!" Janine pointed to a line in the list. "What's that?"

It was a listing in the medical re-supply section. A drug called Medalizam.

Janine queried the computer for more detail and it came up with a short description followed by detailed pharmacology. They read the brief description together and Fuller underlined the key attributes and possible delivery methods.

It was a development of the old amnesia inducing drug Midazolam but with added enhancements. The short term memory, permanent amnesia effect was still the principal focus, however the current version was also an effective anaesthetic and anti-depressant agent. It had the added benefit that it could be used to induce coma long term without side effects.

"It says that the drug can be delivered by ingestion, intravenously, inhalation or by skin absorption. The effects are directly proportional to the dosage applied and all methods are equally effective in the end result, but vary in the time to take effect." read Janine.

"It is kind of perfect for what we want to achieve. I don't want to kill the bastard as unfortunately, we may need his genes in the future for the sake of human survival. Question is how to deliver a decisive dose." Fuller ran his finger down the dimage page. "How do we push the amnesia effect to the maximum. Aha, there it is." His finger stopped and they put their heads together and read.

"We need to see the layout of the complex." said Tom. "I may have been President, but before that I was a Marine and I know a little about strategy, and strategy is all about how good your intelligence information is."

They looked at the schematic based on the entrance tunnel and the vents. There wasn't much to go on.

"Would the repair bot have the complex layout in its on board memory?" asked Felicity. "If something broke down it would have to be able to act independently to some extent."

"Felicity! That is brilliant thinking!" congratulated Fuller. "Shaw, we know the bot model. Get everything you can on it from the computer. Our little friend is going to help us again." Fuller looked at his watch. "By the way, he didn't blow us up." he said with a grin.

A few minutes later Shaw came back to the meeting and pulled up a dimage of the repair bot model. "It is a standard NASA repair bot from about eight years ago. They were replaced by a bio mechanical model based on the same principle as our youniforms. This fellow was in service for about twelve years.

He runs on a fuel cell pack that gives him around forty eight hours of average use, say moving about and doing small repairs. If he is pushed to extremes with heavy work and space activity he drops to about twenty hours. He has a Level two artificial intelligence module and is capable of making simple survival decisions and routine repairs without human intervention. He communicates with his base via multi frequency radio or direct conduction vibration such as audio or surface contact."

"What is his G-mass?" asked Fuller.

"On Earth he would have weighed eighty kilograms, about one seventy five pounds."

"More detail on his radio comms please."

Shaw skimmed the file until he found what Fuller wanted. "Without atmospheric bounce or satellite relay he is line of sight like our suit comms."

"So how is Zardooz communicating with it now?" wondered Tom.

Fuller pointed at the vent mounds and the obs points. "Maybe relayed through antennae in those things. but he wouldn't have known if they were working or not, so one assumes conduction." replied Fuller.

"Our camera view of him has to be by radio transmission. Conduction couldn't carry the data stream in real time for images. Sound yes, moving pictures, no." countered Shaw.

"You're right!" said Fuller. "Where is his antenna? Its not the vent mounds or the obs stations. We would have picked that up. Has to be something the bot brought out of the tunnel. Maybe dropped a surface wire that we missed. We better go look."

"What happens when we find it?"

"Mr Shaw, you may have the pleasure of snipping off well below surface level."

"But Zardooz will know its us!" said Shaw.

"No he won't because we are going to give him a meteorite shower show on the tendril camera and bounce a few rocks off the bot before we snip the antenna. Then we will bounce some large rocks near the bot to give his conduction comms something to chew on, and then..."

Fuller, Tom, Felicity and Shaw had carefully made their way over to the bot. They avoided radio comms in case Zardooz was scanning. Shaw waved his hand and picked up a fine wire that draped over the edge of the bore hole and lay in the direction of the bot. He scouted around and made sure it was the only one.

Fuller started a new image sequence in the pilot helmet that still lay in front of the hole in the cover. Now every so often there was a flash and puff of debris as the fragment ran into space debris. Fuller signalled Tom and Felicity to start throwing small rock chips at the bot. Not an easy task as they had to gouge up the rocks and compensate for the fragment spin. Still some of the pieces hit and the vibration alerted Zardooz. The little thread changed position as the camera came back to the hole.

Fuller picked up a large rock he had dug out and smashed it into the surface near the bot. Then another, this time closer and showering the bot with particles. The next one was a direct hit, shaking the bot enough to cause the tendril to lose its position. Fuller signalled Shaw to cut and grabbed the bot in a bear hug and lifted it.

Botnapped! Zardooz was deaf and blind, thinking a meteorite had blown the bot off the surface. But more important, Fuller had the bot and could download its data.

The others came over and released the pitons holding the bot cover down. Fuller had a few inches of free play to keep the bot off the surface. It needed solid contact for conduction. Fuller's body did not fit the bill.

Together with Shaw's thrusters and the other two guiding, they drifted their prize back to the ship and inside, where they set it down on a bed of foam seat cushions.

Shaw brought up a schematic dimage and located the memory module, which he removed and handed to Fuller. Then he turned off the bot's power and it almost slumped like something dead as lights went out. Fuller headed for the control cabin where he could plug the memory module into the ship's computer.

CHAPTER 62

In the Iranian complex.

Zardooz wasn't taking things at face value. He knew he was facing his nemesis, the Great Satan, the very President of the United States himself. No, nothing would be as it appeared, but he was very confused. The bodies of the women had vanished; could the Americans have done that? But they would have had to enter the complex. No, something else was at play here. Did the Americans really leave?

He might have been a corrupt official of an evil regime, but that was the normal for Zardooz. Even within the criminality of his way of life, he was still faithful to his country's interpretation of the words of the Prophet. He should martyr himself before he could fall into the hands of the unbelievers and take them with him, but if they had left, really left, then it would be a pointless ending and of no service to Allah.

He had to get eyes on the surface somehow and make sure they were gone. He did not have another repair bot and the RABI was only good for boring. There were no space rated suits in the complex as this had never been anticipated.

He sat, slumped in front of the computer and then suddenly straightened in the restraints. He brought up the complex stores manifest and started scanning it, running down the list which was written in Farsi. There was no generic term in Farsi for "Space Suit" but they did have a need for deep water pressure suits when building the complex. What would they be called in Farsi?

He scrolled down, looking for a clue and stopped, finger on a line. "Paragon Diving System" was transliterated into Farsi. Now, was the diving gear actually in the complex and would it work for the vacuum of space? He located the listed storage bay and compartment on the schematic and saw that it was on the periphery of the complex. There were basic security cameras scattered about the area, but nothing directly in sight of the storage bay, so he had no idea if the area was safely pressurized or open to the vacuum of space. The nearest camera showed a dimly lit corridor heading towards the storage area, but that did not mean there was breathable atmosphere down there. The fact was, the diving suit was there because of the deep fissures and caverns that riddled the strata below the site. This maze was probably exposed to space and the storage area was the deepest point in the complex and directly above the caverns.

Zardooz scratched his head in thought as it hit him. Maybe if the storage bay was intact and he could get to the suit, the caverns might give him a way out that would surprise the Americans. A back door! He called for any information about the caverns and was rewarded with a new schematic. They had been explored and recorded with the intent to store nuclear weapons outside the actual complex. This was shown to be impractical as the water table for the entire region was the source of the flooding in the caverns, so one small radioactive leak could have killed the whole population. It was deemed that this was not martyrdom to die in such a way, just sheer stupidity. The caverns were left to themselves.

He looked carefully at the map. As he had no idea where the system was open to space, he would have to explore until he found a way out, or he could try the RABI once he had some idea of the remaining depth of the fragment. Nevertheless, his first job was to secure the diving suit and rig it for a space walk.

He leaned back in the chair and stared at the red self destruct button that would blow the complex to molecules. There were enough demolition charges placed around to vaporize everything. It was his final option, the question being whether he should do it now when he surely could, or do the exploration and risk being captured or stopped by the Americans.

No, he would wait. He really didn't feel much like being a martyr. That was Arjmand's job. He, Zardooz, wanted to live and experience whatever was happening, however strange and however contrary to the will of the prophet. He had always been a rebel deep down.

He got up to go check on Arjmand who was calling from his room. As he drifted towards the doorway, he could see Arjmand moving his limbs about, the leg in the cast immobilized against

---

the bed frame. "Zardooz! Zardooz!" came the weak cry. "Where are you?"

"Here Arjmand. What's the problem?"

"I want to get up."

"You'll hurt yourself."

"No I won't. My leg is in a cast and we are weightless. I want to get up."

Zardooz thought about it for a minute and decided to let Arjmand up. He released the straps holding the cast and moved away as Arjmand gingerly pushed away from the bed. The spinning forces of the fragment drifted him against the wall, which was "down" in this part of the fragment. Arjmand was still groggy from the doses of painkillers Zardooz had administered, but he was able to pull himself along the wall towards the doorway.

"Where are you going?" asked Zardooz.

"To the bathroom."

"It doesn't work anymore. The toilets are all on the ceiling. You have to use a pot with this artificial gravity effect."

"Oooh! Get me something! Quick!"

Zardooz grabbed the pot he had been using for Arjmand while he was out and handed it across to him. "Good luck!" He said and went back to the control room. He strapped in and brought up the inventory list again, scanning for useful items and other obscure entries like that of the diving suit. He was specifically looking for weapons that could be used against the Americans or laid down as anti personnel traps.

He saw a listing for hand grenades that he marked, and another for small arms and ammunition, the Iranian made Satan Stopper nine millimeter pistol, as well as the hundred year old Kalashnikov rifle copies. There were no modern Taser electric shock weapons nor any of the recently developed particle guns that used nano technology. He wondered what the Americans had at their disposal as he consolidated the location information and ordered the server system to deliver all the arms to the same room that the RABI had been sent.

The server system did not reach the diving suit storage which was essentially a dump for useless items. I was easier to leave stuff there than haul it back to the surface, so the area had basic lighting, but that was it.

"Oaahh!" Arjmand moaned as he clumsily made his way in to the control room. He looked a mess, with a strapped up wrist and a leg in a cast, his face a deathly white pallor from the trauma and drugs, accentuated by the shadowed bags under his rheumy eyes. He awkwardly secured himself into a seat and put his head back, sighing in relief. "What is going on?" Was his simple question.

Zardooz looked up from his list and thought to himself, "What a wreck!" then said, "The Americans landed on our property and got into the access tunnel. I was using the RABI to bore through and place another camera at a surface node, but they were waiting for me. We spoke and I warned them to get off our land or I would martyr us and take them along for the ride. They think we have a nuclear device. It appears that they left, although I am not entirely convinced. If we must destroy them, our self destruct charges should be more than enough and we will take the Great Satan with us in our martyrdom."

Arjmand looked at Zardooz with horror written across his already ghastly features. He was, for once, speechless.

Zardooz continued, "I am going to do a recon of the surface using a deep water diving outfit that was left behind after construction. There are caves below this complex that may open out to what is now the surface away from the access tunnel. If the Americans are still here and it was a trick, then they will not expect anything from that side. I will take grenades, a pistol and several magazines of ammunition and blow them to pieces."

"And if they really are gone?"

"Then I will place as many cameras as I can carry over the surface wherever I am able to move. Because of the spin, I will need to use rock climbing gear for the most basic travel. I am not sure that I will be able to reach the American's last known position. It may be too far from the caves. I don't even know if the caves open to the outside."

"How long can you be in the diving suit?"

"It uses a re breather so air is no problem. Other bodily functions are maintained for up to six hours then you are on your own. I will go to the bathroom before I leave. Yes?" Zardooz raised an eye at Arjmand, wondering if the man saw the droll humor in his comment.

"Yes, yes. You should do that. What shall I do while you are away?"

"You will watch the monitors and listen to my instructions. If the Americans come back and you see that they are entering the complex, you will push that red button." Zardooz pointed to the self destruct button that was now without its safety cover. He had preset the release codes earlier and they would not automatically reset for another twenty hours. The button was live.

"What will it do?" asked Arjmand in a quavering voice. He half knew the answer.

"It will blow this rock of ours to dust and the Americans along with it."

"Bu-but it will blow us up too!"

"Of course! We will be martyrs for the sake of Allah!"

"Oh." Arjmand slumped into his chair, staring dejectedly at the red button. "That will be nice." he said insincerely.

Zardooz released and moved to the door. "Time to make this happen. I will trail a cable antenna as a guide through the caves and a way to talk with you. I am counting on you Arjmand." He finished grimly. Arjmand was still fixated on the red button.

"Arjmand!" screamed Zardooz and made him start, grimacing in pain as he jolted his arm. "Get with it!"

"Yes... yes." he flustered as the spasm wore off and he started to watch the monitors, occasionally glancing at the red button.

Zardooz went to the delivery room and examined the ordnance and weapons the supply system had delivered. He already had four camera modules which was about all he thought he could safely transport due to their individual bulk and shape. He hefted the pistol in its holster, slipped it out and checked the mechanism. It sounded perfect and looked perfect, so he slid a magazine into the handle and hefted it. It would do, especially in weightless conditions. He would need to compensate for the fragment spin and intended to test fire in the caves. He took four more magazines and looked at the Kalashnikov. The only advantage it gave was the weight of the round and its ballistic energy. It might be enough to penetrate the skin of a space transport that was designed to counter space debris. Or it might not. He took it with two magazines anyway. He really wanted it for its grenade launching capability.

Finally he looked at the box of twelve grenades that lay before him. These were multi launch, by hand or by the Kalashnikov. The box was too awkward to lug, so after ensuring that each explosive was on safe he popped them into an over shoulder carry bag.

Loaded for bear, he started to make his way to the storage unit where the dive suit waited.

CHAPTER 63

On board the transport.

Shaw had been analyzing the layout of the complex that the repair bot memory module had yielded. Fuller was looking at it from a military strategic angle. Shaw was using it to evaluate and compare the mass calculations for the fragment. Something still did not stack up in the math. Furthermore, Shaw had checked the rotational period of the fragment and found a further anomaly. The spin was ever so slightly slowing; not enough to be of any concern for at least the next fifty years, but it was slowing.

He did some further calculations which came close to verifying his hypothesis and then called a council meeting. The group assembled within minutes, Fuller also ready to present his plan of attack.

Fuller started, "Okay Councillor Shaw, you called the meeting so please start."

Shaw moved to the front of the group and activated a larger dimage of the fragment and the now fully revealed complex. "I have discovered some information that is both of concern and also of a very positive nature." He brought up some equations under the dimage.

"Because we need to know the mass of the fragment as accurately as possible for our future journey, I used the complex schematic to evaluate how much mass has been removed to form all the rooms and corridors and it is substantial. The mass removed still does not account for the estimated mass calculation that I did earlier based upon our rotational adjustments that were fairly accurate.

What this means is that there is a great deal more fragment mass missing or the material of the fragment is very light and spongy and we know first hand that this is not the case." He paused and drew a series of swirls and lines behind the complex representation at the back side of the fragment.

"The only conclusion I could draw from this is that there are more cavities, be they natural caves or excavations, that are not shown in the complex schematic or anywhere else in the bot memory for that matter. Therefore we may have a very different scenario for Councillor Fuller to consider from the military standpoint." There was a buzz among the councillors at this revelation. Shaw held up his hand for silence. "There is one more thing."

He drew in a solid area in the new lines and colored it blue. "The fragment spin is slowing down very minutely, at eight decimal places in the measurements. It is a definite pattern that fortunately will not affect us for decades, but the slowing force means something is causing this braking effect. My conclusion is one possibility. There must be a significant, coherent body of fluid somewhere inside the fragment and based on the rotational behavior it is towards the center.

I am trying to calculate the volume of liquid, and I am assuming fresh water would be logical for the complex reservoir, based on the braking effect of the fluid's coefficient of friction. It is a very difficult estimation without further data but that is not important right now. What is important to us is that there is a LOT of water in there and that means drinking, bathing, washing which are all recycled and when we need it, lost reaction mass."

Shaw sat down and Fuller took over. "Based on these new findings we clearly have to take the fragment, with or without Zardooz cooperating. Councillor Shaw's conclusions are sound and that means that Zardooz may have other exits from the complex if there is a cave or extended unmapped section that has been exposed by the fragmentation. We must examine the fragment surface scans once again now that we know we are looking for openings or signs of internal structure.

I am greatly concerned that Zardooz may be able to poke his head up from somewhere else and see that our lift off was a hoax. I do not believe he will blow up the fragment, but he may try to do damage to us and our transport. I am sure he has weapons in that complex."

"But he wouldn't have a space suit!" interjected Felicity.

There was silence for a moment as the group digested these ideas, then Shaw answered, "There is a large body of water in there, most likely with piping, valves and all sorts of other equipment that might need maintenance. There is a good chance that there is diving equipment of some type for that purpose, and we know that diving suits are not that far removed from space suits."

"I believe," continued Fuller, "that we must consider lifting the transport off and parking it nearby until this is resolved. If Zardooz does do something stupid we do not need to go down with him, and we certainly don't need to make it easy for him to attack us.

This is a fluid situation and may change instantly. We must be ready to react until we know that Zardooz is either contained or... dead."

"I will get ready to lift off." said Janine. "I think we should use explosive shears to cut the tether lines so we are all aboard. You can approach the fragment from the spin axis to get back on later. In fact I intend to park the transport in line with the axis. It makes us a difficult target for anyone not on the axis and we present our smallest profile to any threat."

"Tom, Gerald, Felicity. Take two shear charges each and fix them to the tethers at the ends. We may need the cables again later. Janine will detonate remotely when you are all back aboard."

The group dispersed to do their tasks.

"We are ready to go. Is everyone strapped in?" Janine asked across comms. "This is a tricky manoeuvre and probably a bit gut churning, but it will not last too long. Here we go!"

She hit the switch that blew the tether charges and immediately the transport began to slide against the direction of spin and drift away from the fragment, upside down as it was. Janine applied full thrusters to take it up so that the fragment edge would not swat the transport like a fly. They had some tangential motion already and the shove popped them over the fragment edge with room to spare. Now they were a space ship again and Janine manipulated the jets to bring the transport along side the fragment as she had explained.

Completely without artificial gravity or coriolis forces, the cadets took freedom in not having to be constantly strapped in while the council assembled to work out the next step in taking over the fragment from the Iranians.

CHAPTER 64

Inside the Complex.

Arjmand watched the monitors carefully, constantly glancing back at the self destruct button. He had a crazy urge to touch it, to flirt with danger and feel death through the tips of his fingers. He didn't want to do it, just feel it a little.

He worked his way out of his seat and across to the self destruct panel. He stood, holding himself in place as he stared at the doomsday button, the path to Allah and seventy two virgins.

As he daydreamed about the seventy two, the dead view screen from the surface node that Zardooz has attempted to recover suddenly flickered with snow and lines. A grainy image flashed on for an instant showing the American transport shooting jets and attempting to land. It drifted away and then the screen went blank again. Ejecta from the tether shear explosion had hit the node camera, that as damaged as it was, came on again for that instant as a broken contact connected from the impact and then broke apart again from another strike. But it was enough to excite Arjmand.

"Zardooz! Are you there!"

"Yes, what is it?" came back the tinny reply. Zardooz was in the dive suit and on the move.

"The Americans just landed. I saw it on the outside node camera."

"Impossible. That camera is dead!"

"No! I saw it. Just for a moment, it came on and then died again. I saw their ship landing."

"Fine. They will be there for me to destroy them. Do nothing Arjmand!"

"But you told me to hit the red button if they came back!"

"Do you really want to kill yourself Arjmand?" screamed Zardooz. "Are you so stupid? There are no virgins and there is no glory. It is all nonsense!"

Arjmand was stunned by the outburst from Zardooz. He believed in the Prophet and the seventy two virgins. Zardooz was an heretic. He could die along with them all and not get his bevy of virgins.

"I am pushing the button!"

"Don't be a fool. Think about a religion that rewards you through your penis. That is a physical sensation only for the living. What are any virgins doing in the next world? Not waiting for you. And when the seventy are no longer virgins, what do you do then? Little boys?"

"You are disgusting Zardooz! I am pressing the button!"

Arjmand plunged his hand down on the red button.

"Yes! Yes! He did it!" Howley was so excited. "Charonelle! Did you see that! He actually pressed the self destruct! I pulled all the explosive charges as my interference clause allowed. He did it! He did it!"

"Howley! Calm down! We see it. Now all the interferences are balanced so could we please not have any more? Do I have your agreement? Peepers? Howley?"

"You have mine," pontificated Peepers, "I never wanted interference in the first place. Spoils the au natural appearance of the acts."

"OK!" grudgingly agreed Howley.

"I was impressed that Zardooz came out openly and admitted that the seventy two virgin bit was hard to swallow. I can't quite understand how anyone could possibly believe such nonsense, but that Zardooz did put it succinctly."

"It didn't help though." Said Charonelle. "Arjmand still tried to blow them up."

There was no reaction from the audience. None of them had disembodied from this edition and so had no association with this method of Deity worship.

"I am not denying the Deity in all this. We have the Deity Clause. It is just hugely entertaining to see how these acts over five thousand or so years have twisted the Deity concept and lost sight of what the Deity is all about."

"Please Peepers, this is not an evangelical broadcast," Scolded Charonelle, "This is entertainment at its best and I think these last

acts have done so brilliantly. I would put Arjmand and Zardooz up with the other favorites now."

"You've got to be joking. This has been the most boring segment of the show since the board lit up! I wouldn't give these two the time of day!" said Peepers in disgust. "This is more along the lines of Howley's comedy acts with this virgin nonsense. Good grief! The women we lifted into stasis from Arjmand's orgy were far from virgins and he seemed to enjoy himself there. What is this fascination and fixation on virgins when they treat their women like possessions, like cattle? No these are not winner material."

"All right folks out there. You have heard Peepers opinion. I still hold that these two have something to offer and a chance to win. We will let the acts themselves decide. Let's get back and look at the Fuller team. What are they up to?"

CHAPTER 65

Aboard the transport, now floating free.

Janine had aligned the ship perfectly once she had matched velocity with the fragment. It faced one of the barely visible Dinkshif drives that was counter rotating on the fragment so that it appeared to be travelling along with them as the fragment spun. The fragment loomed around them, blocking the sunlight so they were hidden in the deep shadow that obscured the drive. All the more difficult for anyone on the fragment to see them. Meaning Zardooz.

They would use the Dinkshif drive as a stable work platform to launch their assault on the complex.

Four of the team had carefully surveyed the surface scan of the far side, which had not taken the brunt of the fuel bomb blast that removed the anti-matter. The blast on this side had effectively been parallel to the surface as it curved around, following the charged surface and sweeping away the silver anti-matter layer. The intense heat of the blast had fused the surface into a dimpled, shiny glazing that the shear forces and heat had polished up nicely, completely the opposite of the head on blast effect on the front side. The team had identified deeply colored, shallow concave regions of varying shape. They determined that these were "glass" bubbles covering over the exposed cave system that Shaw had predicted. They did find one anomaly.

One of the dimples, a fairly large one, had a perfectly round, black hole in the middle. An opening into the cave system and maybe access to the complex. The bubble had begun to burst as the blast effect dissipated and the skin of fused rock hardened with the hole formed by surface tension. It was going to be a race to see if Zardooz would find this hole or if he would attempt to smash his way out somewhere else.

Fuller, the President and Shaw were in full jet packs and each carried a two thousand meter spool of mono filament to use for backtracking, just like the story of the Minotaur and the maze. The mono filament graphite carbon was also conductive and would be the antenna for comms link inside the fragment. Fuller carried an extra tether cable spool for their surface track.

The trio jetted off the transport and headed for the Dinkshif drive platform. Fuller carried a pack loaded with their remaining rock climbing gear, as he would lead once they started their crawl across the back surface towards the hole. They had considered testing the fused glass bubbles of closer outlets to see if they could gain entry, but because there was definitely a mass of water somewhere inside the fragment, they did not want to accidentally pull the plug and lose it all. The hole they had found was obviously not connected to the fluid reservoir and Shaw had no success in calculating the position of the main water mass due to the approximations involved.

They started out on their trek, Fuller placing a piton every arm's length and moving along at a snail crawl. Shaw followed him, holding on to the cable and passing equipment as needed, and Tom followed at the back, pulling up nine out of every ten pitons and handing them forward to Shaw. It was slow going, but they had calculated to have a few pitons left on reaching the hole and a permanent path back to the stable platform.

They were passing the first of the glassy bubbles and Fuller moved as close as he could to still drive in a piton without damaging the surface. The bubble was mostly clean and smooth, with tiny pock marks beginning to show from meteorite erosion. It was obvious that in a relatively short time the glass would be sandblasted into opacity and probably shatter. Right now, Fuller was able to stretch over the glass edge and shine a flashlight through it. The beam was swallowed by the intense blackness and nothing could be seen.

"Let's move on." said Fuller, "There is nothing obvious here."

They continued their crawl for another forty minutes, stopping only once more as they closed on the hole to peer into another bubble close to their goal. Still nothing.

The glassy surface before them presented a small problem. The edge of the hole was a good five meters away. They had to either smash through the glass where they were or crawl across to the hole. Fuller pulled a small laser torch out of his pack and began to warm an area of the bubble, moving inwards in decreasing spirals until the center glowed cherry red. He took a piton and pressed it into the elastic glass, then opened the barbed flange at its tip, inside the molten glass.

The area cooled quickly in the zero of space and was soon just warm and hard again. He repeated the process three more times until he reached the rim of the hole, which was polished and smooth. There were no hand holds to grip, so he used the torch to soften the edge of the rim and pushed a piton right through, twisting and sliding it to form a glass handle, and then again two feet away.

Once the grips had cooled, he was able to drape his torso over the edge of the hole and shine a beam inside. The molten glass was purely a surface effect as he could see grainy rock and crystalline reflections within. The bubble had formed over a large chamber in what appeared to be a natural cave system. He could see two black openings that were conduits in the cave system. There were no excavations marks in the walls and stalagmites and tites indicated what had once been up and down. Some of these mineral spears looked menacingly sharp in the bright light.

Fuller pulled back and warned the others about the sharp spikes, then they went to work to fix cables between the hole edge and the cave base next to each opening, after which he designated Tom and Gerald to attach their guide spools to one opening and explore that way, while he did the other.

The comms antennae were transmitting back to the transport where Janine and Felicity were watching as the computer used dead reckoning to plot their movements and thus the cave layout as they explored. From their transmitted description of each area, Janine drew in the features. At the same time, she reported their relative positions back to them via a small schematic image of the fragment.

Fuller's tunnel ran parallel to the surface for some time then turned in towards the fragment center while Tom and Gerald found a fork and split up. Moving inside was relatively easy using the spin forces as artificial gravity. The only problem arose when the tunnel was perpendicular to the spin. Then they had to use the ancient technique of tacking into the wind, taking a small angled push off one wall to reach the opposite wall. The greater the angle, the more distance covered. "Six points to the wind!" Thought Fuller as he brought his leisure time sailing boat skills into play.

"Hit a dead end here!" reported Shaw.

"Me too." the President joined in.

"All right, turn around and head back. My tunnel is still going, so wait for me to report back."

"Hold on a minute!" exclaimed Shaw. "I am taking a close look at the end of the tunnel and it is not natural. It appears to be rough concrete which is why it looked like the cave at first glance. It is also covered with a thin layer of ice in places.

I do believe we have found our reservoir. They must have dammed up the cave system and allowed rainfall to fill it with water, but there must still be a significant single body of water further in, like a huge chamber, otherwise there would be no braking effect."

"What do you see, Tom?" asked Fuller.

"Same thing. Damp concrete barrier. I'm assuming that when there was gravity, the water may not have reached the concrete barrier. Now it is in free fall and it will find its way through every crack or porous area, assisted by the spin."

"Okay, both of you head back my way. There's nothing you can do other than capture some images of what you see. My tunnel seems to be heading around the edge of the fragment, or better yet, around something and heading towards the complex. I am guessing it follows the outer limits of the reservoir system. Catch up with me guys."

The trio carried on for a while, the two catching up slowly with Fuller, when suddenly he called out, "Bingo! This tunnel becomes an excavated conduit. I just hit reinforced concrete walls and I do believe I see light fittings. I'll wait for you here." He sat down against the light pseudo gravity and waited. Soon he saw reflected light flickering from the walls. It was a little disorienting as it came from all around. In fact it was getting stronger, but not from the direction he expected.

He pulled himself as close to the cavern wall as possible, trying to blend in and warned the others not to come any further. It was certainly Zardooz coming his way.

The apparition that caromed into sight looked like a skinnier version of the Michelin Man as it bounced from wall to wall. What was not funny was the black pistol this clown figure was holding. It stopped its motion and looked at a note taped to its wrist. Zardooz had not seen Fuller - yet.

Zardooz raised his hand and pointed the pistol towards Fuller and pulled the trigger. The shot sent up a spark inches from Fuller's head as it ricocheted its way down the cave. There was an "Ow!" from Shaw as the slowing projectile nicked his shoulder. "What was that?" he called out.

"Zardooz took a shot at me, but I don't know how he could have seen me." answered Fuller. "He didn't compensate for the recoil and now he's flying backwards and out of control." Fuller watched as Zardooz struggled to regain equilibrium. After a few minutes he struggled back to his last position and once again referred to the paper on his wrist. He started working his way towards Fuller but stopped short and extracted another paper from his belt pouch, which he stuck onto the cave wall. He was careful to check that the wall was excavated bedrock and not concrete, but all Fuller saw was the bulls eye target hanging on the wall.

"You guys need to get out of here quickly. Zardooz is doing target practice. He never saw me so I will stay put. I don't have time to get out of the way. Go now! Move"

The pair, now together, responded and started back. They were trying for a sharp bend in the tunnel that would afford them reasonable protection from the bullets.

They hadn't quite made it when Zardooz started firing, slow, deliberately aimed shots. The slugs vanished down the curved tunnel in a series of sparks, narrowly missing Tom and Gerald until, "Uhh! I'm hit!" gasped Tom.

They were almost at the bend so Shaw struggled to drag Tom to safety, the sparking bullets coming steadily. They all hit the end wall that the cave presented because of the bend and rebounded into energy sapping ricochets, finally slowing enough for the gravity well to drag them to the rock face where they came to rest. Except for the one that had hit the President and broken his rib. The youniform had done its job, preventing penetration, but it could not stop the impact, just as Shaw would have a decent bruise on his shoulder.

The buddies went to work on both wounded men and started accelerated healing, applying pain suppression to Tom's ribs and soothing Gerald's shoulder.

Even as Gerald looked back, another spark flashed at the end wall as a bullet struck, but this time it rebounded almost perfectly. With few ricochets, the slug travelled back the way it had come and plowed into Zardooz, puncturing his diving suit and sending him tumbling about as his pressurized air blasted out. He was slapping his hands about looking for the hole but couldn't find it as he gasped for the last vestiges of atmosphere. Then he blacked out.

Fuller moved quickly to the prone form. He had seen that against all odds, Zardooz had shot himself. He didn't think twice about saving him. It had to be attempted.

Zardooz was out and close to death. Fuller found an emergency youniform patch and applied it to the obvious bullet hole in the dive suit. There was no blood so it was likely the bullet had buried itself in the tough suit as there was no exit hole. Once patched, Fuller took what was clearly an extra oxygen bottle and attached it after removing the exhausted one. The suit began to inflate and bring oxygen to Zardooz's starved brain. Fuller thought about taking Zardooz captive but decided they did not need the difficulty involved in guarding him. Instead he took all the weapons and ammunition Zardooz had strapped to himself.

Finally Fuller looked at the paper on Zardooz's wrist and carefully removed it and folded it into his belt pack. Zardooz was coming to, his eyes just visible behind the diving face plate fluttering into consciousness. Fuller wrapped Zardooz with his own cable to disable him, and pressed his youniform faceplate to the diving plate.

"Zardooz! Can you hear me?" Inside the helmet Fuller could see the sudden confusion and fear in Zardooz's eyes as he fully awoke, his head splitting with pain from the oxygen deprivation.

"Whaa? Who?" he rambled and then focussed on Fuller's face, inches from his own.

"Do you hear me?" demanded Fuller.

"Yah..." Zardooz gasped.

"You know who I am. We spoke earlier."

"Yah... yes."

"Zardooz, I can kill you right here. I could have left you to die when you shot yourself. I did not. You need to cooperate with us. I am not going to kill you. I am going to take your weapons and let you live. Go back and think about this. I saved your life so you owe me. Go and think hard Zardooz. The next time we meet, if you are not with us, I will kill you."

Fuller pulled away from the helmet to helmet contact. This was non-negotiable. He stood over Zardooz and pointed the pistol at his face. Zardooz was frozen, but began to wriggle and struggle when he finally realized he was trussed up. Fuller held up a palm in the universal stop signal and Zardooz calmed, as Fuller released the binding on his wrists. The first thing Zardooz did was to look at his wrist where the paper had been attached, then he looked back at Fuller who just smiled and tapped his belt pouch. Zardooz slumped in defeat as Fuller backed away, now laden with guns and grenades. Fuller stopped for a moment, still illuminated in the edge of the flashlight beam, Zardooz watching him, as he bent forward a little and signalled "think" by tapping his head, then he turned and vanished into the darkness of the tunnel.

Zardooz unwrapped his ankles and got up, slowly making his way back to the emergency air lock to the caves from the complex, his mind now racing. If places had been traded, he would not have hesitated to kill the American. Zardooz was puzzled.

CHAPTER 66

Aboard the transport.

Tom had his youniform stripped off to the waist allowing Amy Young to apply the Bio-Meter to his tender ribs, while behind them Felicity examined Shaw's shoulder. The Bio-Meter indicated nothing broken and applied a topical analgesic and bruise treatment.

In the front Fuller had laid out the weapons he had taken from Zardooz and Janine asked him why he had allowed Zardooz to go. He explained his reasons, stressing the point that as they were not prepared to kill a prisoner and due to Zardooz's profile, he would be impossible to hold as a long term prisoner, so it was kill him or let him go, but with a lesson in mind.

"He's just going to come back and try to hit us again." reflected Janine.

"I don't know." mused Fuller. "I think this time I got to him. I guess we wait and see." He picked up the paper he had taken from Zardooz and unfolded it. "Look at this. We struck gold."

Janine peered at the faded sheet and saw it was a map printed off an ancient laser printer. It showed the complex layout in plan and from one side, but in addition there was an attempt to depict the cave system behind and under the complex. The center of the cave section showed a substantial void that must be the water reservoir and the tunnel where Fuller had encountered Zardooz was marked with a red line. That tunnel diverged away from the reservoir leaving a substantial and increasingly thick wall the further it digressed. Zardooz had chosen this area for his target practice so he would not pierce the reservoir.

"Look at these intakes from the water storage to the complex," said Fuller, pointing at a series of fine lines in the side view. "I wonder if there is water getting into the complex now? This system was gravity based with pumps moving water to small storage tanks in the complex. Gerald? Are you done there? Come take a look at this and tell me what you think."

Shaw came over and took a good look at the paper and the

diagram and then applied his usual analytical thinking. He applied a set of lines to both views saying, "That would be the probable water level based on piping and access tunnels here and here. Now spin up the fragment and watch where the water goes."

Shaw overlaid a transparent blue representing the water volume in the reservoir and any attached cave openings. A large part of the cavern plan was not inundated by water until gravity was removed and the dimage began to turn and emulate the real spin of the fragment. Shaw did some calculations based upon the measured slowing rate of the spin and now that he had a reasonable location for the main bolus of water, was able to calculate the volume required to cause the slowing effect. He applied that value to the dimage and suddenly the picture changed dramatically.

Much of the water ran back into what was the empty cavern system and some of the previously full areas emptied back. The bolus was gathered to one side of the reservoir space by the pseudo gravity and the intake pipes were left high and dry.

Shaw looked up and said, "Zardooz has only the water in his storage tanks."

"Freeze the image." ordered Fuller. He moved closer to examine the cave system. "Give me surface topography for this area."

The surface showed translucent with the caves below. Fuller traced the surface point from the entry hole bubble back to the first bubble they had encountered. It was filled with water.

"Someone is looking after us!" Fuller exclaimed. "Imagine if we had smashed through there. We would have lost the lot and blown this fragment off trajectory with no hope of recovery."

"So how thick is this glass bubble?" asked Janine with her characteristic wry look.

"Right now it doesn't matter because it, and I assume others, are holding. We'll have to look at protecting them when we know what resources we have from inside the complex."

"You think Zardooz will cooperate?" asked Janine.

"Whether he will or not is irrelevant. We have the Medalizam up our sleeve and we know where his water supply is. I will drug him if he won't work with us. Fact is, we are still here and he knows it and he still didn't blow up the fragment. I think we called his bluff."

Back in the complex, Zardooz had unsuited and returned to the control room, his face red with anger.

"You WHAT?"

"I pressed the destruct button when I saw the Americans landing."

"You liar! You spineless worm! why are we still here?"

"I don't know. Look!" Arjmand plunged down on the red button before Zardooz could stop him. Zardooz's heart leapt into his mouth as he screamed at Arjmand, "FOOL! It is no use now!"

They both froze, staring at each other as they waited for the final, searing blast to vaporize them.

Zardooz blinked and looked around slowly. He was still alive. The destruct system had failed.

"Thank Allah!" he thought to himself and then aloud, "What did you do to the destruct system Arjmand?"

"Nothing! By the beard of the prophet! Nothing" he was crying, bawling like a baby.

"It is clear to me that Allah does not desire our martyrdom. We will no longer consider self destruction as an option!" commanded Zardooz.

Arjmand was still whimpering, but gathered himself enough to ask in a tiny voice, "What happened out there? Why are you back so soon?"

"There is nothing for us out there. Just empty tunnels and no way to the surface." lied Zardooz. "We will..."

His words were interrupted by static on what was a blank screen and garbled noise coming through. It resolved itself into a picture of the American who had accosted him in the tunnel. This time both sides could see and hear.

"Zardooz, I am Col. Fuller of the United States Armed Forces and you have met our President. I spoke with you in the tunnel and meant every word. You have not destroyed your complex or this fragment so you are clearly bluffing. There is no time left to play these games. You either cooperate with us fully or suffer the consequences."

Zardooz wasn't about to capitulate without extracting as much as he could in the way of concessions, an old tradition in his genes. However Arjmand had seen and heard the exchange and now gaped at Zardooz, mouth hanging open in astonishment. "You said.. you said..." stammered Arjmand.

"Shut up!" ejaculated Zardooz from the corner of his mouth.

"But..."

"SHUT UP!"

Arjmand cowered back and stopped his questioning, the expression on the face of Zardooz putting him in fear for his life.

"What do you want?" Zardooz asked Fuller.

"You will surrender all weapons and give us free access to your complex. In return we will work together and take you and any survivors on our journey to another star system, where we will look for a new home planet to re-establish humanity. I think that is a pretty good deal."

"And if we refuse?"

"You will find out... just before you go space walking without a space suit."

Zardooz could not help but gulp at the overt threat. "I need time to think about this."

"Fine," replied Fuller. "You have thirty seconds."

"Or what?" Now Zardooz was truly alarmed.

"You will figure it out next time you see me. I will be inside and you will be outside - without a space suit. Think fast."

"Fine. You win. But you live on your ship, not in here. There is insufficient room."

"There will be no conditions if you wish to live. I will decide where people live."

"Can we continue to worship Allah in our own way."

"Provided it does not result in any further violence or suicide attacks, you may worship freely. Keep it to yourself."

"What about Arjmand here?"

"What about him?"

"I cannot control his actions. The fool actually pressed the self destruct button at least twice. Fortunately for all of us there was a malfunction."

"Zardooz! You are so predictable."

"Huh?"

"This nonsense about the self destruct."

"No! It's true. Arjmand did it. Ask him yourself." The view swung over to Arjmand still cowering in a corner seat. He leaned forward and his face changed to a snarl, "Yes I did it!" he hissed, "And I will keep pressing it until it works you infidel dog!" He started to move towards the destruct panel again but Zardooz grabbed him and they wrestled for a moment until Zardooz used a carotid block and put Arjmand to sleep.

"Now do you believe me?" asked Zardooz as he returned to center screen. "Look, I carried the prophet's flag as far as I could in the name of the Iranian Empire. I am a reasonable man and I know when to give up, but this fruitcake really believes you are the Great Satan, and coward as he is, his fanaticism will override his fear. We are all at risk with him around."

"We can take care of him. We have a way that will not harm him. Now let's work out how we enter the complex without losing atmosphere. Your corridor segment is too large to evacuate. We need to make it smaller. And while we do that, we are going to swing past what is left of the moon. There may be survivors behind it waiting for contact."

"You are going to leave me here?"

"No, the whole fragment is our space ship. We are going to redirect its velocity for a slow pass by of the moon and look for our friends."

"How can you do this? The fragment has no means of propulsion."

"It does now."

Zardooz shook his head in wonder, congratulating himself for even having survived in the face of these seemingly invincible Americans. "Move the fragment?" he wondered to himself.

The Dinkshif drives were running perfectly. Only two of the four were deployed, one on each end of the axis of rotation of the fragment. Janine was now the pilot of the largest artificially driven object in all history. The tiny specks of the Drives seemed insignificant, almost invisible, mounted as they were, but the incremental punch of their powerful reaction drives gradually altered the path of the fragment as Janine redirected their thrust by turning them in tandem on their gimbal mounts. Instead of pointing straight back they now slewed in parallel to about a thirty degree angle from their original trajectory. The side thrust component was accumulating and the path was describing a wide arc which would bring them around the moon at a safe distance. The traverse across the hidden region would give them some hours to locate other survivors. They would lift them off with the transport.

While Janine was redirecting the fragment, Shaw was discussing an idea with the President and Fuller. They did not have the resources to cap the glassy cave seals and protect the irreplaceable water supply, so Shaw had come up with another plan.

"Once we have passed the moon and picked up anyone Commander Carver will redirect the fragment towards interception with Alpha Centauri in a projected five year journey. Before we switch into the Dinkshif Drive stage, I propose that we stop the fragment spin and bring all the water back to the central holding reservoir, then block the openings to the cave system to remove the problem entirely. With the mass as one, central consistent bolus, we can ascertain the orientation of the complex and reservoir to was originally "up" and "down". We move the Dinkshif drives to optimum position to give us linear acceleration so that "down" really is "down" and we have a non rotational LINEAR psuedo gravity for the duration of our journey. For the deceleration segment we do a one eighty degree flip. Same thing again."

Fuller diagrammed the proposed traverse to Alpha Centauri. "That looks like it could work. Can you run all the parameters we know of through the computer and see if any anomalies are revealed?"

"Already did that Councillor Fuller," replied Shaw with his usual cheeky grin,"and there is nothing obvious that would prevent this from working."

"I guess we present it to the whole council and vote. I do have one question that needs answering. What happens to the reaction gold trail when we reverse direction. We will be flying into our own trail."

Shaw answered, "Nylast Dinkshif anticipated this issue but there is no practical application or experiment that provided an answer, so the solution was very simple. We give away a small vector of our thrust for a five degree offset on each Drive, countering each other. The gold trail flows past us to either side during deceleration.

Once we understand the Drives after using them for some time, I would like to devise experimentation to resolve such questions."

"Yes, without blowing us up." laughed Fuller. "If Janine can join us for a while, call the Council meeting."

Shaw presented his idea to the full council, resulting in a unanimous vote of approval. For now, the moon rescue took priority. They had several hours transit until they would come into line of sight communications. Everyone took a holiday and relaxed.

CHAPTER 67

Behind the Moon.

Back in the Shuttle, Sheila, Martin, Graham and Corcoran, now recovered, sat together and swapped information. Martin explained how all the passengers had simply vanished at the time of the mutiny without any obvious cause.

Sheila was writing the points on a dimage, but only got to two before they hit a wall. "Your passengers vanished and here the whole fleet population seems to have vanished. What are we dealing with? If it was the anti-matter then you and Corcoran would have been affected also."

The group sat, speechless, thinking hard. Nothing made any sense.

"Aliens?" Graham broke the silence.

"God?" Martin added.

"Spontaneous human combustion? I read about it in history books." Corcoran chipped in.

"Whatever it is, none of us have actually seen it happen," said Sheila, "and at this point we will use that as Rule one. We always stay in sight of one another, including my passengers." She turned around and surveyed her charges in the cabin. They were all busy doing small things or snoozing. Nothing was out of place in the scene.

"So what's Rule two?" asked Martin.

"Rule two is enforcing Rule one by keeping in groups of four with two people designated to watch another group of four at all times. That way we are all being watched by one or two others. If any more disappearances occur, we will see it happen. We have to nail whoever or whatever is doing this to us. There can be no slacking off on this. We will roster four hour shifts so that sleep times are covered. There can be no privacy at any time until this is resolved."

"We have twenty eight people aboard," said Martin, "so we have seven groups. I think we should also roster the groups on watch staggered four hours each with two hour overlaps. That will give full coverage."

"So what do we do if anyone does vanish in front of us?" asked Graham.

"Hit the alarm and circle the wagons. What else can we do but watch?" replied Sheilah. "Meanwhile, we need to set up a signal beacon that is not going to cause epileptic fits in case any of the other transports made it through. Then we need to do an inventory of our supplies and our people skills. Martin and Corcoran, please organize the security groups and roster. Do Graham's group first. Graham, take your group, and another if you have to, and do the resources inventory, without losing sight of another group. That is the key I think."

The group broke up and security groups were arranged. Sheila took her group to set up a signal beacon and survey the fleet. Even with the anti-matter coating, they knew how to break through it now and there would be essential survival materials aboard the other ships.

"Well! This is quite a turn about Peepers!" Charonelle was almost breathless in her excitement, except she didn't have any lungs. "Zardooz has joined the Carver team and Sheila's group has become highly suspicious because of the disappearances. I said it was too obvious to pull all those people into stasis."

"Oh come now!" blustered Peepers, "Who would have thought they would find a way to get through the anti-matter. In fact I thought they were stasis fodder long before that, when they did the catch thing with Martin."

"This puts a whole new spin on the act by Sheila's troupe. They know something is up and they even suspect outside interference by aliens." Howley snorted a chuckle. "Aliens indeed. Are WE aliens?"

"Your brain has always been strange Howley!" retorted Peepers. "Maybe you are an alien, from the comedy universe."

"And a migraine to you Peepers! If I had a middle finger it would be up right now! Hmph!" Howley went silent.

"You know guys, we could mind wipe the lot of them and put the fleet people back."

"Charonelle, there's been enough damage done," pontificated Peepers, "so we will let it run its course. If you restore it back this whole segment could run on for years. Let it be. What are we down to now, twenty eight in Sheila's group and thirty on the fragment? That is enough to finish this series with a grand final like never before!"

"Agree with Peepers Howley?"

"Hmm!" Howley agreed, still angry with Peepers.

Down in the control room, Nickle had been watching the exchange in growing horror, the anticipation of mind wiping all those people a logistical nightmare. He gave a sigh of relief when the judges decided to carry on as is.

Nickle looked at the board. Everything was dark and quiet. There wasn't even any betting traffic going on since things has quieted down. He sighed, took a swig of his beer and sat back to watch an old football game replay from thirty five thousand years earlier in Game Series Four. He loved the boot knives and exploding football shrapnel effects of that version of the sport.

CHAPTER 68

On the fragment.

"We come over the comms horizon in two minutes. We monitor every possible radio frequency, visual comms and even look for bottles with notes floating in space. We have no idea if our friends made it, or if they are disabled. Our searching must be pro-active. If you have any idea that something might be a message follow it through." Janine looked at the intense young faces in front of her. "Take your places people."

Most of the cadets and the President's staff ranged themselves around the cabin next to port holes looking for visual signals.

Fuller, Carver, Shaw and Hannaford took up positions at the instrument panels. Shaw brought up a regional dimage showing a real time scan of the visible region. As the fragment progressed on its journey he peered more closely at the moon's horizon and increased the scale. He could see some irregularities but was unable to make out what they were.

After a few minutes he started pumping the air with his right hand and chanting "Yes! Yes! Yes!"

Fuller looked up from his screen, "What? Gerald?"

"Ships. Transports. Shuttles. I see them. As we move further I can see more of them."

"Go full visual. Image up." Fuller commanded the computer.

The view that appeared brought a collective gasp of despair from the four. The ships were all coated in anti-matter.

"Beacon! Beacon!" shouted Felicity excitedly. I have a signal from a Space City Shuttle. "Shuttle commanded by Sheila Johnson. Twenty-eight survivors aboard, including two Transport Pilots, Martin and Corcoran. Beware anti-matter coating everything. Need rescue. No reaction mass. Ship location follows." A series of numbers giving a three dimensional location relative to a distant know star sight streamed in. Shaw plugged the coordinates into the computer and the dimage zoomed in on a dark grey spot that resolved itself into the shape of a shuttle in deep shadow. There was no anti-matter on this one.

Fuller played up and down the comms frequencies hailing the shuttle until a squawk came through the speakers and Sheila's voice was heard, loud and clear. "This is Shuttle SC11. Sheila Johnson commanding. Please identify."

Janine, as commander, replied, "This is Skyhook Transport X3 in conjunction with Air Force One, Janine Carver commanding. Commander Johnson, I am not familiar with you. Please identify fully."

"I was promoted in the field by Commander Bob Evans who was in command of this fleet - until he and all the personnel vanished. I was originally Cook's Assistant on Space City with a Doctorate in Stochastic Processes on the side."

"What is your situation Commander Johnson?"

"We used the last of our reaction mass in rescuing two Transport Commanders, Martin and Corcoran. They report that their passengers vanished while they were outside their ship, however there was no anti-matter involved there. All the crews and passengers of the fleet were here some hours ago before the anti-matter attacked. After we returned from our rescue mission the ships were covered in anti-matter and the people gone."

"How can you be sure that they are not trapped inside?" asked Janine.

"We devised a way to penetrate the anti-matter safely and looked inside the nearest transport. It was empty."

"You said you penetrated the anti-matter. Did you record your method?"

"Did you say Air Force One?"

"Yes I did. Can we get back to the anti-matter matter?" Janine giggled when she realized the silliness of her words.

"Is the President aboard? Alive and well?"

"He is."

"May I speak with him please?"

"I guess so. I will call him." Janine asked Tom to come to the cabin, explaining the situation briefly.

"This is the President." He put on his most imperious voice. "To whom am I speaking?"

"It's me Uncle Tom! Sheila, your niece."

"Sheila! Good lord! Thank God you survived!"

Janine rolled her eyes back and shook her head in disbelief. "The President's niece!" she said to no one in particular. "Who woulda thunk it?"

Janine broke into the happy reunion, "Sorry people but this has to wait. We have a very small window to pick up this crew and no time to waste."

"Sorry Commander," Sheila apologized, "we will catch up later. But WOW! My Uncle made it!" The joy and relief were almost tangible in her happy expression. "What do you want us to do Commander?"

"We are going to try to grab your shuttle as we pass by. We have access to a fair quantity of reaction mass in this fragment and we have refuelled our transport in anticipation. We plan to come to you with the transport, offload a full reaction mass bladder and take your empty aboard. You will then be able to rendezvous with the fragment.

There is no time now to tell you all that has happened and what we have planned. We need to catch you in the next thirty minutes, so please remove the empty bladder and be ready to receive the full one. You follow us immediately. If you do not catch us, there is nothing we can do to assist you, so plan carefully."

"One question Commander Carver?"

"Go ahead."

"Have you experienced any strange disappearances of personnel?"

"Not directly, but another survivor we picked up did say something to that effect."

"Oh! Others. Good! Well we had better get outside and get that bladder ready. Err... what about the rest of the fleet?"

"In spite of the fact that you did beat the anti-matter, it is still too dangerous to become involved in salvaging. We have good resources here so the risk is not worth it, especially if there is no one aboard those ships. Proceed Commander Johnson."

"Acknowledged. Seeyalater Unc!" Sheila couldn't resist throwing that in.

Aboard the transport Tom smiled and said, "She's a real fighter that Sheila. Got a lot of her Australian mother in her. You know, she's a martial arts master. Some seventh Kishka in Pirogi Cholent which was used by elite Israeli agents, cute as a button and brilliant at math."

"Hmm, a daunting combination for any man." murmured Janine. "Let's move. Gerald, how much water did we get from that storage tank?"

"We topped up both our bladders and about half a third one before we lost the feed and couldn't push our pipe in or around any further. The bore hole has been plugged and fused to prevent any leakage."

"Poor Zardooz, no more showers for a bit." Janine put on a sad face and Felicity cracked up laughing.

"I'm amazed we got that done in such a short time." said Shaw.

"Helps not to have someone shooting at us!" replied Fuller. "Is the laser borer secured in the cargo bay?"

"Yes, Felicity and I locked it in as soon as we brought it back. How did you make out getting into the complex?"

"We managed to seal off a small section of the entry tunnel and inflated it with carbon dioxide waste gas just to check the integrity. We didn't try an entry yet. We'll leave that until after the recovery and see what has happened to the gas pressure."

"Will Zardooz try to interfere with it?" asked Felicity.

"I don't think he will," replied Fuller, "because he doesn't have any appreciable water left in his storage tanks and we are the only hope for him to retrieve water from the reservoir. He has a vested interest in keeping us healthy now."

"Ready for docking with the shuttle." In the time the short discussion had taken place, Janine had taken the transport to the shuttle and matched relative velocity to zero. She worked the transport into position with the side thrusters, moving as close as she dared to make the bladder transfer as fast as possible. Fuller, Shaw and the President moved to the lock to go out and shift the full bladder. Janine could see the figures of the shuttle crew and the open reaction mass bladder bay with the empty bladder rolled up and ready to go.

In moments the crew had egressed and the fuel tank open light came on. She watched as Fuller's team drifted the huge, wobbling bladder towards the shuttle in slow motion. The process was a docking manoeuvre in its own right, with precision acceleration and deceleration involved.

The three figures from the shuttle moved forward to assist and together they bedded the bladder into position. Graham, identifiable by his physical size, made the conduit connection and then the three shuttle crew recharged their personal reaction mass tanks from a small nipple off the main conduit. They were all running on empty.

Fuller's crew took the empty bladder and jetted back to the transport, but not before the President and Sheila had hugged each other for a brief moment.

The transfer had gone off without a hitch.

Now both ships had to catch the fragment as it hurdled past at two thousand miles an hour. Martin piloted the shuttle as they moved off in tandem, Sheilah looking back with tears in her eyes at the abandoned fleet as they dwindled to faintly luminous points and then were absorbed by the dark silvery disk of the moon. Soon even the moon shrank as they drew away from the last vestiges of their home.

Sheila rested her head on Martin's shoulder as she wept and he brought up his hand to trace her tears with a finger. He came closer to her and brushed her lips with his, making her open her eyes to look deep into his soul. She relaxed completely and snuggled closer as the couches allowed.

Aboard the transport, with the first moments of relaxation in days, Felicity and Gerald were snuggled together, whispering and giggling like two teenagers, exactly what they were.

Up front in the pilots couches, Janine and John were vigilant, but comfortable like a pair of well used, loved gloves. In fact in both ships, couples had isolated themselves as much as possible in their groups of four, which had also been adopted by Janine's ship, cadets, secret service, presidential staff and space city passengers. Peace and love were in the air.

The board in front of Nickle started to sparkle with blue flashes, something he had never seen before. He had no idea what it meant so he rummaged through a rarely opened drawer in his desk until he found the quick start user guide card that had been there for over thirty thousand years. The colors were a little faded after all that time, but it was otherwise in as new condition, never having been used more than five times by new keepers.

He scrolled down the card until he came to the board color coding. Red. Yellow. Green. There was no blue listed. Then he noticed the asterisk next to the green code. He vaguely remembered that asterisks meant look somewhere else on the card, usually at the bottom in fine print. Nothing on this side, so he flipped it. Yes, there was something there right at the bottom. He squinted to read it.

*"In the unlikely event of the board turning blue, prepare a system wide shock jolt or the collective euphoric state of the audience and all participants, including judges, could become permanent and the Game Series will be automatically terminated without a winner. This will mean a further Game Series for the incumbent keeper after reviving as many brains as possible. Apply shock only if board is partially turned to ensure some brain survival. Applying at full blue is of unknown consequences and could result in total loss of immortal population."

"Oh shit!" Nickle scurried to the board controls. He didn't want to spend another five thousand years pampering a load of slimy brains, no matter what his reward at the end. And yet he was scared to be without them.

"Nickle! What's going on? We are losing our audience. Private channel now! Explain!"

Nickle was working furiously to set the charge for the system wide shock. "Not now Peepers, got an emergency on my hands. Stand by for system wide shock!"

"What?" screeched Peepers. "Nooooooo!"

Nickle pushed the button.

BZZZZZTTT!

CHAPTER 69

Approaching the fragment.

"We will dock at the closest axial platform that you can see straight ahead, Martin." Janine instructed the shuttle pilot. "Once I dock the transport, I want you to dock along side us, parallel. Our first task is to check off all personnel and profile skills, then to check inventory. We are all well rested," she paused and grinned at Fuller, who reached out and brushed her breast intimately, "so there is no reason to delay these tasks."

"Understood." Martin replied.

The docking process was quick and while Janine's instructions were being carried out, Fuller and Shaw jetted over to the tunnel, matching rotation once again and entering. They were able to raise Zardooz immediately and told him they were coming to test the air lock integrity. Zardooz illuminated the inner corridor and waited.

The pressure gauge on the makeshift partition was at the same reading as when they had departed. It looked good.

"Zardooz, we have a good pressure seal here. The next stage is entry if you agree."

"I agree Col. Fuller. But let us not waste the entry effort. What can we achieve by this entry?"

"We wish to survey the access to the main water supply and examine the pipe system. You have no water left in reserve..."

Zardooz interrupted, "So I noticed."

"...and we have a plan to restore regular water supply and stabilize the psuedo gravity. We want to begin by sitting with you and explaining our future plans. You and Arjmand are part of these plans whether you like it or not. I would prefer to have your willing cooperation."

"Could you bring a little vodka to this meeting?"

Fuller looked at Shaw with a huge grin at Zardooz's request. "I'll see what I can do. I thought the prophet said your lot are not allowed alcohol."

"Medicinal purposes Col. Fuller. Strictly medicinal."

Fuller switched to private comms and told Shaw to jet back and pick up a bottle from the Airforce One supplies that had been shipped aboard. While Shaw did this he ran the gas sniffer around the seals once more to be sure, then just waited for Shaw to return.

Zardooz was getting impatient. "What is taking so long Col. Fuller?"

"We are double checking the seals. We have time and no need to take any risks. We will do everything with the maximum safety of all personnel foremost, and that includes you two if you are with us."

"Well thank you. I trust that our earlier differences will be put aside sir. We are most prepared to forgive your country for what it has done to us."

"Zardooz, I suggest you don't go there. Do not go there ever again. You are in no position to be assuming any high ground, moral or otherwise. We are under martial law and I tell you that any such talk from this point onwards will bring unpleasant consequences for you and Arjmand. Make sure he knows to shut up as well!" Fuller dropped all pretense at diplomacy with his last words and pushed his message through harshly. "We are on our own now, just you and me Zardooz. So you get one warning. Step out of line just once, and I will happily lose your genetic contribution to the new human regeneration into the vacuum of space. Your prophet will be mightily pissed at that. Got it?"

"Now now Col. Fuller, no need to become belligerent with me. I wish to live. We will cooperate to the best of our ability." Zardooz was trying hard to control his anger. He almost sounded friendly.

At that moment Shaw returned with a bottle clutched in his gloved hand. The contents were almost solid courtesy the chill of space. Zardooz would have very icy vodka.

"We are coming in Zardooz. Are you ready to release the lock?"

"Yes. Your repair to the circuit is holding. We are showing green to go."

"Okay. Evacuate the lock."

Zardooz activated the pump that sucked most of the carbon dioxide test gas back into the general atmosphere. It would be scrubbed out in the normal cycling course. The temporary entry light on the outside went green so Fuller pushed in the small, makeshift port. There was no puff of escaping gas. The system had worked well. He and Shaw climbed through the round hole and pushed the door shut, dogging it into place. The whole structure had been cut away from the secondary hull access point of the transport where it would not be missed. A patch plate had replaced it and access was available from the forward section of the hull. Just inconvenient if it was needed.

"Zardooz, pressurize the lock please." commanded Fuller.

They saw a tiny puff of vapor as moisture in the first air into the tiny lock froze on contact with the extreme cold. In moments the whole lock had fogged up but there was enough visibility to see the inner access door which was still scorched and streaked on the outside from the anti-matter and subsequent fuel bomb blast, as deep as it was inside the tunnel. Fortunately it was superficial damage. The seals had held, although Fuller and his team had to replace fused wiring when they installed the temporary lock.

The door swung open into the corridor of the complex. They could see the bloody smears where Arjmand had come to grief earlier. Shaw pointed to the marks and Fuller nodded that he had seen them. They knew that someone had been injured here.

"We are in Zardooz. Closing the air lock door now." Fuller pushed the door closed and the dogs latched into place. The pressure was left in the temporary lock ready for departure.

"Come straight down the corridor Col. Fuller. You have two more equal pressure locks to pass through."

"Where is Arjmand?" asked Fuller.

"Still asleep. I sedated him after I knocked him out. I hope you have something as you mentioned earlier."

"Yes I do. We are approaching the last door."

"I will come to meet you."

The three sat in the complex control room strapped into chairs. Arjmand was still curled in a foetal position in the corner couch, and would stay that way for some time. Fuller had administered an injection of Medalizam that would set Arjmand's memory back a few steps if it worked as advertised. A doctor aboard Sheila's shuttle had worked out the dose and frequency of administration to take Arjmand back to the days before he became the president of the Iranian Empire. It was going to be an interesting experiment.

Zardooz carefully picked up the bottle of vodka from the makeshift restraint and examined the label. The contents were now oily thick as the temperature increased. He pursed his lips and nodded his head in appreciation. "The real thing. Stoli. You treat yourself well Col. Fuller."

"This is a gift from the President of the United States Mr Zardooz." Fuller had decided to become formal and see where it all led. "Our President trusts that you will make a medicinal toast to our future friendship and cooperation."

"By all means! Here, let me load some drinking bottles with a little for each of us. We have to find solutions to these new conditions for everything, even drinking."

Zardooz had three empty bottles ready, their caps unscrewed. He carefully unwrapped the neck of the vodka bottle and broke the seal, surreptitiously inspecting it for any tiny holes or signs of interference, but Fuller noticed. He oriented the bottle so the psuedo gravity kept the precious liquid away from the mouth and placed a plastic drink container tight against the glass vodka bottle, then sealed it with a strip of adhesive tape, also cut beforehand.

"You seem to be well prepared for this Mr Zardooz."

"Yes Col. Fuller," Zardooz relied, noting the change of attitude, "I was certain you would follow through with your agreement to find a bottle. If you can move this fragment then a bottle of vodka should be child's play to you."

Fuller laughed, "It may be easier to move the fragment than find a bottle in the future. Don't get the wrong idea in your head. Oh, just do one for me. My companion is yet of drinking age."

Shaw caught himself before he reacted with an objection, realizing that Fuller still did not trust Zardooz and wanted Shaw to watch his back in case the bottles had been tampered with.

Zardooz shrugged and handed Fuller a bottle with a generous

amount of vodka. He lifted his own bottle in a toast and called out, "Le chayim!" and took a good swig. Fuller waited and did not react, actually surprised that Zardooz had used the national toast expression of his most bitter enemy.

"Colonel, you do not drink? Aha! You still do not trust me. A wise man. Here, give me your bottle." Zardooz reached out and took Fuller's bottle, then holding it away from his lips, squirted a stream of vodka into his open mouth. He wiped the stray drops away with his sleeve and gave a sigh of appreciation and handed the bottle back. "See Colonel, no poison!"

Fuller took the bottle and looked at the top, then back at Zardooz. A fast acting topical poison could still be on the drinking cap, so he unscrewed the cap and carefully put it in his belt pouch, then squirted a bolus of vodka into his own mouth without touching the bottle. Zardooz gave a faint smile and said, "You will find nothing on that cap Colonel. I have no bad intentions towards you. It would not be worth my life."

"Mr Zardooz, there is a creature that I recall changed its color instantly to save itself. A chameleon lizard. It was still the same lizard underneath the color. Think about it. Now let's get down to business and I will explain what we are planning."

CHAPTER 70

"It is a difficult docking sequence Martin, but I have done it once with the fragment tumbling, not just spinning. Gerald Shaw has calculated the two rim positions for the transport and the shuttle. We will dock one at a time to avoid collision. Once in place and tethered, we will apply gradually increasing thrust against the spin of the fragment until we reduce the spin to relative zero. Unfortunately, the downside of this plan is the loss of a large amount of reaction mass, namely our water supply, and the catch to the scheme is that we cannot get more water until we stop the spin. We have to use everything we have available and this is truly do or die. When the spin has been stopped, we will apply the Dinkshif Drives to build linear acceleration that will create a pseudo gravity in the correct orientation to put the main body of water back into the reservoir where it can be accessed by the pump system."

"Janine, why can't we use the Dinkshif Drives to take off the spin?"

"The Dinkshif theory states that a trail of ionized gold is the exhaust of the system. We have no idea of the properties of this gold or what it would do to the fragment or us. If you look at the spin mechanics you will see that we would collect exhaust residue from the de-spin on the facing edge of the fragment as we travel into the exhaust material off the leading edge. We cannot take that risk. Your group detected the relationship between the gold residue and the anti-matter."

"I understand. You know, I always wondered why the metal gold was considered so valuable. You couldn't eat it at the end of the day. It had to be an artifice of the human mind that gave anything value, but now I see that this gold residue comes from a reactive drive, it makes a bizarre sense to see that there is something special, almost unworldly, about gold."

"Hey Martin! That's what alchemy was all about. Creating gold from base metals. Just when we get it all figured out, wham! There's no one left to appreciate it. OK you ready to dock? Your tether team on stand by?"

"All ready Janine. Here we go!"

Martin took the shuttle into an inverted trajectory over the thin rim of the fragment, a zone about fifty yards wide with a sharp edge where the fracture from the Earth's crust had occurred. He made it look too easy as the shuttle eased down on its back and then he held it in place with the thrusters as his tether team boiled out of the ship and took their positions. With guidance from Janine's prior experience, they got the cables set and the ship secured. There was about a five degree angle from the perpendicular to the fragment that was taken care of by the gimballed main drive.

Then it was Janine's turn and she did it like an old hand. The space crews were the best of the best that Earth ever had to offer. Tom, the President watched with pride the perfect execution of the plan, then felt a huge mood of depression as he realized yet again that there was nothing to be proud about. He went back to thinking about Zardooz after hearing Fuller's report of the encounter.

The bottle cap had tested almost clean. There was just an infinitesimal trace of something so obscure that it took the Bio-Meter three hundred and fifty three milliseconds to identify it, instead of the usual three to five. The substance was a very rare snake venom, native to Iran but believed extinct on Earth for some two thousand years. That it was even in the data base was astounding, an apparently beneficial adjunct of the Iraq-Iran wars of the past century where no holds were barred by either side. The Iraquis had identified this threat and put aside a sample. US Desert Storm forces has captured all the documentation and samples which over the ensuing years had been tested and cataloged for its esoteric and maybe medical, value.

There were just a few molecules present on the cap. Just enough to kill. Just enough to blame on a snake living somewhere in the complex near a water source.

Tom was thinking furiously whether to space Zardooz and Arjmand or try to live with them like the two poisonous snakes they were.

In the cabin, Janine was coordinating the thrust build up with Martin under instruction from Gerald Shaw. He was manipulating the dimage at an incredible speed, running what if calculation scenarios to narrow down the effects of unknown factors. On Martin's shuttle, Sheila was following the math as fast as Shaw could manipulate the equations. Already genius level, Shaw was moving to another strata of human intelligence never before seen. The other councillors watched in amazement and admiration as the teenager took physics and mechanics to new heights. Felicity watched with a glow of possessive pride as the solution took shape. She too was understanding math that she had never been trained into. She could not innovate like Shaw, but she could follow.

Sheila watched Gerald's dimages flash past and added her own interpretation, seeing one place that he had missed a variable, simply because he had no idea it was there in her ship. She corrected and a fleeting "thanks" scrolled by.

The main engine thrust gradually came up, the tethers taking the strain and applying the anti-spin force to the fragment. The cable anchors were the weakest link in the plan so there were people in pairs watching each anchor outside the ships. The fours had to be sacrificed for the moment.

They had some redundancy in the tethers in case of breakage and the observation teams were set back out of the danger zone if a break occurred. Or so they thought.

Inside Janine's transport there was a sharp noise, like a firecracker, transmitted through the hull as a cable anchor pulled free without warning. Outside, the two cadets watching the cable never knew what hit them as it sliced them in half like a grass trimmer. The ship did not move but the gory remains of the pair drifted and spiraled outwards as the others watched, horrified. The two lower bodies were left tied down where they had been watching. The loose tether had finally whipped around and passed through the thruster blast which cut it and it flew off into space.

The remains stayed put. Nothing vanished. The gore was splattered everywhere it could stick. The buddies were dead too.

"Everyone hold position!" commanded Janine. "We go on!

There is only one shot at this. Hold position and keep right down low. We will mourn later. Now we have a job to do people."

Outside, two of the cadets in sight of the grizzly scene were being violently ill, but their youniforms and buddies took care of the upchuck before it could do any damage. After a few minutes they all settled down, spirits dampened and without enthusiasm.

Nickle watched the board. There were more red dots again, those brains that had not been strong enough for the electric shock treatment. More mush for the recycling system. He looked at the judges' monitors. Uh oh! Howley wasn't back on line yet. He could hear moaning from Peepers.

"Oooh! My head hurts! What happened? Where am I? Oh my back is killing me? Why is everything dark?"

"Peepers? It's Nickle. Your old friend."

"Nickle? Nickle who? Nicklodeon? Ha ha!"

"Aahhg! What hit me? Peepers? Howley? Are you guys OK?"

"Who are you?"

"Charonelle, Peepers don't remember nothing and Howley hasn't come back on line. I'm afraid he may be brain mush."

"Ohh! Nickle! What happened?"

"I had to do a system wide shock. Too many brains was going into one way euphoric addiction mode. They would never have come out of it and the instruction book said I had to do a system wide shock before everybrain got caught up in it."

"Gracious me! What about the audience?"

"We seems to have lost quite a few of 'em as red dots. Lot more than last time. Doesn't matter though. Theys all went out smiling."

"Nickle, the game must go on! What of our erstwhile performers?"

"Well, while you lot were all in happyland they had a little accident and a couple of the cadets got kinda messed up."

"Did you catch them and put them is stasis?"

"Naw. I was too busy sorting out you lot and the main board. Likes I says, they got messed up as in little pieces. They was too dead before I could do nothing."

"Those poor dears. I guess there is no point in crying over spilled

blood now. Oh well." Charonelle was reflectively silent for a moment then, "Can we do anything for Peepers. He seems to think he has a body once again. The shock jolted his memory back over twenty five thousand years. Is this permanent or will his memory come back?"

"Ah don't know Miss Charonelle. The hand book say that the amnesia be temporary and memory come back gradually, starting at earliest regression, so I guess Peepers has twenty five thousand years of memories to live through. Could take a little while."

"Oh my! Is there any sign of Howley?"

"Well that's an interesting question. I been watching his monitor light and I thought we lost him to red, but he keeps swinging through a range of colors, mostly in blue and purples and there ain't nuttin in the book about that, so I'm guessing he's getting brain screwed big time and loving it. The jolt didn't seem to affect him at all." Nickle stopped talking as Howley's light changed from the odd color to a steady green.

"You guys been talking about me?" came Howley's cheeky voice.

"Oh Howley!" gushed Charonelle, "We were so worried about you! What happened?"

"Char, if I had a face I'd be smiling to split. I just had the best brain-sex mind-gasm blast in the universe with a lady brain friend. We let go to the euphoria stream just right and then Nickle gave us a tickle," Howley giggled at his own rhyme, "Nickle tickle huh? Well that little helper kicked us both off together in a shared mind-gasm like never before. It made the long gone love tackle orgasms look puny by comparison. Whew! I'm still coming down from it."

"Oh," said Charonelle with a touch of dismay in her voice, "I just blacked out and poor Peepers has lost his memory. He still thinks he has a body."

"That was probably the last time he had an orgasm, when he had a body. Makes sense he would regress there. He always struck me as being anal retentive."

"Well just us two now as judges and Nickle told me we actually lost two finalists to death, which has never happened before."

"That is sad. And what's worse, from what I can see not one of the audience saw the death episode. What waste of actors. Can we do *anything with the body parts in stasis?"*

Nickle cut in, *"We can't touch them any more. They know something is fishy and have even set up watches round the clock to stop the stasis collection. Peepers messed up big time when he snatched the fleet people. These performers are really clever, better than any before. We can't afford any more mistakes."*

"OK Nickle, no more snatching unless it is totally concealed." said Charonelle.

"So audience!" announced Howley, *"Who is still with us and what are the odds now? Let's hear some betting people. That IS what this is all about!"*

The network began a subdued hum. *"Hey! Cometfart! You still cerebrating?"*

"Wotchit Moonballs! If I had just one leg I'd hop over to your galaxy and boot you in the balls. How much you want on Sheila and Martin. I kinda fancy them..."

CHAPTER 71

After five solid days of de-spin the fragment was almost at relative zero rotation. The stars stayed in place and the sun was now behind them as they drifted towards the pinpoints of the Alpha Centauri system. They were still well within the solar system and had not come close to the orbital path of Mars, which was across the other side of town on the far side of the sun.

Martin and Janine were working the thrusters like precision surgical instruments at Shaw's instruction. Their goal was to remove all appreciable wobble and rotation to ensure the most perfect vector for the Dinkshif Drives. Once in post-relativistic drive, there could be no further adjustment so there was no time limit placed upon getting it right.

An error of one thousandth of one percent could see them missing the Alpha cluster by irretrievable distances, adding years to their journey in recovery. Once the Dinkshif's took over there would be no celestial navigation, no view of the stars. Once again it was do or die.

When all the pilots and Shaw had checked and double checked the instrumentation, there was consensus that the fragment was in perfect configuration for the journey. The water bolus had settled to the correct position even before the acceleration of the drives, due to the tidal pull of the sun. It was miniscule, but enough to be helpful. The pumps would now work, bringing the priceless, life giving fluid to the holding tanks. With no further need for reaction mass, other than personal jet packs for emergencies, every molecule of water would now be recycled at what amounted to one hundred percent efficiency.

The two pilots, Martin and Janine, settled their craft for the last time until half way point turnover, on each side of the complex entrance. The vessels required only light tethering as their own inertia would hold them in place against the pseudo gravity. Everything of possible use was transferred to the complex after the temporary lock was replaced by a sturdy, permanent structure devised by Graham. The final job was to permanently seal the

---

RABI bore hole at both ends.

All four Dinkshif Drives were deployed, the two extras being placed where the ships had anchored to stop the fragment spin. The reasoning was that having an independently controlled drive on each of the principal axes would allow directional correction, and considering that this had never been tried before, Shaw wanted every possible control advantage.

The launch group sat in the complex control room. The dimage module from the transport had been brought in as it was far superior to the ancient Iranian US surplus equipment. The Dinkshif's were linked and controlled from the module. Shaw sketched an envelope shape around the fragment dimage, leaving sufficient room to move the ships if required. The smaller the envelope, the more power the drives could apply to acceleration. He pushed back and made way for Janine, Martin and Sheila to examine his design. Fuller, Tom and Graham looked on.

"Would it make a huge difference," asked Sheila, "if we had a kind of tail and a bulb on it trailing back here?" She moved her hands and a tubular extension appeared, like a sting ray tail. Then she added a bulb to the very end.

"What is that for?" asked Janine, already suspecting the answer.

"Disposal. Sort of a burial area if we ever needed it."

"Makes a lot of sense." Janine looked around at the others for agreement. They all nodded affirmative. "Can you factor that in Gerald and see how it affects us?"

Shaw took the dimage addition and broke it down to surface equations which he pushed into the dimage above. The computer generated the most efficient envelope shape that finally looked like a fat and skinny ten pin. "There's our shape. The effect of the added tail reduces our coefficient of thrust by only one quarter of a percent. We can go with this shape."

The group patted Sheila on the back. "Good call commander." said Fuller.

"Please Colonel, I'm no commander."

"You were promoted in the field I believe?"

"Yes sir."

"Very well. Carry on commander. That is your rank until further notice. Don't ask for a pay increase. There is no pay." Fuller smiled at Sheila who shrugged her shoulders and accepted the inevitable.

Fuller looked around at everyone present, including Zardooz who sat at the back, watching. "This is it people." he said across the comms system to all in the complex. "Any last thoughts or ideas? Any concerns? State them now. We are about to leave our solar system and what was our home. For ever." He waited for a few seconds. There was silence. He nodded at Janine who was to initiate the Dinkshif first stage of envelopment and then to engage the drives. The trajectory was locked in to the dimage system. "Let's go." he said calmly.

Janine touched the activation switch and everyone tensed up.

Nothing happened.

No Change.

Except... yes, the outside monitors were changing from a view of the sharp pinpoints of stars and fuzzy galaxies to a uniform, featureless grey. The large orange digits of the distance panel lit up with its four lines all ticking over, elapsed time, time to go, elapsed distance and distance to go. Two smaller lines showed total time and distance. The time was in hours, minutes and seconds, the distance in kilometers. They were leaving miles and gallons behind as the dimage system was completely metric.

Of course the first thing heard was, "How far is that in miles?" from Felicity.

She cringed when Gerald turned around and shook his head in mock disgust.

"Two and a half years to turnover. Let's make this place home!" said Fuller. "Full community meeting in one hour. We will use the large room two doors down as our permanent "town hall". Maintain the groupings of four and the roster at all times. "Sheila, Martin and Corcoran, please join me now."

The complex went into a relaxed state for the hour, while Fuller and his companions discussed the disappearances in the control room. They didn't have anything to add in the way of detail and did not come closer to a solution or identification of the cause.

However Zardooz was still sitting quietly, listening in. He stood up carefully in the low gravity and sidled over. "Excuse me." he interrupted. "I have some information in this matter."

They turned to him expectantly. "Yes?" said Fuller.

He told them about the women who had died during the fuel bomb blast and how the bodies had vanished from this very room. He had searched the complex later but they were nowhere to be found.

"During my search for these women," he continued, "I also found evidence that certain vermin had entered the complex. There were rat droppings and I found a small, but very deadly snake in a store room. Even its venom alone can be toxic. We must be careful and eradicate these things."

"Why didn't you tell us this earlier?"

"I killed the snake. It was not so important that you should be distracted."

"What else have you chosen not to tell us Mr Zardooz?"

Zardooz looked down and turned his lips into an inverted crescent while shrugging and throwing his palms upwards. He shook his head rapidly indicating that he could think of nothing he had omitted. Sheila watched him closely, noting the body language and analyzing it through her Pirogi Cholent training.

They moved off as a group to some down time before the meeting. Sheila whispered to Fuller, "He's lying through his teeth Colonel. There's more he hasn't told us. Body language analysis is mandatory training in my discipline."

"Are you sure you can read oriental body language?"

"It is partially nurture, but the underlying signals are all nature. I read this slimy bozo loud and clear sir."

"Can you nail a specific subject?"

"He lied about the snake and the rat droppings. He was telling the truth about the women. And he blew it at the end with the whole palms up act. He's good. Just that I'm better."

"Thank you Sheila. I will be very careful."

CHAPTER 72

The meeting resulted in the appointment of standing committees to take care of the functions encountered by any small community, from agriculture to zoology and all points in between. Zardooz had been present but had not been given any specific job or position. When the meeting broke up he made his way across to Fuller and waited for him.

Fuller turned to leave and saw Zardooz. "Yes Mr Zardooz, what can I do for you?"

"Colonel Fuller, this is my complex. This is part of Iran. May I play a part in all this?"

"Mr Zardooz, we wish for you to be able to relax and enjoy this new life. Your primary task is to keep Arjmand under control. He could still do a lot of damage because we don't know his state of mind, even with the amnesia. We are not disrespecting you sir. On the contrary, we are supporting your privileged position."

"Thank you Colonel Fuller. I do appreciate your consideration, however I do not wish to be viewed as a parasite and a user by everyone else. I believe I should have a public position."

Fuller could see that Zardooz was going to keep biting his ankles until he gave in. He thought quickly and came up with a solution. All the essential functions had been covered by committee appointments, so he needed a function that appeared to be essential but actually made no difference. The disappearances were the answer.

"Mr Zardooz, we have one position left, possibly the most important function on the whole fragment which I was going to assume myself. I think possibly that you may fill that position, as you have first hand experience of the phenomenon. Would you consider taking on this important task?"

Zardooz couldn't help a small smile curling on his lips as he pretended to consider accepting the job. "What would my duties be Colonel?"

"You would need to maintain a baseline observation of the whole complex with a personnel distribution overlay. Any sudden differences must be reported immediately to an investigation team. While the team is directed to the anomaly you will be monitoring external monitors and electronic signals, also for anomalies and overt signals. Our conclusion was that we are being monitored and interfered with by an alien civilization with advanced technology. We have yet to find direct evidence, but all the signs point to aliens."

"Hmm. All things considered Colonel, I will be honored to take that position. Will I have any assistants?"

"Of course. Since we tragically lost two of our cadets we have had two teams of five. The two cadets left will now join you and Arjmand to make a team of four once again. Part of our vigilance strategy is that teams are together all the time without exception... even in the bathroom."

"I'm sure that I don't need full time assistants Colonel. I have not been part of a team up to now..." blustered Zardooz, realizing he painted himself into a corner."

"No, those are the rules Mr Zardooz. There are no exceptions. Not me, not you from now on."

Zardooz saw he was beaten again and rolled with the blow. He would find a way to steal some private moments. He had plenty of time to work out a scheme to take over the complex that belonged to him, but for now, he would play along.

"Thank you Colonel. I will assemble my team and get on with the job. You will make known my official position to others please?"

"Certainly."

The ongoing needs of the group were undergoing careful analysis based upon current knowledge. There was an assumption that the youniforms would not last forever so food would become an issue. There was seed stock aboard destined for experimentation on Space City. No more experimentation. This was the food of the future.

Hydroponic farms were built in the caves, using artificial lighting and water from the readily available reservoir One group took the RABI and set it on coarse cut, carving away a chamber into solid rock. The chamber was a side benefit because they wanted the residue as soil. Upon further exploration of the cave system, a whitish strata streak was identified as a phosphate based mineral deposit which they mapped out. They could mine it safely for use as fertilizer to which they added a source of bacteria, the only source of bacteria, human feces, to start breaking down the rock particles and cellulose refuse from around the complex. There was not going to be a planting of seed stock until the soil was safe, some generations of bacterial activity down the track.

Even though hydroponics would be sufficient, keeping the idea of soil based agriculture alive was the primary aim. The sanitation team was closely allied with the agricultural and water teams as they struggled to build a balanced eco-system. They could not afford any mistakes.

Fuller had told the President of Sheila's observation about Zardooz and what he had done to keep him under surveillance around the clock. That jogged the President's memory about something Rafi Ben-Gurion had revealed to him during the hostilities. There was a patch of nano-bot varnish on a desk in this secret complex, the problem now being lack of equipment for receiving and controlling the varnish, plus it was not a US design. Rafi had sent the President one thing, a specification document, but it was in Hebrew, which no one on the fragment knew as a native language.

"Hang on! I do recall Zardooz toasting us in Hebrew. As head of Iranian security he surely must know Hebrew, the language of his enemy! But then, there is no joy in that. We need him to translate the very thing we want to use to watch him."

"How about trying the computer translator?" said the President. "It may not have the power of an on-line facility, but it may give you a sensible text, or something close."

"Worth a try." Fuller worked the computer, retrieving the file sent by Ben-Gurion and loading it into the on board translator. After a few seconds the Hebrew resolved itself into a series of number sequences, which is what Fuller had been expecting. These were the communication frequencies and wavelengths for the nano-bot paint control that the dimage would be able to control. It seemed all to simple for such a sensitive system. The dimage flashed up a message, "UNABLE TO CONNECT". There was an ingredient missing.

The President moved closer and said, "See that symbol up there in the top right corner of Rafi's document? You just went with the main text. Rafi was secular but had a religious bent. I think if you use that sequence in front of everything it may work. His message is that God always comes first... That's it! What is the Hebrew for God?"

Fuller typed in "GOD" for a reverse translation. Four Hebrew characters appeared, which he copied to the original document.

The same numeric sequences appeared, but this time a short numeric line with four numbers, separated by commas, appeared first. 10, 5, 6, 5.

This time the dimage accepted the data and produced the nano-bot paint control screen that was embedded in the numbers. An image coalesced on the screen, but it made no sense... until it moved as a piece of paper that covered the nano-varnish on a desk that was bolted to the floor of a secure conference room revealed...

Zardooz, seated at his desk. He was leaning back working his way through the remainder of the vodka and reading through documents, clearly looking for something. He suddenly stopped and looked around, as if he felt he was being watched. He settled back and gave a start once again, then shook his head to clear it and looked at the remaining vodka in the squeeze bottle. He pulled out a drawer and carefully set the bottle down, cap closed.

In the control room, Shaw jumped to shut and lock the door while Fuller directed the nano varnish to gradually make its way off the desk and move to the ceiling, changing color and texture as it encountered new surfaces. Zardooz was just in the picture as the varnish slid over the edge of the desk to move to the leg. He was head back and snoring from the vodka, papers scattered everywhere on the desk, his two cadet assistants and Arjmand in the annex, separated by a glass door.

"What are you looking for Mr Zardooz?" said Fuller more to himself.

"Nothing good for us I wager." said the President.

"He knows something or is looking for something that will give him an advantage. He's pretending to cooperate and I don't believe he is a suicidal fanatic like Arjmand. He knows that damaging what we have here will kill him too and he can't threaten to blackmail us when he can't follow through, so what can he do?" Fuller touched some dimage buttons and personnel files came up. He spoke out, "Find psychiatrist, psychologist, profiler."

Moments later two names appeared in a list. One was a Space City doctor from Sheila's shuttle who listed psychiatry as a second discipline, and the other was one of the President's Secret Service detail who was a former FBI agent specializing in criminal profiling.

Fuller noted the locations of the individuals and sent Shaw and Felicity to bring them to the control room. He felt that the rule of four was unnecessary since the self destruct charges had been "vanished" from the complex before Arjmand had hit the button. He also had a gut feeling that something had changed with the alien interference. There had been no sign of them for days since the fragment had been taken into Dinkshif drive mode. He had personally felt a nagging anxiety that had been part of his life, and thus unnoticed, lift from him when the Dinkshif envelope was activated. He hadn't quizzed any of the others about this feeling yet. He was waiting to see if any unsolicited comments revealed a similar feeling, and he had certainly noticed a lightening of spirits of many of the population.

He did however notice, every so often and not at a regular interval, the feeling of anxiety trying to invade his mind anew, but now that he had identified this artificial emotion he was able to block it as soon as it manifested itself.

He decided he would discuss this with the doctor of psychiatry after looking at Zardooz.

Shaw was entering with a short, stocky, middle aged man,

obviously well kept and fit, a twinkle in his eyes and a smile on his face. His youniform revealed well defined muscles and the edge of a receding hairline. "Doctor Peter Lewis, Colonel Fuller and the President." introduced Shaw.

The doctor shook hands with both and moved aside as Felicity ushered in the Secret Service agent. "Mr President," she said,"you know David Lucas of course, David, this is Colonel Fuller."

The introductions done, Shaw and Felicity moved to the back of the room while doc Lewis and agent Lucas were seated in front of the dimage and monitor screen. Fuller did not waste any time and went into a full disclosure of everything that had occurred since first contact with Zardooz. He did not give any impressions or draw any conclusions, just straight fact.

When he finished, he looked to the President and Shaw and asked them if he had missed any detail, or if they had anything to add. There was nothing.

Fuller then brought in the first analysis of Zardooz that had even some remotely justifiable basis. Sheila's view that Zardooz was lying about the snake venom on the bottle. Fuller connected the event with Zardooz later volunteering that he had killed such a snake and that there were snakes, rats and vermin in the complex.

"Now gentlemen, I will play back all security auto recordings of our interactions with Zardooz."

Fuller hit the start button and the screen showed the first contact, from the episode with the repair bot, the interaction in the tunnel, right through to the present. Fuller hit fast forward in the static sections and the intelligent system stopped to play when the scene had any significant change.

"Hold it there!" the doctor called.

The scene was Zardooz speaking about the snake venom and rats.

"Can we replay that part but slow it right down please?" the doctor asked, then looked at Lucas.

"I see it." said Lucas. "Sheila Johnson is good. She picked it up too."

The clip ran in slow motion showing Zardooz face on, looking up at the person he was speaking to, probably Fuller. While Zardooz spoke about the disappearance of the women he looked directly at his audience. The moment he started to talk about the snake venom, his eyes flicked down to his left momentarily, then he caught his physiological reaction to lying and he forced his eyes back up again, the small muscles of his face clearly tensed as he fought the lie reaction.

"Can we bring up a still image from before the eye movement and set it beside an after image please?" Lewis asked.

Fuller manipulated the controls and rolled back to an earlier frame, asking the doctor if it was suitable. He nodded affirmative. Then Fuller found the after frame and had the dimage put them side by side. Another command produced three dimensional dimages of Zardooz's face that slowly rotated through ninety degrees, back and forth. The differences were subtle, but remarkably telling.

Doctor Lewis bent closer to look at the small motor muscles. When Zardooz was speaking the truth, the muscles were smooth and relaxed. The moment he had to lie, they tensed up and caused bunching under his skin, especially at the corners of his eyes and mouth. Not having the comparison, or the training and knowledge, one would not see a difference. Here it was obvious.

"Please continue, if that is OK by agent Lucas?"

"Go ahead."

Fuller pressed play and the scene rolled on. The final part showed the recent capture from the nano-bot paint, that Zardooz certainly did not know about. This segment too was most telling, the very first part showing Zardooz relaxed before the sensation of being watched has taken hold, then his reaction to the "watched" feeling somehow caused by the nano-bot paint, followed by his disbelief and blaming it on the vodka.

"That's it." said Fuller. He handed each man a slim file, and said, "This is everything we had on Zardooz before the Destruction Event. Do not remove these files from this room. It has been swept for spying devices and all Iranian communications have been cut off. Everything stays in here.

Doctor Lewis, Agent Lucas, what is Zardooz looking for? What is his plan? That is why you are here."

The pair nodded agreement and put their heads down to read the file material, both adding to the notes they had already taken. Fuller withdrew with Shaw and Felicity to leave them undisturbed.

"Nickle? What's going on? Why don't we have live feed? The audience is getting restless." said Charonelle in a perturbed voice.

"I'm not sure Miz Charonelle. I've tested all the circuits and checked antennas and transmitters. Everything is working OK. We are receiving from all galaxies throughout the universe. I zoomed in on the solar system and everything is in place there. I can see the fragment. It really is moving now and picking up speed. Uh oh!"

"What is it Nickle? What is uh oh?" Charonelle was getting worried and agitated, very unlike her usually clam demeanor.

"I can see a shape that is kinda like the fragment, but it is much bigger and smoother and it is leaving an ionic trail of... wait... of... gold particles behind it. Its like a huge ten-pin flying through space. We can't see inside the shell. Wow, at this rate it will hit light speed very soon."

"Light speed?" This was Howley, now back to normal, if he ever was in such a state. "How did they manage to go from firecrackers on sticks to beating light speed so fast?"

"Who cares Howley! The problem is that we can't see them!" shrieked Charonelle, losing it completely. "What are we going to do? We'll go crazy with nothing to watch. There are no other acts left! Our audience will commit brainicide out of boredom. Howley we have to DO something!"

"I can do a stand-up comedy routine."

"Don't you be a fool Howley!" exclaimed Nickle. "You cain't do stand-up comedy! You ain't got no legs to stand up on!"

Nickle looked at the board and saw a faint green glow come from many of the nodes. The humor of his retort had not gone unnoticed by the audience. Thinking quickly, he announced to the network in his best recording voice, "We apologize for this break in transmission and ask you to be patient while we rectify the problem. Please enjoy the comedy routine from our very own funny man, Howley from the Mandelbrot quadrant, or replays of the goriest incidents in this edition of the World Game, featuring lions tearing apart and eating Roman prisoners and some wonderful footage of guillotine executions during the French revolution. If you do watch these replays, please pay particular attention to the heads bouncing off the cobblestones as they are chopped off and miss the catcher basket.

Other violent atrocities are available through the channel index. Enjoy and we hope to be back on line very soon. This is Nickle Gannon your World Game compere."

CHAPTER 73

The Dinkshif Drives performed as advertised and brought the envelope and contents up and past the speed of light in the universe. Inside the fragment life went on, with days, weeks and months passing as time within the fragment slowed to almost zero relative to the universe they were speeding through, as hundreds of relativistic years passed by in the first weeks of travel.

As the Dinkshif drives accelerated them even faster, the theoretical limits were breached without notice and they entered multiple speed of light velocity, the time dilation effect changing to thousands of years passing in the universe to their months and single digit years.

Inside the complex, the hydroponic garden team had nurtured the small seed stores into burgeoning crops of lush vegetables and fruits. There were no trees, but vines thrived in the low gravity effect and watermelons grew to three times their normal size. Strawberries were as big as a fist all the time. All the produce was huge, tasty and more importantly, nourishing.

Protein came from varieties of beans and one other unexpected source. Fish.

The water conservation team had detected unusual ultrasound reflections when they were surveying the reservoir and caverns still in use. The shadows that appeared in their scans resolved into goldfish and a few lively pike that had been native to the streams that fed the underground system. How these fish had got in was any ones guess, but they were here and the team learned about fish farming and algae control in the process.

The offspring of the goldfish were growing larger than their forebears, whereas the pike stayed essentially the same size. These early generations were nurtured and not farmed at all, so the population increased rapidly, which produced a new problem. What to feed them. Fortunately they took to soy bean meal as an algae and weed substitute, so the closed ecology study group were able to balance their equations to account for this wonderful bonus and to preserve it.

Within months of the discovery, there was sufficient fish population to start culling and delicious fish dinners began to appear on a frequent basis. Bones, offal and waste went back into the garden system as fertilizer which made a difference to the soil growth plants. Small fruit trees were sprouted and controlled using topiary to direct their growth in the enclosed spaces.

The ecology equations were not identical to surface living, but were certainly panning out to be close to correct, with little loss from the total cycle.

All in all, the fragment colony was in good shape.

In the control room, Fuller and the President were meeting with Lucas and Lewis. The observation of Zardooz had confirmed that he was lying but early in the piece, had not revealed what he was searching for. He had not made any overtly threatening moves and had in fact been keeping Arjmand under strict control since the amnesia drug administration. He had been spinning Arjmand a new reality to bring him up to the present, telling him that the world had faced a cataclysmic natural disaster and that Iran and America had teamed up to save some humanity. And that even though he had lost his memory after being struck by a falling rock, Arjmand had been regarded as one of the most important men on the earth and so had been included in the survival program.

Fuller asked doc Lewis, "So do you think this will stick with Arjmand?"

"One can never tell with drug induced amnesia. If we take him off the maintenance level of the drug it is possible his subconscious will restore some or all of his previous memory. His problem will be the confusion of the contradictions, because his current belief is as real to him as his former memories were actually real. He could go into total breakdown."

"We will continue to watch them. So far he has been rendered harmless which was the alternative to spacing him. We don't have that option while in Dinkshif mode. What else can you tell me about Zardooz since we last met."

Lucas pulled out a sheet of precious paper. The notes on Zardooz could not be trusted to the electronic system in case Zardooz had compromised it in any way. Even personal tablet computers were not safe as they linked into the main system. He placed the sheet where all could see it as they moved in closer.

"I have some slight indication that Zardooz has a more than passing interest in the small nuclear reactor that has been powering the complex. He seeks subject matter that skirts the reactor, or has some indirect association with it. Over the past months I have correlated all of his search parameters across dozens of apparently unrelated subjects. The only common thread has been these light touches on the reactor data, always in different areas of the data.

I'm not a nuclear engineer or expert, so what I have done is to list each point where he touched the nuclear database and then afterwards I went in and found the subject matter for each touch. I have a sequential order of his searches, but I do not know if chronology is important. We need a nuclear expert to run over this."

"Doctor Lewis, in light of this information, can you add anything to your evaluation?"

"I think I can Col. Fuller. Zardooz is a very complex personality. Much more than the average person. He has his private persona which he believes we do not see. The nano-paint has revealed the true nature of Zardooz's character and it is this that is driving him. When we assess everything in his public record, and by that I mean your security records and profile right up to the nano-paint insertion by you, he is a walking contradiction. His public face is showing cooperation and withdrawal from the self destructive religious tenet. He appears to be most reasonable and helpful.

His private persona, what I have seen and the little I have heard, seems to indicate that he is still deeply dedicated to his religious beliefs, a contradiction to his public presence, clearly in essence, the destruction of the Great Satan America, in the name of Allah at any cost. He does not believe in the seventy virgins nonsense as Arjmand apparently did but he does appear to have an element of self preservation that will override self destruction if there is even a minute chance of success and self survival.

Other suicide terrorists in the past have had the same last

minute reluctance, and therefore there has been some third party or fail-safe to ensure their destruction. If Zardooz was totally dedicated he would not have reacted as he did when he told you about Arjmand pressing the complex destruct button. I have viewed that recording several times and what I see is genuine relief that Arjmand did not succeed. This contra-indicates the total fanaticism required to self destruct.

My feeling is that although Zardooz is looking to gain some control of the nuclear reactor, he will use it for blackmail purposes rather than self destructive. He will threaten to self destruct but will not follow through unless there is absolutely no way out."

"Mr Lucas?"

"I agree with the doctor, Col. Fuller. Profiling is an inexact science because we only have the known parameters and I do not have access to the computer programs that used stochastic processes to perform the "most likely" analysis. However going back to profiling 101 at Quantico I would agree that Zardooz was and still is a consummate actor and blackmailer. Whether he would self destruct or cave in at an ultimatum, I could not judge at this time."

"Stochastic processes? That is probability and distributions? I had to touch on it during my training." said Fuller. "It just so happens that we have a doctoral graduate in Stochastic Processes who also happens to be an assistant cook and an excellent shuttle commander right here with us. I want you Mr Lucas, to get together with Doctor Sheila Johnson PhD and see if she can help you redevelop the software you need. We have several excellent programmers who can work with you.

I do not want to terminate Zardooz or take any action until we are certain beyond reasonable doubt, the basis of our whole legal system, that he is planning our destruction or a mutiny of sorts. Maintain observation, but proceed as we have discussed with all urgency. I will find our nuclear engineering expert and run this by him, then get back to you. Our code word to meet back here without delay is..." he looked around the room for inspiration that would not result in confusion,"... our word will be elephant." He had spied a small trade mark on the side of a filing cabinet that sported an elephant image, a word unlikely to come up in general conversation. "Use the term "I have an elephant size headache." in some context. Thank you both gentlemen."

The pair shook hands with Fuller and went about their tasks as Fuller contacted Sheila Johnson and cryptically filled her in without any incriminating detail that Zardooz could interpret, if indeed he was listening in somehow. She understood that there was some urgency in what Fuller was implying and immediately set off to find Lucas.

Fuller sat down to devise a simple code in order to pass on orders over comms in the matter. Elephants were the beginning. He sighed in frustration, thinking how the eons old historical, irrational, animosities were sticking to the fragile remains of humanity like superglue. "Will this never end?" he said to himself.

"Nickle? are you there?" Charonelle's voice was crackly and sounded tired.

In the control room, a very old man with long white hair and a skeletal frame woke from a snooze and rolled his chair to the blank board. His rheumy eyes roved over the board as he squinted to see if there was anything amiss.

"Here Miss Charonelle." his voice croaked. "What's up?"

"Have you got any other recordings we can put to the network that haven't been replayed so many times already?"

"I tol' you last time you axed me that. There ain't any more and we can't start another Game. Our systems have broken down. We can't pull players into stasis any more. In fact, I don't know what we CAN do.

In any case Miss Charonelle, my contract finished fifteen thousand years ago just after the system wide shock. The Game was supposed to finish then. OK so no one knew that these performers would take such a huge technological jump and leave us sitting holding our dick if you had one, but I want my retirement and benefits. Look at me now. I'm too old to get it up and I have missed out on life. That ain't fair."

"You are right Nickle, but there's nothing I can do about the situation. Peepers never came out of his amnesia and still thinks he has a body after all this time. Howley disappeared off the network and I haven't heard from him. What can I do on my own?"

"I wasn't gonna upset you Miss Charonelle, but Howley's maintenance system failed and he is now a dried up piece of jerky about the size of a walnut. I'm afraid you really are on your own."

"Oh my! On my own you say? What about Peepers? Is there any chance he will recover?"

"He's been this way for the whole time Ma'am. I don't believe so. I had to use an emergency sub-routine that sends lunatic asylum restraint impressions to Peeper's brain so he thinks he is strapped down in a straightjacket. That keeps him quiet for a time. I think you are really on your own."

"This going from bad to worse. What about the audience? Have we got one still?"

"Looking at the board, we are down to about twenty five percent of what we had at the peak, fifteen thousand years ago. A lot of the audience committed brainicide out of boredom and there was nothing I could do to stop them. Some have gone dormant and others formed their own clubs and are playing Scrabble and Chess. Thousands of games, over and over and over and over..."

"I get the picture Nickle. What can we do to recover this? I can't run it on my own. I don't know how. Peepers was the brain behind it all. Do we have any idea what is happening with the performers?"

"I did some research Miss Charonelle, about six thousand years ago. I think what has happened is that they are travelling faster than light speed inside their bubble towards another star system but we see them moving at a snail pace between their old solar system and Alpha Centauri where they we know they is going to. That's why they have taken fifteen thousand years so far. Time inside their bubble has almost stopped by our standard and the mass inside their bubble is almost infinite, but from what I can see it all happens in alternate universes so this infinite mass doesn't mess us up. So what we didn't know before was how this Dinkshif stuff worked. That came as a total surprise to us. What I found out is that the fifteen thousand years we have been waiting for them, well only two and a half of their years has passed according to this here computer, and they is about to hit the half way mark of their journey where they's have to flip their Dinkshifs and start decelerating."

"Is there any way we can get back in for the audience to watch again, now that you know what is going on with them?"

"I contacted an expert in astrophysics and relativity and he is working on it now, but doesn't hold out a lot of hope because of the random universe generator that their Dinkshif drives use. He said we need to synchronize with their drives to have any chance."

"Nickle! We have to do something. We would have to wait for another fifteen thousand years until they arrive before we can see them again! We can't even start another Game series until this one if finished. It's in the rules."

"There is one remote possibility Miss Charonelle."

"What? What?"

"Well from what I remember, that Zardooz fellow was not as honest as he appeared when he was confronted by Fuller and I know he was looking to get into the nuclear power plant to do some damage. If he succeeds then it may force them back into normal space and THEN we can get back into transmission. My expert said if we can get a drone on board then we can auto synch from inside and pick up transmission even if they manage to get back into Dinkshif mode."

"Oh Nickle! Do you think....?"

CHAPTER 74

Fuller dandled baby Jodie on his knees as she held on to his thumbs and chuckled in glee. Baby Jeffrey crawled up to Fuller's legs and started pulling himself up towards Jodie. Felicity and Sheila looked on with motherly pride at their firstborn as two more crawlers bumped into each other head first, rolled on their backs and started howling out of shock more than hurt. The appropriate mothers jumped forward and cuddled their offspring into quiet sobbing then laughter as the clash was forgotten and tummies were tickled.

Felicity took Jodie from Fuller and Sheila picked up her Jeffrey and took them off for a feed. Fuller returned to the cabin where Janine was working over the turnaround computations.

The rule of fours had been relaxed quite some time ago as it became apparent that there was no further evidence of interference, presumably from the Dinkshif effect. Life was as normal as it could be under the circumstances.

Fuller saw that Janine was engrossed as she glanced up, gave him a smile and went back to her task, so he headed to the secure control room where Shaw was on duty.

The door security had been beefed up by adapting a Bio-Meter as a DNA reader, so Fuller placed his hand on the reader and waited for a moment while the sequencer identified him. The entry light went green and the door unlatched. Fuller entered and was greeted by a warm smile from Shaw who swung back to the monitors.

"Anything doing?" asked Fuller.

"Don't know. All quiet until about ten minutes ago, then I lost track of Zardooz."

"Huh? How's that? We have him nano-painted from head to toe. That's impossible."

"Impossible or not, we've lost him off all tracking."

"Check the reactor room cameras."

Shaw worked the dimage and brought up multiple views of the reactor area and surrounds. Nothing.

"Call up the security teams and get them searching. Activate auxiliary power from the ships to the drives in case he is up to something. Route power to this room and the cameras as well."

"All done sir."

"Secure the nursery and send all off duty personnel to domiciles at ready status. Put out code yellow. We have to find him."

The complex became a buzz of activity as everyone took up their assigned positions or hurried to their quarters. The nursery was locked down with two armed mothers at each entrance, Felicity and Sheila included. No one was going to mess with their babies and they wanted their partners, Shaw and Martin, to be undistracted in their duties. They all knew Zardooz was dangerous. Now they were going to find out just how dangerous.

Suddenly the lighting flickered and whole sections of the complex blacked out. Fuller's preemptive measures kicked in immediately, resulting in the flicker at the millisecond interruption to power.

"Yes! Yes! We're in!" Nickle was elated. The drone had teleported into the complex in the split second of time that the power had cut, the fact being that the space time anomaly of the Dinkshif effect had not fully dissipated but there was enough trans-universal stability to allow the drone to sneak through the interface. Almost.

"Nickle, what is it?" Charonelle had roused from her depressed stupor.

"We got in. Something happened and they came back to our universe for a moment."

"Nickle! I'm so happy I could piss in my pants if I had any!" shrieked Charonelle. "How soon can we get a feed going again?"

"I'm trying right now. I am getting image and some sound pickup, just very garbled. I think it needs time to synch and then transmit out of the bubble. We have to give it time."

They waited, and gradually the image cleared, although the sound transmission remained full of crackling static. Part of the drone's structure involved the use of second generation transmatter gold that was stable in a fixed universe environment, but volatile in a variable interface. The drone had dropped through a very messy interface and had barely made it. The transmatter gold had been partially transmuted back into standard gold and lost its out of universe properties. The drone could not fully penetrate the bubble. What Nickle had was all they were going to get.

"It ain't getting any better Miss Charonelle. I don't think it will get better. We gotta go with what we have."

"All right Nickle. Let me make an announcement about it and then transmit."

Charonelle spoke up and the network started to come to life again for the first time in fifteen thousand years. Nickle monitored the commentary that started up and watched as the private clubs broke up in anticipation of live feed starting again. He started to get up to activate the feed when heard an ominous "crack!" and collapsed onto the floor.

He lay there, moaning.

"Nickle? What are you doing?"

"Oooohh!" he moaned again. "I think I broke something. Oooh it hurts. I think my hip is broken. I can't move. Oooohh!"

"Where is your medic-bot? This shouldn't have happened to you."

"Oooohh!, Haven't seen a medic-bot around in five thousand years. Last time I had a physical. I think maybe it broke down. This is the first time I have tried to stand up since then. I was supposed to be retired ten thousand years ago, fifteen even."

"Well we have to get you fixed up. Can you get back to your desk and chair?"

"It hurts so much! I'll try and drag myself to the desk. AAAAHHHH!" Nickle screamed in agony as he crawled to the desk, his emaciated, twenty five thousand year old body looking like a sack with old bones poking out the fabric. He finally reached the desk and was able to slide out the lowest drawer. He raised himself on an elbow, gritting his yellowed teeth, and felt around in the drawer. He found the box he was looking for and pulled it out. Squinting through myopic eyes he could make out an expiry date on the analgesics he had used seventeen thousand years ago when he had a whopper hangover. "Hmmph! Expired seventeen thousand years ago. But what the heck, it was all he had. He popped three of the opiate based pain killers and dry swallowed them, then laid back on the floor waiting for them to work - or not.

After twenty minutes, he gingerly tried to move a little and found that the pain was just above tolerable, but not excruciating as it had been. He eyed his chair and steeled himself for the effort and agony of climbing back into it. He would then be able to roll about and find the medic-bot. Even if he couldn't fix it, it had stronger stuff in its pharmacy compartment.

An hour later, soaked in sweat from the effort, his broken hip grinding and centering his focus on absolute pain, he was able to roll himself to the activation panel and press the switch to send the drone feed to the network. Then he rolled to the closet where the medic-bot rested, and there it was.

Its power light was dead. It was a hunk of inert metal and plastic and Nickle Gannon, game show compere and all round nice guy, had to become an electronics and nano-technology repair expert.

He could see the pharmacology access hatch on the bot and got to thinking that there had to be some way of replenishing the bot when stuff got used up or expired. Stood to reason that the closet had some interaction with the bot, so he looked carefully at the inside walls. There it was, the outline of a panel that corresponded with the bot's panel. Struggling to reach, and against the bolts of pain that shot from his broken hip, he touched the edge of the wall panel outline, which started a whirring noise. There was a crunch and grind of clogged, corroded machinery and the panel began to open jerkily until it swung out about forty five degrees.

Nickle got his fingers onto the lower edge of the panel and pushed a little, which helped the wheezing motor to complete its job against the detritus of five thousand years. A small probe extended itself once the panel was fully out and moved in and out several times, looking for the bot. Not finding the bot, it withdrew and the panel started to swing back, more easily now that the adhesions had been broken.

"No you don't!" Nickle grabbed the edge and pulled down and the panel movement reversed.

While he held on, he peered behind the bot to see how it was supposed to interface and recharge its power supply. Looking hard, he could see a socket that was supposed to mate with a wall outlet. The protruding socket was apparently spring loaded and would have slid into the wall receptacle under normal circumstances. But what he saw wasn't normal. He looked again, blinking. There was a stringy thing hanging from the join and he could see some tiny bones and ribs covered with scrappy fur. On top of the socket he made out the tiny skull of a rat that had got itself stuck in the socket before the bot had tried to recharge.

"Damn rat!" swore Nickle. But at least he didn't have to be an engineer to fix the bot. He just needed a pest remover. He thought it over and decided it was going to be worth any pain to get the bot working again. He would have to physically man handle the bot off the socket, clean it up and push the bot back, then hope it would recharge and do self maintenance.

"Nickle...." wheedled Charonelle, "we have a little problem with the feed?"

Nickle threw up his hands in exasperation and swore again, "Screw the feeds! I'm injured and hurting!"

"But Nickle, you have to put the audience first at all times. That's in your contract!"

"Lady, get this straight! My contract finished fifteen thousand years ago. I am in pain. Stuff your feeds!"

"But Nickle, the feed is frozen! Nothing is moving!"

"Lady! Use your brain!" He stopped and giggled at what he had just said. "We have a drone in there, but that doesn't alter the time dilation effect. Every second inside the bubble is and hour and forty minutes out here. You'll get more excitement watching grass grow. It's moving all right. At the speed of light! Now leave me alone to fix my hip."

Charonelle went into silent shock at the revelation that they would be waiting for another fifteen thousand years before any entertaining events would happen in relative real time. This was disaster beyond all proportion.

"Nickle?"

"WHAT!" he screamed.

"After you fix your hip... is there anything we can do to help Zardooz sabotage the reactor? We need to get this Game finished."

"Grrrrr! I'll let you know!" He cut off the comms and was isolated. He looked around to see if there was anything he could use as a tool to lever the robot back from the socket and allow the rat remains to fall away. Swivelling back and forth, he saw the outline of another long closet on the other side of the room and remembered back twenty five thousand years when he had to use a broom and pan to clean the floor one time when the jani-bot had broken down. There was also a manual fire extinguisher and an axe in there. Perfect. Except he had to get there and back. He popped another two of the ancient analgesics and started rolling his chair using the desk edge and anything he could grab onto. Wincing in pain at every tiny jolt, he got around to the other side of the desk closest to the broom closet. He had about ten feet of open space to traverse.

"Geronimo!" he yelled as he pushed off from the desk. The swivel chair flew across the open space without slowing and smashed into the closet, bashing Nickle into the wall with another sickening crunch. This time he had broken his left arm. Fortunately he had tied himself into the chair and it had not tipped over.

"Damn!" he swore again. "At least the pain killers are in before the hurt this time."

He opened the closet with his good arm and reached in for the broom which was hanging from a forked rack. The fire axe was inside a glass cabinet and just out of his reach. He could not stand, so he used the broom handle to force the cabinet open and dislodge the axe, which fell with a loud crash to the bottom of the closet.

He retrieved the axe and then using the broom like a gondolier, poled his way back to the medic-bot closet, where he immediately attempted to move the bot using the broom stick as a lever. The stick bent alarmingly, never designed to take such strain, but the bot had moved just a little. The rat remains were still in place. Nickle stopped to think it out.

With only one arm working he needed some leverage he could lock into place so he could use the axe as well. He untied himself and set the swivel chair in the best possible position to push the broom stick behind the robot. With his right arm he levered the stick back and wedged it under the arm rest so the small movement of the bot was held. Using the axe edge as a smaller lever he pried the socket further apart until he could see the whole flat rat. He wiggled the axe and the molded shape of the rat pelt came loose and swung down, just held in place by some strands of fur. With a last effort, the rat fell free and the socket was clear. He pulled the axe out and the socket sprang back into place, only the broomstick preventing it from closing.

Nickle reached under the arm rest to release the broomstick which flicked up as the robot's weight was released into the socket.

WHACK! The broomstick hit Nickle across his right hand, smashing several fingers.

Of course he swore again.

After some choice invectives, he calmed down enough to check out the medic-bot. The lights were on and it was charging its ancient batteries. Now he had to hope that the pharmaceuticals and supplies were still good. The bot could fix him. He didn't bother trying to move again. He would wait for the bot.

CHAPTER 75

"Have you found him?" Fuller asked the search team whose chatter had increased without explanation.

"No sir." The cadet leading the party offered no explanation for the noise so Fuller queried him for the reason. "We found a small hatch in the wall of the tunnel leading to the reservoir sir. It is not marked on any plans and the only reason we noticed it was the rim shadow and some dislodged chalky dust. The hatch is locked sir, or at least we are unable to open it from here.

"Wait there. Do not attempt to open the hatch. I will be there in a few minutes. Be on your guard."

Fuller pulled up the dimage of the fragment with all known tunnels and the complex superimposed. He brought up the beacon of the search team to locate the position of the hatch and zoomed in on the area. Most notably, there was a convergence of the tunnel system with the chamber housing the nuclear power plant, other than the one actual entrance. Now Fuller knew what Zardooz had been looking for. Some obscure documentation revealing this back door to the reactor control chamber. Whether it was there officially or not, it made a great deal of sense to have an emergency exit. Fuller called Lucas and Lewis.

They arrived in short order and Fuller filled them in on events.

Lucas said, "Sheila's program predicted a moderate range non self lethal threat from Zardooz. The very fact that he turned off the power and did not blow up the reactor, well knowing that the ship power would kick in, is a strong indication of his will for self preservation. We have identified a strong internal conflict in his psyche that stems back to his childhood where he was thoroughly brainwashed into the martyr persona, a subconscious reaction that arises every time an opportunity presents itself to do damage to the imagined enemy of his militant religion.

In his later formative years as a youth, spent as the son of an ambassador to the Western World, he discovered the reality that there are far more people existing in peace and harmony outside of his upbringing, other truly peaceful religions that do not demand forced conversion under the shadow of bloodshed. He was fully exposed to the Western educational system according to his profile and was constantly re-indoctrinated with the fantasy of the seventy virgins and the absolute rightness of Islam over all other peoples and religions.

He is a very strong personality, in spite of the apparent wavering between social normality and the instilled, mindless bloodthirstiness of his madras learning. He is able to resist a lifetime of brainwashing and has come to a compromise which has transferred his loyalty from religion to state. By doing this he has partially assuaged his internal voices that urge him to martyr himself, by reasoning that he must remain whole and alive for the sake of his country.

Col. Fuller, all the indicators are present that he will not self destruct, and will capitulate if driven into a corner, provided there is some small way out of the predicament. If he is totally trapped with no out, he may well act out the martyrdom persona. It is imperative that we do not drive him into an absolute situation."

"Thank you Doctor Lewis. Mr Lucas, anything to add?"

"Yes Colonel. Working with the same data, but applying profiling methods that the FBI developed, I tuned my analysis to be a little less in depth on the personal side, although the profile matches precisely that of Doctor Lewis, and looked for possible scatter effects. We knew he was searching for something and never pinpointed it. Now we have this event which fills in the blanks, but I have not had time to fully integrate this new data into the profile, so I am going to risk an analysis update on the fly. With Doctor Lewis moderating, I think what comes out will be close to accurate.

Taking up where the doctor left off, Zardooz is the type that will pad himself with extra protection if he can find it. I would suggest at this moment that we determine the whereabouts of Arjmand, who would be his first level of protection, and then head count all other personnel, including children. He is a classic hostage taker. He will have levels of negotiating using each threat level until he gets what he wants or he takes the ultimate step and destroys everything."

Fuller immediately called and emergency alert across the comms and ordered the head count. He sent a security team to check on Arjmand who was usually locked away in a room talking to himself.

"Mr Lucas," asked Fuller, "We have determined that Zardooz will only self destruct if he is painted into a corner with no way out, and I do not intend for that to happen. If we do get hold of him he goes into the next room to Arjmand for the rest of the journey." The comms interrupted.

"Colonel Fuller, Arjmand is not in his room!"

"There you go." said Lucas.

A further urgent comm squawked out, "Col. Fuller, the head count shows Felicity and Jodie not accounted for! Gerald Shaw has taken a weapon and is heading for the hatch. We have warned the team there!"

Fuller switched the comms to Shaw's personal frequency. "Mr Shaw! Report in please."

"Go away!" came the growled reply. "This bastard doesn't touch my family!"

"Mr Shaw, we have the situation under control. Your action could trigger an immediate self destruction by Zardooz who is using Arjmand. Gerald, calm down and report here to me. We will get Felicity and Jodie back safely and not blow us all up in the process."

Shaw slowed down his headlong charge towards the tunnels and then stopped. A security team in front of him warily eyed the weapon he held and kept back. He looked up at the pair, suddenly realizing the fear he had put into them. He put the gun down and signalled then that everything was okay. They moved in and gently patted him on the back, telling him to report to Fuller. One picked up the weapon and the trio moved off.

"Shaw reporting for duty sir." he replied to Fuller, the dismay clear in his voice.

That crisis averted, Fuller turned back to Lewis and Lucas. "How do you recommend we proceed gentlemen?" The pair looked at each other and Lewis indicated to Lucas to speak.

"If we were not in this bizarre situation, I would compare it to a classic terrorist hostage scenario of the jihad movement of the last century, typically the aircraft hijacking. Usually the actual mastermind was not present at the hijacking and used his drones as perpetrators and cannon fodder. As the atrocities proceeded through the decades, the soldiers died and were replaced by more brainwashed automatons who also died thinking they were going to get seventy virgins when they could often not get even one in real life. It was national intelligence services and their active teams that took out the head terrorists and that tended to calm the activity for a time until a new engineer of terror rose out of the murk.

We have a small scale event being conducted by a schizophrenic half statesman half terrorist accompanied by a totally brainwashed follower. I believe that Zardooz will use Arjmand as his weapon. His threat will be serious, even paralyzing to us, but he will be in a safe place until the effects of his attack dissipate or until he can find further safety. He will sacrifice Arjmand without compunction and Arjmand will do it willingly, whatever it is.

Zardooz is fully acquainted with the capability of our youniform and buddy combinations. He also knows we have drugs that can incapacitate, Arjmand being the give away, so he will be doing something that he believes we cannot stop using any of these tactics, or if we do apply them, the hostages will also be harmed by our own actions.

It is clearly in his own interest for us to reach and achieve landfall on a new home planet, or his purpose is totally negated unless our profile is completely wrong.

I am puzzled as to why he has made his move now instead of in another two years or so when we approach Alpha Centauri. I must conclude that he has some other agenda other than the purist jihad focus. We need to figure out what it is very fast, as the turnover time seems to be the trigger for his action."

There was the silence of thought for a few moments before Fuller asked the doctor, "How do we handle the hostage situation.

That is my first concern, to get Felicity and Jodie out unharmed."

"The key," the doctor answered, "is to keep that small chink of hope open for him at all times. Throw doubt on his premise, whatever it is. Keep him negotiating and that will keep his moderate, Western influenced persona dominant. He wants something, so he needs to give something back to get it."

"I have an idea. We need to call Sheila and Martin in." said Lucas. "She mentioned something in passing while we were setting up the program that may give us a clue to what Zardooz is up to. I suspect it may have something to do with the aliens and the disappearances."

"Do it." answered Fuller.

Minutes later Martin and Sheila showed up at the door. Fuller let them in and seated them, signalling Lucas to proceed.

"In the manner of Sherlock Holmes, when you eliminate the impossible, whatever is left, however improbable, is the answer. I do believe, since we have eliminated every logical reason for Zardooz to strike now, that only leaves an expectation of alien intervention.

Zardooz is quite warped, mad if you will, but still a scientist under all those veneers. He has had enough time to work out the Dinkshif effect and to understand the theory behind the practical application. He also experienced the alleged alien interference first hand and has been privy to the fact that since we entered Dinkshif space, there has been no sign of the aliens. This whole episode appears to hinge around the mid journey turnover when we reduced the drive thrust for just enough time to rotate them for deceleration. The nuclear power cut off came at the precise moment of lowest Dinkshif effect.

I was able to discuss some of the theory with Graham who explained that the glitch in power during ship turnover, that exact moment when Zardooz cut the reactor, could have exposed the fragment to full or partial normal space in our own universe for nanoseconds. I do believe, putting all these jigsaw pieces together, that Zardooz wanted to let the aliens back in on the principle of "the enemy of my enemy is my friend" even though the aliens are clearly no friend. Which brings us to Martin and Sheila.

You two have had the most exposure to the disappearances presumably orchestrated by some all powerful alien civilization. Starting with you Martin, what were the exact circumstances of your event?"

"You know," Martin had a far away look on his face as he thought deeply, "As wierd as it sounds Corcoran and I didn't actually see the passenger disappearance happen.

But before that, when the original mutineers were sucked out into space, we could see the agony on their faces as they asphyxiated and boiled out, apart from the lacerations from broken glass. They were in terrified agony. As they were swept away into space I followed their path using the youniform zoom to keep them in sight as long as possible. They simply winked out on me. One moment there, then gone. I thought they had drifted into a lunar shadow and about then I had my hands full with the rest of the passengers who were rioting and had locked myself and Corcoran out of the transport. We could see in and it was an absolute shambles. We got back in and blasted off in a hurry. Ten of the passengers had vanished when we went back to check on them. During the prep for ejecting the useless stuff we were both occupied and when we went back to the passenger area the ship was empty. We knew something weird was going on but there was nothing we could do about it."

"Thank you. Sheila, your experience with the fleet and Bob Evans please?"

"I can't add any more to my original report. Our shuttle was almost out of reaction mass as we headed to join the fleet behind the moon to escape the anti-matter swarm. Corcoran and Martin had used a laser reflecting off the anti-matter to send out a Mayday signal and the reflected laser frequencies from the anti-matter set off grand mal epilepsy like seizures in people who had no history of the affliction. If they were not removed from the source very quickly the seizures stressed the body beyond limit and the person died, which is what happened to our pilots and one passenger, who subsequently could not be found." She reached out for Martin's hand and squeezed it reassuringly, for no matter that no one could have predicted such an effect, he still felt bad inside and his expression had saddened at the verbalizing once again.

Shelia continued,"We figured out what the message was and by then we were in line of sight communications with the fleet. Commander Bob Evans had taken charge and put me in command of my ship. He worked out an intercept with Martin and Corcoran but we had to lose their transport. It was calculated but risky, however the alternative was to see them go by and continue into space forever.

When I called for teams to help from among my passengers, I had to quell a small mutiny by some of the guys using my martial arts skills. Incidentally, these guys, one in particular, have redeemed themselves many times over. The incident needs to be forgotten. We performed the rescue that went pretty well as planned, including the scenario for a miss of the catching net, and I caught Martin who had missed the net. We reeled back in after sharing my youniform and buddy melding as he was out of recyclable air after such a long time." As she spoke of the suit sharing she looked at Martin with a melting smile that he couldn't resist and he very unprofessionally reached out and hugged her.

"Okay lovebirds, that'll do." chided Fuller with a grin.

"When we got back to the shuttle we tried to call the fleet but there was no reply. At first we thought our radio was malfunctioning but then we looked with some focus on the anti-matter swarm passing and saw that the distant view of the fleet under magnification did not look normal. The ships were all coated in anti-matter.

We couldn't assume that everyone inside them was dead and it explained the non response to our signals. The anti-matter had damaged the fleet equipment, so we decided to approach and observe. In any case we had to do something because we had no reaction mass left and we were as stranded as the fleet."

Fuller stopped her there for a moment. "Doctor? Mr Lucas, anything you would like to ask at this point?"

"Yes, I do." said Doctor Lewis. "I am seeing a pattern emerge here that at this point is as tenuous as a soap bubble, but it may lead somewhere. Martin, when you were drifting, after missing the net, what was your state of mind?"

"I was worried, but more for the person who was risking everything to come after me. I was confident that if I could be saved, our service dedication and loyalty would bring me safely home, and it did. I never gave up hope. I guess it was the best few hours of my life because I had my first date with Sheila!" Martin laughed.

"Without going into too much detail, that was my next question for both of you. I have no idea what your previous "dating" experiences were in life, so if you do have a comparison, how was this any different?"

Sheila and Martin looked at each other. She was suppressing the urge to crack up laughing and he was biting his bottom lip for the same reason. "It was an out of this world experience Doctor." Martin spluttered and then regained composure. "Physically, I guess for me it was a perfect ten out of ten, and I think Sheila would agree?" she nodded assent with a huge grin, "However on an emotional level, I can say that I would never have imagined that two people could merge their psyches as we did at that time. I had not one speck of doubt that Sheila was perfect for me, that our love for each other, as new as it was, was the most perfect love in the universe. This was not artificial that would dissipate like taking a party drug. This was real."

"Sheila?" queried the Doctor.

"I agree absolutely. In fact since then, Martin and I seem to think alike and anticipate the other's thoughts before we get to verbalize. It's almost telepathy. I would like to say something about the whole event that normally would not leave a person's bed room, but considering the circumstances and where I am guessing the Doctor is heading with all this, well I have had a couple of experiences from time to time, but they didn't work out with the guys. Coming together with Martin, and I mean that in EVERY sense," she grinned again, "I had the longest and most intense orgasm of my life along with the emotional bliss and total joining with Martin. I think the intensity of our tryst must have generated some effect in the universe. I am suggesting that we go back and look at any recordings we have of background radiation, anything, that happened, changed or peaked at that time.

Now one more thing. Felicity and I were talking women's stuff, and she intimated that she had a similar experience with Gerald Shaw, so we must look at that time as well."

"The pattern is becoming clearer, the more I hear." said Doctor Lewis. "Can we get those readings Col. Fuller?"

"I'm already on it Doctor." Fuller was working the dimage system, inputting the dates and times of pivotal events since the first observed disappearance. He brought up multiple images, each displaying a simple line graph of a measurable parameter, such as background radiation, radio frequency transmission, solar radiation and subatomic particle measures. They all appeared unremarkable except for the universe background radiation. That had some interesting corresponding blips. Fuller tweaked the vertical axis and the blips became definite peaks that EXACTLY matched the pivotal events and then vanished when the Dinkshif drives had been activated.

The group moved in to look and marvel.

"It appears that Mr Zardooz has an amazing intuition that we had to prove using science." said the Doctor. "So Col. Fuller, who can explain what this background radiation is to us laymen?"

"That's easy." Fuller touched a question mark on the dimage screen and the computer spoke, explaining about the ambient radiation that filled the universe and confirmed the big bang theory of creation. Until this very moment, the radiation had been a constant factor, diminishing in intensity as the universe continued to expand. There had never been measurable glitches in recorded history.

"I think we have found a sign post pointing to our aliens." said Fuller. "We need to look closely at the corresponding events and peaks."

He removed the other dimage screens and increased this one to take the whole wall, revealing a constant variation level between the spikes, like teeth on a saw. "Look at all that activity," he exclaimed, "and we had no idea. Uh oh!" He stopped short, pointing to the far right end of the time line. The smooth line from the Dinkshif activation until the present was broken by a single spike that matched the turnover point and Zardooz's knocking out the nuclear power. Fuller magnified this spike until it revealed that it had a flat top and had lasted for ten microseconds, the area under the spike representing the energy level of the event.

"Call Graham in here now!" Fuller urgently ordered Sheila. He went back to the other spikes and examined them closely. They were all irregular in their profile, exhibiting some randomness. The squared off spike was something else all together. But what?

"Here's Graham." said Sheila and went to let him in.

Fuller went over the discoveries and the Zardooz situation and got Doc Lewis and Lucas to summarize their analyses, which were rapidly turning from the realm of ephemeral theory to solid fact.

"So this spike," said Fuller, pointing to the squared off anomaly, is the first indication since Dinkshif space and certainly out of character."

Graham perused the earlier spikes then concentrated on the last one. "The flat top is absolutely indicative that there is an artificial radiation source here. Let me think this through for a moment."

The group was silent as Graham stared intently at the dimage. He moved the fingers of his right hand as though he was playing the piano in the air. Doctor Lewis pursed his lips as he watched Graham processing and gave an almost unnoticeable nod of admiration for the mental aclarity and ability he was observing. Nothing unusual in this group of the top minds in the space program, but still worthy of appreciation, like viewing an old painting masterpiece actually being painted.

"Do we have any other observation recordings, anything, for this time segment? I believe there should be a Dinkshif envelope integrity record in the system. You didn't look at it before because it has no relationship to external radiation or other phenomena."

Fuller immediately pulled up the record Graham wanted and displayed the relevant time line segment below the universal radiation graph.

There was an obvious bump in the line corresponding to the flat topped glitch. The rest of the line was essentially smooth.

"We could say that this glitch occurred due to the power fluctuation when Zardooz did his thing, but by my calculations that should have resulted in a net deficit to the envelope integrity charge. What we are looking at here," said Graham with authority, "is an increase in charge where the envelope was doing its job, trying to prevent a foreign body penetration by repelling it before it could hit. The power fluctuation just at that instant weakened the envelope integrity enough to allow something to pass through it. Looking at the flat top radiation blip here reinforces that theory because the energy represented by the area under the blip is significant. In fact I think we can work out the approximate mass and size of whatever penetrated by using the energy variable which will give us the mass, and the envelope resistance variable which will give us a cross sectional area of the object size. Then we will know what to look for. Maybe not where to look for it is the rub."

Fuller turned to the group. "People, we obviously have a security breach that unfortunately puts Zardooz on the back burner. I don't believe he knew the extent of what he was doing, however the damage is done. Mr Graham, please do your calculations and take anyone you need to assist you. As soon as you have a result, publish it to all personnel and we will escalate the search from anything unusual to something more specific.

Sheila, I want you to gather a strike team, those with combat and hostage experience, maybe three others, and work out a plan to pay a crash visit to Zardooz. We can't spare any more people. Shaw must not be one of the team, regardless. Report to me when you have something."

"Col. Fuller," the President had been sitting quietly at the back of the group through the whole series of meetings and developments, "there is one thing we need to consider."

"What is that please?"

"We have the nano-paint transmitter. The aliens have somehow been observing us from time immemorial in some fashion.

The Dinkshif effect obviously upset their observation system as we have just proved, so isn't it logical to assume that whatever has entered our habitat was possibly not just a single observer device, but maybe a container for something like our nano-paint? Something that could spread through our spaces and observe, even cause disappearances again?"

"Point taken Mr President. Get Mr Shaw in here. We need some way of identifying alien stuff that could be dust, paint, anything. Everyone else, move on your tasks and report in anything you feel out of place, even if it is a fleeting gut feeling."

The group dispersed except for Fuller, the President, Lewis and Lucas.

Fuller pulled up a corner of his mouth and his eyes twinkled with mischief. "Oooookay gents!" he drew out to raise anticipation. "Here's a first for psycho-analysis and FBI profiling. Can you profile our aliens?"

"Worst case," laughed Lucas, "is we'll end up with a great Science Fiction story that no one will ever read, or we get a little lucky and come close."

Nickle lay sprawled in a stupor, dulled by the painkillers he kept popping. Every so often he lifted an eyelid to peer back at the bot's charge light. it had gone from red to yellow. He needed green so he slumped back again.

"Nickle? Oh Nickle, are you there?" sang Charonelle in her sweetest, most innocent little girl voice.

"Bugger off!"

"Nickle! I'm shocked! I just wanted to check on you!"

"Sure you did. Like a fly checks on cow shit. Bugger off. I'll call you when I'm ready."

He saw something change in the corner of his eye and was relieved to see a green light on the medic bot. He wasn't entirely sure how to activate it to help him, so started with verbal commands.

It didn't move. But something flashed across the view screen on its front. He strained to move a little to read the scrolling message. It said "manual re-activation required. Press and hold on/off switch

---

for ten seconds."

It was going to hurt again, but he had to worm his way closer to reach the switch he could see on the side. He slid out of the chair onto the floor like jello out of a mold.

He stretched his right hand out and with excruciating pain from his broken fingers used his knuckle to hold the power switch down for the ten seconds that felt like ten hours. He heard the welcome message spoken by the bot and flopped back on the floor, completely spent and spread-eagled.

The bot rolled out of its closet right over Nickle's broken hand and he let out a shriek like never before heard in creation.

"Sorry sir!" said the bot. "Still calibrating. What can I do for you sir?"

Nickle gritted his teeth and said, "I have a broken hip, a broken arm and several broken and now crushed fingers. I am starving and dehydrated. What else do you want to know?"

"What is your mother's maiden name sir?"

"WHAT?"

"Your mother's maiden name please sir. I need to validate your identity before providing treatment. You have a co-pay of thirty five credits if you check out okay."

"Aw!" moaned Nickle. "Mother's maiden name was Gunston."

"That is correct sir. However, you said WAS, not is. Where is your mother now sir?"

"She's dead you dickhead robot. Has been for twenty five thousand years."

"My sincere condolences sir. As she is dead and I am unable to verify your response, let me ask some other security questions."

"JUST HELP ME YOU MORON!"

"Abusive talk will get you nowhere sir. What was the name of your first pet?"

Nickle thought clearly for a moment. The idiot bot said "was" the name. Won't matter if the pet is dead. "My first pet was called Rocky."

"Good sir. Now was Rocky one of the following, a squid, a porcupine or a dog?"

"A DOG! NOW HELP ME!"

"Excellent sir. How would you like to do your co-pay sir? I take credit card or direct debit of your account on file."

Nickle sighed in defeat."Direct debit."

"Thank you sir. Please enter your pin number on my number pad sir."

"I can't. My fingers are crushed because you ran over them."

"I do apologize sir. I will request a ten credit discount for your inconvenience. Now please enter the pin number."

"I just told you I can't. One arm is broken and doesn't move and my fingers don't work on the other hand."

"One moment please!"

The bot made some whirring noises and rolled around Nickle's body, stopping at his only working limb, his right leg. "Please enter your pin using your toes sir."

"AAAAHHHGGG! I HAVE SHOES ON YOU IDIOT!"

"Your ten dollar discount is cancelled due to further verbal abuse. Please remove your shoes."

"I can't move."

"I will remove them for you sir. That will require a further thirty five credit co-pay."

"Fine. Do it. AAAHHHHGGG!" Nickle split the air with another scream of pain as his broken hip was wrenched by the bot pulling off the left shoe. It then did the right shoe.

Nickle didn't see the board going green all over for the first time in eons, as Charonelle surreptitiously routed feed to the control room. The network was getting off on Nickle's agony because the real show was static.

"Please input your pin sir."

Nickle raised his working leg and squinted at the pin pad six feet away. Even with socks on he figured he could hit the right four numbers. He went for it.

"Sorry sir, incorrect pin number. Try again."

He tried again.

"Almost sir. One number wrong. Try again."

"Please remove the sock on my right foot robot."

"Yes sir. That will be another thirty five credit co-pay." The robot pulled off the sock, pinching and breaking the middle toe in the process. Nickle just whimpered. He had no scream left in him. He carefully aimed and pressed the correct sequence.

"Very good sir. I need to do an IME sir to determine what procedures should be followed."

"What's an IME?"

"Initial Medical Examination. I will determine if I can treat you sir or if we have to send you to a trauma center."

"Robot, is there any way we can skip the IME and get down to treatment. I am in agony here and close to dying."

"Oh sir, I will immediately reclassify you as an emergency. All the co-pays are cancelled. Triage commencing!" The robot started making all sorts of dings and whistling noises as it ran around Nickle, sending probosci into his body, measuring and recording. "Most serious deficiency is hydration sir. I am inserting an intravenous feed of fluid and nutrients."

Arms and tools popped in and out of the medic bot and gradually Nickle started to look like an Egyptian mummy as his fractures were taped. The bot trundled into its closet and came back with an inflatable half body cast to immobilize the broken hip. Once applied, the bot lifted Nickle and placed him on his sleeping pallet and put Nickle into a deep sleep.

The board went yellow and then blank.

"Nickle? Oh Nickle?" wheedled Charonelle. "Nickle?"

CHAPTER 76

"We may have an identifier!" said Shaw excitedly. He and Corcoran had been using the nano-paint as the basis for the possible alien infiltration device. They had nothing else to go on. They had looked at detecting the emissions from the nano-paint but nothing was apparent unless an actual transmission was in progress, and even then it was almost impossible to detect as the nano-paint was programmed to detect the detector and shut down.

What Shaw and Corcoran had found was that a spectrum analysis of the interface between the nano-paint and the base paint or varnish layer showed a distinct spectral variation. As good as the nano-paint was, it was programmed to fool the human eye, not a precision instrument that was not anticipated by the designers of nano-paint. The spectrum analyzer viewer consistently showed a line when nano-paint was present.

"Okay Gerald, let's go look around with this." Corcoran led off with the spectral analyzer held in front of him like a flashlight with a view screen at the back. It was standard equipment on the transports for detecting micrometeorite hull leaks. The escaping molecules of gas altered the spectrum of reflected light off the hull, just as it had detected the nano-paint earlier.

Corcoran paused and turned to Shaw, saying, "If you were an alien hooked on voyeurism and getting off on violence and sex, where would you put a spy? And especially if it was your favorite X-rated couples, Hannaford and Shaw and Johnson and Martin?"

Shaw looked at Corcoran wide eyed. "Not in my bedroom they don't." He took off, Corcoran trailing with the spectral analyzer. At least Shaw's mind was temporarily distracted from the predicament his wife and child were in.

They reach Shaw's living quarters and burst in, looking about and swinging the spectral analyzer all over the place. "Hang about." Corcoran stopped. "This isn't going anywhere. Let's be scientific about this. Stop, look and think. Where would you get the best view of the hottest couple in the universe?"

"Above the bed!"

They moved into the master bed room and turned on the lights. The walls had pictures and mirrors attached. The ceiling was flat white with illumination panels strategically set for gentle illumination. Above the double bed was a clean expanse of ceiling.

Corcoran aimed the analyzer at the center of the ceiling, above the bed, and peered at the screen. "Well what have we here?" Shaw looked over his shoulder. "What we have here is an interesting spray of spectrally different dots, but we are not getting a line definition." He hit the magnification times twenty which brought a small area of the scatter into focus revealing dots within the dots. Further magnification was unable to resolve a final particle size. It was too small for the analyzer's optical function which could get down to cellular level, but not molecular or atomic.

"We need a sample for analysis." said Shaw, climbing up on the bed to reach the low ceiling.

"No! Don't touch it! You'll tip them off that we found them."

"Doesn't matter, they won't know for days or even weeks. We look like a frozen movie screen to them because our time has virtually stopped relative to the universe. That they even inserted this stuff doesn't make sense to me and there have been no disappearances since it happened." He reached up and carved a circle of paint away with his utility knife, peeling the circle of emulsion away like wallpaper and dropping it into a bag.

Corcoran had the analyzer pointed at the spot. "The dots are moving in to fill the space. They must be autonomous like our nano-paint. Hold up the bag for me." He trained the analyzer on the bag. "They have grouped to the center of the patch. About the size of a cent coin. Let's get back to the lab."

Now they knew what they were looking for, Corcoran kept scanning walls and ceilings all the way back. Apart from a true patch of dirt, the complex was infested with small, strategically positioned patches of alien transmitters.

Shaw had notified Fuller of their success and he was waiting for them, after giving Sheila and her team the go ahead on their rescue plan. The rest of the personnel were searching for the alien delivery vehicle while Lewis and Lucas were close to developing the likely alien profile.

Sheila's team had the most intensive job at that moment. Fuller had search teams close by ready to back Sheila up in an instant and the Doctor and Lucas were ready to drop their task and assist her in negotiating.

The four team members were at the access hatch and already cutting away the lock mechanism with a small laser torch. It fell away to the pseudo gravity and the hatch swung open easily. The tunnel behind was simply an unlit crawl tunnel, so they crawled. Sheila carried a flashlight and locator that was fed by the central computer. As they moved, it added the unknown, new tunnels to the map.

She stopped suddenly so she would not slip forward as the tunnel sloped sharply down. She could see small ridges in the floor ahead, obviously for friction to allow movement up the incline and prevent uncontrolled sliding down. If not for the youniform, her knees would have been shredded. She moved on cautiously, noting that the tunnel was man made of concrete and not carved from bed rock. Up ahead she could see an end wall and a deep shadow to the right where the tunnel turned.

She signalled her team to stop, turned off her flashlight and moved forward, feeling her way to the edge of the corner. She peeked around and pulled back, expecting to see more darkness. The latent image in her mind showed a grating with a little light slipping through. A ventilation duct screen. She signalled to move forward, complete silence.

At the screen Shelia took out a syringe with a long tube instead of a needle and slipped it through the lowest slot, right in a corner where it would not be noticed, and depressed the plunger for one drop of the liquid to be expelled.

The thinned nano-paint flowed out and onto the chamber wall, returning an image to their youniform viewers instantaneously. It was not a scene that anyone had expected. Fuller and his group watching in real time were astonished and horrified.

The view was of the annex to the main reactor room, with

control panels and screens around the perimeter. The focus was the group in the center of the room.

Felicity was taped to a chair by her wrists and ankles, a piece of duct tape over mouth. Next to her, looking frantically wide eyed at the vent and wagging his head negatively, was Zardooz, similarly taped up. Beside them stood Arjmand who had wrapped some cloth around his head to make a turban, holding little Jodie and talking to her in Farsi, waving his free arm about and with a wild look in his eyes.

On closer observation Arjmand also had something clutched in his hand with his thumb pressing down on a button.

A dead man's switch.

Arjmand stopped his ranting as Fuller's voice came across the comms system. "President Arjmand, how are you feeling today?"

The bland, unthreatening line took Arjmand by surprise. His delusional state had prepared him for an all out assault, not a friendly greeting. Taken aback, he blinked, lost for words. Then it started.

"You must address me as "Your Highness" the incarnation of Sal-A-Din, the greatest warrior of Islam, ruler of the world and chosen of Allah!" he screamed, startling Jodie into crying and reaching for her mommy. "Bah!" Arjmand dumped Jodie onto Felicity who could do nothing. He reached out and ripped the duct tape off her mouth without warning.

"I will let your whore here talk to you. She knows what is required by Allah! If you do not comply immediately I will kill this brat first, then I will cut Zardooz to pieces and then to her, and then I kill her very slowly. If you still refuse I let this button go and the reactor blows up." He turned and ripped the tape off Zardooz. "Tell them Zardooz. Tell them that I know exactly what I am doing."

Zardooz, face raw where the tape had ripped out a day's growth of beard, gasped in pain. "He knows... he knows, Col. Fuller. I was just going to take control of the fragment for Iran. I brought Arjmand down here also and he somehow got loose and stunned me. I had no idea he was this mad..." Zardooz was cut off by a vicious backhanded blow to his face that rocked his whole body and tipped the chair over backwards, smashing his head onto the concrete floor. His eyes rolled back in his head, unconscious. Arjmand continued to kick and punch Zardooz, only stopping when he saw that it had no effect on the man who was out cold.

Arjmand slowly looked up and around, his thought processes coming together to realize that Fuller could see him. He stopped and a crafty look came over his face. "Colonel Fuller, I wish to see you immediately on screen, or the whore gets the same treatment!"

In the control room Fuller did not hesitate and projected himself to the comms screen. He pressed the background omit to keep a slight edge and looked to the Doctor. Fuller had to be constantly on screen so they resorted to writing fast notes. Fuller's first was "He doesn't know about the duct?"

The Doctor wrote back, "Clearly not. He would have done something about it by now."

"Dragged in unconscious or drugged by Zardooz?"

"For certain."

While all this scribbling was going on, Arjmand was ranting at Fuller's image, nothing intelligible and in a mix of Farsi and English.

Fuller wrote, "Warn Sheila to be ready to move - risk - but have to stop him."

"Done. Your call. Nothing anyone can do right now."

Fuller wrote to Lucas, "Recommendation?"

"Move fast. He is totally unstable."

"Dead man switch?"

"Confrontation - no kill - Sheila move fast - martial arts - only way."

"Tell Sheila I will enrage him - distraction - get vent loose and ready to enter - explain non-lethal, switch is target."

Lucas instructed Sheila precisely while Fuller waited for the ranting to stop. The longer the better for Sheila to prepare.

After a few minutes Arjmand calmed down, so Fuller started. "Your Higness Sal-A-Din, I would like to discuss this situation with you man to man. Will you allow me to join you?"

"This will do Col. Fuller. I want none of your satanic tricks."

"Okay Your Highness. But I am concerned that your brilliant plan to honor Allah has been far eclipsed by the exploits of one much greater than Your Highness."

Arjmand reacted to this by stiffening up and closing with the screen, as if face to face with Fuller. "And who is this greater than myself person?" he screamed.

"There was a great leader of a group called Al-Quaeda at the beginning of this century who claimed to be fighting the war of the prophet for the same sake of Allah..."

Arjmand cut Fuller off shrieking, "You do not compare me with that pig dog Osama Bin Laden! He never set foot near an action and lived like you western decadent dogs. All he did was send others to be killed. I am here doing Allah's work myself, just like my name sake, Sal-A-Din. If I die now it will be for Allah, in glory, not shot down among whores and dumped out of a helicopter into the sea. I will..."

There was a loud crash from off picture as Sheila and her team tumbled into the room in a controlled avalanche of bodies. Sheila was focussed on Arjmand and his hand holding the switch.

She whispered "God help me!" and dived at Arjmand who instinctively kicked out a leg, blocking her move.

Arjmand's mind went blank and he released the switch.

CHAPTER 77

Time stopped. The Universe stopped.

God spoke to a human being once again.

"I am with you Sheila."

Sheila found herself transported to a place where she was surrounded by all her friends. No one was injured and all looked at peace but a little puzzled.

"Your faith in Me is its own reward Sheila. I have created a new Universe for My creations to begin again. I give free will to My creations to choose to seek Me and do good for each other. This is the purpose of My creation. There is no other purpose. Your son Jeffrey and the daughter of Felicity, Jodie, will be renamed Adam and Eve and will be the only remainder of this creation to be placed in the new universe, to populate it and through your children, bring glory to My Name. You and all your friends will be brought to a place by My side, to exist in My radiance and to marvel at your children on the new Earth. Now please, you and Felicity, give your children a final word."

Neither Sheila nor Felicity felt panic or fear of losing their children. This was their God and Creator, all Truth and Love.

Sheila picked up Jeffrey and hugged him, whispering in his ear, while Felicity did the same to Jodie, finally holding her out and looking deep into her brilliant blue eyes for the understanding. It was there.

EPILOG 1

Still drifting through the old universe, the fragment continued its journey, the nuclear blast having been stopped by God, who now spoke to Arjmand and Zardooz in a dream.

They awoke in astonishment that they were still alive.

"I should kill you now Arjmand, for what you did to me!"

"You can't. Allah just spoke to me and said we are both immortal. There is no one left but us on this fragment. Zardooz! We have finally won the war!"

"Oh Arjmand! You are really nuts!"

"I asked Allah when the seventy virgins would be provided. He said it would be after I died."

"But we are immortal now!" replied Zardooz. "We will never die!"

"Yes I know." said Arjmand smoothly, eyeing Zardooz's ass. "Come to me Zardooz... come!"

"Nooooo!!!!" Zardooz jumped up and ran, pursued by Arjmand, unbuckling his belt as he chased him.

EPILOG 2

Jodie, now known as Eve, her mind fresh and unsullied by the past, wandered about the lush garden, full of fruit trees and flowers, food plants and creeks of crystal clear, sweet water. Under the soil of this paradise, small worms tunnelled and fertilized the growth. This was a new world where even the lowest life form communicated in some way.

Two worms bumped into each other.

"Oof! Who is that?"

"Charonelle?"

"Peepers?"

"Where are we?"

Above them, Eve looked at the most glorious tree in the whole garden. She knew that she must not take anything from that tree. It was the one rule God had given to her and Adam, who was resting in some shade across the clearing. Eve gazed at Adam's beautiful, exciting form and felt a flutter in her belly. Adam lifted a lazy hand and waved to her as he drank in the most enticing beauty of her body, the perfect curves, all designed by the Creator to urge him to join her in the pleasure of procreation. He could sense the life already growing within her from their very first joining.

A tall, thin figure lurked in the shadow of a fig tree, blending in with the dark and light dappling. It did not move and was invisible to the slender woman who was totally absorbed in touching and examining the fragrant fruit of another tree, scant feet away from it. It had bandages on some of its stubby digits and was strapped up around its middle. Another bandage was around its tiny head. The bandages looked almost like natural stripes.

The woman had long tresses of golden hair and was perfectly formed, other than a slight swelling of her belly, that in itself was beauty.

She suddenly balked and tensed, sensing the presence of something unknown, feeling eyes upon her. She looked about, without fear, just curiosity, scanning past the being and then swung back, suddenly fixing her brilliant blue eyed gaze upon it.

"Who are you?" Her voice was pleasant and lilting, her smile innocent and enchanting.

The being cocked its narrow, bandaged head to the side and stared at her silently through tiny black eyes that were ringed by vivid yellow circles.

"I am Snake." it hissed. "It had tried to say "Nickle" but Snake hissed out instead. The Nickle in the Snake knew that his only hope was to get this woman to break God's rule, then he would revert to Nickle and live in comfort on this planet. "You are staring at that tree. Why don't you eat from it?"

Eve moved closer to Snake and replied, "Because God has commanded us not to touch this tree!"

Snake answered, "That is because if you eat from this tree you will have all the knowledge and power of God and be like Him. Believe me..."

Eve didn't let him finish, her Mom's parting advice to a tiny child now flashing clear and understood through her mind. She put Snake's lights out with a right cross that would do Smokin' Joe Frazier proud, standing straddled over the unconscious form.

"Not this time Buster!"

* * *

The ~~End~~ Beginning.

www.ingramcontent.com/pod-product-compliance
Lightning Source LLC
Chambersburg PA
CBHW051230260626
47162CB00002B/357